PYRITE PRISON

VAST COLLECTIVE BOOK VI

Nicole Hayes

IONA PRINT

Library of Congress Control Number: 2021916511

ISBN 978-1-7356713-6-9 (Hardcover Edition)
ISBN 979-8-9894105-9-0 (Softcover Edition)
ISBN 978-1-7356713-5-2 (Ebook Edition)

Printed in the USA

Iona Print

nicolehayesauthor@gmail.com

https://nicolehayeswriter.com/

THE VAST COLLECTIVE SERIES

Last of Daylight
By the Pale Moonlight
Asylum in Firelight
Nox's Verse
Glass Chains
Pyrite Prison
Restraining Silver
Korac's Verse
Thirst
Levee
Flood
Featured Verse
Cascading Light

Here's to those of us who fuck up.

TRIGGER WARNINGS

Please consider my entire series 'Rated R.' These books are meant for readers sixteen years and older. Read with the following triggers in mind:

- Graphic Violence
- Graphic Language
- Graphic Sex Scenes
- Psychological Warfare
- Bondage/Domination Sadomasochism
- Almost Sexual Assault
- Relived Trauma
- Vague Memories of Childhood Abuse
- Torture
- Gaslighting

CONTENTS

ACKNOWLEDGMENTS

Thanks to my book family for following me on this journey. I hope everyone brought a helmet because shit *will* hit the fan.

Beware of shrapnel and tears.

Batman—husband, partner, reluctant reader—Thanks for always providing the casual reader's perspective.

Firefly, thanks again for talking me into keeping a certain silver-hair Icarus alive in Last of Daylight. Otherwise, this amazing story wouldn't be possible.

Jasmine, thanks for hanging in there with me. Our Sunday morning venting sessions provided much needed relief and inspiration.

To my fan club, enjoy the creeping chaos.

ONE

THE DESTRUCTION SHE WROUGHT

{EARTH}

"UNCLE CAEDA! Uncle Caeda!"

Tameka Phillips, Sovereign Ambassador of the Two Worlds, opened her green eyes and scanned her surroundings. Smashed hardwood planks cut trails over otherwise aesthetically pleasing waterways. Gray-painted, busted walls. Overturned plants. Buried waterfalls. The scent of exotic flowers and millennia of old rock dust.

Xelan's underground stronghold.

Slabs of rock collapsed onto the kitchen and dining area. The explosion in the cylindrical entryway, miles under the Egyptian desert, blocked their exit and any rescue attempt.

The voice of her two-year-old son cut through the structural rumbling again. "Uncle Caeda!"

"Pax? Where are you? Be careful!" Trapped in a pocket of rock, Tameka rolled onto her back and pressed palms flat to a chunk of limestone. Push! Her tawny brown biceps bunched and ripped. Ligaments popped. She screamed through the pain and pressed, anyway.

"Mommy!" In his searching for her, that sweet baby jumped right on top of the limestone with enough weight to send it crashing back down on his mother.

Tameka curled on her side surrounded by her waist-length red curls with her arms folded inward like a bug. She suppressed sobs in the dirt as the soft tissue repair system in her nacre—the nano computer in her chest—healed the damage. Before round two. Coughing from the dust and dirt, she answered, "I'm here. Under the rock."

His brown face with darker brown freckled cheeks, like her own, appeared in a small opening. "Mommy, Uncle Caeda gone."

A hot tear slid down her cheek as she relived it all. They sat down to dinner when Chris, resident hero and bodyguard to the King Regent of Earth, got a call from Kyle at the Iona Medical Ecology urging them to find shelter from Imminent attacks.

Rocks exploded from the entrance.

Caedes. He stood over her and her son. Shielded them from the collapsing structure. His deep green, almost black eyes, filled with so much pain as slab after slab of rock fell on him until he disappeared.

Tameka smiled weakly as her son tried to pry his way into the pocket with her. "It's okay, baby. We'll find Caedes. Have you seen the others—"

"Karter?!" Chris shouted through the mess. Some rocks shuffled around and debris stirred, indicating his excavation. Coughing and croaking, he asked, "Are you all right, Jack?"

"Alive. My leg was broken in two places, but it's already healing. I've got Ross. She's unconscious, but breathing." The eighteen-year-old King of Earth reported their status from closer to the exit.

Oh, thank Elden. Tameka waited to hear from the Valkyrie.

Chris moved about the space, disheveling bulky rubble and shifting dust. "Karter?" He crawled closer to the dining room table. The last place they saw the tall, muscular Icarean warrior before she pushed Ross out of the way of the collapsing ceiling.

Tameka closed her eyes and hoped the two Icari survived—

Crashing and rumbling erupted from the entrance, and rocks caved further into the cylindrical lift. Slabs chucked into the smashed living room.

"Pax! Get down!" Tameka cried out and reached to her son through the hole. As fresh dust plumes rose and fell, he disappeared. "Pax! PAX!" No. No, she wouldn't watch someone else she loved die. "Answer me!"

"I've got him," Chris called to her from only a few feet away.

"Batman gave me gum." Her son sounded pleased in the man's arms. The codename suited the black veteran's one hundred percent heroic ass.

Shuffling around the rock out of her sight, he assured, "We'll get you out, Fury."

Tameka smiled slightly at her self-chosen codename. "I can almost push it off, but I need help."

"We need Rayne." Jack said it first. And his voice squeezed as if in pain as he said it.

"Is it time?" Chris' question rang through the collapsed cavern.

Tameka gripped the chain around her neck. It just might be—

"Stronghold. Batman. This is Bones. Come in. Over." The comms device, boosted by Tritan alien technology, allowed them to communicate with team members across the world. Bones, another Icarean warrior, currently watched over King Rayne of Earth and Cinder as she slept.

"This is Batman. An explosion took out the entrance to the stronghold. Jack, Ross, Pax, Tameka accounted for. Searching for Karter and Caedes. We need help. Repeat. We need assistance to get the hell out. Report. Over."

Xelan. His hidden home. Damaged and forever compromised.

"How did they find us?" Tameka rasped with emotion clogging her throat. It hurt to think of her lover's heart breaking at the loss of fortitude after thousands of years of secrecy.

"No idea. A spy? Maybe we weren't discrete enough. Although, I can't imagine anything more discrete than Seamswalking," Jack offered reasonable deductions.

"Batman. We're sending help. Try to keep calm and avoid structural weaknesses. We'll fill you in on the other instances once we arrive. Over and Out." Bones disconnected.

"Other instances" hung in the air. What the fuck happened? How were they blindsided so badly? And with all of them in secure locations.

Rubble shifted around. "I'm coming to help you, Tameka. Pax, stay and watch over Jack and Ross for me. Can you do that?"

"Yesss."

Tameka's heart squeezed at the sweetness in his excited voice. "Get me out of here, Batman, so I can hug my son."

"Yes, ma'am." Did he salute? She wished she could see if he saluted. He stuck his face in the small gap. "Are you injured? Palpate for me to check for neck injuries."

She wanted out so badly she almost screamed in frustration at his perfectly reasonable request. After following his instructions, she checked out fine. "No headaches. No nausea."

"Okay. You know what to do. On the count of three. One. Two. Three!"

Nacres imbued their bearers with strength and increased healing. As a Progeny—the hybrid of an Icarus and a human—Tameka inherited a few enhancements, including greater strength and faster healing. Not to mention the unique ability to drain energy from anything with a nacre. Time and place, and this wasn't it.

Again, she pushed and screamed as if drawing her might from her voice. Chris' groans harmonized. Almost there. A little more—

It lifted suddenly with ease.

"Uncle Caeda!"

Caedes stood on the other side, revealed in the settling dust. The tall, bald, gruff Icarus needed a med unit, badly. Blue blood soaked his face and the back of his head.

Scrapes swelled along his back. After settling the limestone away from Tameka, the warrior wrapped his arms around his ribs and collapsed to his knees. He vomited a wash of blue.

She bolted from the dusty floor to check on him. Chris, the only one in the room with official medical training, immediately checked the Icarus' vitals. While Batman searched for injuries, Caedes stared into Tameka's eyes. Breathing. His primary focus. Inhale. Exhale. Don't die. The effort to keep going written in his eyes.

"Will he make it?" Jack called out from the more structurally sound side of the room.

Chris answered for the Icarus, "We need to get him to the Medical Ecology. The hard tissue repair system will work overtime until then. We'll get you across the room, and then I don't want you to move unnecessarily. You got me?"

Caedes nodded so very slowly.

Chris threw one of the Icarus' arms over his shoulder. Tameka took the other. For a brief moment, her bright green eyes met Caedes' deeper ones. No wasting time. "Thank you—"

A boom and a crash interrupted her. The place vibrated with the shock of it. Another explosion?

The comms device whirred and Bone's voice came on the line, "We're here to get you out."

Chris snarked, "With what? A bulldozer?"

"The crawlers."

{EARTH}

Tameka died. No, Pax did. Kyle burned in the fire. Lucas died in the chateau. Tempest and Dolor sank with the quantum comm system at the Hoover dam. But Andrew knew better than these Probabilities. He followed the guide that Kyle made in his memories.

His childhood.

School.
Meeting his friends.
And then…

{EARTH | 2004}

"Andrew, I want you to meet someone." Rayne nervously wet her lips and wrung her hands before she looked to the sky.

A heavy thud sounded behind him with a whoosh. Andrew turned to see what made her eyes so big. The nondescript parking lot lost its lights long ago, but he still made out the figure surrounded by black wings. They unfurled and retracted, revealing a handsome man. Tall. His skin was pale and kinda gray. With a fantastic smile. Jeez.

"I'm Xelan." Calm and kind, he held out his hand for Andrew to shake.

Sure, why not? "Andrew. She told me about you."

The girl in question walked up beside him and nudged him with an elbow. Rayne teased him, "I didn't make him up."

"Yea, yea." He rolled his eyes and slapped a five-dollar bill in her palm. "So you gonna tell me I'm descended from a hybrid species and need to train for the upcoming apocalypse, too?"

A look passed between Xelan and Rayne. They already had secret looks after a month since she told Andrew of the close encounter. Eventually, the winged alien turned his attention back to the younger man. "I'm glad she got some preliminary information out of the way. And yes. The five of you will save Earth."

"What if I don't want to join your little army of underage heroes?"

"Rayne, can you excuse us a minute?"

She scoffed a little at Andrew before groaning and walking away. "Fine!"

Left with Xelan, the teenage hybrid shrank and shuffled awkwardly. "Yea, well. What do you wanna say to me?"

The tall man crouched to half his height, meeting Andrew's eyes even kilter. Black with a deep blue ring around the iris. "If you don't join the cause, the worlds will fail. If you join us, you'll only see the truth after we've succeeded. You'll look back on this moment many times and remember how pivotal you were to the salvation of this unit. Tell me, is that something you're willing to let down? To let go?"

Andrew glanced across the parking lot at Rayne, who punched the shit out of a tree. With every blow, she yelped in pain. Dedicated. Certain in her trust. The gravity of this moment strung between him and the people he cared for. The world.

"Okay. But I want a statue made of me when we win."

That fantastic grin again. "Deal."

{Earth | Present Day}

This was a bad time to bring up that statue.

"Kyle isn't dead," Andrew announced to the terrified people he loved, gathered in the Iona Medical Ecology lobby. Other voices—other of his voices—echoed those words in his head. The many Probabilities he filtered through to anchor his proper reality.

The glass walls and ceiling displayed a scorched field at the top of a cliff overlooking the ocean. The Ecology hung from the cliffside in a building of glass and concrete. A quarter mile from the entrance, the conduit leading to the Iona Arsenal spewed a column of fire.

Lynn Renee, Chief Weapons Engineer, sank to the floor, staring out the window in shock. Her deep skin tone contrasted with her white coveralls. Black hair coiled in locs draped over her face, hiding her tears. Hoarsely, she repeated, "I tried to stop him. I tried..."

Her husband, Chief Medical Officer, Dr. Pablo Suarez, swept his white lab coat off and draped it over his wife's shoulders. "You're in shock, honey." He kissed her temple before turning serious brown eyes on Andrew. "I hope you're right, but how do you know?"

"Because in a gazillion Probabilities that matches our current path, he lives on to crack a few more jokes."

Lynn faced him with eye contact and sat straighter.

Silence, the mysterious amnesia-stricken Icarean woman, spoke up from the suspension staircase's landing. "If not dead, then what happened to him?" The youthful cadence of her deep voice belied the age in her steely gray eyes. Eons lingered in there. Empty ones.

It struck Andrew as interesting and convenient that Kyle, the memory-reading Progeny known as Story Taker, vanished right as they found a way to hack into her memory. But she asked an excellent question. He shook his head and offered nothing. "I don't know." He turned back to Lynn and put as much reassurance in his tone as possible. "But I know he's alive."

"We trust you." Lucas, resolute and gorgeous, shot Silence an unexpected glare as he passed her on the stairs. Did he suspect her of something? The sandy-blond Icarus with golden eyes nodded at the disaster outside. "We can worry about Kyle later. In the meantime, what can you do to stop that fire, Lynn?"

The human woman survived a load of bullshit in the last few weeks. It leadened her shoulders with the heft of its burden. "I need a comms device."

"I got you, boss." Smith, her second officer, jogged up the stairs. He also shot Silence a strange look as he ran passed before handing a comm unit to his superior.

Lynn allowed a moment, as if she physically switched to the commander hat. Her voice came firm and clear. "Weapons Division Max. This is Chief. Over."

Andrew and Lucas exchanged curious glances. As the agricultural team in Australia, they rarely encountered protocols for this area of Iona's asylum operations.

"This is Weapons Division Max. We're glad to hear from you, boss. What are your orders? Over."

The Chief swallowed and wet her lips before ordering, "O.P. 324. Seal it off. Over."

Smith's brown eyes widened twice their size, and his mouth gaped open. "Chief..."

She cut him off with a firm shake of her head.

The engineer's voice stuttered, "3—324. Yes, Chief. I need your code before I can execute. Over."

Heavy, tired, Lynn hung her head as she confirmed, "Iona. Banana. Yellowstone. Treehouse. Delete after reception. I'm compromised. Over and Out." The woman acknowledged her husband's kind smile before standing and shuffling to the glass outer wall. And waited.

They watched with her. One second the fire roared from the spiral it created inside the Arsenal's tubular entryway. The next, it ceased altogether as if they sucked out the oxygen.

Her back to everyone, Lynn's voice trembled. But not with fear. The brave human female demanded, "We save Kyle. Then we find Imminent. We kill them. Then we get our lives back." She turned with her deep brown eyes burning. "For Earth and Cinder." When she pounded her fist to her chest over her nacre, the others followed. Even Silence, who looked perplexed at the gesture, seemed to understand its significance.

"Iona Medical Ecology. This is Bones. We need help at the Stronghold. Over."

"The nightmare continues..." Lucas stated dramatically.

Smith looked to the ceiling and groaned, "We need a miracle."

They needed a Seamswalker.

{GAIT}

Vanilla and darker things. This scent...what did it remind her of? Old iron. Blood-soaked eons.

Sagan Sterling bolted awake and almost walked into the Seam on instinct. Everything felt wrong. Her body craved for something. She patted herself down and checked her mental inventory. Purple Lyriki armored coat? On her body. Twin battle axes? Holstered on her belt in the corner. Chain necklace? With Matt. Boots? No boots. Where were her thigh-high boots? And—

She patted a hard metal plate on her chest over her nacre. Round and about the size of a golf ball. The nacre port. She allowed the surgery for the implant that enhanced her interactions in Razor's Emporium of Exotic Experiences. As promised, she awoke in a small infirmary space with only a cot and a door. If they kept all their promises, the Progeny Seamswalker's human friend and fellow covert operative, Matt, guarded her beyond that door. Guarded her from—

A knock sounded, followed by Razor's muffled voice, rich and eerily soothing. "The monitor alerted me you regained consciousness. How do you feel, Seamswalker?"

"Where's Matt?" Sagan not only croaked as if dehydrated, she also failed to conceal the suspicion in her voice. Waking up smelling like the man on the other side of that door elicited that kind of response.

Muffled exchange. Then, "Hey, Sagan. I'm right here. Never took my eyes off you with video proof and everything." The auburn-haired twenty-year-old's assurances soothed her.

She sighed and let her head fall back against the wall. Eyes closed and everything. Working this mission took more out of her than usual. Her stomach growled hard enough to cramp. "Ugh..."

As if he heard it, Razor called, "I can have food and water brought to you. But I came with news from Earth."

That got her attention. "Come in." Before he entered, she straightened and haphazardly reseated her axes while searching for her—

The tall man with bright red, spiky hair, tanned skin, and no fingernails entered holding her boots. The friendly smile on his face freaked her out a little. And he grinned wider, as if he knew it. "I had them shined for you."

"Thank you." Sagan accepted them with no creepy handsy attempts. Razor always subverted her expectations, leaving her feeling bitchy for her initial mistrust. Sliding them on, she asked, "Did the surgery go well? Anything I should know?"

He hitched his gray slacks at the knees before sitting in a chair positioned in the corner. "It went splendidly. No post-treatment instructions aside from hydration." He pointed to the cot. "I hope you don't mind. I brought my own pillows up." He held up a pitiful excuse for a hospital pancake—formerly a pillow—before tossing it to the opposite corner.

That explained the smell. It irked Sagan how much she considered whether that gesture bothered her. Eventually, she allowed, "Thank you. You're more thoughtful than I first assumed." That craving hit her again.

"No, I'm not. But I like you. You challenge this old alien, and that comes once every three lifetimes."

Sagan leaned forward, careful for the two axes on her hips, and stared into his eyes. Vertically split with green in the outer half of the iris and orange in the inner half. Softly, she asked a question she wondered a few years ago before she ever met him, "How old are you, Razor?"

He mirrored her, leaning forward and putting those strange eyes dangerously close to her own. He whispered in a voice gone deep, "Guess."

The colors of his eyes swirled like a pinwheel the longer she stared. Hypnotic. Dizzying. Headache-inducing. Sagan winced and looked away first, fingers pressed to her temples.

Razor shifted in the seat without touching her. "We need to hydrate you before you leave."

Okay. Yes, she planned to leave. But… "Why am I leaving?"

"Sagan."

He rarely used her name. Concerned, she looked back into his eyes with a question on her lips.

"There were several attacks on Earth. Enki declared war on Imminent in defense of your worlds."

"Several? Where?" No panic. Just pure resolve. She already survived one interplanetary war. Depending on the locations, she trusted the other Progeny to manage a few terrorist attacks—

"The Brethren's chateau and the quantum communicator."

The Seamswalker jumped to her feet with her hand cupped to her mouth before she realized it.

He stared up at her and continued, "There are rumors they targeted other Progeny-specific locations. Although, nothing confirmed—"

Sagan looked down at the man with infinity in his eyes and coldly articulated, "If you had anything to do with these attacks while I was unconscious—unable to help them—I will rip your world apart."

Razor stilled into a statue. No outward response. Only the irises of his eyes moved with the orange and the green dancing synchronously. After a tense moment, he suddenly stood, standing over her even in heels. He kept the scant distance between them, but managed a sense of encroaching on her personal space. In that soothing tenor, he assured, "I want to establish a friendly business relationship with you. Perhaps, even a liaison partnership for the potential market on Cinder and Earth. Angering you risks my ambitions. Afford me more credit than that. All that aside, I am curious."

He scanned her muscular build from her short blond hair, over the swell of her substantial curves hidden beneath her armored coat, to the four-inch heels of her boots. Not sexually appraising, but something else. When he returned to her violet gaze, he asked in a voice so deep it resonated in her chest, "How would you fulfill your threat, Seamswalker? Quick and professional? Or would you take your time and draw out the pain? You'll want to know the answer before you make good on your offer."

The tiny room shrank. Suffocated Sagan. Without another word, she stepped into the Seam between conduits and walked to the other side of the door. Matt leaned against the wall beside the door he guarded into the tiny infirmary cell. He waved a greeting as she appeared out of thin air. "Hey. Did he tell you the news?"

"Yea. I—Do you know how bad it is?" Sagan wanted so badly to scrunch her hair in frustration, but displays of weakness fed the people on Gait. "The casualties?"

He waved her down. "No reports of casualties yet. The last attack took place barely an hour ago."

"Imminent—"

"May not be responsible."

At the sound of his voice behind her, Sagan spun on Razor. He stepped out of the infirmary looking much looser and friendlier than a moment ago.

"How so?" She kept the suspicion from her voice that time.

"T.A.O. supposedly perpetuated the attacks," Matt filled her in. "She's not a known player in the cell, is she?"

Sagan frowned. The last time she saw her ancestor, The Afflicted One—T.A.O. for short—Celindria stole the small black woman away. Along with the rest of the First Wave Progeny. Created by Xelan in 6,000BCE Egypt, the Icarean-Human hybrid experiment launched with Celindria. They learned from Nox's Verse that the First Progeny convinced her maker to develop four more like her based on specific ancient Icarean lines. They theorized that's what led to the special abilities gifted to the Progeny—ancestor and descendant alike.

T.A.O. and Sagan were the only known Seamswalkers. If Celindria corrupted or even controlled T.A.O.—

"I'll save her," she announced.

Razor chuckled, annoyingly warm and charming. "I'm impressed with how much sentiment the Progeny assign their enemies. Although, it proved fortunate for Cinder and the Icari."

Sagan withheld any reaction to his toothless barbs. He enjoyed testing her. To watch her craving grow stronger. She cut her violet eyes to Matt's dark brown ones, conveying a message.

He gave a single nod.

The scenery changed from the Emporium's mezzanine with its corrugated steel floor and glass shelving. But not to the Iona Medical Ecology where her friends no doubt needed her.

No.

Sagan wanted five minutes alone with the one person she loved most in the Vast Collective before she broke down and begged for an experience.

{GAIT}

Korac, General of the Icarean army and convicted war criminal, paced a rut into the black corrugated tiles comprising the floor of his prison cell. His swift stride back and forth along the nacre-resistant energy barrier kicked up his ankle-length black leather duster. Odd to find a replica of his Invasion Day gear among the clothes Lucas collected for him. That a certain gorgeous blond woman provided him.

No.

Don't think about her. His thoughts might leak into her consciousness and distract her. Let her focus on the crazy shit happening on Earth. Worry about her later when it caused the least interference—

Sagan, General of the Two Armies, walked into the all-black cell with his battle axes on her hips. The Icarus hesitated only long enough to scan her for injuries before opening his arms to her. He tried not to linger on the nacre port in her chest as she melted into their embrace. Korac's lover squeezed him tightly with a desperation he gladly relieved for her. Shorter than him by eleven inches, Sagan made up for it with four-inch heels and badassery. Her short blond hair nestled against his collar with her arms wrapped around his waist beneath the coat. He smoothed a circle between her shoulder blades and kissed the top of her head.

"What do you know?" He despised breaking this moment by asking, but he wanted to know how her people fared.

She shook her head against him, her nose pressed cutely into his chest. "I came here first. After..."

Hiding his appreciation for her priorities, Korac stepped back to examine the port. "I understand it's painless?"

"That's right. Pain free." Sagan's beautiful violet eyes refused to meet his pale ones as she took in the cell decorated in gifts from her travels.

Gently, he captured her chin and lifted her gaze. "I know your task evolved to require the port. Pehton delivered your message. Your dedication to the mission is admirable. Reminds me of a certain handsome, fair General." He smirked at her with an extra crook. Just the way she liked it.

Elden, Sagan looked adorable when she blushed. And her scent... watermelon. Sweet and fresh—

He frowned. Vanilla. She smelled of—

"Razor gave me a pillow while I was unconscious," Sagan offered, as if sensing his confusion. "Matt watched over me the entire time. I was careful." She fidgeted with an axe blade in a nervous gesture, implying she feared Korac's reprisal.

The Icarean male swiftly took the Progeny female's hands in his and squeezed tenderly. "No matter what happens, I will not let you go."

Relaxing visibly in the fall of her shoulders and the heavy exhale, Sagan repeated her vow, "I promise to never go where you can't find me." After a thoughtful frown and a cute scrunch of her nose, she asked, "Do you think he did it on purpose?"

"Definitely."

She tossed her hands up and groaned. "I don't get it. If he wanted sex, I think I'd understand—"

"I want sex."

Sagan brushed off his blockmate's intrusion without missing a beat, "—Hi, Remorse—But Razor genuinely doesn't seem after that. I don't know what he wants from me. I have no money. No power."

Korac held up a finger, and she gestured for him to speak, "You have more power than you know, General." He smirked a little extra for that one. "You're one of only two Seamswalkers in existence. He wants you. Whatever that means to you, he'll try to take you."

Sagan hugged herself and leaned her side against the wall with a clang from an axe. He hated her delicate shudder. The lost look in her eyes. As she tried to make sense of the world around her. Fragile, it broke and crumbled. And in her powerful position, people expected her to piece it together again. With that in mind...

"I love that you came here. It means more to me than you know. But your people no doubt need you." Korac went to her and chafed her arms. Kissed her forehead. Anything to relieve some tension. "When you have some time to spare, update me. I can't help from here, but I care about...at least two of those people."

Sagan bubbled into precious laughter until it melted away and left her older. "I'll be back. I'll bring mushrooms."

They kissed goodbye, deep and lingering. But comforting. Korac knew what he wanted from her. There wasn't time for it now. Later. Later sounded good.

She broke away suddenly and glanced down at his attire, recognizing it. After gaping, she quipped, "I swear Lucas is stalking us."

He laughed, and her eyes sparkled in response. They loved each other despite the bizarre odds of their relationship working out. She, a Progeny, fought on the side of Earth when the Icari of Cinder invaded. He, a dashing Icarus, led the invasion with millennia old vendettas to settle. Both so lucky their two leaders understood and permitted it even with their own differences.

Nox. Rayne. The giant and the sprite. A legend arose from the ashes of their rivalry. They loved each other in secret. Nox staged the public assault on Rayne to throw off their enemies. Likewise, Rayne claimed to kill him when she actually freed him during their ultimate battle. So that one day the Icarean King would return to free the sleeping sprite from her imprisonment in the Martyr Complex.

Unfortunately, Korac knew better. While Nox intentionally assaulted her in public, it wasn't staged. And Rayne definitely killed Nox. What happened to the executed King of Cinder's nacre after? Well, the Icarean General never received full confirmation. But he suspected—

"Memory lane?"

Korac blinked and shook himself from his thoughts with a gentle smile. He eyed their shared axes as he said, "Reflecting on my good fortune to have someone who looks at me the way you do."

"I plan to do more than look when I get back." She pointed an axe at him in warning as she backed into the Seam.

"I look forward to it as always, General."

With Sagan gone, Korac restrained himself from fretting. She was safe. She would be all right. But more importantly, his woman was a badass, and more than capable of looking after herself.

"If you don't ask her to marry you, I will."

Ahh...Remorse. Korac's blockmate kept quiet over the last few days. "What's kept you occupied?"

"My sleep cycle differs from yours." The alien of unknown origin sounded defensive. "But you've entertained quite a few guests. Discover the identity of our wayward brother in the basement yet?"

The Icarus ran a hand through his white hair and absently noted its increasing length. Almost to his shoulders. Elden, it would take five years to grow back. On an afterthought, he muttered, "No."

Silence stretched between them. One heartbeat. Two...

"She wrapped up with Razor?" Remorse's voice held an edge of...concern? Tenderness?

Korac stepped to the nacre-resistant boundary and called, "Why?"

"Girl's got one of those hearts you read about. Big and soft. We don't deserve the love of the likes of her, you and me. With that said, Razor doesn't even deserve to know hearts like hers exist. Do you understand?"

Taken aback, Korac considered the man's sentiments. After another silent moment, he asked softly, "What do you know about the Pain Curator?"

"He eats little hearts for breakfast and will make a feast of your girl."

{Earth}

With Kyle gone, Silence predicted dissension among the nervous lesser beings.

There.

The Progeny's people finished discussing their plans and turned. Turned and looked at her. These were not friendly looks.

Of course.

Silence remembered little of her life. The time and place of her birth. Who raised her. How she came by her training. All lost to her. But she retained a decent comprehension on the behavior of sentient creatures in mass.

In a time of crisis, turn on the outsider.

She considered opening her blue wings, breaking through the glass, and flying away. To find Kyle, the only person with a key to her memory and her forgotten mission. Another, more disturbing, temptation presented itself. Slaughter them all. End their confusion, their concern. As if answering the temptation, a wave of blue light pulsed beneath her skin.

They stepped back. Except Lynn. The young woman with her dark complexion and fun twisted hair visited an unexpected kindness on Silence since her arrival at the Ecology. The human shared her clothes with the Icarean woman. Fixed her hair. Showed her how the toothbrush worked.

Now the woman known as "Chief" gazed at Silence with harmless curiosity. Decision made, the Icarean female brushed the blue stripe in her otherwise black hair from her eyes and walked over to the Chief. The males watched in suspicion.

Chuckling wasn't polite. Silence gave them a decent amount of trouble since her arrival. None of it intentional.

But, alas, it left a lasting impression. So, when she reached Lynn, the Icarean female held out her hands squeezed together at the wrists. "You may arrest me, but not the males. I'm in your custody now, Chief Lynn."

Silence broke her last pair of nacre cuffs. She felt the seam in them, the weakness, and split them apart so they shattered into precious dust. Kyle took custody of her after that. He promised to restore her memory. For their benefit, she wouldn't destroy the cuffs this time. But... "I want to find him to learn why I was awoken."

"No cuffs. We'll confine you somewhere comfortable until we understand better what your role is in this current catastrophe."

Lucas said those words. He reminded her of...someone or something from her past. His golden eyes fueled the urgency in her to continue her mission. He also loaned her clothes with legs almost as long as her own. The t-shirt she wore now belonged to him. Barely long enough to brush the tops of her thighs, she liked the males' reactions to her exposed skin. Especially Kyle's. Except Smith. He never reacted to her, not even so much as widening his brown eyes. She caught him staring at her only from the peripheral occasionally. Like now.

Silence searched Lynn's eyes, waiting for her judgment.

Mrs. Chief nodded. "I hate to do this, Silence, but we don't really know you. And the man that vouched for you—"

Lynn's breath hitched, and she swallowed her words. The memory haunted her.

"Yes." The Icarean female offered nothing to console the stricken human woman. Kyle survived somehow. Conscience—Andrew—believed that. The younger woman's brown eyes found her gray ones again. So great was their height difference that Silence slouched to maintain eye contact. Meanwhile, that mysterious purpose screamed for her return. "Let's begin."

Smith accompanied Lynn to Silence's new cell. The others scattered to rescue trapped Progeny. Her two jailors deliberated on the subject. Bored, she let her thoughts drift. How could she find Kyle? Scouring this planet, even on wings, might take her a year. Cinder, two years. These people underestimated the task ahead of them, but without knowing the full potential of their resources—

The resources that survived the attacks, anyway. Whoever wanted to cripple them knew exactly where to hit. That implied a spy. Silence understood spies. But not why. She hoped the Shadow would let her help. At least long enough to find Kyle—

The Icarean prisoner of war, Twenty-One, waited at the glass front of his cell as they rounded the corner. Everyone paused awkwardly in the corridor. The very, *very* large Icarean male gazed at Silence. Not with attachment. With kinship. For a moment, they reconnected as Icari. Proud warriors of Cinder. Why not?

Silence broke into a smile, implying that she looked forward to the next time. He returned the expression. She suspected it was his first one in a long time. Even as the two pulled her along, she kept her gaze locked on his. The both of them up to a special brand of mischief only Icari understood. Fun, casual sex as escapism from the horrors they survived. Getting caught only enhanced the experience. Impressed, he shook his head playfully at her trouble-making and left the entrance before they shoved her through a door. The extra secure cell they kept the Imminent prisoner. The same one the ancient Seamswalker murdered him in before causing this calamity.

Silence clicked her tongue and turned on her jailers. "How long?"

Lynn stood in front of Silence and faced her like a proper warrior. "So much happened. We need to assess the damage and find out if there are any casualties. I know you understand."

The taller woman nodded slowly.

"I know you can break out of here." She sighed and gestured exasperatedly. "But on good faith, please stay here until we can interrogate you. Andrew seems better, so maybe he can search your intentions. And if Kyle is alive, we'll find him."

"I want to help." Silence meant it.

Smith took a step closer and reasoned, "We know. The best way you can help is to stay here for now until we know more. Can you do that?"

Lynn also looked up at her, expectant and entreating.

Silence hated this. The unknown mission clawed at her muscles, her lungs, and her heart. They stood in the way.

No...

She took a deep breath and calmed herself. No. The amnesia stood in the way. They wanted to help her.

"Very well." Silence sat with her legs stretched out in the middle of the floor and looked up at them both. "I will stay here while I wait for you."

Obviously expecting more resistance, they shared a bewildered look before Lynn sighed in relief. "Thank you." They both took their leave.

With them halfway out the door, Silence called out, "Send in Twenty-One whenever you like."

Lynn's groan echoed in the cell.

TWO

THE STAKES ARE HIGHER THAN YOU REALIZE

{EARTH}

SAGAN WALKED INTO A SPACE MEANT ONLY FOR HER. Bed, dresser, walk-in closet, entertainment center, and desk furnished the impressive room. Framed pictures of her and her friends covered every surface. Xelan wanted the Progeny to feel at home in the stronghold. He decorated each of their rooms to suit their individual personalities down to the sheets.

The room looked undisturbed, so the damage must be closer to the entrance. She Seamswalked six feet at a time, mindful for signs of structural fallout. Every time her foot stepped into the Seam, she peered around the empty world between worlds. Grayscale cathedral halls stretched white bone to an arched ceiling so high a mist collected in the vaults. The hard floors were stone, a softened shade of black.

The Seam went on endlessly. Forever. When the Icari spoke of the afterlife, Eternity, she imagined it looked like this. Ash fell like snow, slow and unceasing. It left her so lonely. It didn't help that only she and T.A.O. could step foot into it. None of her friends, nor Korac, could tread in the place. They stepped through it and into the next conduit.

Sagan flashed through it about a dozen times before she heard the first cry.

"Karter?"

Tameka. They were in the kitchen, and, as Sagan neared, dust plumed from the ravine Xelan used as a stairwell.

Sagan Seamswalked next into a massive wall of wreckage. The reality too overbearing, her heart stopped as she cried out, "Tameka, can you hear me? It's Sagan. Are you all right—"

"Thank, Elden!" Jack cried out. And Sagan immediately sighed with relief. He went on, "We've accounted for everyone but Karter. Caedes is badly injured and Ross is unconscious."

A boom resonated through the rocks, rumbling the gravel and dust.

"What's that?"

Tameka answered this time as Chris called again for Karter, "Bones and Cypher in the crawlers. Para and Colton are watching Rayne. Para wanted to help find Karter, but we need at least one Icarus with the King. I have to bring the other Valkyrie good news. Can you get us out?" The edge of panic in her voice freaked Sagan out. The redhead always maintained her composure.

"Hell yes, I can. Anywhere in the room where I can fit? Describe a spot in the room as it looked normal, and I can pop in." Man, she wished she wore clothes under her coat this time. It'd help to take it off. Keep it from getting dirty. But then again, Korac's eyes shone with celestial light every time he opened it to find no other barriers between them—

Focus. Elden, why? She gripped her stomach and doubled over with a hunger cramp. Every one of her appetites hit her all at once. Talk about fucked up timing. While she dealt with her selfish first world problems, Tameka gave her instructions.

Sagan walked into the kitchen closest to the stove. A small empty space housed the group. Tameka's long hair draped around her like a dusty cape. All her scrapes already started healing. Chris recovered from a bleeding bump on his head. Jack couldn't stand. His legs looked mid-healed broken. Even so, he held Ross in his arms. Blood seeped from the back of her head. Caedes...Sagan hadn't seen that much Icarean blue blood cover a man since Rayne defeated Nox.

"I need to get you out."

Chris, codenamed Batman, shook his head. "Not without Karter."

The next boom shifted a shelf of bedrock and a waterfall of rubble crushed the dining room into ruin. They all took cover. By the time it finished, Sagan resolved herself to washing the Lyriki armored coat and polishing the Icarean axes. "Okay, Chris. But I have to get Pax out of here. I'll take them to the Ecology and come right back to help you search for Karter. But promise me you won't move from this spot until I return."

"I'll stay put. Don't be long."

The group gathered together with Sagan in the middle. "Cross my heart—" Poof. Drop off. "—And hope to die." She returned, leaving the other group abruptly in the Ecology for treatment. The lobby looked full, so they'd be fine. "Where did you last see her?"

Grimly, he pointed to the recently demolished dining room table.

"Right."

Another boom.

Chris got on the comms. "Bones. This is Batman. Hold for now. Structure too unstable. Seamswalker on scene. ETA ten minutes. Over."

Cypher, one of Xelan's first Iona employees and currently Kyle's right-hand man responded, "Roger that, Batman. Over and Out."

While he set to that task, Sagan flitted around the open concept space. Everywhere she went, tiny rock slides increased her anxiety with their foreboding of the inevitable. Nacres were a blessing of Tritan technology.

Without them, the people in this room couldn't survive this cave-in. That being said, she never wanted to know how long a nacre-bearer might survive while pinned under a collapsed stronghold miles beneath Egypt.

"Karter? Can you hear me?" She Seamswalked closer to the dining space, warily. "Are you there?"

Nothing.

Chris looked on, concern naked in his dark brown eyes. He loved that tall, muscled Valkyrie female with her rainbow colored mohawk and crazy *Mad Max* fashion sense. Sagan found no fault in it. Karter was truly loveable.

"We'll find her," she assured while carefully dislodging some rock.

"Let me help."

She held out a hand and tried to keep her voice gentle, "I move faster on my own." She lifted another mid-sized slab. "If I sense so much as a belch, I'll be over by you before you can blink—Hey. Hey! I think I found—"

A new nightmare.

{Enki}

John and Tumu took turns asking after everyone on the comms device.

"Sagan said Karter looked so bad she doesn't feel comfortable Seamswalking with her." Tameka updated them with an exhausted sigh. "I'd hate to tell Para that."

The two Icarean Valkyrie served Cinder for millions of years together. Over all that time, they developed a strong relationship where one rarely worked far from the other. If they couldn't move Karter because of the extent of her injuries…

"Don't worry, Tameka. We'll get to Sparkles." Tumu, a thirteen-foot tall when compressed, sixty-five foot tall when decompressed Gargantuan Tritan, sounded genuinely caring in his deep booming voice. Stationed as Officer of the Third planet in the Vast Collective, he acted as liaison between Earth and Enki. The latter being the Tritan's supposed homeworld, a Dyson's Sphere.

While the giant blue alien's allegiances swung toward the ambiguous, John believed he had a soft spot for the Progeny. Probably because of his friendship with Xelan. Today, they'd take advantage of it. "How will we get to her?" John asked, knowing full well Tumu never learned the stronghold's location.

He turned his lidless eyes like black circles in his face onto John. "Sagan can take me to the stronghold without ever showing me its coordinates."

Okay. True.

Tameka also liked the idea. "Go to the shrine for Earth, and I'll let Sagan know to meet you there. Waste no time. I won't. The second she returns, I'll tell her." After a thoughtful pause, she added, "John, it might be best for you to stay. I want to know more about what exactly it means when Enki declares war."

Tumu placed his hands on his ear holes and loudly hummed to tune them out. Plausible deniability and all that. After the Tritans learned of Tameka's pregnancy, they "asked" her to live in Enki. John and Caedes accompanied her. Two years later, they still refused to let her move back to Earth. In the meantime, they spent every waking moment scouring the Dyson's Sphere for helpful or even secret intelligence. They coincidentally visited Earth the same week a shit ton of terrorist attacks hit home. It smelled shady.

"I'll look out for anything suspicious," John assured. "I'll ask to shadow Abresson like he's the boss around here. He'll like that."

The blue alien snickered in his fist. "You're right." His voice deepened as he turned serious. "But he has a temper and the power to support it. Do. Not. Fuck. Up."

The human saluted with a fist to his nacre. "Yes, Office of the Third, sir."

Tumu recoiled as if unsure how to respond and flattered all at once. At a loss for words.

Tameka giggled. "He is good at feeding that ego—Okay. Yea? She's awake? Good. Jack said Ross regained consciousness."

John sighed in relief. Kyle's little sister breathed fresh life into their group. They all hoped to find the youngest of Story Taker's siblings, Bethany. Taken by Icari during Invasion Day at twelve-years-old, she was fifteen now. Recently, Tumu picked up a fresh lead that the Lukemore textile mills bought her.

Once everyone recuperated, John planned to join them for the rescue mission. He always wanted to see the planet of the Luks. He met two during the Volcano Day battle—the battle that ended the war between Earth and Cinder. X and R were invertebrates with jellyfish caps of varying colors and designs at their waists like skirts or kilts. Their hair was kelp, forming deep green dreads. They consumed their prey like spiders, setting electric webs and draining their victims dry. The planet must be quiet given the Luks whispered when they spoke. As an educator of Vast Collective culture, he looked forward to the trip.

"Earth to John?" Tumu prodded as if he repeated it several times already.

"Sorry."

Tameka continued as if she waited for his attention, "Find out what you can. Tumu head to the shrine. I'll get Sagan."

"Wait." John stopped her from ending the call. "What will you do with Karter, Tumu?"

The Tritan sort of frowned. Hard to tell without eyebrows or a nose. "If she's this badly injured with little outward signs of healing, we'll bring her to Enki for an upgrade as a special courtesy to the King Regent and Sovereign Ambassador, or however the hell I have to word it. We will take care of her. Which brings me to my next concern."

There went those ambiguous allegiances again.

The redhead on the line groaned, "What?"

"They want you to return to Enki. And Jack and Ross come this time. They don't like the most important figures on Earth at this much risk."

Silence stretched between them.

Eventually, Tameka asked, "Why Ross?"

"Kyle is missing, as I understand it. The Eminents suspect they can awaken a trace of his abilities in her. This makes her a target. Do you understand the implications?" Tumu's body went rigid with tension. He even clenched his fists.

John interrupted the second quiet moment, "That's understandable. But what about the embargo, Tumu?" Enki forced the woman on the line to stay on Earth before the attacks because of a virus that afflicted Jack. As Rayne's sibling, he qualified as a Progeny technically. They banned the Progeny from traveling to the Dyson's Sphere for quarantine.

Tameka huffed bitterly. "Let me guess? They'll conveniently lift it because of the state of emergency they no doubt had a hand in creating?" Her censure oozed through the comms and infected John like a toxin.

At the shamed look on the Tritan's face, John scoffed, "Are you serious?!"

"I will get to the source, Peaches. I promise."

Okay. Tumu knew better than to use that nickname for her unless he intended to keep that promise.

Voice icy, the Progeny woman tersely repeated their mission, "Recon. Shrine. Karter. Over and Out."

A heavy quiet filled the room when suddenly the Tritan muttered, "Hey, John?"

"Yea?"

"Abresson would prefer it if you applied lip balm before kissing his ass."

"Fuck you, Tumu."

{EARTH}

"Yea. I'll tell Para. She'll insist on going," Bones responded to Chris and Tumu's most recent update from the depths of the Earth. The crawler he operated hugged the inside wall of the stronghold's cylindrical entrance. With the bucket extension, they unearthed a third of the chute. But there was still so far to go. He lamented telling his casual lover that her longtime partner, Karter, needed to travel for reconstructive surgery.

Barely recognizable.

That's how Sagan described her. Hard to imagine one of the most powerful Icarean warriors to exist—a Valkyrie, no less—lay down there reduced to a bloody pulp. He shook his head and waited for confirmation before returning to work.

Chris, a pretty decent guy for a human, assured, "Tumu said it'll be tight, but he'll find an excuse for her to visit once 'the Chef' arrives to replace her on King Duty. Please pass that along to her. And my love."

The Shadow—the collective group of apocalyptic elites—loved one another. King Rayne, in her glass coffin, kept the conduit between Earth and Cinder open to allow the Icari to evacuate. Her brother, Jack, supported by Chris, Karter, Ross, and Colton ruled Earth-side and negotiated with The Brethren—the Two Worlds' governing body—for the good of both races.

Kyle and Cypher guarded the conduit, with the former screening memories of entering Icari seeking asylum. Andrew screened intentions and headed the agricultural restoration of the Vittle crop, the Icari's primary source of nutrition. His Icarean GQ model, Lucas, headed up Progeny interests with The Brethren.

Tameka, the fieriest redhead that ever gingered, ran the diplomatic division with Caedes, one loyal Icarean warrior, and John, the traveling educator. Sagan, the Seamswalking Progeny, was hands-down the most overpowered being in the Vast Collective and the most down-to-Earth.

Pablo and Lynn ran the medical and weapons research divisions, respectively. Matt and Lucy... killed things very, very violently. Bones and Para completed the teams as necessary.

Not a single member went underutilized or underappreciated. Love. Kindness. The world Elden wrote about in his Verses. This was family.

Bones twisted the pendant on his chain. Proof of his official initiation. He looked up the chute to Earth's sky through the plume of rock dust. With these kinds of emergencies, was it time—

Fuck this. "Cypher, I'm heading back to Cinder. I'll be back in an hour. Do you want a lift anywhere?"

"Roger that. I'll await instructions here. Say 'hi' to the King of Earth and Cinder for me."

Rumor had it Cypher once had a thing for Rayne. If someone ever asked Bones—and not that anyone would—who he thought made a comparable partner for the force of nature that was his new King, he wouldn't say a pretty decent but otherwise average human soldier recruited by Xelan to run the first Iona out of Little Rock, Arkansas. No. The Icarus that came to Bones' mind surprised him. Especially given said Icarus was currently deceased.

Wild reality they were in.

Those musings entertained Bones the entire flight to Nox's Castle on his majestic-as-fuck wings. Approaching the open square tower high in the sky, the Icarus hated the message he came to deliver. Through the vent of black rock, he soared into the pit. It housed a lake in its center. In the middle sat a lone island with a glass box.

The Martyr Complex.

Sheepishly, he nodded in reverence to the King that slept within it. Not as if his brain didn't disrespectfully suggest minutes before that she belonged with the man who built the thing.

Colton, another decent human, waved from the modest kitchen in the corner. He held a finger to his lips and pointed over to Para sleeping on the couch. Shit, he needed to wake her with the news. He approached cautiously, making gentle noises along the way. Never—ever—wake a sleeping Valkyrie with stealth mode on. Bones heard what happened to Chris. Without a nacre, the human might still be a soprano.

"Para, wake up. I brought news."

The Valkyrie opened her shiny black eyes and bolted upright. Her short blue hair fluffed similar to their post-coitus sessions. At the terror filling her eyes, Bones mentally kicked himself for letting his thoughts even drift there.

Gently, he shared, "Hey. They found her."

The tiniest of the Valkyrie at five-foot, eight-inches, Para released a shaky sigh of relief that made her appear fragile. She even spread her hands over her face and held her head. He almost choked when her shoulders shook with soft sobs.

Shit. "That's the good news."

She snapped back to him with her eyes bloodshot and glistening.

"Chris, Jack, and Tameka are taking her to Enki." Para made to stand, and he gently gripped her substantial biceps in a comforting squeeze. "She needs upgrades to her nacre. Tumu promised to arrange a visit for you once that new Tritan guard for King Rayne arrives."

Bones released her, and she leaned her head back onto the couch with her eyes open to the vent above them. He took a cursory glance around the pit and noticed that Colton left them alone. So many decent humans.

"We've been together so long now—millions of years—I couldn't imagine my life without her," Para choked out the confession. The muscles in her throat strained with the words, and tears poured freely from the sides of her eyes into her hairline. Even softer, she added, "I like Chris. Love him, really. But right now, I resent him because he gets to go with her and I don't."

He winced at the truth in her words. Then gently, he offered, "We know him well enough that if you say the word, he'll switch places with you."

Para turned, and Bones watched the wreckage salvaged in her eyes. "I know. That's the only reason I won't kill him." The longer she stared at him, the more her eyes shifted into something . . . else. The sweet, exotic scent of mango filled the air.

Ahh. The rumors of Valkyrie appetites increasing during times of grief weren't exaggerated. Para looked at Bones like someone lost in the desert looked at water. Thirst. Hunger. Need.

She moved for him.

Against all of his instincts, Bones held her aloft. "I don't consent." Shit. Why did he say that?

Para pouted, and his bones hurt. They kicked his own ass for saying "no."

"It's not a good time for you, and Colton is around here somewhere. Would Karter approve?"

"Karter would insist on joining even with her injuries." Para almost purred the words and ended them on a growl.

Bones resisted a shudder. Not a bad one. Her scent intensified with every intoxicating inhale. Stronger than he ever smelled it. Fuck. Him. Please.

"Let's go to the King's chambers this time."

"Race you there."

{Gait}

Matt fidgeted with the chain Sagan entrusted to him before her nacre port implantation. It tangled with his matching one throughout his day of shining the Martyr Complex Bar & Lounge's bar tops and polishing the Emporium's parquet flooring. When he saw his face reflected in the hardwood of the main area proper, he took a break before starting the floors in the addition. The kitchens boasted exotic eats from all twelve planets within the Vast Collective. Fancy shit for the upscale crowd that frequented the eccentric auctions and the Divine Booths. The major attraction allowed for guests to experience the lives of others, specifically their pain.

The ginger human set aside all the fancy fixings and hit up the ham and cheese. The human fare appeared in the fridge after his second day employed under Razor. Strange to admit it, but this job made for the cushiest gig so far. And Matt only worked undercover jobs. And only ones that fed him. Not sandwiches, either.

Nope. He agreed to help Sagan with this mission to explore the pain market. He stayed because of Lucy's letter. The one she left him six months ago when she disappeared.

Find men like Justice Lee in the worlds, and you'll find me.

Once you do, I'll explain everything.

Always together,
Morning Star

Matt considered Razor. Not exactly Justice Lee. More like the man Lee aspired to be. But the Pain Curator served men like Lee with vices like the ones hidden in the basement. Every day, Matt went down there and performed for the circus. Every day, hopeful that Lucy would appear undercover as one of Razor's hapless victims. And every day, Matt surfaced disappointed—

"Hey don't let the boss catch you listening to that."

"What?" Matt lowered his massive sandwich to find one of the aggressively ripped drones from Monarch 3 standing across the counter from him. Only then, he noticed the music in the background. Oh. Night Rayne. "Someone else left it on. I didn't realize it was them."

With shimmering, multi-faceted eyes, the guy looked left and then right before leaning forward all conspiratorially. Quietly, he shared, "Between you and me, it's worth pissing him off to see a show."

"Yea?" Not that Matt gave a shit. Only two things satisfied him, and he'd gone six months without his favorite.

The drone—Puke? Puk?—nodded. "I worked security at a show two months ago. They set people on fire with the pyrotechnics. And Rayne? Hot. So hot." The facets in his eyes glimmered with excitement. "Hey, I heard you know her. The real one."

Matt shrugged nonchalantly. "Sorta." Who the hell discussed his business with the coworkers?

"What's she like in person?" He fully leaned forward on the counter, eager to know more.

How to describe Rayne in one word? "Dangerous."

The guy's head bobbed approvingly. "Hot."

They bumped fists.

Matt watched over his sandwich as Puk headed to the basement entrance. The redheaded human's shift started soon. Dusting the crumbs from his hands, he headed for the addition. Voices carried around the corner to the shop.

"I know it's hard, dear." Razor's voice at his most convincing.

Someone sniffled. "No more," a girl pleaded. Young. Her voice sounded small.

Gently, the alien pushed, "A little more then we can stop for the day. Does that sound good?" After a pause, he called, "Matt?"

Shit. Caught eavesdropping. He turned the corner to find a blond girl facing Razor with her back to Matt. "Boss?" He always reacted well to the title. Indeed, the Pain Curator smiled before whispering something to Puk's identical drone beside him. The Mon3 alien took the girl gently by the arm and escorted her out of the shop. Matt never saw her face, but he'd never forget her voice.

"Night Rayne offed another prime client at the most recent show," Razor announced.

Apparently, the band ate away at the Emporium's more prestigious visitors. Too bad, really. Matt asked, "Have you ever been to one?"

"No, but I am curious. I might even consider it. To scout out the competition, of course. I have no intention of participating." Razor's gray eyes shifted as he passed a dark blue hand through his pale blue hair. Time for a change of subject. "How long before the Seamswalker returns, do you suppose?"

Matt tilted his head to the side as he considered. Not Sagan. No, he considered the man before him. What the hell did Razor want from Sagan? Or Pehton? Or him, for that matter? The Pain Curator had more angles than a myriagon. After some thought, Matt ticked the list off on his fingers. "With The Brethren down, possible Shadow casualties, and Progeny facilities damaged?" He knew for a fact that Imminent hit three massive ones. But they were hidden installations best kept secret from current company. "Give her a week. Maybe two."

"Three days at most." Razor held out his hand to shake. "A week of your menial tasks on it."

A wager. Should Matt feel some type of way about betting on his friend? No part of him minded, personally. But the precarious position he balanced between working with the good guys while living like a bad one always tipped to the danger zone.

Matt gripped the offered hand and ignored the fingernails missing from Razor's nail beds. At the man's telling smirk, the younger one observed, "You either know something I don't, or you underestimate her sense of duty to the Progeny."

"I know something you don't. I know *her.*"

{???}

The monster hit Rayne in the throat, so she couldn't scream. Couldn't say no. Then he threw her onto his throne and climbed on top of her...

Kyle relived this memory often. It spun in an endless loop of horror and shame. Because it wasn't the monster stripping off her clothes or settling between her legs that broke Kyle. It was her eyes. The look in Rayne's bright blue eyes as she accepted her fate. She didn't—

With a shout, he threw himself out of the tortured memory in his sleep. With the recent emergent issues, he quit smoking pot to clear his mind of the haze he preferred...

To...

Live...

Where the fuck was he? A small red waterfall splashed into a basin below a rock bridge that spanned the colossal cavern. Purple-leafed, orange-blossomed flowers lined the cave walls. It smelled fresh and alive. He awoke on said bridge that combined two tunnels. Naturally formed with no balustrade.

Shit. Kyle recalled all his trauma before remembering the giant fireball that blew out of the arsenal to claim him. How the hell did he survive—

"Don't move."

"Fuck me! T.A.O.?!" Hers was the last voice he heard before he lost consciousness. Kyle ignored her order and spun on her. He intended to cuss her out. To ask her why all the crazy threats and bombing people. But his words drifted into space the longer he looked at her.

The tiny black wraith of a First Wave Progeny wore a crazy black leather catsuit with cutouts and perforations. Gold lined every hole. Ribbons of it adorned her long black hair. Spiked gauntlets made from the stuff. As a blacksmith who specialized in gold weaponry for the war, Kyle admired the sleekness of it. Cute outfit on such a tiny person.

Her expression was anything but cute. With her eyes locked in Atramentous form, the solid mauve color glowed around the black slit of a pupil in the center. It glowed in terror.

Kyle took a friendly step toward her. "T.A.O., tell me what's wrong. What happened? You've helped Tameka and Sagan. You helped on Volcano Day. They told me. What has Celindria—"

"Don't," she snarled and trained the small nacre tranq gun on him.

How many times would he see one of those pointed at him in one lifetime? "Okay. What do you want from me?"

"We're recruiting you."

He glanced from T.A.O. to the utterly psychotic bitch who stepped out of the tunnel.

Internally. Holy shit.

Externally. "Celindria."

Truly beautiful. Long black locs to her waist with gold beads and ribbon intertwined. Skin the same shade as a dark calla lily. Dressed in all white linen that covered any indecency while enhancing her curves. But her eyes always arrested Kyle. The same bright blue as Rayne's. She gracefully picked her way on bare feet across the grotto to him. "Story Taker is an interesting moniker for a memory-reader." Melodic and rich. Seductive without trying.

Why were crazy women always so hot? Or the hottest women always so crazy? He ran a hand through his tangled hair to give it something to do. Damn, he wished he had a joint. "If you're coming to me for help—with T.A.O. under your control—then you lost Devis somehow."

Her eyes hardened into sapphires.

"How are you controlling her? And how does this contribute to Imminent's aims? What are you doing, Celindria?"

The celestial statue remained silent so long, Kyle wondered if she astrally projected somewhere. When he opened his mouth to ask, she cut him off, "Submit your blood and spy for us."

"You already have spies." This entire scenario gave him flashbacks to Colita.

Her lips quirked into a smile that gave nothing away.

"If I agree to your terms, I'll use it to the Progeny's advantage. I'll learn how you're controlling T.A.O. and set her free. Give me too much time, and I'll tear Imminent down by the foundation. Do you understand me? I will never submit to betraying her again." In his fury, Kyle worked his way across the bridge and got in Celindria's face, only an inch lower than his own.

Beyond the First Progeny, T.A.O.'s solid-colored eyes flared in warning.

The crazy woman's smile never wavered. She never flinched. Nor took a step back. Breaking eye contact to breeze around him, she continued pitching her scheme, "Well, if you can accomplish all that, then we're evenly matched and you've nothing to fear from my proposal. You've much to gain."

Kyle hated her at his back. He whirled and found Celindria teasing a bloom. Expecting the poor thing to wilt at the toxicity of her touch, he stepped between them with a cutting glance at the enemy. "What do you expect from me?"

"Agree to my terms, or we return you to your people after carefully planting evidence pointing to your complicity in the attacks."

Fuck. He wanted to argue that his friends would never believe her. To rail against her heinous schemes. But Kyle knew better. They'd believe it and lock him up next to Korac in Gait. Then he'd have to endure listening to Sagan and the Icarean General make up for lost time.

"What do you gain from my submission?"

Celindria spared a glance over her shoulder to the stone-still other First Wave Progeny posed on the bridge. When she looked back at Kyle, her eyes sparkled. "Have you heard of Elden's Tenements?"

Kyle rolled his eyes. The Icari placed a lot of faith in Elden's writings, but sometimes their recital of it made him itchy. "Nox went on about the Tenements of Vengeance to Rayne once. I never read them."

"I want you to sign the Tenements of Volition."

He recoiled slightly. "Volition? My will?" Shooting a terrified glance at T.A.O., he tried to suppress any outward signs of disgust. "You want me to sign over my will to you? Under what circumstances would I ever agree—"

"We'll activate the sleeper with only one objective."

No. "Rayne," he breathed. Who the fuck was the sleeper?

Shaking her head, her locs swaying softly, Celindria waved a hand at him. "No. But I enjoy your flare for the dramatic. Rayne is quite safe. However, your sister is not."

Without thinking, he gripped the First Progeny by the collar of her linen halter and lifted her bodily off the ground. She made no move to defend herself. "Do not. Fuck. With my family." He spat the words in her face.

In a flash, T.A.O. snatched him and disappeared, releasing Celindria. She Seamswalked them to the highest point in the cavern and held him over the edge of a shelf.

The shallow basin below would only grow redder with the addition of his blood.

"You've no wings. You'll die," Celindria reminded him, as if he would ever forget.

The other Progeny received their wing upgrades while Rayne refused him a pair. Not for forty-eight more years as penance for his betrayal. And here was her ancestor, threatening death by fall to betray them. They'd hurt his sister and further damage his reputation.

He put everything he felt into a single sigh. "I fold."

As Celindria beamed like an angelic maniac, two things crossed his mind. What were the Tenements of Volition? And would Rayne find it in herself to forgive him for a second betrayal? Would she trust him to act in Earth's best interests, the Shadow's best interests, and hers?

No matter the cost to Kyle.

THREE

THE PAIN IN YOU

{???}

NOX CHAFED AND MUTTERED, "I CAN'T FATHOM THE DISRESPECT OF THOSE TWO."

Rayne's laughter chimed, beautiful and bright. He appreciated the presence of it in the wake of the recent troubling news. With a kind smile, she teased him, "Aww. What happened to 'Do you think for one second Para and Bones feel anything less than the utmost respect for you?'" She fell gracefully onto the couch and stared up at him with that light in her eyes.

He turned his back on her and raked a hand through his hair. A little gruffer than he meant, he elaborated, "For *you,* of course. But those are my chambers."

"They're mine now."

The former King of Cinder hid his wince at the reminder of his demise. Nox found their current situation more than he deserved. Beyond what he imagined for Eternity. But it still made for an in-between existence. What of its permanence? Would he spend forever as a second personality in Rayne's mind? If not, how long before she exiled him to the dark? Only retrieved as needed?

Still, better than he deserved.

"Nox..." Rayne called to him softly.

It forced his eyes closed. He loved the sound of his name from that kind, hopeful woman.

More than he deserved.

The leather of the black sofa creaked as Rayne stood. Closer now, she called again, "Nox."

At her will, she shared in his thoughts and emotions. He wished it wasn't always so. As he turned to face her, he wished certain ruminations remained his own. Rayne stood within reach, and he wished more than anything to air his regrets. All of them. With no pressure on her to forgive him. Or to absolve him. He sought only to make them known.

That Nox was wrong.

But this bastard mind of his wouldn't stop admiring how captivating she looked. Standing there, straight and tall, yet still only reaching his chest. Rayne had to fly to his height when she took his nacre from his sternum during their penultimate fight. Then, she wore fitted battle armor, all in black. Now, she traipsed around her mindscape like a sprite in flowing tops of purple, burgundy, and blue the color of her eyes. The color of his blood. With her shoulders and back exposed, her skin shone like moonlight. Elden's Verse written in gold ink across her shoulder blades and down the small of her back. He caught himself reading it more here than ever in his studies.

Rayne swept her long black hair over to one shoulder before addressing him, "Your concerns are understandable. For now, I've no intention of exiling—"

The exsanguination mechanism kicked in. The Martyr Complex acted as Rayne's prison where she served a fifty-year sentence for war crimes against the Vast Collective. It also served as the lock for the conduit between Earth and Cinder. Her blood was the key. As long as her blood flowed through it, the conduit remained open.

So, the Complex mined her blood with sixteen golden cylinders every hour. They fed her anesthetics and nutrients as they filled the glass coffin with her life. Her nacre kept her from drowning in it.

"Every hour, I curse myself for designing that damned mechanism," Nox growled softly. If one could soften a growl. The giant Icarus tried his best not to raise his voice around her. He gave her no cause to feel unsafe in this mental space of hers.

Rayne searched his eyes intensely before accusing, "You didn't design it. I know you didn't."

He looked away and shifted his weight between his feet. Uncomfortable. Caught in a lie.

Shifting, she eyed the rope on the couch. The one she routinely braided from their nacres and knotted whenever her hands idled. Quietly, as if saddened, she explained, "I know the mechanism was Korac's idea. He never told me. But you mentioned in your Verse that he created certain components. The cylinders were the most artistically designed and fine-tuned for pain."

"He only followed my orders—"

"It's okay. I won't punish him for it. But . . . " She turned back to him, looking up their height difference to meet his eyes. "I'm so curious that you would lie for him. Shoulder the responsibility. Almost on a reflex or out of some instinct." She closed her eyes and concentrated. He sensed her rummaging through his conscience. "You love him. And you want to protect his happiness. Even after he betrayed you, Nox?"

The former King of Cinder walked away from her again. He needed a better coping mechanism. This farce of escaping her scrutiny solved nothing. With his back to her, he confessed a hard truth, "Korac was right to betray me." How could he fault his second-in-command for choosing Rayne's side? For protecting the Seamswalker—the woman Korac loved? No. Their diversion was inevitable. Not unlike—

"Let's change the subject," Rayne offered with a tension-relieving exhale.

Nox released one himself. "Let's continue your education." Hearing the sigh of the couch once more, he turned to find Rayne curled against the leather with the rope in her hand. He stepped over to collect the free end, careful to move slowly with his arms loose. Retrieving shards of his nacre as she showed him, he wove a piece of himself into the strange mental construct. *"A net, a noose, or a bridge,"* she'd said. Peering at her, he imagined the woman intended to build a bridge. A representation of the ability she harnessed to reach Pax and her other loved ones in their dreams.

"Tell me again of the reproduction program."

This subject burned Rayne. She resented that certain Tritans, the unnamed Primary and Abresson, intended to force her into reproducing with them. Ironically, it burned Nox as well. The Primary used his mother in the same way, producing Xelan. "Including everything I've already mentioned? Not much is left to tell. All the civilizations of the Vast Collective can reproduce with the Tritans just not all in the same way."

"What does that mean?" Her nose scrunched cutely whenever she frowned in confusion. It distracted him often.

He kicked himself and continued on with his work. "Recall the people of Monarch 3?"

"That's right. No live birth," she pondered aloud.

Nox chuckled. "Xelan threw such a fit over that."

He caught her staring and met her gaze. "Am I not allowed to speak of him—"

"You miss him . . . " Rayne tossed the rope aside, stood once more, and crossed the space to search his face. Her heart wide open in her eyes. This was it. "Did you think you'd punish him and somehow everything would work out? That he'd survive and acknowledge you were right? That you'd be brothers again?"

She never raised her voice, but allowed Nox to feel the full brunt of her bewilderment. Her pain. He looked away. It hurt too much to face the truth in her words.

But Rayne was finally ready. "What were his last moments like, Nox? What was the last thing you said to him? What did you do to him? Because I *know*—Elden, do

I know—he survived that explosion. I know he wouldn't leave me alone in a world with you in it. Not unless you killed him, yourself."

Nox shut his eyes. The projection flared to life behind him, allowing her to see the memory. To experience it as he did. To feel his emotions and read his thoughts.

"You won't like what you see," he warned with no attempt at reproach.

"Show me." King Rayne of Earth and Cinder stepped in front of the projection and prepared to watch the death of her guardian with his killer at her side.

Nox kept his eyes shut to the scene and tried to ignore the words from his own mouth. He never once believed they'd be the last between him and his brother. There were no excuses. His anger didn't conquer him. It wasn't the high of his impending triumph. It was scalding hot venom and malice. Toxic and necrotic. He wanted to hurt Xelan. And then he killed him.

Rayne's sharp gasp as he told Xelan of his intentions toward her so near the end shattered Nox.

It's true, he never expected his baby brother to remain deceased. Squabbles and tantrums were common in their household. Usually, after Nox returned from a hunt with a prize for his brother, the tension settled and they got along again until the next time.

The routine of siblings.

But Xelan didn't perform a resurrection trick. Didn't fly out of the ashes like some phoenix.

Rayne did. And into a lonely world without her guardian for guidance.

Nox was a bastard.

The fire consumed Xelan's remains. Nox collected his nacre, turned his back on the ashes, and flew off to commit an even greater sin. For which she executed him.

The End.

Without so much as a glance, Rayne opened to him. All of it. The full force of rage and grief coalesced until it towered into a tsunami of emotion and pain that consumed Nox.

He fell to his knees, gripping his scalp to relieve the heart in his figurative skull. He stared up at her with more than tears—his heart's blood—pouring from his eyes, awaiting her righteous judgment.

Rayne turned to him with his planet's star glowing in her eyes. Tears, hot enough to scald her cheeks red, streamed down her face. Or was that her heart's blood? The strongest being in the Vast Collective clenched her fists. She opened her mouth, and he prepared for her to mete out her justice.

A tear fell from Nox's face onto the abyssal plane. Then another.

His victim. His rightful end . . . stopped. Her fists unclenched. The glow in her eyes dulled until only the shimmering blue remained.

Nox watched it all from his knees, deserving of her punishment.

He hurt.

More than ever in his life. Sharing in Rayne's mourning of Xelan intensified his own loss the day he killed his brother. A remorse he allowed to trickle, but now the dam burst open. Flooded him in grief and regret.

Why? Why did he ever allow their relationship to disintegrate so badly? Why did he resent Xelan's happiness so much that he doled out such cruelty in the end?

"I've had eight thousand years to think about what I would do to the brother that betrayed his people. Betrayed me! I thought I'd torture you for the next eight thousand years."

Manic. Bitter. And remorseless. So close to retribution and righteous culmination. Eight thousand years, Nox waited to prove to Xelan he chose the wrong side. And he refused to show restraint or mercy—the same deference Xelan showed him.

None.

"Force you to watch as I reduced the planet you forsook us for to ruins. As I defiled Rayne. But you know, brother. I'm in the mood for instant gratification, so I think I'll finish what I started all those millennia ago."

Those were *it*? Those were his last words to his baby brother?

He lowered his head in shame.

She vanished. He understood. In no way did he deserve her presence.

The lights shut off as Rayne left Nox in the dark where he belonged.

FOUR

A WAR IS STARTING; BEST KEEP YOUR HEAD DOWN

{EARTH}

TAMEKA EAGERLY AWAITED WHATEVER NEWS, REPORTS, INTELLIGENCE—ANYTHING—THAT TIPPED THE SCALES IN THEIR FAVOR AND ALLOWED THE SHADOW TO TAKE A SINGLE PROACTIVE RATHER THAN REACTIVE STEP.

Hell! She'd settle for a plain, active step.

That'd be a welcome change to this pandemonium. The flight to Enki's conduit in Siberia hurt all the more because of the silence. It strained with the weight of sheer terror and unexpected failure.

That's right.

The gorgeous specimen of Icarean female strapped to an alien stretcher with all the bones of her face smashed in counted as a fucking failure. The truly decent human man watched over Karter with his head bowed to hide the fear, no doubt.

Oh, Fury would live up to her name today. Enki. Imminent. Anyone and everyone responsible would feel her wrath. The Shadow's wrath.

"Mommy, your hand hurts." Pax kissed the mottled knuckles of Tameka's clenched fists. "All better."

Relax around the kiddo. Xelan wouldn't want him to feel the tension. Only security and love. Gently, she reassured, "I'm fine, baby. Do you want in my lap?"

He nodded emphatically as Tameka unbuckled his seatbelt and tucked him comfortably against her. She kissed the top of his red curls and resumed staring out the window. It hurt to hold him and relive the moment Tumu, Sagan, and Chris appeared at the Ecology with Karter between them. Damaged. Busted. Unhealing. All three of them coated in her cerulean blood. The look in Chris's dark brown eyes . . . If someone gave her a mirror right after losing Xelan, Tameka imagined she looked as haunted.

Tumu insisted on flying them himself. She glanced away from the window when he popped out of the cockpit and checked on Jack. Autopilot altitude. Not much longer before they landed, then.

"Your legs are fine?"

Rayne's brother nodded and cleared his throat before speaking, "Yea. Thanks, Tumu. Sorry you keep having to volunteer for an emergency infusion."

A martyr. Just like his sister. Tameka shook her head and scratched Pax's back for her own comfort.

The blue alien gently admonished, "Stop saying that." Then to Ross, "How's your head?"

Damn, the Tritan's genuine concern for them warmed Tameka despite her mistrust of him.

Ross smiled prettier than her brother ever could—

Shit. A slight pang hit Tameka in the heart. Not that she could stand him, but where was Kyle? How did Imminent know where to find the Arsenal? Why did they hit the chateau when The Brethren weren't assembled? What did they gain by any of this?

"Peaches..."

Tameka closed her eyes against the convincing warmth in his tone.

"Uncle Tu! Hee." Pax held out his arms for the extra-compressed Gargantuan Tritan to hold him.

With a nod from her, the ancient alien obliged. Standing over her and bouncing her son, Tumu assured, "We'll get answers."

How did he know? But really, what else would she think about right now? One thing came to mind. Cinder's star, Li, held a nacre in its center. One she powered up a few days earlier. She needed answers for that. Did Earth's sun have a nacre? Could she drain it like all other nacres? Was that how the Tritans manipulated it to expand into a red giant? Was it reversible?

Lightning illuminated the sky.

Caedes emerged from the cabin where he rested most of the trip. He held one of many devices he kept for communication or intelligence reports. "The weather... It's hazardous on Earth *and* Cinder. Elden's sphere nearly collapsed."

Tameka shot a sharp look at Tumu. That only happened when—

"Something's wrong with Rayne," Jack muttered in horror. "Who's with her?"

"Bones, Para, and Colton," the Officer of the Third informed. "I'll contact them immediately."

As Pax grew tense, Tameka squeezed gently to relax him. "It's okay, honey."

He looked up at her with those eyes so like his father's and pouted. "Auntie Rayne is sad."

From the open cockpit, Tumu called out, "What?!" He rushed back from the comms to ask again, "What was that, Pax?"

Tameka glared at him as her son stiffened and shrank back from his urgency.

Despite that, Pax timidly repeated, "She's sad. Mommy has me to hug her. But Auntie Rayne gets no hugs." Then this beautiful angel of a Progeny hopped out of her lap and went to Tumu. He hugged the giant blue alien around one leg. Rushed over to Jack and squeezed his side. Hugged

Ross' arm, careful for her slow-healing bruises. Chris swung him up for a big hug and let the boy blow the covered Valkyrie a kiss. On the last, he toddled over to Caedes, who held out a pinky—the only uninjured part of his body—for Pax to squeeze. Even that tightened his eyes in discomfort.

Once finished with his precious errand, Pax returned to his mother for the warmest embrace of her life. Tears warmed her eyes and threatened to spill from her lashes. "My baby," she whispered against his hair.

"She needs a hug, mommy."

Tumu stared at the black carpeted floor, hanging his head to hide his black eyes. In shame? In grief?

Tameka caught Jack watching the alien. The entire plane observed the Tritan compartmentalize his ideals. A crisis of faith. Once upon a time, he and Xelan were friends. Quite the rogue in his day, Xelan led an epic chase across the Vast Collective, and Tumu—the Officer assigned to his case—tracked him. The Tritan once regaled her with many of the adventures they shared. But two years ago, when the Progeny sought their own nacres from Enki, it became clear that Tumu never completely chose a side. So, they survived many encounters with the Tritans where the Officer of the Third did little—if anything—to help them.

The worst being Rayne's Tribunal. Eminent Wiw, Eminent Lance, and Eminent Abresson sentenced her to fifty years in the Martyr Complex with Eminent Celindria as witness to her crimes. Utter. Betrayal. In the end, they charged Tumu with the execution of her sentence. This allowed him to assign the Progeny as her guard. It was the only positive out of the entire ordeal.

But that left Rayne alone and afraid in that box. Asleep in her own blood. She requested it to keep Cinder open to Earth, but...How awful was it to miss living out life with her friends? To miss all their shenanigans? All their progress? Shit. Miss finding a partner and having a life of her own? When they delivered bad news, her rage manifested in some serious climate change and other bizarre effects. Like storms and tectonic disturbances.

"One day—I vow to you—everything will be clear." With that, Tumu stomped back into the cockpit and flew the plane through a thunderstorm.

Caedes plopped in the seat beside Tameka and Pax with a groan he attempted to suppress. On an exhale, he muttered, "Callahan is safe. I'm sure nothing could best her even in her sleep." The Icarus rubbed the center of his chest—over his brain—as if tending a headache.

Checking on the group, Tameka glanced back at Chris. No change. She much preferred him cracking jokes and doing hero stuff. Jack turned to Ross, and the two conversed about Enki. Plans of utilizing resources there to find Bethany on Lukemore. Possibly taking a break from Story Circle.

"You'll need to make an address, Jack," Chris called out from the back.

The young man turned for some eye contact. "Right. You're right. I'll do that when we land."

"What will we do? From a global leadership standpoint?" Ross asked some hard questions.

They all looked to Tameka as the highest-ranking officer on the plane. A Progeny, she earned a certain amount of leadership more esteemed than that of the King Regent. She looked down at the future in her lap. After his beautiful display of pure kindness, Pax tuckered out and snored in the hammock he made of her skirt. They were fighting for him.

"When we land, I'll call an audience with the Eminents to discuss the terms of the declaration of war. Ross, I want you with me. It's the best way to check on travel permissions to other planets. While we do that, Jack, you reach out to Earth and enact a state of emergency. But only mention the public places, okay? The chateau and the quantum communicator. Don't mention the Arsenal or the nacre chamber. Caedes, I know you're hurt—"

He gruffly chuffed at her understatement and winced from the movement.

"—But I need you to reach out to The Brethren and find out their next steps so Jack can report the public-facing ones. Chris, you get Karter to medical and you get me some good news. If you speak to a Tritan, stay civil but discuss nothing in detail. Are your objectives clear? Do you have any questions?"

"We heard you loud and clear, Fury," Ross answered firmly.

Caedes nodded gently with pride shining in his eyes.

Chris answered with a soft, "Roger."

As she met their gazes with renewed hope and love, Tameka gripped her chain. Jack noticed and did the same. Ross and Caedes followed.

From the back, Chris repeated the Shadow's pledge, "We will always remain."

{???}

The bit in 324's mouth only protected their teeth from chipping and muffled their screams. The hood over their head prevented them from identifying their abuser and suspended them in pure darkness. An abyss of pain. Restraints kept them still on their knees. The floor hard and cold. Sweat and gas coalesced into a frightening aroma. Sweat meant fear. Gas meant a flame for boiling.

324 tested the restraints, imagining which boiling liquid this time. Water? Oil? Or worse? They recounted the last few sessions. No. It was too soon in the cycle for water or oil. It must be—

Scorched and scalded. Blistered and bubbled. The most unimaginable pain. This was the worst. The worst it ever got. The liquid poured onto 324's skin and took the first few layers with it as it found a course down their bare shoulders, naked chest, and exposed stomach. It hardened. Crystallized. Sweet and harmless, the boiled sugar formed a sticky system of scars down their body. Blood followed and cooled. It soothed. But not long until—

More sugar. Hotter than anything, it never let go. It clung and peeled. A copper taste filled their mouth. 324 punctured their tongue again as the bit's design allowed. They were so tired from screaming. From sitting upright against their will. The smell of their skin boiling made them vomit against the bit.

The abuser paid no mind and poured another ladle on.

For. Hours.

This went on for hours. Until they choked on their vomit. Until they dehydrated from the tears. Until there was no skin left.

324 wanted to die as the abuser cradled their raw body and laid them tenderly in their bunk. No outward sign of remorse from the abuser. Just 324's shame in their exposed nudity and regular mistreatment. They cried out as their skin touched the sheets. Too raw. Too bloody. Heat roiled off their scalded wounds. They gripped their abuser by the wrist before the hooded person could leave.

One word of kindness. Please. Such a small mercy. Please.

But it never came.

As the bunk door closed, 324 removed their hood and stared into the same darkness that filled their heart. With no hope left, they resigned themselves.

It was time.

{GAIT}

Korac hit one thousand two-hundred and twelve pushups when the air brakes sighed on the lift. He turned and rolled the platinum plate weights from Pil off his back in time for Executive Warden Pehton to stop in front of his cell. The charmingly tiny Lyriki woman spared him a glance. He smelled her reaction to him on her neglected scent, but she remained otherwise professional about her physical attraction to him.

The Icarean war criminal took no offense. Most people's scent shifted when he entered the room. Maybe it was the white hair, the pale eyes, or the ripped and tall figure? The only one of his kind in the Vast Collective. Exotic rarely covered it. It harmed his allure very little that he insisted on cladding himself in expensive clothes. All tailor-fit to flatter him best. He smirked to himself. No harm at all.

But the Executive Warden kept her eyes forward on the hall. She refused to acknowledge him with any of her growing fondness. Must be here in an official capacity. He settled for observing her rigid posture and her mighty carriage. Those orange feathers—comparable to human hair—stopped at her shoulder-blades. They contrasted starkly against her pitch-black skin. The electric-blue Lyriki armor, grown from within her, wrapped around her legs, hips, breasts, and shoulders. Protected her modesty and her vital points. Even with her stomach exposed, she'd meet few foes able to wound her. The Lyriks were genetically designed to defend the Tritans and their assets. Such as Gait, their prison planet.

Pehton's gliders—orange extensions from wrist to elbow—flared in anger as she commanded, "Request time. Place your orders."

Korac popped his brows high. Requests? One inmate called out for a Reipon film of a pornographic nature. Another asked for certain foods. As each of them listed one or two items, he recalled a conversation with Pehton upon his incarceration.

"We take care of our prisoners here."

So it would seem.

A prisoner down the hall and around the corner shouted, "Where's Razor?"

Her solid red eyes hardened like garnets. "You know he wouldn't dare show his face here and besmirch his establishment's respectable reputation."

The same one snarked, "What I want, you won't give me. I miss the old days before your ridiculous laws."

No words. No facial reaction at all. Pehton walked over to a panel. Into it, she sang a special combination of pitches and bled on the seal it produced. A hot whoosh of air blew through the halls. The smell of the prisoner cooking lingered longer than his cries of pain.

"Anyone else miss the old days?"

Damn. Korac whistled and smirked when he caught her attention. "Executive Warden Pehton in action. What a badass."

She flushed prettily before approaching the nacre-resistant barrier separating them. Softly, she asked, "Have you heard any news?"

"Sagan is checking on the situation. She'll return soon." It took some time to figure the Lyrik out, but the Icarean General understood people at their core. Despite whatever past she buried, Pehton's heart bled like the Progeny's people. She belonged to the side of the heroes. But like him, she might hesitate to accept it. Hell, Korac still shuddered at all the warm, huggy shit they got up to. His capacity for compassion only afforded him so much, and he reserved it exclusively for Sagan. Maybe Rayne. Now, his curiosity, on the other hand, never tired. "What's with the order fulfillment?"

She fluffed her feathers and blew out a sigh of frustration. "The prisoners make one request per Collective month. Pay with chores like linen press, information, or other favors. Razor fulfills the orders."

Something nudged at the back of Korac's mind. In his memory. But if it came from his time as prison labor, he'd rather keep it repressed. Thanks very much. Pehton scoped out his cell, filled to the brim with wonderful and exotic gifts from all over the Vast Collective. Sagan truly spoiled him, and he loved her more than he could ever express for it.

It was the Lyrik's turn to whistle, impressed. "I don't think you want for anything."

He smirked. "Not as such."

She stomped her boot and looked away. "Elden, I hate when you do that. And put a shirt on."

Korac laughed to himself as he stripped out of his shorts and activated the shower's spray when he stepped on a specific black tile.

From behind him, the Lyrik growled, "I hate you."

"You wish you could."

"Does Sagan know you're like this?"

"Hah! Who do you think revived me?" He shut off the shower and covered himself with an Egyptian Cotton towel from Earth. When no word came from the Lyrik, he peeked over his shoulder, expecting to find her drooling at him with pretty black lips gaped open. But she was frowning in confusion. "What is it?"

The Lyrik gave him her back for privacy as she explained, "It's an odd way to phrase it. 'Revived.' What do you mean by that?"

Korac mastered the art of keeping his mouth shut and refusing to divulge much about himself. But with the warmth and comfort of Sagan's regular presence, he noticed his usual stoic icy exterior melting slightly.

His bad.

But working with Pehton required a delicate balance of quid pro quo. If he shared with her, the Lyrik returned in kind. It became tricky when he wanted to share only enough to tip the scales in his favor. Balance. "I'm sure you've heard of the Vacating?"

He climbed into worn black leather pants and a band tee. Who the hell was *In this Moment*? Whatever, he appreciated their aesthetic. When Pehton answered with a nod, he turned his back and continued, "Well, I died. In a way. All the Icari did. And Sagan revived me." Vague, but clear.

"You're lucky."

Unable to contain it, Korac rudely barked out a bitter laugh. "Until recently, luck isn't something I'd accuse myself of having."

Adorably, emphatically, she swore, "Fuck it!"

He whirled to find his cell open, and her stood waiting, expectant. Hopeful. A little wild, even.

"Korac, do you wanna make some trouble with me?"

He skipped the smirk and went straight to a magnificent grin even Xelan would envy. "What did you have in mind?"

Pehton told him her plan, and a strange combination of exhilaration and concern washed over him. Korac finally identified the look on her face.

Suicidal.

{GAIT}

"Remember. His terms with Sagan permitted you one memory retrieval in a Divine Booth," Pehton repeated for the fortieth time as she escorted her prisoner down Mercy Row.

In glass chains, Korac never stood taller. She came to his elbow. "*Contaminant* thug." That's what Razor called him. Dressed in a band tee and distressed leather pants, she appreciated the "thug" sentiment. Although a high-classed one, the Icarus was still a convicted war criminal.

The "*Contaminant*" part itched her. Razor served upscale addicts from all over the galaxy. He never seemed one to discriminate against race or origin. The Pain Curator wanted pain history and credits. The venom as he spat those words never left her.

And here that thug glided gracefully across the slushy pavement wearing motorcycle boots. Snow recently melted. The Icarean General, fond of titles, carried an elegance in squared shoulders and a raised chin. All around them, derelict space-scrapers pierced the atmosphere. Even they couldn't match his elevated sense of self.

Pehton liked Korac. His looks. His attitude. His humor. Hell, even his taste in women. Sagan complimented him spectacularly in a peculiar but endearing match of innocence and corruption. Intellect and cunning. Kindness and ruthlessness. Pehton shipped them harder than the Vast Collective shipped Nox and Rayne.

So that made this brief field trip to Razor's Emporium of Exotic Experiences even more hazardous. She agreed to keep the perfect couple separated in exchange for unlimited access to her memory. But as Sagan recruited her own friends to help Pehton recover her memories, the Lyrik couldn't shake the guilt gnawing at her. The Progeny went out of their way to include Inanis—the Warden's personal crusade—along with their other objectives. And now they were suffering.

Karter. Para. Kyle.

Elden dammit! Time to switch tactics.

"Are you ready, Executive Warden?" That elegant cadence from his smooth tenor... How was she ever supposed to resist?

"Ready."

Razor waited in the center of the Emporium proper. He was expecting her. Even with a crowd surrounding him, he watched with intensity darkening his brown eyes as they traversed the revolving door. The carbon fiber coveralls fit him well. Tall and athletic, she imagined he kept fit working out in some small corner of his establishment. Alone and out of sight. He held a small Enki-tech tablet in his hand for noting the prisoners' orders. Without a word, a threat emanated from him.

Not that she saw much of him. Korac shifted himself between the two. Taller. Broader. Simply better, to put it frankly. Cinder produced nice, sturdy warriors. The Lyrik planned to schedule a return visit.

Clients dressed in casual clothes—discount night for the local junkies—gawked openly and gasped at the Icarus in chains. What a spectacle they made.

"Peh Peh." Icy, Razor ladened his voice with reproach, "You brought a guest."

Pehton stepped out from behind the shield Korac made of himself. She plastered a sweet smile on her face. "I did. And I have the orders. General Korac joined me to fulfill your agreement with the Seamswalker." Gripping the Icarus' considerable forearm at eye level, she led the pale prisoner toward the rows of booths. She kept his back angled away, preventing scrutiny of the nacre cuffs.

Razor walked ahead and stepped in her way. "I'm afraid my favorite guest isn't here, at the moment." He spared

Korac a jovial glance. Except for the ice in his gaze. "You'll have to return with both ladies as chaperons."

Okay. Now to play hardball. Pehton clenched her fists until the knuckles popped to prepare for this delicate performance. Wide-eyed and sweet, she cried loudly, "Razor! The public knows you always honor your debts. General Korac here won't cause trouble. I promise. I'll keep him good and reined in."

Overhearing, people gave the trio conspicuous glances and whispered to one another. Make a scene for the desired effect. Lashes batted. Chest heaved. Feminine petiteness emphasized. One glance at the Icarus for a rating.

Faint, but there, he winked. Oh, and with a little crook at the corner of his lips.

Well, Korac's approval certainly lightened her step.

Razor used that cold tone again. "But you don't always honor *your* arrangements according to the agreed upon terms, Peh Peh—

"*Executive Warden.*" Korac, Icarean General of Cinder and convicted war criminal, just corrected Razor, the Pain Curator of the Vast Collective.

The air in the room thickened as the two men locked gazes. Zealous clients gave them some room with furtive glances. Pehton halfway wanted to step back. The redheaded human male peered over the railing of the mezzanine with a look of curiosity and apprehension she expected on her own face. Was Razor self-conscience of the inch difference in height? So slight, but some men really chafed over that shit.

Brown eyes sparked against pale white ones.

After a few heartbeats, the Pain Curator smirked with flames glittering in his eyes. "One session." He turned and waved for the redhead—Matt—to come down the stairs.

Pehton shot Korac a relieved glance. But he never took his eyes off Razor. He also gave off a scent. Like cold air on a winter's night. It chilled her more than Razor's stare.

Interesting.

Matt pushed through the crowd, and Razor ordered him, "Take them to the furthest booth. Peh Peh knows how this works." He handed him a memory capsule. "Take good care of her and get the orders for the prisoners."

Shit. Pehton wasn't expecting an escort. She needed Razor occupied for some freedom around the Emporium. But Matt—

"Okay, so he said you know how to use this thing?"

Matt spoke to her, but she inconsiderately tuned him out. Too busy watching her world fall apart. After affording her a small salute, the Pain Curator walked toward the mezzanine's wrought iron stairs. His expression said he'd contend with her later.

Subdued, Pehton set Korac up in the booth, hoping to engage the correct memory. She'd done this once on herself, but the science shouldn't vary that much between their species. "Okay. So you put on the goggles after you submit your capsule there. Good luck." With an affirmative nod from him, she headed for the door. But something gnawed at her. She turned back and asked, "Korac, what would you have done if he struck you?"

He peered at her curiously, as if surprised she didn't know the answer. "He wouldn't."

"But how could you know that?" Pehton frowned, hard.

"Men like Razor don't resort to physical violence. He'll wait and corner me when he decides there's something I have that he wants." He popped the unsealed cuffs off and checked out the space for surveillance.

Her eyes grew wide as the realization struck her. "Sagan."

Korac nodded solemnly. "But he underestimates her. She's more than a match for him." He grasped the goggles and examined them.

Chewing her bottom lip, Pehton soaked that in. It didn't sit right. "I'm afraid *you're* underestimating him."

Another graceful shrug. "Then I'll reduce his empire to rubble if anything happens to her."

On that cheerful note, Pehton exited the booth to start some sleuthing. Only one problem.

"He warned me you might try to walk around unescorted. I'm afraid I can't let you do that."

Matt. The human complication. Nice guy so far, but really in the way right now. "Human, I am the Executive Warden of Gait."

He shrugged, not graceful like Korac. But he argued with some sound reasoning, "Yea. And my boss is Razor. No offense, ma'am, but who would you be more concerned with pissing off?"

Daring to look, Pehton peered down the aisle of Divine Booths and up to the mezzanine. Razor stood up there, hands spread across the banister with him leaning forward on it. His brown eyes glowed through the din of the whiskey lighting. What fresh hell was he imagining for her? Would he hurt the others? Take his anger out on them?

She hoped Korac distilled something from this event. Otherwise, Pehton risked her good standing with her jailer for nothing.

One day. The Executive Warden vowed she'd scour this den of vice and pain until she found the rest. And then she'd give up her life to free them. If that's what it took.

{GAIT}

The sight of Karter's face would haunt Sagan's memories like Rayne's arm after her first fight with Nox. She needed a shower, a meal, and a hug. Imagine her disappointment when she arrived at Korac's finding only the first item on her list. Maybe Pehton took him for a routine physical?

Too exhausted and starved to spare it more thought, she showered away all the dirt and blood. Didn't bother stripping from the coat either. Not until the water ran clear. It also rinsed the axes for her. Under the spray, she remembered she removed her chain. No reason to worry. Matt would hold onto it for her.

Moments later, she hung everything to dry and slipped into a ripped tee. Nothing inappropriate peeked through the holes. Not that she'd care. She climbed into those white silk sheets from Lukemore with every intention of sleeping until the bruises healed on her heart. To wait for—

Korac.

He was screaming for her.

Sagan threw back the sheets and ran through the Seam to wherever he called her from—

Razor's Emporium. On the mezzanine.

The Pain Curator stood against the banister with his back to the crowd. His gaze shot from her bare legs to the over-sized shirt to her shower-wet hair. Never with lust in his eyes, but always with something more predatory shining in them.

At the sight of him, with Korac's fear screaming in her head, Sagan lost control. Atramentous, defined as dark mode for Icari and Progeny alike. The iris swallowed the eyes, wings often detracted, and voices triplicated in pitch.

With her eyes transformed to a solid purple and a black slit for a pupil, Sagan stalked toward Razor. Her wings opened from her back and decimated shelves of his precious wares. She closed her eyes and accessed the more important sense with a deep breath.

When she opened them again, the conduit Sagan sought split beside her just a crack. With her voice in three pitches, she demanded, "Where is Korac, Razor?"

The Pain Curator handled this a little too well. Fascinated and studious, but not frightened. Exhilarated and impressed, but not concerned.

This bothered Sagan immensely.

In his smooth rich voice, not at all trembling, Razor answered, "While you dealt with matters on your homeworld, I invited him here for the memory dive I promised you. Under Pehton's supervision, of course."

So reasonable. So courteous. Damn him and damn her. Razor was a creep. Sagan felt it in her bones, but the man never once gave her concrete evidence to believe it. Let alone punish him for it.

"Seamswalker, where does that go?"

Oh, yea. All that growling and snarling to their side came from the conduit she'd left slightly cracked. Maybe that's why her head swam. Or maybe the adrenaline she barely mustered to rush over and save Korac left her dizzy. Yea, that was it—

The conduit closed, and Sagan felt weightless. The crowded Emporium floor tipped to the ceiling. She groaned. Something warm dripped to her lip from her nose, and honestly, she couldn't take anymore.

Razor stomped forward to catch Sagan when her knees gave. Too much. So hungry. So tired. Vanilla smelled nice on him. But the blood—

"Sagan."

Her name from Korac's lips spoken with so much love and concern. Warmth suffused her like a hot fire against the cold of a winter's night. She opened her eyes. The moment they found him on the first floor, Sagan caught her second wind.

"Korac."

With one Seamswalk left in her and a barefoot sprint across the floor, she sprung up into his open arms. Unsealed nacre cuffs fell to the floor. He enveloped her with a secretive smirk, and she wrapped her legs around his waist to further cement herself to him. Deep breath of his scent. Feel his pulse through his clothes.

The Seamswalker kissed over the war criminal's nacre, uncaring of their audience. Korac would protect her, and Sagan would save him from whatever made him scream. There were no two people safer in the entire Vast Collective.

Clinging to him, exhausted, she glanced up at his face. She caught him glaring beyond her to the mezzanine. Within the same heartbeat, he looked down at her. Softly, he asked, "Are you all right?"

Karter's face flashed in Sagan's conscience. The subdued cast over her friends' eyes followed. All their progress—the Vittle crop plantation, the education halls in the chateau, and the quantum communicator—utterly destroyed. And then, for a moment, she thought—

Well, she wasn't entirely sure what she thought. Korac went missing. She sensed his fear and need for her. Here. Did she think Razor chained him in the basement? If so, why would she continue interacting with such an unstable engagement? The mission. That's why.

"No." Sagan swallowed and muttered, "Can we please go home?"

"Take from me what you need." He kissed the top of her head and glanced down at Pehton where she appeared beside him.

She gazed up at the mezzanine with fear tightening around her garnet eyes.

"Executive Warden, I apologize for the cuffs." Korac startled the Lyrik.

"Fuck it. I'll never hear the end of it, but the scene you two just put on more than made up for it. Hope you're prepared for the backlash because here he comes."

Pehton nodded toward the open floor, but Sagan didn't need to see. Korac regularly held her without an ounce of strain, but the Pain Curator's approach caused his muscles to tense as the Icarean General tightened his hold.

Sagan cherished it.

Razor made certain to stand where she could see him, even with half her face pressed into Korac's chest. His voice set to kind, he offered his farewells, "Warden, General, I hope you found the memory an immersive and responsive experience. Please take care of the Seamswalker for us. Her presence always lights up the Emporium." He met her eyes momentarily. The orange and green looked subdued, like muted stained glass.

Sagan hurt his feelings when she accused him of ill-will toward her Icarean General. If she thought about it, Razor was nothing but gracious to her. Creepy, of course. But twice in the last two days, she got in his face over offenses without a shred of evidence to implicate him. And she did it with pure conviction.

She startled Korac when she reached out for the Pain Curator. Razor stared at the offered hand and then into her eyes, reticent. It affected her. Eventually, he reached out two fingers and pressed them to the pulse point in her wrist.

Razor wanted them to start over. This was his greeting. He kept his orange and green eyes on hers, sparing nothing for Korac or Pehton. Everything between them passed through her head, reliving every moment. The world spun, and her head fell back against Korac.

"Sagan?" Her lover whispered her name. Their audience would never hear the threat in it. The threat against anyone who tried to harm her. He wanted her permission. Korac's love warmed her.

"Hungry. Tired."

"I can set the buffet?" Razor offered. Genuinely or not, she couldn't tell and no longer possessed the energy to try.

Sagan opened her mouth to accept the offer. The food here rocked—

"Executive Warden, would you join us for some grilled mushrooms? Sagan knows a great vendor."

The Seamswalker almost protested until Korac rubbed a circle in her back with his warm hand spread wide. Slender fingers kneaded into her sore muscles. Yes. More of that, please. Wait, did she purr aloud?

Pehton chirped—no pun intended—cheerfully, "I'd like that a great deal, General. Let's get you back to your cell where I will absolutely separate that girl from you." She gave them both an exaggerated wink.

The ridiculousness of it made Sagan snicker into Korac's band tee. Oh, dizzy.

"Thank you for an eventful evening at my Emporium. Seamswalker, until the next time. Warden, we'll talk soon. General, submit any further requests through the proper channels." Razor took a tablet from Matt—where did he come from—and the two left to eat all her yummy food.

Sagan fell asleep the moment they left the Emporium. Cradled in Korac's arms, she knew nowhere safer. By the time Korac woke her, they were back in his cell without

Pehton. She was awesome, so it made Sagan a little sad not to say goodbye.

"She'll be fine. I'm more concerned with you. Try to eat something."

She could tell he and Xelan made for a good couple. They shared certain nurturing traits. But as Korac handed Sagan the mushrooms they relished not a week ago, her stomach turned at the smell. She shook her head and pushed it away.

"If I didn't smell any better, I'd ask if you were pregnant." Her man just dropped that bomb on her out of nowhere and diffused it in the same second.

"Come again?"

He quirked a brow at her choice of words. It made her goofy smile and only then did he elaborate, "Maternity affects the scent of females. Only higher nacre upgrades can smell it, and only if they knew what to look for. Don't worry. You're not, but..." He pressed the back of his hand to her forehead before cupping her jaw. "You're losing weight. I know everything went critical recently. Is taking a break out of the question?"

Sagan barely tracked him. Too much happened, too close together. She needed to rest and find something that agreed with her stomach to eat. Not to mention her mind spiraled out of control, thinking of babies. Parenting with Korac. What would that be like—

"Hey! What're you doing?"

The Icarean warrior scooped her off the black tiles of his cell and carried her to the white sheets of his cot. "Time for you to rest properly. Nice shirt, by the way. Elden, I don't know if you could've worn anything more perfect."

Sagan blushed. "I wasn't trying for a statement."

"Oh, but you gave it. Loud and clear. Might as well get a collar with my name on it."

She yipped when he playfully slapped her ass hard enough to sting, encouraging her to crawl faster across the bed and wriggle under the sheets. Korac slipped in behind her and spooned her body with his. His warmth contrasted deliciously against the coolness of the sheets. And that's when it occurred to her, "Hey, Korac?"

"Hmm?" He swept her hair back from her nape and kissed her.

"This is our first time sleeping together."

"I recall our time very differently." He chuckled.

"Ha. Ha. You know what I mean." She huffed and settled in.

Korac draped his arm over her side and squeezed. "Good night, amos."

Uh oh. That familiar bug bit her. Alone in the dark, questions raced through her mind. It happened when she'd sleepover with Rayne. A curiosity needled Sagan and refused to let her sleep until she asked, "Korac, before I started this mission with Razor you said the pain and control...That it was done to you?"

He kissed her hair and assured, "I won't ever keep anything from you. But tonight, I want to hold you. I don't think it's the right time for this story."

A thought occurred to her and elicited a giggle.

"What is it?" He propped his elbow on the pillow and rested his head in his hand. The bewildered grin suited him.

The next she said in tandem with her snickering, "Maybe you can put it in your Verse to Rayne."

"Hah! The only way I'll write a Verse is if I dictate it to you while you're at a typewriter dressed like a naughty librarian."

"I still have my old glasses." Not a beat missed.

Korac purred against her back and kissed her cheek. "Get some sleep."

She perked up once more, "What about your memory—"

He swallowed her words with a hungry kiss over her shoulder. It left her breathless. Even his voice sounded hoarse with it, "Sleep."

"Aw, c'mon, you two are killing me with this toothache!"

Sagan bubbled with laughter. "Sweet dreams, Remorse!"

FIVE

ARRANGE THE PIECES ON THE BOARD

{Enki}

"Now?"

Ross looked up hopefully as Tumu entered Karter's room. Chris hopped to his feet; his eyes dragged down by dark circles. He refused to sleep. John, Eminent Lance, and Eminent Abresson took Jack on a tour of Enki. Mandatory leadership duties never ceased.

The thirteen-foot Tritan solemnly gripped Batman's shoulder. "They finished with Caedes. Tameka took Pax home to rest. They're ready for her."

Chris spared a glance at Ross. "You good here alone?"

"I won't be alone. Officer Tumu promised to stay with me." Here's hoping Ross remembered how to tell a lie. It'd been so long since she had to.

The Tritan's eyes widened a little before Chris turned to him for confirmation. He cleared his throat and assured, "That's right. I'll watch over the human. You take care of our Valkyrie here."

Voice gruff with emotion, Batman thanked the alien and followed the two Tritan technicians outside with Karter's hovering gurney.

Please. Please let her be okay.

"You mind telling me what you want with me?" Tumu didn't sound unhappy. But he sounded awfully suspicious.

Ross tossed her curly brown hair over her shoulder and took a deep breath before unloading, "Please take me to Reipon."

So. Tritans could bark out in laughter. "You want me to smuggle you through an official conduit during a galactic crisis onto a planet that enslaves your kind? And I suppose you want to go alone?"

"Well, as it happens, everyone else is busy. You know? With the galactic crisis you mentioned." At his incredulous huff, she pressed on, "I'm not contributing anything here, Officer Tumu. I'm in the way. But if I go, I can search for my sister."

His lipless mouth frowned, and his forehead sorta furrowed. "When they find Kyle, your brother will wipe my memory clean if he finds out I helped you—"

"He can do that?"

"—And I'm not convinced you'll find her before endangering yourself. You'll be alone and unprotected. And I'm a stupid-crazy Tritan for considering it."

She perked up at that. "Really?"

"It's the best time to go. This disaster scenario means all eyes are on the Progeny, but you won't be noticed if you slip away. Reipon is preparing to host a special gala for the Eminents. It's never canceled, even with this emergency. Perseverance and all that." Was he trying to roll those black voids he called eyes? "Security there is high. If you get into official trouble, any mention of my name will get you shipped straight back to Enki."

Ross smiled up at him, optimistic—

"But. If a slaver catches you, that's a different kind of trouble. There's a possibility you'll disappear. We may never find you. Whatever you do, stay away from anyone who mentions Razor."

The guy mentioned in the anonymous Verse. In Xelan's diaries. Any passage with him in it made her shiver. "Why?"

"He trades in the pain market. You avoid that like the plague. That said, I think I know someone who might consider helping you. Get your stuff. We're leaving now."

She reached out to stop him. "Wait, Officer Tumu—"

"Just Tumu."

"—I don't wanna sound ungrateful, but why are you helping me?" She retracted her hand and stared earnestly up at him.

"In truth, with your brother missing, we need another Story Taker until we find him. We won't unlock that potential in you by hanging around here. And frankly, you distract the King Regent. He takes the role bequeathed to him by his sister very seriously. Everyday Bethany is missing, Jack thinks he's failing you. He needs to worry about failing the world. Anything else you want me to be candid about?"

Ross absorbed his words into her marrow. "No. That's quite enough. Thank you."

"Anytime. Now grab your things."

She did as he told her, only then realizing she brought nothing with her from Earth. Rootless. "What will you tell the others? To keep them from coming after me?"

"I'll tell them the truth. But only after they've noticed you're gone, which may buy you a few days." Tumu led her out of the infirmary and down the hall.

Ross struggled to keep up with his impressive stride. His words twinged her heart. Useless. "Right. They won't notice me missing for a few days. Shows how much I contribute to the group."

Tumu stopped and whirled on her with one long finger in her face. "Listen here, Little Tree. The last week was the hardest these people have been hit in a long while. They wouldn't notice if I went missing if it weren't for my Enki connections. Give yourself a break. You're the newest member. And frankly, with what happens to the big contributors, I'd be thankful for the tiny target status. Do you get me?"

Feeling overwhelmed with her gratitude—genuine progress—Ross squeezed the trunk of his leg. "Thank you."

He blinked down at her before shrugging her off uncomfortably. "Well. Are you ready?"

They walked forever. Through a billion conduits, spanning several platforms in the middle of the ocean, and finally exited in a glass box so seamless she almost mistook it for thin air. They were at the heart of the Dyson's Sphere with the star powering it closer than ever, but not so close to blind her.

Tumu graciously let her absorb the spectacle. Ross looked back up at him. "Is this the shrine for Reipon?"

"It is. I'll chaperon you as far as luo—he owes me a favor—then you're on your own. Take this."

He handed her a strange disc, and she looked at him questioningly.

"It's enough credits to sustain you for a month or two. It should keep you out of trouble."

Her eyes bugged wide. "A month or two?"

The Gargantuan Tritan adjusted his orb and compressed a further six feet of his usual height. He stretched with a pained groan as he explained, "I hope you return in a few days at the most. I'm not looking forward to the backlash once Jack and Chris realize you're gone. But just in case, those credits should buy you out of anything."

Ross held out her hand. "I'll repay you somehow."

Tumu took it. "Yes. You will, Little Tree. Now let's go."

{EARTH}

Silence laid out on the floor of the detainment pod and counted the imperfections in the ceiling. She folded her arms behind her head and relaxed. Distracting herself. For the fiftieth time, she sang Elden's Verse, both parts.

Imminent.

They set up the Progeny's people masterfully. The nacre fortification virus. The disabler. The decryption. All designed to unlock one man's memory bank in time for the fireworks to start. And not for the first time, she wondered if she comprised a piece to that puzzle.

A distraction. A diversion. Or...something worse.

Silence rolled onto her side, stretched out languidly. Her reflection came back to her from the two-way mirror. The shirt covered little as it rode up higher than her hips. Nudity never bothered her. But it sure made this generation of humans and Progeny blush.

Kyle wouldn't turn away. He'd professionally keep his eyes on her own. She liked that about him.

That smirk.

Was Silence a sleeper?

And so the cycle of racing thoughts continued.

The door opened with Dr. Suarez calling behind him, "No. He demanded to see her."

Silence straightened the shirt for the married doctor's modesty. She liked Chief Lynn too much to leave herself exposed to the other woman's husband. He turned to her then and shook his head, incredulously. "You won't believe this. But T.A.O. returned with Kyle. And he refused to explain anything to us until he saw you. Can you please assure him we didn't mistreat you? He's upset."

She pulled herself onto her feet as if by strings and sidled by him. Twenty-One waited at the nacre glass front of his cell. They gazed at one another, and she took her time. But not smiling, no. She was sad for the Icarus.

"You understand why we need to monitor you, right, Silence? We're not cruel. We're concerned." The human male sounded genuine and kind. His expression reflected his words.

"Will you punish him?"

The doctor recoiled as if she'd slapped him. "No. Of course, not. I'm not sure how to explain it, but I don't think either of you are necessarily at fault. It's an aspect of your biology. My primary concern is learning if the virus we tested on him transmitted to you."

Twenty-One spoke through the glass, "You can trust the doctor. He's saving us."

Silence pressed her hand to the glass and smiled when the imprisoned Icarus reciprocated. Trust. With a sweeping gesture, she put her faith in the doctor. "Lead the way."

Dr. Suarez led her to the cafeteria where Kyle waited with the short woman from the sky. Lynn pointed at Silence behind him. Kyle turned.

And Silence fought not to claw her way out of the room. His eyes. There was something wrong with his eyes. Empty. Blank. A soulless void with no light inside. She looked away to hide her reaction.

"Good." He nodded to her before continuing, "Celindria can control T.A.O. I don't know how to stop it. All I know is that it's intermittent. Probably because she's a Seamswalker. During one of the 'off' intervals, she rescued me. I brought her here to save her."

The small woman with beautiful black skin and solid violet eyes peered around the room, but never met a single person's gaze. When she looked in Silence's direction, the Icarean female quickly avoided her. Soulless. Like Kyle. This was wrong.

Dr. Suarez kept his hands out as he approached the First Wave Progeny. "Can I examine you? I only want to check your vitals."

While he checked out the waif, Silence peered around the room, looking to see if anyone—anyone at all—noticed. Chief Lynn kept staring at Kyle in disbelief, but not horror. So wrong.

Kyle caught Silence's gaze then. He approached her, and her skin tried to crawl off her bones to shrink away from him. Despite that, she held firm. He searched her eyes with those empty green marbles. "Are you okay? Did they hurt you?"

That wasn't... No. Even that question was wrong. Kyle spoke wonderful things of the Progeny's people at Iona. Never once would he assume they'd harm her, and she knew that. Still, "I'm well. Chief Lynn treated me very kindly."

"Good." *It* turned Kyle's back on her with a hand on his hip as It took charge of the room. Also, unlike the man she met two weeks ago. "Listen up. I gathered some intelligence regarding Celindria's plans for Imminent's next strike—"

"Not before you're checked out." Andrew walked into the room without his partner. Lucas went to investigate the bombing at the chateau with other members of The Brethren and Smith.

Surely Conscience would sense the change in Story Taker. If not, the unusual intentions of the one called T.A.O.

Silence expected the thing inhabiting Kyle's body to protest an examination, but to her growing concern, *It* agreed. "You're right. Vitals check and blood tests all around. Lead the way, Doc."

Pablo visibly warmed at the nickname. "I'm glad you're back."

Lynn joined the two with relief naked in her eyes. "I thought... I thought I watched you die."

The parasite shook Kyle's head and chafed Chief Lynn's arms. "You're not that lucky."

With all their laughter, the remaining tension drained from the room.

And into Silence. She lost hope until she caught Andrew looking at her. Maybe someone else noticed after all. He looked away almost immediately, and she felt more alone than ever.

She turned on her heel and made to leave the room. The wrongness of everything picked at her skin like fiberglass. A shower. That would help.

"Silence."

The urge to vomit from the toxin in the room almost cost her her control. Instead, she mustered every ounce of it for this performance. She even smiled as she faced what was wearing Kyle. "Yes?"

"One sec, Doc," *It* called as It led Silence from the room. In the hall, It made a show of confessing, "When the fire almost took me, I couldn't stop thinking about you. It's crazy. You were almost my last thought in this world. Of how alone you'd be without me. Here." It removed the necklace she'd seen Kyle toy with often and donned it over her head. "If you ever get in trouble, use this."

"What about Ky—you? If you get into trouble?"

The shell grinned. "Don't you know? I'm always in trouble." Then, in an act of pure torture, *It* kissed her cheek. "Let's talk after."

Green pools gazed at her, expectantly.

Regret. Silence filled with so much regret. For not engaging him with her needs sooner. For not learning him more. Because surely whatever inhabited him now killed him for that smile that once warmed her through and now chilled her to the bone.

She stared into the face of the most familiar person in her lost world and fought back tears. "I'd like that." Gripping the chain after the abomination disappeared, Silence swore to avenge Kyle.

Even if it meant killing him.

{Earth}

Pablo drew another vial of Silence's blood. "Okay. One more and then you're all done here. Good?"

A mute nod. The Icarean female sucked all the gratitude and relief of the last few hours out of Pablo. Her melancholy prompted the examination in the first place. He only met her a few days ago, but her personality made an impression. Alive. A little wild. Living every moment with an earnest fascination and appreciation for the heartbeats around her.

So what happened? With his back to her, he asked, "Are you feeling all right, Silence?"

The warrior woman lived up to her name.

Facing her with his back leaning against the cabinet, he pressed, "You were livelier when we escorted you to the detainment pod. Does this have to do with Kyle?"

Silence's head snapped up. The search she gave his eyes opened his soul to her. What did she want to see there?

Confounded with it, she finally opened up her mouth, "Haven't you noticed—"

The knock on the door startled Pablo, as enraptured as he was with Silence.

"It's Andrew."

The doctor pinched the bridge of his nose and groaned at the spike in adrenaline from the jump scare. "Come in."

Silence returned to staring at the tile floor, no longer willing to talk.

"Sorry for interrupting. We heard from X and R." Two aliens from Lukemore who set traps for the Volcano Day battle. Tumu contacted them as part of the declaration of war against Imminent. "Enki's letting them through. They'll be here in the next day or two. Legir, too." The Leader of Yu's history went deep in Earth and Cinder. One of his son's, Bin, befriended Nox. Through a cruel twist of fate and manipulation, Nox killed Bin. This prompted Bin's twelve brothers to seek revenge. They all fell to Nox. Legir eagerly joined the Volcano Day battle, providing medical help across the field. Recently, he mentored different members of the Shadow. Including Pablo and Sagan.

"I'm looking forward to seeing him again." Pablo smiled fondly. The centrifuge finished. "One second."

Andrew peered curiously over the doctor's shoulder as he dripped Silence's blood onto a plate. Under the microscope, he carefully introduced an element of Lynn's nacre disabling weapon to the nanites in the female's blood. The results disturbed him. "Shit." He spun on his stool to face Andrew. One shake of his head had them both looking at Silence.

She stared with a subdued alternative of her typical curiosity. Her voice stripped of her usual force of personality, she softly asked, "What is it?"

"After Twenty-One...you contracted the nacre fortifying virus. We can't let you leave the facility. Not until everything settles down." Pablo watched her reaction to the news. From the squeeze of her fists to the flitting of her eyes between him and Andrew, she absorbed it.

Silence tried to speak twice, clearing her throat. "I can't help with the reconnaissance?"

Pablo shook his head, and Andrew took over. "It would set us impossibly far back if they captured you." He held up his hand to stave her arguments. "I've heard of your fighting prowess. You're an incredible warrior. But we've been blindsided so much we can't risk you."

"Can you take it out of me?"

"I don't have a cure yet, I'm sorry. We weren't planning to make one, but if you want, you can help me do that. We can test with you. If you'll let us?" Pablo considered a few avenues where they could start. As a physician, he sincerely wanted to help her despite his suspicions. Silence seemed so lost in this world. And she saved them from Imminent's first attack during the Twenty-One transfer.

Convenient coincidence or Imminent sleeper? Either way, he wanted to help her.

"Yes. I'd like that. I want to help Kyle." Some of the earnestness returned.

Pablo failed to see the connection, but he appreciated her eagerness. "You and Twenty-One will spend some time together this way. I'll get some consent forms ready."

Andrew crossed over to the exam table and took up in front of the female Icarus. "You do that. I'll test her intentions. I thought you'd be more comfortable if we were alone for that, Silence."

She peered at Conscience a long time before flashing those big gray eyes at Pablo. "Yes. Thank you, Dr. Suarez. I'll be fine with Andrew while you retrieve your papers."

Pablo sensed an exchange taking place. An accord of sorts between the two. He left them alone with curiosity burning in his veins. Until he caught the figure approaching him from the opposite end of the hall.

Lynn looked infinitely better since Kyle returned. That said a lot, considering their rocky terms. Alone for the first time in days, Pablo opened his arms to Lynn. She fell into them and squeezed tightly. "I just want off this ride."

"Shh…" Pablo kissed her locs. "We'll get through this." He stepped back and pressed her hand to his tattoo over his nacre. Over their wedding vows.

She traced the words. Never endanger this. "T.A.O.'s window ended. She's returning to Celindria. Shit…I can't believe this. It's so convoluted."

"If you think about Nox's Verse, it makes sense. We're hitting the location on Reipon first. T.A.O. promised to take us there. No one's heard from Tumu. I don't like any of this—"

Pablo kissed his wife, deeply. Pressed her firmly against the wall and planted both hands on either side of her face. He ground into her hips with his own, and she purred for him.

Lynn broke away with a stern finger in his face. "I know what you're up to. You're trying to distract me. As much as I usually love it, I can't imagine this is an appropriate time for it. Even by our standards."

"You're right." He backed off, hands on hips, and bit his bottom lip to restrain himself. "Silence agreed to tests for the cure to the virus. She definitely contracted it."

"Do you think it was intentional?"

He shook his head, bewildered. "I honestly don't know anymore. At first, I suspected it. But now…"

"We're adopting her. And Twenty-One. We do this. Pick up strays and make them official Shadow." Lynn shrugged and thrust fingers in her hair. As two of those lucky strays, they found little room to complain but… "I just want to blow stuff up."

Pablo chuckled once. Twice. He opened up and laughed. Despite her best efforts, Lynn joined him. He kissed her forehead with all his love for her and smooshed them together. They both gripped their own chains over their vows. The Shadow.

After a long, comforting minute basking in his wife's love and the love of their family, Pablo asked, "Have you heard from Sagan? It's been a few days since Kyle returned."

Lynn sniffed and nodded. "Korac answered her device—so much for prison. He said she needed to rest. He'll wake her later today."

Pablo smiled timidly and headed for those documents. "We wore her out."

She followed down the hall. "Well, let's hope she got plenty of sleep. Because we'll need her for this. I don't trust T.A.O. as the only Seamswalker on a forbidden planet."

"Sagan's like all the Shadow." Pablo glanced back to see Lynn waiting for him to elaborate. "Strong and resilient. That's how we always remain."

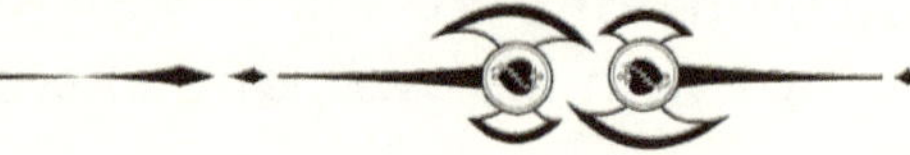

{Gait}

Korac watched as Sagan slept. For two days, she snored gently into the ostrich feather pillows she acquired from Reipon. She needed more rest, but the messages he received on her comms device required her attention. After waking her, they'd have breakfast. This time he'd sit on her and force her to eat. If that's what it took. With all the activity, she shed almost fifteen pounds in three weeks. At first, it cut her muscle tone nicely, but now it ate away into her mass. He was losing her.

No idea to what. But he strongly suspected—

"Razor..." Sagan muttered in her sleep. "Leave Matt alone. Please..."

Time to wake her. Korac crossed the room and sank on the bunk beside her. The war criminal leaned forward and kissed his sleeping princess. Sagan inhaled deeply of him and returned in force. Her fingers found his hair, shoulder-length now, and pressed him closer. He purred for her before breaking away. The prominence of the hollows of her cheeks worried him. The dark circles, despite her sleep, tightened his chest.

But that smile—Lazy. Silly. With her blond hair stuck up all over. Freckles glittered across her nose. Her eyes finally opened. Bright and happy. Unused, her voice came out rough, "Morning, General Korac."

Korac smirked. "Good evening, General Sterling."

Sagan sprung up, frazzled. "Evening? What time is it on Earth? I—"

"You slept for two days."

She gaped. "Why—Why did you let me sleep so long?"

He clicked his tongue and crossed the room, gathering her comms device. "I'd prefer you sleep longer. As much as you seemed to need it." Korac slipped out of his robe, silk that matched the sheets. When it hit the floor revealing his bare backside, a squeak erupted from behind him. His smirk widened into a grin. "But I've taken calls from your Shadow. They seem quite incapable without you."

"I should thank you for taking care of me." He turned in time to see his woman stand from the bed and strip out of his shirt. Gloriously naked.

Korac fell to his knees at Sagan's bare feet. They could play this game forever, one-upping each other. But despite his dominance in bed, the Icarean General knew his place. He served her.

"Take from me what you need. Give to me what you want. Until Eternity takes me, I'm yours." Korac tilted his neck, exposing his carotid. "Feed from me. Honor me."

Given their height difference, Sagan stood barely a head higher than Korac on his knees. Accepting his reverence, she swept the hair from his shoulder—

The air brakes on the lift sighed as it descended with its passenger. They shared an abashed look.

"Shit!"

"Pehton."

They scrambled to cover and dress. At least make some effort not to take advantage of the Lyrik's graciousness.

"She's still here?!" The Executive Warden of Gait rubbed her forehead and groaned, distraught. "I'm so demoted."

Korac hid his amusement as Sagan gave a speech straight from the heart. "I want to thank you so much, Pehton, for being so understanding about this—"

"You're talking to me about this while wearing a sheet."

"—I know it's put you in a difficult position. One that I respect—Hey!"

Korac picked Sagan up and threw her over his shoulder. At Pehton's bemused brow, he held up one finger to stave her wrath. Adorably, the General of the Two Armies slapped his ass, covered now in jeans. "Let's get you dressed. Then you can assail yourself of the Executive Warden's wisdom and grace." He carried her over to the Japanese silk screen in the corner and handed her the Lyriki armored coat. Then the hip harness for the axes. And, apparently, a hairbrush at her request.

Pehton called with her back to the cell, "Save it for later, General Sterling. I consider this a favor to be repaid. In the meantime, you're needed on Earth. They've been calling you for days."

Sagan finished dressing and reached up to cup Korac's face with both hands. "Thank you," she whispered, warming him through. Intelligence flashed in her eyes. "What about your memory? The one that upset you?"

He gently clasped her wrists. "Nothing to resolve at the moment. We'll talk next time. I've already extended the limits of my selfishness by keeping you to myself for two days in the middle of a war. I'll try to keep my thoughts of you to a minimum."

Korac appraised her from head to toe. Cute short-cut hair. Sexy corset coat with nothing underneath. Thigh-high stiletto boots. He gave her a wicked smirk. "Even at a minimum, it'll prove quite the crucible."

She shoved him cutely.

He sobered for the next bit. "The Ecology first. Then Tameka needs you in Enki. And Sagan?"

Sagan paused in her supply check to peer up at him.

"Go see King Rayne."

Her face fell. He hated reminding her, but the longer she postponed it, the harder it became. But something else darkened her eyes. A shadow. She bit her lip and looked away. The nonverbal tell.

Sagan craved a pain experience. She even spoke of them in her sleep. Asked Razor for more. She slept the withdrawal off, but with each passing experience, her body depended more on the rush of endorphins.

Korac kissed the top of her head and drew her gaze back to him. No sexy smirks. No winning smiles. He whispered, "You come before the mission. Don't risk yourself more than necessary. And if you ever need me, I'm one step away."

The shame melted from her. Only love shone in those purple eyes. She put a fist to her nacre and winced when it hit the port cover. Despite that, she promised, "I'll be seeing you."

"I look forward to it as always."

The scent of fresh watermelon lingered in Sagan's wake. He wished she'd fed. Ate. Rested longer—

"Korac."

This.

Right.

Korac turned to face the dainty Lyrik and acknowledge a nightmare he'd rather ignore.

"I've waited two days, but now it's time to answer my questions. What is the Atheneum? And how does it concern you?"

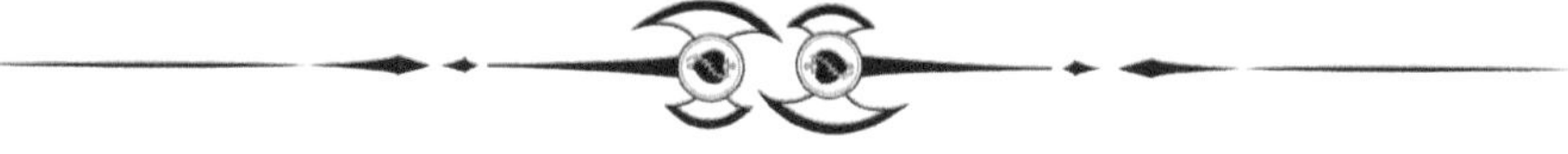

{EARTH}

Andrew hated tightroping. Especially with the multi-Probability shift that shadowed every face, every room, and every moment. Everything so eerily familiar and unbelievably foreign all at once.

Kyle illuminated Andrew's history in his mind. He could see from their shared past where he took a step, what he wore, the breaths he held. And separate those events from all the others that existed at once.

Going it alone from here might prove difficult. And terribly lonely.

"Hey, are you ready to go?" Sagan arrived a few hours ago after they tried reaching her for two days.

Andrew memorized the features of her face. The pretty eyes, the cute smile, and the sweet freckles. So much warmth emanated from this one person. He designated her a pillar.

Few people qualified as a pillar, a foundation for his sanity. Their Probabilities aligned to match the core of the person in every instance. Sagan was a pure soul, and Andrew welcomed her presence.

"Everything squared away with Kyle, Pablo, and Lynn?" he asked as he turned back to the cliff overlooking the Mediterranean. The sun set beyond Earth's Sphere. He voted in favor of renaming it after Rayne, the only other person who qualified as a pillar.

Sagan paled. "I'm still coming to terms with—"

Andrew *suggested* she not finish that sentence and shook his head sternly.

"Right. I'll drop you off. Then check on Tameka. And then hopefully come back to welcome Legir." As she listed off her tasks, her genuine smile grounded him. "I look forward to seeing him again. And of course X. Maybe not so much R."

Conscience chuckled at her eyes widening in bewilderment. "He takes some adjusting." Playing the part for her, Andrew ignored her screaming intentions. The real ones. At the first opportunity she could separate from her obligations, she intended to visit Razor's Emporium. He glanced at the metal disc over her nacre and fought the urge to frown.

They survived so much without breaking. The Two Worlds trusted them to bend only enough to test the enemy's strengths and rebound even stronger. Andrew held out his hand. Sagan took it and walked them to western Australia. Daytime here, he gazed out at the black fire that changed his world.

"What's it like?" Even her curiosity sounded innocent and sweet.

"Like I'm living a billion lives at once with some differences being only slight but…" Andrew turned back to meet her gaze. "I fall into the major ones like bottomless pits drilled to capture me. Throwing me off and spiraling me into all the potential unknowns."

"Andrew?"

Sagan stepped aside, clearing the view to the zeppelin.

Lucas, a sight for Andrew's sore eyes, triggered the worst fall of all. In an equal number of Probabilities, he betrayed them. And Andrew couldn't discern if this was one such thread. He hated doubting a face, a voice, and a presence he came to love.

No matter how much the paranoia confused him, Imminent bombed Lucas' chateau. That's a loss, and the Icarus's golden eyes dulled. He looked as if he needed some comfort.

Andrew crossed the field between them and wrapped his arms around his lover. Tightly. The powerful Icarus returned in kind and kissed his neck. Sagan appeared beside them, hopeful. They both laughed heartily as they pulled her in for a three-way embrace with her so tiny she barely reached their shoulders.

Warmth. Love. Sincerity.

Quite a break from the shit happening at the Ecology. And that's when he decided not to share his assumptions with Lucas. Trust needed reestablishing before any further exchanges of "need to know" information.

A keening howl drew him from the nest of arms. "Pisces came home?" The night someone dropped all the Cascading Light on the Vittle crops, their pet Hellkite, Pisces, disappeared. He worried someone harmed her. He called out to her as he ran behind their home.

The red-scaled, twelve-foot tall beast with a croc's snout and six arms whooped and fell to the ground. Instantly exposed belly.

"Aw!" Sagan cooed from behind him and rushed by to fawn over the beast.

Lucas sounded genuinely relieved. "I actually lost sleep over her. But the tart went and impregnated herself." Interesting feat considering they were asexual and reproduced as such. He joined Sagan in spoiling the critter.

"Do we need to find a vet or something?" Andrew indulged the monster with his foot along her snout.

A light bulb went off over Sagan's head. He'd testify in court that he watched it happen like in a cartoon. She peered up at Lucas. "Hey—"

"What is it this time?" As if he saw the look on her face, too.

She dared look sheepish in response. "Well, it's wardrobe related."

"Of course it is. You know I contribute in a dozen ways to the Shadow, but you three girls only ask me for clothes." At her pout, he relented with a grin. "Go ahead."

As Sagan put in a request for a dress, Andrew gazed out over the burning field. Cascading Light burned forever. He frowned.

One. The black fire only consumed the entire crop in one Probability. This one. The billions shifted and churned. The vines and vegetation mostly clear of ruin. Except this one.

Lucas' hand on his shoulder startled him. The Icarus removed it immediately with remorse in his golden eyes. "I'm sorry."

Fake it. "You're fine. How's progress on the new fields?"

He beamed with the good news. "Fifty acres planted already. Twice the amount here. We'll restore it. Make it right."

"Good to hear," Sagan cheered. "Now, if you don't mind, I have so many places to be. Love you both." She kissed a cheek for each, waved, and walked into thin air.

"Has she lost weight?" Lucas asked once everything was all clear.

"Stress."

"There's plenty of that to go around. Speaking of which, I was drawing a bath when you arrived. Care for a soak?" As Andrew searched his face, Lucas' expression fell. He covered it well. "Of course, you should rest alone. I can take one after—"

Andrew pulled those soft lips to his own and ran his fingers into Lucas' sandy-blond hair. With permission granted, the Icarus melted to the Progeny. The kiss deepened, and Andrew moaned into his mouth. Should he hate himself for testing his lover's intentions the whole while? For *suggesting* they fuck without complications or discussing current events? Feeling how much Lucas enjoyed the arrangement, Andrew decided the guilt could wait.

Sex now. Apocalypse later.

SIX

WHAT LIES IN OUR DREAMS

{CINDER}

"ARE YOU EXCITED TO MEET YOUR RELIEF TEAM?" Bones rushed down the ramp to find Para staring into space again.

She looked ill. Pallid to her gray skin. Dark circles under her black eyes. Hair frazzled from gripping it. The hollowness of her voice would haunt him forever. "I can't think. I..."

Silence filled the pit. Only their breathing sounded between them. It was cruel poetry that the females among their race built best for war suffered the most from grief and loss. Almost as though one could not be had without the other.

Sagan Seamswalked into the pit with Tameka. The blond girl headed straight for the fridge. "I'm starved. Anybody want anything—Hey!"

"Sorry." Bones nodded toward the smallest Valkyrie. In mourning, she cleaned out their entire supply. "All gone. I meant to grab some at the fortress."

She smiled sadly. "It's fine." Seamswalking over to the couch, Sagan sat next to the stricken woman. "Para, I'm taking you as soon as Tumu gets here. I saw Chris. He said good things about their progress with Karter."

No response.

Tameka took the skid to King Rayne. "Hey, I brought your girlfriend with me this time."

Bones took a few steps away, respecting the Progeny's space.

"So, it's true. She can hear you?" A deep voice called from behind.

Bones whirled around to find a Tritan standing on the ramp overlooking the lake. The seven-foot tall man was green. Not blue.

Fury glared from the island.

Sagan Seamswalked beside him and put an axe to his throat.

Para went full Atramentous and growled in three pitches, "I didn't know they made Tritans in your color."

"I'm not your typical Tritan." He took in their team and chuckled in a strange, high-pitched yowl. Like a hyena. The almond-shaped black buttons for eyes bounced manically between them. "She's got nothing to fear. Am I right?" The Tritan leaned over the banister and called to the Martyr Complex, "Don't worry. I'll take good care of you."

Bones shifted uncomfortably as he looked to the Progeny for orders.

Tameka shouted up at the stranger from the island, "So you're 'the Chef?'"

Dramatically, the stranger pressed the back of his arm to his forehead and groaned. "Oh, no! They told you *that* name." He straightened and locked eyes on hers. Serious, stern. "Now I have to kill you."

"What the fuck?" Sagan cried out.

Para flew to the ramp and got all in his personal space.

But Bones restrained from laughing. Something in the Tritan's posture, his eyes...He was taking the piss, but the poor bastard picked his audience badly. These were not the girls with whom to fuck while protecting their King.

The Chef matched Para's gaze without patronizing her over the height difference. The tension loosened a notch as he frowned at the tiny woman's apparent condition. "Sparkles will be fine."

Para startled and took a step out of his space. Tumu's nickname for Karter softened the moment, allowing them to breathe.

"Why do they call you that? Is your specialty knives or something?" Tameka asked as Bones rounded the lake to the ramp.

The Tritan turned his green back on Para and bounced his brows at Tameka. "Flambé."

"Dammit! Why do I keep falling for men who like to keep the mystery going?" Tumu finally rounded the corner from the tunnel. "Lamassau breathes fire."

The Chef—Lamassau—growled, "The 'air of mystery' fetish keeps your ancient ass young, Tumi." He leaned over the banister again, all conspiratorially for Tameka. "Sounds like 'do me' in the bedroom. Get it?" He winked extra big.

And then ... they made out. Bones gawked as the two lipless aliens exchanged very tongue-heavy kisses. Talk about inappropriate timing. Although when Enki sounded so stiff and regimented, a pair of Tritans might take advantage of any opportunity for affection.

Sagan's unexpected giggling brought everyone out of their shock and broke the pair up.

Bones reached Para at that point and barked out a laugh as he chafed her biceps.

Tameka shook her head, bewildered. "I know so many things I didn't want to know five minutes ago."

Sagan Seamswalked to the island and beamed up at the odd couple. She declared, "I vibe with it."

"I knew you were always my favorite, Star." Tumu nodded to her and took Lamassau's hand, bringing him further into the pit. As he passed Para, he offered, "Let me on-board him, and then we'll take you to see Sparkles."

Para nodded in response, fading back into catatonia.

Bones muttered against her hair, "Soon. Okay? You'll be leaving me alone with a most interesting character." He kissed the soft blue strands.

Hey, she laughed a little and squeezed one hand he offered in comfort. "Thank you."

Behind them, the girls introduced the Chef to their King. "Rayne, keep the morgue pranks to a minimum. The last thing I want to hear is that you spooked him and he promptly cooked you." Tameka made a good point.

Sagan's voice went quieter than usual. "Can you give me a minute with her?"

The grouped back way off. Lamassau and Tumu went to the corner. To make out. More. And Bones took Para over with Tameka where they all watched, unable to look away. In approximately five minutes, Sagan returned to the lake's shore and the two Tritans finally came up for air.

The blond Progeny took Para's hand. "Ready?"

"She's allowed visitors. You'll be in the room with her," The redheaded Progeny assured.

"Bones."

He turned to Tumu, prepared to receive security orders.

"Don't let Lam convince you we have an open relationship. We don't. And he likes to make me jealous."

"Aww, Tumi. You spoil my fun. I'd planned to immediately seduce the strapping Icarus. Now how will I entertain myself?"

Tameka shook her head incredulously. "I swear to Elden, all Tritans do is cause trouble—"

And Sagan took them through the Seam, leaving Bones alone with the Chef.

"So, why do they call you Bones?"

{GAIT}

Matt adhered himself to Razor like a good bodyguard. This required an upgrade in dress. What would Lucy think of the fancy black tuxedo? To him, clothes covered and provided him with pockets. That's it. But maybe she'd appreciate the tailored-cut shoulders and the cufflinks at his wrists? Nah. The inside jacket lined with throwing knives might impress her, though. All perfectly sharpened and balanced. With all the lethal in his suit, he slicked the fringe of his auburn hair back and tried his best to melt into the crowd.

The boss wore red tonight. It contrasted strangely against his navy blue skin and pale blue hair. A phenomenal host, he greeted his guests and escorted a few select clients to the booths himself. Matt observed the shifts in his personality with each individual. The life in his eyes, the ease of his posture, and the congeniality in his voice. Everything varied based on the company.

Matt learned a lot shadowing that man.

"Surely, it's low risk enough tonight for you to engage one of the young ladies with a dance?" Razor spared him a friendly grin and nodded in a Lyrik's direction.

Before the evening started, the black-skinned, yellow-feathered woman—and the rest of the Lyriks—followed the Pain Curator upstairs from that abyss he called a bedroom. Also, the location of his personal office and vault. Come to think of it, Pehton was the only Lyrik Matt noticed from outside the Emporium.

The exotic female caught them looking and hurried over. She. Curtsied. To Razor. It was...bizarre. From Matt's limited understanding, the Lyriks warded Gait. Why in the hell would they physically bow to a merchant?

Her yellow eyes ducked low, never meeting Matt's.

The Pain Curator offered her to the redheaded human. "Will this one suffice?"

Perplexed, Matt shook his head. "No, thank you." He plastered a warm smile to relieve any impoliteness on his part.

"You're dismissed, Oleen."

The Lyrik returned to the party, volunteering to entertain other guests.

Razor tsked. "You have a one-track mind. It's dangerous to leave tensions unattended. Makes you sloppy in your work. And since your work is protecting me or handling wares around my Emporium—I think you see where I'm going with this." He gestured at the pitch-black woman once more with the glass in his nail-less hand. "Oleen is fair game. The other Lyriks are also fairly receptive. Except Triss. She's mine. Keep your hands off."

Matt nodded along at the strange turn in the conversation when a thought struck him. "What about Executive Warden Pehton?"

"She's still her own. For now." Razor smirked with a menacing intensity.

It distracted Matt so much he almost didn't notice Puk, the Mon3 drone, approach from the rear. The man leaned in and whispered to Razor, who turned with an inconvenienced frown. "Again?"

Puk nodded solemnly.

"Switch shifts with Matt. I want him on 324." Razor turned to him and explained, "324 is special. But I understand you have a certain gift. No emotional scarring. Got it? Remember, the goal is not to break them but to ease them into this way of life."

Eager for a shift change, Matt tore out of the tuxedo jacket while rushing to the black basement entrance. Stripped off the white shirt. Collecting a black bodysuit and hood, he finished changing in the locker room. Matt took a deep breath before donning the anonymous gear. He wore it. The Numbered wore it. Only his height lent to any identity.

Everything black. Floor, ceiling, walls, rigging, instruments—Abyssal. A vacuum of pain. He hurried down to the third floor of Hell. Located the correct bunk and the small Numbered inside. The unimpressive height concerned him, and he flashed back to all the underage girls he delivered to Justice Lee at the Cult of Night compound.

But this wasn't sexual. The Numbered exchanged their pain for credits. Paid pain-workers. That excused some of the hedonism—

Sniffle.

Sob.

324 cried in their bunk. The hood muffled the sound enough so Matt couldn't discern gender. But definitely clocked the age as under eighteen. He scooped the lightweight person in his arms and carried them three floors back upstairs to the zones. The rotation chart marked flogging for tonight. Well, if they weren't crying before, they certainly would after. It was one of few instruments that soothed him. Matt took it seriously.

The person whimpered as Matt laid them on the cool black floor. No, not person. The Numbered. He tied the restraints from the walls and ceiling until 324 formed a sagging X. A small one.

The young man shook his head and took a deep breath. He always broke the most important rule. Not to assuage his conscience. Matt wondered if he ever got one of those. No, he broke the rule to leave them more pliable. To improve the results of the follow-up evaluation. The more Numbered he accrued, the more he found himself in Razor's favor.

So he leaned forward and whispered against their hood, "We both know I have no choice but to hurt you. But I want you to know that I don't want to. One day, you'll fulfill the contract, and he'll release you. Play the part until then."

324 broke down and racked with sobs. This was the usual reaction to the reintroduction of hope. He absorbed the response and observed their emotions. Emotions he'd never understand.

Perimeter lighting illuminated the floors and ceiling only enough to see the blood splatter the walls and drip to the floor. Drains set around the room would take care of that. The black space soaked in the red like a vampire. Or an Icarus.

Matt ripped and tore into 324's back and shoulders. For hours.

Razor required six-hour shifts out of each Numbered every two days. 324 differed with this daily schedule. He wondered why. They weren't particularly resilient. Quite the opposite.

They cried more than anyone he worked so far. Begged at times. It meant Matt stuck to a completely professional approach. Strikes evenly apart, allowing them to heal. None harder or lighter than the last. No aggression or perversion. Strictly business.

By the end of the shift, the Numbered passed out three times. He took 324's shivering, unconscious body to the spray and washed away the blood. The water revived them, and the tears started anew. Soft, silent ones.

When he returned them to the bunk, he carefully tested for the least painful position. Professional. No undue harm. As he turned to leave, the small person grabbed his arm. A question passed between them. One he couldn't answer. When he took their wrist to pull them away, he squeezed gently.

324 wept as if their heart broke.

Who the fuck was this person, and why the hell did Razor put them through daily shifts? As Matt stripped in the lockers and hit the showers, he took small comfort in knowing that at least now he took responsibility of 324. No telling what kind of abuse the others put the Numbered through. Easy to get carried away and all that.

Matt broke into the kitchens, starving and exhilarated. A familiar voice reached him from the addition.

"You haven't really done anything to deserve how I've treated you," Sagan offered Razor.

If she only knew.

"Well..." Damn. The amount of charm Razor laid into his voice impressed even Matt. "I'm sure I've done something to deserve it."

She laughed as if despite herself while idly fingering an axe. "I appreciate the food. I was starving."

Matt peered around the corner at the buffet the Pain Curator laid out for the Seamswalker. He only loaded that thing down for parties. And her. Matt ignored it, preferring the simpler fare. But wow, Sagan loved that shit.

"You've been busy. You haven't slept, have you? Here let me get that." Razor reached over and brushed a smear of food from her cheek.

The Seamswalker blushed lightly under her freckles and let him. With her chin cupped in his hand, Matt expected the alien to linger or worse—kiss her. But to both his and apparently Sagan's surprise, the Pain Curator dropped his hand the moment the food disappeared.

"I slept a few days, but I've been all over the Vast Collective since then. I'm a little exhausted. But I still plan to attend the gala with you. As promised."

Matt shook his head and stepped away. He grabbed some ingredients for his sandwich as the pair wandered closer.

"I'm delighted to hear that. But please don't feel obligated. So much transpired since I extended the invitation." Razor stepped into the kitchens with a friendly nod to acknowledge Matt's presence.

Sagan beamed. "I already have a dress in the works."

The Pain Curator smiled at her with a flash in his gray eyes. "I looked forward to seeing it. But that's not the only reason you came to me. Is it?"

She looked away for a heartbeat.

Through the tension, Matt took a loud bite of his sandwich. Lettuce and pickles crunched in his teeth.

Breaking into a bright fit of laughter, Sagan shot the redheaded human a pretty smile before turning back to Razor with something akin to embarrassment in her eyes. "An experience? I wanted to try this port before I got rid of it."

"Ahh. I'm still curating your next one. But if you don't mind something less personal—"

"I'm happy to try anything."

Wow. She said that awfully fast.

Razor turned his back on her for a moment, and Matt caught the most disturbing, satisfied smile on his face. When he faced her again, the Pain Curator held a capsule. "I can ease your troubles. Allow me one second to load it." He headed for the booths.

In his absence, Sagan shivered. "I hate when the green shifts around with the orange in his eyes. Don't you?"

Matt fought to swallow the colossal bite in his mouth to question her. "Sagan—"

"I'm ready for you!"

"Be back." She Seamswalked across the warehouse.

And left Matt with another mystery to solve.

{GAIT}

Pehton felt pale. A gray cast covered her pitch-black skin. She kept checking her hands to see if the color washed away. Korac's past, what little he shared with her, left her sick. Bruised. And that was only a quick overview. The way he talked about it, too. So clinical. Cold. Dead.

She shuddered and chafed her arms, freezing. Her boots splashed along the wet pavement on her way to Razor's Emporium. The purple Overseers droned through the sky. Unmanned, they swept for escaped prisoners or persons of interest. She received their reports every hour to her palm device. The uncatalogued faces of Prisonborne required the occasional followup, but otherwise the prison planet was quiet.

As she crossed to the warehouse's revolving door, Pehton considered her reasons for returning. She no longer trusted the memories Razor granted her. It freed her from him in a sad way. Her liberation was a consolation prize for forgetting the beautiful faces of the little boy and girl—

The door was locked. She pushed, but it refused to spin. Unheard of. A little frantically, Pehton knocked on the glass. She came here to ask Razor about the Atheneum. Ever since she was made, Razor was always here. He might know something.

If he'd answered the door.

The ginger human came to the glass. "He said if it was you to tell you to wait. He'll be with you in a minute."

"I'm—"

"The Executive Warden of Gait. Yea, yea. Anyway, he'll be right over." Then he took a sloppy bite out of a massive sandwich.

Well.

Pehton stepped away and reflected on her conversation with the Icarean General. *"The one man I can't see in my memory asked the man in white pants about the Atheneum. As if they were assigned to guard it. Hide it, even."* The devastation in Korac's gaze kept her from pressing. He was famous for the perfectly cultivated mask. The most nonreactive leader in the Vast Collective's history. Devastated, and he let her see it.

"You're shivering, Peh Peh."

If she wasn't before, she would now. Razor's voice was pure ice. The other night with Korac and Sagan was the first time she truly defied him. It was a bad idea, but Gait's Warden would never regret it. For once, people took her side and had her back. It warmed her through, even at the memory. But how did she proceed from here?

Pehton turned and offered him a professional smile. "That's Executive Warden Pehton. May I come in? I'm conducting a Vast Collective investigation, and I have a few questions to ask you."

It bothered her so much that Razor smirked as he gestured her inside. "Quite the return to form, *Executive Warden*. If you'll follow me this way." To the ginger human, he instructed, "Matt, please see to our guest."

"Sure, boss." The ginger winked at Pehton and walked off while stuffing his face with the last of his sandwich.

Up the wrought-iron stairs to the mezzanine. Across the corrugated metal to the vault. Which he opened and indicated for her to follow inside. Odd. Pehton hesitated at the blackness inside. So seamless, she startled when Razor sank into a staircase in the floor.

He raised a questioning brow. "Is there a problem, *Executive Warden*?" As if this sort of clandestine set up was normal, and she was the weird one.

Still, Pehton followed him below. It dropped them into a barely lit black cavern that spanned the entire basement of the original warehouse. An Olympic swimming pool of a bed took up the center, sunken into the space. The sheets struck her as odd. They were a purple silk and familiar. A colossal desk overlooked the bed. Enki tablets and stationery neatly arranged on top.

Razor called out, "I'm home."

Oh. This was why he wanted her down here.

The Lyriks poured out of the dark space. Scantily clad or entirely naked. They slipped the tuxedo jacket from his shoulders. Pulled out the desk chair for him. Handed him a drink. All while Pehton stood across the desk from him.

Oleen pushed in the chair under him. Triss, the brightest red-feathered of the Lyriks, walked up with a sultry sway to her hips, got on her knees, and ducked her head out of Pehton's sight under the desk. In Razor's lap. Her head bobbed a bit, and the Executive Warden felt bile rise. Before she vomited, Triss stood with his loafers in hand.

Smug. Perversely gratified by Pehton's disgust. Bastard. He kicked his feet up on the desktop, and Triss snatched a pillow to place under them. Such a gross display of power. Power Pehton gave him. Power he now threatened her with.

Razor leaned back with his arms folded behind his head. "How may I help with your investigation, *Executive Warden Pehton?"*

Shamed, she trembled. She did *not* pity these women. They brought this on themselves, and she wasn't entirely sure they'd yet served the extent of the sentence they deserved. She would never be like them.

"What do you know of the Atheneum?" Professional.

He chuckled and sat up straight as if relenting the display for the conversation. "A long time ago, the Tritans scoured the planet for it. It's a myth. Something about the Ancients. I've lived here for millions of years. I've known no one to find it."

Bullshit. "During Inanis—"

"Peh Peh." He admonished her gently. Filled the familiar endearment with kindness and a warmth close to love. The follow-up sigh sounded with pity.

"—Two men discussed the preservation of it in the prison yard." The Executive Warden didn't acknowledge the interruption. She held her chin high and squared her shoulders.

Razor stared at her across that immense desk and looked impressed with her. He rapped his knuckles on the surface before offering, "We haven't been very nice to each other over the last few days. Have we?"

The charm, when he laid it on thick, tempted her. Return to the status quo. The familiar. The safe. In his good graces.

"I'll do something nice for you. No favors in return. Just to show you there are no hard feelings between us, and we can return to being friends."

So tempting. The tension with someone like him truly unnerved her.

He slipped his suspenders off and finished his drink in one gulp. As he rolled up his sleeves, Razor finished his proposal, "I'll ask around and cash in on a few favors. The Atheneum. Inanis. Your whole crusade. Free of charge."

Pehton's eyes widened in surprise. Razor did not do charity. Cautiously, she prodded, "I hope you understand I find this offer too generous."

When he stood, she almost flinched. "I like you, Peh Peh. If I didn't..." He spread his arms wide to once again remind her of the worst-case scenario. "I don't want to fight with you. Hell, the little show the other night brought in so many customers over the last few days, I might even owe the three of you credits. The highest rollers arrived from all over the galaxy for the chance to glimpse the sainted Seamswalker and her sinful Icarean General. It's adorable."

She reluctantly sighed in relief. With enough credits, Razor could forgive anything. "I'd appreciate your participation in this investigation."

Razor held out his hand with a kind smile. Pehton hesitantly placed hers in it. He pressed two fingers to the pulse point in her wrist. As he did when they first met so very long ago. "Let's start over."

They emerged from his creepy basement in time to find Sagan exiting a booth, looking exhausted and hauntingly satisfied. The young woman forgot to close the port in her chest. She also lost some weight—

"Hey, Pehton. I still owe you an apology, but I'm heading out. Didn't want to be rude and leave without saying goodbye." Sagan nodded to Razor.

The Executive Warden stepped over to her and closed the nacre port. Into that shamed smile, Pehton said, "You eat something and get some sleep somewhere other than Korac's cell."

"You can always sleep in the infirmary," the Pain Curator offered.

Matt appeared from the kitchens and glued himself to his employer. "Yea, I can stand watch."

Pehton didn't like the proud beam Razor shined on his human employee for vouching.

Do not tell that grown woman how to live her life. Do not adopt her like some little sister and sway her from sleeping where she shouldn't. The Seamswalker could handle herself. Although, given her current condition, maybe not so much.

"I appreciate that, but I promised Tameka I'd stay with her in Enki. She gets kinda mad if I break a promise. I'll see you, later." After a wave, she disappeared.

Razor looked visibly disappointed. He wiped it clean off his face as he turned to Pehton, "I'm returning to my home. Unless there's anything else?"

"No. Thank you. I look forward to news on the Atheneum."

A strange ripple coursed over the Pain Curator's body at the word. Like his muscles shifted and rustled. "Of course. Good night, Peh Peh."

He nodded to Matt, who led Pehton to the door. "See you next time, Executive Warden." Even the young man sassed her.

On her walk to the prison, she considered how someone like Razor slept. That's when a figurative bolt of lightning hit her. Recognition dawned.

The sheets were violet. The color of Sagan's eyes.

"Motherfucker."

{ENKI}

"I'm sure Ross is fine. Tumu will be back any minute. We can ask him then," John assured Jack for the third time in the last hour. The uncertainty left him equally nervous. Between Karter's procedure and the changing of Rayne's guard, Ross disappeared. John accompanied Jack on his diplomatic responsibilities through the upcoming war efforts while everyone around them lost their shorts.

Except the Tritans. They seemed to like the King Regent.

Jack rushed down the corridors of the glass and stone colony established in one of several oceans in Enki. The teenager and his sister shared a certain air in these situations. Severe, strained, and focused. Tackle the problem and solve it. Now that problem was a missing girl. Kyle's sister. There was nothing to physically tackle.

At the bungalow they all shared, John popped his face in front of the scanner. It dropped a nacre-resistant barrier and let them inside. He heard sounds coming from the kitchen, "Tameka, you back?"

"Yea, in here."

Pax echoed his mommy, "Here! Here!"

As they rounded a corner, Sagan stomped her foot in a mock-tantrum. "All right. That's it. I want one."

They all turned to her, confused. Even Jack frowned at her.

"Pax, you're the most adorable critter I've ever seen. And now I want one just like you."

The boy responded with a bashful smile that he hid behind brown fingers. He fled from the room, leaving Tameka gaping and wide-eyed at Sagan. "Are you serious? I mean...that would explain the weight loss and why you turned your nose up at dinner. You love my cooking—"

"You are looking a little thin in the face," John pointed out.

The Seamswalker laughed incredulously and threw her hands up in frustration. Those axes, a symbol for her relationship with Korac, gleamed on her hips like a proud reminder. "For the last time, people. I. Am. Not. Pregnant. Although, now I'd like to be—"

Jack whistled loud with his fingers in his teeth. After everyone gave him their undivided attention, he pressed, "I'm sorry for interrupting, but I don't have much time before I'm needed elsewhere. Tameka, have you seen Ross?"

John crossed the kitchen for an apple as the redheaded Progeny frowned. "No. Not since Caedes finished at the infirmary. She was in the waiting room with Chris and Tumu."

"Thanks. I'd like to see Caedes before I go."

The apple crunched wonderfully as John took a bite. "Me, too."

"Is something wrong? Have you not seen Ross?" Sagan hugged herself in that armored coat. Concern drawn in the features of her face.

John shook his head. "No. But there's only two people left to ask now. Chris and Tumu. Did you bring the Officer back with you?"

Tameka nodded with all those red curls in a foaming wave. "He took Para to the infirmary."

"We'll visit Caedes, first. Then we'll head there," Jack announced as he pointed up the stairs questioningly.

At Tameka's nod, he climbed up to the next floor. John followed with an extra apple. Assuming the Icarus had any teeth, he'd appreciate it. He knocked, not on the bedroom door, but on the door to "the room." A hidden closet Tumu kitted out with Enki tech for Caedes to keep them connected. If he could breathe, he'd be in this space.

A pale imitation of John's favorite Icarus answered the door. No obvious injuries, but he moved so stiffly. He squinted at the light in the hall. The dark circles under his eyes implied a lack of sleep, or worse. He needed to feed. As the only volunteer in the house, John needed to pencil in some time to feed him. Straight and asexual, he got nothing out of the typically intimate experience. But

Caedes' gratitude went a long way in Pax diaper duty or potty training instruction.

"Thank you for saving Tameka and Pax." Jack said as severe as if he were Rayne.

Caedes planted a fist to his nacre and half-bowed with a wince.

John knew the right thing to say to mark this moment. "I'm so relieved your head is harder than bedrock." At the humorous slip in the Icarus' formal mask, John slapped Caedes on the back. Hard.

The bald man hissed on a groan, all the while glaring at John with "I'll remember this when it's your turn" in his deep green eyes. In a tight voice more gravelly than usual, Caedes said, "If you're done being an asshole, I want to show you the map I've compiled of all the known routes in Enki so far."

They stepped inside the cramped space and took a peek at the screen. John pointed at the circle on the far left. "So this is us?"

"Right." Caedes swept his hands over the touch-sensitive device, and it expanded into a three-dimensional visual of the Dyson's Sphere. "I'm not sure when the design came to me, but the lines represent the conduits we enter."

The young King frowned. "This looks familiar."

"I thought so, too, your majesty. But I can't place where I saw it before."

A small knock came from the door.

Caedes tried twice to call out, "Come in, Pax."

The two-year-old entered with wonder on his face. "How?" As in, how did Caedes know it was Pax.

John broke into a grin, and Jack's anxious frown softened.

"It's my super power, kiddo."

"Hee!" Pax toddled under the desk and resumed the storytelling of various deities throughout human and Icarean history. With disturbing accuracy.

Back to the screen, John nodded at the center. "Primary Bol is the closest conduit to the Pantheon on the northernmost point of the sphere."

Tameka called from below, "Jack, Tumu is here!"

The teenager bolted from the room while John stayed behind to review likely points of exploration. He handed the Icarus an apple and quietly offered a donation. "I can make time in an hour. Jack's schedule is busy, and I don't want to leave him unattended. But I'll make time."

Gruff and dry, the Icarus grumbled, "Thank you."

"You did what?!" Jack's voice thundered through the bungalow.

Severe.

John burst down the stairs to find the King Regent red in the face, glaring at a thirteen-foot alien.

"How could you abandon her like that? I've never thought of you as reckless. Tumu, you'll get her killed!"

Tameka and Sagan moved behind him, ready to reach for the kid at the first sign of aggression.

The membranes over Tumu's eyes blinked. "I left Ross with a trusted associate and plenty of funds. She's as safe as any interplanetary traveler. Safer. Iuo won't let any harm befall her. This way she stands a better chance of finding her sister."

The bungalow was crowded. Tameka always left the glass partitions open to let the salty air breeze inside. Angry and shocked breaths stifled the otherwise airy space. Sagan's voice cut through the tension. "I'll check on Ross. She's staying with Iuo on Reipon, right? I'm visiting there in two days. Give me that long, and we'll pop here for a quick check-in. Tumu's right, Jack. She can't wait around on us to find her sister. I'd do the same."

Tameka stared at her. She searched the girl's face with frantic glances, as if soaking in her features. "I wouldn't wait around either. I'd find you. And don't you ever put me in that position."

"Jack, think. If someone took Rayne, again, but you could do something about it this time. Wouldn't you?" John offered cautiously. "We know Rayne would do exactly what Ross did. For you. For the Shadow. Hell, for Bethany."

The young King's muscles uncoiled by millimeters, then inches. Until finally he relaxed from the spring he coiled into as if ready to attack Tumu. Eventually, he shoved his fingers in his hair and folded onto the sofa. Tameka rushed to his side and knelt to check on him. When Jack's face reemerged from his hands, it was red. His hazel eyes blotchy with unshed tears. In a broken voice, he confessed, "I only want everyone safe."

"The young ask for so much," Tumu said as he gripped Jack's shoulder.

John blew out a sigh of relief when Jack let the alien comfort him. "We're all tired." He nodded over to Sagan, who all but withered on the spot. "Let's cancel the rest of today's schedule and rest up because we all know. This isn't it. Not by half."

Their enemies always waited with more.

{EARTH}

No. More.

Kyle resisted every step, every look, every opening of his mouth. With every failure to do so, he betrayed his family. He wanted to die.

In a dark recess of his mind, he pressed his head to the floor and wept. Again.

"You'll come to appreciate our designs." Celindria repeated her promise. She occupied the space with him. She occupied all the spaces of his control. At the wheel, the sociopath put on a good deep fake. With all his memories and thoughts at her disposal, she'd make a terrible arch nemesis if she didn't.

This hurt. Kyle ached with mental exhaustion. It rode him down. On more than one occasion, he resisted until he slipped out of consciousness. Lost a day or two. No. He couldn't afford that again. The entire reason he agreed, never minding the threats and blackmail, was so he could glean some Imminent secrets. To help the Shadow once they retrieved him.

But now he understood how truly impossible that was. The only way to break the Tenements of Volition was the same way he agreed to them. The words came out of the mouth of the willed upon. Andrius' stolen ability—the power of suggestion—amplified Elden's old labor agreement. But it required the initial agreement of the participant for the suggestion to take hold. To end it required the body to protest.

The words must come from Kyle's mouth. And be damned if he wasn't trying.

Celindria turned a stony expression on him. All of her expressions were some variation of icy or hard. He'd like to think every time she glanced at him that way, it meant he almost pushed through. Almost broke down her control. Maybe a tic appeared to the person she was talking to. Something to let them know it wasn't him inside. Elden knew he tried screaming and begging for help without a single outward response.

"Your body reacts most to Silence," the psychotic bitch observed.

Kyle expected her to gloat and bait him. Live up to her cruelty. But the puppet master reined him with an icy control while physically hidden safely in her grotto hideaway. It was the same for T.A.O. The first Seamswalker agreed under threat of harm to her brothers. She'd get no blame from him.

"That girl, Lynn, she's relieved you didn't die on her watch. But I catch her glaring at you. Is she still sore from the original betrayal?" After a pause, Celindria turned and faced the figment of Kyle in his conscience. "You dislike that. The reminder of it. That it led to Nox assaulting Rayne."

Please let the banter start. Anything to change the subject.

"I was there."

Well, that was a turn of events. He held up his head only long enough to meet her gaze.

Celindria turned back to the view from his eyes. Softly, she said, "We both know the truth, do we not?"

Fuck, Celindria made for terrible company.

"Okay. So this is the best location to hit Imminent first. Is that right, Story Taker?" Lynn approached with a tablet of plans.

Celindria spoke the words that left Kyle's mouth. "That's right. We'll strike there first. A little payback."

He cringed so hard.

Pablo added, "T.A.O. will have to work for transport. Sagan isn't available at that time. Something's keeping her busy on Gait."

"I wonder what that 'something' could be?" Celindria as Kyle quipped with emphasis on the sarcasm.

Kyle's skin shriveled and tried to run away.

But there.

Lynn and Pablo exchanged the barest of glances. Unnerved. Did they suspect—

No. He didn't imagine it.

Beyond them, Silence stepped into a pair of detainee coveralls wearing only a bikini. Rather than slipping into the top half, she tied the sleeves in a knot around her hips. Pablo walked to her and handed her some forms to sign on a tablet. She smiled at him. A thousand-watt beam. They were taking her in. Adding her to the family. And she trusted them because he told her to.

Kyle wept. Again.

"Are you okay? You're crying," Lynn whispered beside him.

A shift in the current. A turn in the tide. Kyle looked up to find Celindria staring at him. Astonished. Dismayed. Maybe even a little...scared.

Quickly, she addressed the Chief, "I'm fine. After all this stress, I'm missing my usual fix."

There was a way. A weakness she missed. An emotion she couldn't account for in her calculations.

And Kyle knew it.

Won't be long now.

SEVEN

THIS MIGHT STING A LITTLE

{ENKI}

SIP.

Tumu helped Tameka lay out pallets for everyone in the open living space. When no one wanted to confine themselves to a room alone, Sagan tossed all the pillows to the floor and insisted on a slumber party. So now the Sovereign Ambassador of the Two Worlds snapped sheets in the Officer of the Third's face.

It was passive aggressive, but the punishment fit the crime. Although Tameka sided with Ross' decision to find her sister, she still couldn't believe the Tritan left a teenage girl on an alien planet unattended. One that bartered and traded humans like slaves.

Eventually, he asked, "Is that fury I'm detecting?"

Sullen, she admitted, "Maybe." After rolling her neck along her shoulders, she exhaled out all the frustration. "I know you saved her from sneaking off on her own with no resources. I know you did the right thing."

He set to assembling the next makeshift bed. After a minute of comfortable silence, he muttered, "Thank you."

Tameka whipped her waist-length curls over her shoulder. Again. One more time. She'd give it one more time. To distract herself from the irritation, she asked, "So, Tumi." It proved difficult not to cringe. "You and Lamassau. Did that happen after your crush on . . . " Damn. Couldn't she even joke about him without the knife twisting in her heart?

"He's an on-again/off-again obsession of mine. Well, we try anyway."

Sip.

"Shower's free!" Sagan joined in the conversation then, having Seamswalked into the living space with more pillows and wet hair. And of course the axes. "What do you mean by try?"

Clutching a pillow to her chest, Tameka took a break on the sofa while Sagan helped with the pallets. Engaging in girl talk with a Tritan. But why not? "Is Lam too much of a cheater?"

The Tritan chuckled, but the sound was sad. "The cheating is my fault. Punishing me for running off after . . . " He cleared his throat as if ridding himself of a bad memory. Guess he couldn't bring himself to say Xelan's name, either. "Our relationship is forbidden. Lam and I. As a scientifically curious people, Tritans genetically enhanced our species until we could no longer breed females. Now we're expected to remain celibate until we find a suitable one from the various races we cultivated."

"Is that why I see Tritans with Lamias and Lyriks on Gait?" Sagan offered.

Tameka raised an eyebrow in bewilderment. "They date their historians? That seems unethical."

Tumu shook his head. "No. I mean *one* suitable female. The Mother." Tameka recoiled when he looked rather intently at her as he continued, "The reproduction program collects a chosen few females to broodmare less and less diluted children. Until they're interbred more and more into purer Tritans. Until we produce females on our own again. We aren't permitted to interact with males until such time. Nor anyone outside of the program."

"That's why Abresson wanted Rayne." Sagan gasped. Followed up with a sour face.

Tumu nodded solemnly. "She was one." He glanced over the living space at Tameka.

The room spun. She swallowed hard as the color drained from her, and she clutched her chain for strength. After two tries, she shared, "Primary Bol called me that. He called me 'The Mother' when I asked to visit Earth." She caught her head in her hands. A warm hand scratched along her back, comforting her.

Sagan.

"All three of you are candidates. But Sagan is off limits. I don't know why. I didn't press, given the small mercy." Tumu approached, and Tameka rolled her eyes to glare at the constant bearer of bad news. He retracted the hand offered in comfort, as if he thought better of it. Smart Tritan. "No one has claimed you yet. There's a hesitation until we see how Pax turns out. If results are favorable, then I'm afraid they'll try to push me onto you. But I assure you have no intentions—"

"If my nacre would let me vomit, I would have just now," Tameka confessed on a disgusted groan. Her hair fell over into her face, forming a suffocating curtain. "That's it. Sagan. Please. Cut it."

Sip.

"What?! Are you sure?" Sagan's eyes widened to the size of a silver dollar.

Tumu backed off and gave the girls some space.

Tameka recognized the gesture for what it was. While she appreciated it, her gut still reeled from his earlier horrendous revelation. Sweeping her hair back behind her shoulders, she affirmed, "I'm certain. It's in the way and a battle hazard. If we . . . If we ever get back to a time where shit isn't blowing up around us, literally and figuratively, I can always grow it back out. I'll get the scissors."

As she rushed off, Tameka overheard Sagan ask Tumu, "'Off limits?'" While upstairs, she checked in on Jack and John in "the room." For a second, they drew her in with Caedes' map—an amazing feat—before she broke away to check on Pax. He passed out in his room while playing with a train. A black, gray, and white one. She let her heart soak it in for a moment before approaching the only bathroom. It worked fine for their household. Spacious and lots of storage. Nacres recycled energy in their bodies, preventing waste. They only needed the shower, and not very often. Mostly out of comfort.

With everyone else in the house accounted for, Caedes must be in the shower. And Tameka needed the scissors. He loved her. She couldn't love him. She couldn't think of anyone that way. Not after…

Swallowing hard, she opened the door like a grownup. No curtain. Only tiled walls peppered with shower heads. Two drains drank in the run-off.

Tameka never forgot the communal showers in the Ionas. It was uncomfortable, but not impossible. People mostly acted professional with her, save for the occasional curious glimpse. For the same reason she wasn't curious then, she wasn't curious now.

Sip.

Cupboard. Scissors. Where were the scissors? "Shit."

"What do you need?" Caedes asked with that familiar gravel in his voice. A little extra rattled given the state of his throat. His trachea busted all the way out during the collapse. While he protected her and Pax.

A good man wasted on her. "Looking for the scissors."

"Try the second shelf down. No. There. In the back."

Right where he said. "Thank you."

"You're welcome."

Tameka stopped herself from fleeing. Rigid, she left something unfinished. "No. I mean it." She turned all the way around and faced him. "Thank you. Even if we'd survived the cave-in, because of you, Pax never knew pain like that. Thank you."

Do not look down.

Icari were not modest by human standards. Still, Caedes blushed until his bald head turned blue. He looked mostly uncomfortable. But he still didn't turn away or hide himself. Nor should he. What Tameka allowed herself to see was perfectly honed and in great warrior condition. Yup.

Do not look down.

"I'm glad that you're both alive, and if any part of that was because of me, then I'm honored for serving you." Caedes' impressive chest visibly swelled. Impressive, considering it concaved under the weight of the rocks that fell on him like a nine-car pile-up. His missing chain implied the reason for his survival. Thank Elden, he used it in time.

When Tameka reached for the door, an internal debate finally resolved itself. "John's human blood is a little on the weak side. Tonight, you can feed from me to help with the healing."

Without turning around, she imagined how the proposal affected him. "No sex" went without saying. The Progeny woman wasn't over her lover. Her soulmate. But she cared for Caedes, and he showed his love for her and Pax in so many ways. All the ones that counted.

With that in mind, Tameka cut off the unseen protest before it could start, "Tonight. There's no need to argue with me. I trust you."

"Thank you."

Tameka headed downstairs, ready to tackle the next item on her agenda. Including her excursions throughout the week, they learned Sagan could Seamswalk around Enki without detection. It was time to confirm with Tumu if this was truly the case. And to test the limits of that particular advantage with one specific objective in mind.

The Pantheon.

Sip.

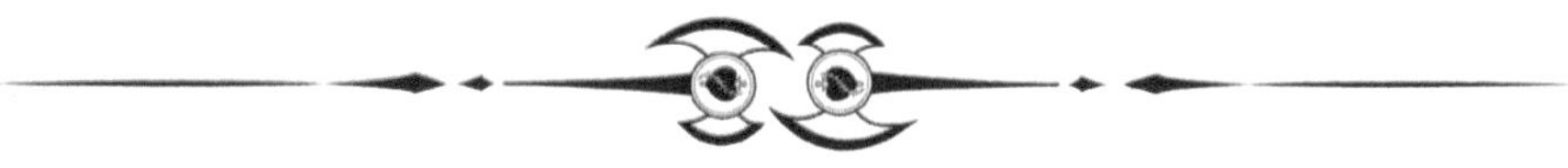

{ENKI}

In one of Enki's glass-tech infirmaries, Para fell asleep leaning on Chris' side. Her chain mingled with his. They shared in the exhaustion. Let her rest. Three days, they told him. He waited at Karter's bedside for three days already. No sleep. No food. The idea of eating turned his stomach. The thought of closing his eyes longer than a blink terrified him. For what if in that one blink, her last breath left her and he wasn't there for her?

No.

Chris straightened in his seat and squared his shoulders. Moistened his eyeballs. The small woman next to him trusted Chris not to leave Karter to die alone. And be damned if he wouldn't keep her faith.

A resurrection casket. That's what they called the thing they laid Karter in. The glass box emanated a soft red glow. It resembled a more-technical, less-decorative Martyr Complex. It knit her bones together using her own bio-organic materials fused with synthetic fibers crafted of nacre glass. Engineered specially by the Tritan scientists. They told him many times how they "eagerly looked forward to testing it on an Icarean specimen of such worth."

He shivered. No. The place wasn't cold, and in her mourning, Para transformed into a tiny furnace. The Valkyrie's body produced more heat than Li. And the poor girl tried to climb in his pants three times since she sat down and started waiting with him. With Karter laid out in reconstruction, Chris couldn't find it in him to comfort Para as needed.

He liked her. He did. But Karter was the glue that held their trio together.

Wow. Whoever thought it'd come to this. But his heart hurt. His lungs ached. Could breath bruise? Because that's how he felt with every inhale.

Karter's face would haunt him forever. He'd seen some shit overseas. Some shit working hospitals. Some more during Volcano Day. But... he never imagined seeing the woman he loved pulverized. Reduced to so much meat. Not without expecting to put her in the ground the day after. Waiting to see if she pulled through—in a Dyson's Sphere—yea, that definitely never occurred to him. With all the crumbling, she still found time to use her chain.

The red glow on the casket softened and cooled into a blue light. Dare he hope? Chris let one hand hover over Para, to wake her in case this was it. In case—

A weak thud. Then another one. Stronger. "Para. Para, I think..." He shook her gently, not willing to risk death at the hands of a sleeping Valkyrie.

She sat upright and stared at the vessel. Another thud pounded. They stood together and warily approached the casket. Through the glass top, Karter stared up at them with green and black eyes groggy from anesthesia. When Chris met her gaze, she stopped pounding and relaxed.

He explained, "You're in Enki. Tumu and Tameka brought you for recovery. Para's here." Letting them take a moment together, he sucked in all his emotions when they broke down as the Valkyrie locked gazes. Let them have this moment.

After a few seconds of sniffling and sobbing, he continued, "You had a nacre infusion and reconstructive surgery. I'll find a technician and see if you can get out."

Karter nodded. With her beautiful face intact. Tears sprung to Chris' eyes, and he choked them back to find the nearest tech. Two seconds, and a little rough handling later, a Tritan re-prioritized his to do list to open the casket.

Good for him.

Chris took the slender fingers that reached for him. Para took her other hand. Karter's dark gray skin glistened, unnaturally. She caught him looking and frowned at his concern. He kissed her hand. "Trying to catch myself from admiring you too much. You look amazing."

Para let out a sniffly laugh. "You're glowing—"

Karter's face fell. The color drained from her skin. Her eyes went wide and searched them over frantically. Gripping their hands, she lurched them closer and whispered, "The bomb. It wasn't meant for Jack or Tameka. It was meant for me."

"What? How could you know? Calm down, they monitor your vitals." Chris tried his best to mitigate the distress without delegitimizing her concerns.

Para looked less concerned. Hell, she looked placid. "Do you really believe that? It's been so long—"

"I know. And I know who did it." Karter was dead certain.

"Then it's time you told us, Sparkles," Tumu slipped through the doorway. He turned the lights off and disconnected all the monitors. Holding a finger to his lips, he leaned in with the rest of them. "Tell us about Thailea. Quietly."

In pitch darkness, Karter sucked in a shaky breath and told a story too insane to believe. Calmly. Rationally. And the proud Valkyrie shared it as if she didn't expect them to believe her. As if, her entire long life, people tried to convince her she was crazy. It broke Chris' heart.

Tumu glanced at the smaller woman beside him.

Karter shook her head. "Para was out for three days. She never saw him."

Chris gripped her hand. "I believe you." The relief and surprise on her face choked him from further reassurance.

Para also nodded. "I never doubted you. You made sure we both survived the rings. I'll never understand why Umbra and Amolot insisted . . ." She also choked.

"Because they knew the truth. I think I know what became of your baby, Sparkles. But I need you to trust me. It's better you don't know for now. Give me time to confirm my theory first, and I'll tell you everything."

The Valkyrie winced as she drew herself closer to him. "Vow on Elden. Vow on Cinder and Li. Don't you let me go one more day than necessary living with this persecution and loss."

Chris squeezed her hand while staring at Tumu. Para chafed her lover's arm but refused to look up. She'd lived it with Karter. The smaller Valkyrie was probably the only person who came close to understanding her pain.

The Officer of the Third pounded a fist to his nacre. "On Elden, on Cinder, and on Li—I will discover what happened to your youngling."

Hot. Damn.

{Lukemore}

"X. This is Pipe Bomb. Have you located it? Over." They broke out the super discrete Enki-tech earpieces for this one. In all black, Lynn tried to blend into the acres of open silo field. Only the mills operated above ground, releasing pollution into the pale yellow sky. It smelled terrible. Fabric and wood pulp. Nasty.

"Pipe Bomb."

Lynn startled and rounded with the confiscated Imminent rifle aimed at X's chest.

His kelp dreads and jellyfish cap for a kilt made squishy sounds as he approached. Luks, inhabitants of Lukemore, spoke everything in a whisper. "Sorry. Don't kill me."

With a sigh, she dropped her sights. "Did you find it?"

"Yea." He waved for her to follow. "It's halfway across the field. The purple silo. That one holds all the textile labor. The people that require sunlight, anyway."

Shit. "Can we evacuate it?"

He shook his head. "It's the most populated. Nothing short of a bomb threat would shift that herd."

She pinched the bridge of her nose with a gloved hand. Think. "X?"

"Yes?"

"What exactly did you see?"

The squishing amplified as he held out his palm. A digital feed played back on his implanted device. Two hundred and eighteen floors. Twenty-eight bunks, apartments, or whatever they called them on each floor. The laborers retired for the evening, all worn and drab from their hard work. But the eighteenth floor made her double-take. Soldiers dressed in the same gear as their recently deceased Imminent captive. Rifles. Enki tech. Carbon fiber jumpsuits and decorated jackets. The Shadow still wasn't clear on the rank system. Hell, they weren't clear on anything. Wait a minute…

"Son of a bitch. Is that Abresson?" Lynn took no offense to X shushing her. She knew better. But it was hard to hold in all this rage as the same Tritan requesting the nacre disabler and fortification virus walked among Imminent troops looking suspiciously comfortable. Smug, even. "That bastard. All right. I've got an idea."

Ten minutes later, they squared that away. In one minute, T.A.O. arrived to Seamswalk them to the rendezvous. To pass the time, Lynn brought up a possibly inappropriate topic with X. "I'm sorry about your sister." Sister-in-law, but Luks referred to them as brother and sister after union.

X's body wriggled before restoring to a rigid state. A sign he was emotional. More hoarsely, he whispered, "After the mudslide, we excavated the bodies..."

"And you found it then?"

"Imminent carved into each of the windows? Yes." X looked up from his feet with sadness straining his pink glowing eyes. "R raised the children. They weren't home at the time. A playdate with the neighbors saved them."

The pair walked along the silo's shadow as the suns traveled across the sky. Waiting. A thought struck Lynn, and she frowned. "Where was R when it happened?"

"He—"

"Ready?" T.A.O. Seamswalked onto the field. "Smith and Kyle finished on Reipon. I'll retrieve Cypher and Andrew from Lacceirus-Capra."

Lynn remembered from Nox's Verse that the Icari and Enki poisoned L. Capra's atmosphere. It rendered the Caprents into a life below ground. Eventually, the sky detoxified enough for resurfacing, but they liked their existence below ground.

She worried about team members in the caverns, given the Shadow's luck with cave-ins lately. The chain around her neck weighed heavily. Each link may as well represent a person she loved. Kissing the pendant for luck, she nodded for T.A.O. to take them.

They stepped into a plaza on Pil. Lots of brick domes set in rows, and walkways lined in pavers. The Dwarves originally traded as masons, and they took pride in their heritage. Now, they specialized in physics and engineering. Their sky came the closest to Earth, but without a Sphere of nacre glass between them and all that blue. Cooked meat permeated the air. Surreal, Lynn reminded herself this was an alien world, and she was standing on it—

"Hey!" Kyle whisper-shouted across the concord.

Time to apply the mask again. Professional. Earnest. They rushed to his location, and she led with, "Did you find anything?"

"No, you?"

Lynn and X exchanged a look before she answered, "We found it. It's all prepped."

"I must fetch Andrew and Cypher. One moment." T.A.O. disappeared.

Smith rounded the dome and nodded at Lynn. "You good?"

She blew out a shaky breath. "Tense."

"Tell me about it." He chuckled and leaned against the building, arms folded and ankles crossed. Relaxed.

Two quiet seconds passed before T.A.O. returned with Andrew and Cypher. They collected into a huddle as Andrew reported, "A heavy Imminent presence on L. Capra, but I don't think the civilians are aware. They're posing as Yu researchers, testing the soil."

That set off alarm bells for Lynn. Wasn't their soil—post atmospheric contamination—an ingredient for the progenitor? The one that eventually led to Xelan creating the First Wave Progeny. She glanced at T.A.O. who lingered beside Kyle.

Something felt wrong.

"Let's return to base and ask Legir if he's heard of a similar project. Who knows? It might have a legitimate basis." Kyle sounded awfully casual regarding a stack of coincidences ready to topple over and land on the Shadow.

"Agreed." T.A.O. said before reminding everyone, "I'm halfway out of the light. Not much longer before I retreat." They formed a chain to Seamswalk back to the Ecology.

Beyond the glass lobby and passed the cliff's edge, twelve tornadoes formed over the ocean. Andrew muttered, "Rayne."

Lynn took a step closer to the clear wall. Rain and hail pounded on the glass ceiling. Lightning flashed against the dark night, illuminating the storm. Unable to contain her concern, Lynn asked, "Is she all right? I mean...Should we check on her?"

Kyle assured, "The new Tritan guard and Colton are with her. She's fine."

"I miss that spitfire," Smith confessed. He even gripped his chain.

Pablo climbed the suspension staircase from the lower floor. A beautiful sight. Until he frowned and confirmed, "Cinder looks worse."

Andrew clutched the pendant on his chain, silent and thoughtful. Lynn wondered how many Probabilities included the treasures meant only for the Shadow. X regarded them with respectful silence. He and T.A.O. shared a similar expression, confusion mixed with intrigue.

"King Rayne misses him," Cypher quietly offered.

No need to name "him." They all glanced at the Iona Medical Ecology sign above their heads. They'd forever miss Xelan. And in his name they continued to do good. Here's hoping he'd approve of their measures this day.

Or Elden save them all.

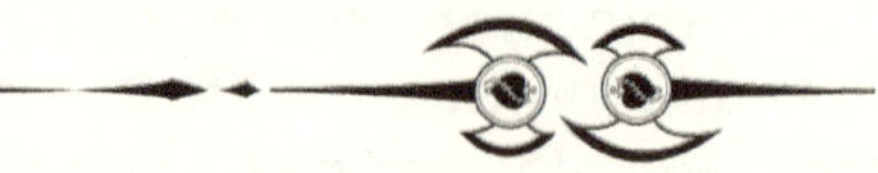

{Enki}

Sagan stared at the ceiling of Tameka's Enki bungalow. The salty breeze from the open glass panels carried the fresh smell of the ocean. The soft sheets breathed like Earth cotton. No lumps in the pad beneath her. Her family's comforting breathing surrounded her. Comforting aside from Tumu, who stayed and snored like a foghorn. And if the redhead beside her would quit kicking her, maybe Sagan could close her eyes long enough to sleep. Her only consolation? The tiny redhead in her best friend's arms kicked his mommy more. What went around came around.

With that in mind, she muttered a prayer to Elden for her friends in the galaxy, staging payback against Imminent. She hated leaving them to T.A.O. with everything they suspected of her. But they reassured the youngest Seamswalker of her own mission and restored her faith in theirs.

Okay. One dilemma solved. Truthfully, nothing would ease her completely. Except...

Itch. Twitch. Pinch. A gnawing need. Sagan craved pain. The sear of fire, the lash of a whip, the concussion of a good right hook. All of it. Any of it. Top it off with a trip to the prison and engage the real thing at Korac's expert hands...A cocktail better than sex.

She needed to stop. If the gala proved fruitless, Sagan would refuse the next experience and detox. The entire balance of the arrangement fell off kilter with Razor landing on top. Never again. She'd never allow a man made of control to exploit her ever again. Addictions of her own making, included.

That said, she absolutely planned to sneak to the prison for a nap. There was no better sleep than snuggling with her Icarus.

And food. Delicious food. Her mouth watered at the thought of barbecued bore and steamed Caprent pike. Starved, she looked at her hands and frowned. Her already dainty wrist lost some mass. Forearm muscles lessened and overly defined. She burned more fuel than she put in the tank. But nothing appealed to her aside from the Emporium's buffet. Promising herself to eat before she left, Sagan closed her eyes.

Exhaustion claimed the Seamswalker eventually. Sometime later, she awoke to a tiny kick. Too tiny for Tameka, Sagan opened her eyes and restrained from gushing at the sight of Pax tucked into her. His curly red hair laid against the dark freckles on his cheeks. Thick red lashes fanned above them. The poor baby would run if he knew he slept against her. Toddler crush.

But that led to an interesting question. Where was Tameka? Not in the blanket palace. Probably her room. Now seemed like a good time to seek guidance regarding the addiction. Sagan stood and Seamswalked into the master suite.

"Tameka, I—"

Oh. My. Elden.

Knocking.

Knocking would've been good.

Tameka sat on her bed and gaped at Sagan, bewildered. Her eyes grew wide and glittered like shocked emeralds. Caedes didn't bother looking up from where he fed on the bend of Fury's arm. The sucking sounds of the intimate act never to be forgotten. Nor the gruff Icarus' gentle purring.

Sagan immediately Seamswalked back to the living space. Well, almost. As she hurried away from Tameka, the blond Progeny paused in the Seam.

The moment her feet touched the bone-white stone, she sensed it. A shift. A change. A—new. Something new. The young woman spun in a circle, trying to catch it. In the corner of her eye, she swore a shadow jumped between the cathedral's pillars.

"Hello?"

The empty never responded . . . before today. A rush of incoherent whispers flooded Sagan. Some from a distance. Some directly in her ear. It startled her, and she batted at it. Unarmed and dressed in her pajamas, she never imagined facing a threat in this unpopulated place. Terrified and overstimulated, she closed her eyes and breathed. Deep inhale through the nose. Exhale through the mouth. Center and focused, like Xelan taught her.

Whispers. Soft. Rushed. Couldn't make them out. Couldn't understand—

"Atheneum."

The voices formed into a chorus and repeated the single word until the whispers shouted at her. "Atheneum."

Sagan clutched her chain and blindly Seamswalked the fuck out of there—

"There you are. Here I thought you finally learned to knock—Sagan, what's wrong?!" Tameka clutched Sagan's biceps to keep her from falling.

She was back in Tameka's place. In the second-floor hallway by the master bedroom. Everything was fine. She was safe here. The Seamswalker backed against the wall and sank to the floor. Not on the verge of tears. No. On the verge of screaming. For hours. Days, even.

That place was dead. It was empty. Where did those voices come from—

"I don't know what happened, but I can see you're spiraling." The redhead took the blond's hand in a warm, familiar grip. Safe. She even brushed a strand of Sagan's hair behind her ear. "It's okay. You're home. Nothing can touch us here. Tell me what happened."

"Atheneum."

Tameka recoiled. "That old legend? About a library? There was a brief mention of it in the archives here. Is it significant?"

So she didn't hallucinate it. The voices. The word.

It was real.

Sagan gripped her best friend by the shoulders and tried to contain the crazy as she demanded, "Tell. Me. Everything. Tameka, the Seam. It told me to look for it."

Okay, back to the wide green eyes. "The Seam? It talks?"

"It did. Just now."

"Sorry to say, there isn't much to tell. Some old text mentioned a library, kinda like Alexandria on Earth. The Tritans searched for it and never found it. Contains a lot of knowledge about the Ancients, so they wanted it." Shoving Sagan's bangs aside, Tameka checked her for a fever. "Your nacre seems fine despite that ugly port thing."

Sagan gently nudged away the concerned gesture. "I'm fine. I need to find the library. Who would—Razor might know. I can ask him."

Fury folded her arms and glowered at the Seamswalker. "You know you picked up Rayne's habit of sleep-talking. You mentioned Razor a few times."

That shut all kinds of things down in Sagan's brain. "I did?"

"Mhmm."

Oh, shit. Did she do that around Korac? She tried to conceal the panic from her friend. The topic was a little sensitive. Speaking of, "Sorry for earlier. I—"

"Save it. Learn to knock. And not that I need to defend myself to anyone, but I want to be clear. I fed him potent enough blood to help him heal properly. That's all." The redhead shifted uncomfortably before changing the subject, "We need to visit Karter before you pick up your dress from Lucas." She rolled her eyes at the last. "Dancing with the enemy. You and Rayne. I swear..."

"The storms...do you think Rayne knows what day it is?"

Tameka's eyes softened. She stood and held out a hand. "There's no way she couldn't. Rayne's connected to us, so even unconscious, she knows."

Sagan took the offered hand and stood. Both girls gripped their chains. Today was hard on all of them. They honored it each year. It was the reason they tried. The reason they hoped. And the reason they loved.

We will always remain.

{GAIT}

Cagey. No amount of running in place, push-ups, or pull-ups could relieve this pent-up frustration. This sedentary uselessness. Korac paced the halls of Infernus block while the other war criminals slept, read, or indulged in their Lamia porn. And he thought he'd seen it all.

Atheneum. A forgotten curse. A word whispered in his nightmares. They held him down. They hurt him. And all the while they asked him for the Atheneum. His muscles too weak, limbs too short, and mind too young to fight them off—

Korac flexed his fists. He chewed on nothing to pop his jaw. Rotated his neck and shoulders. Relax. His control waned, and the mask slipped. Prison wasn't exactly the ideal place to advertise his vulnerabilities. But Pehton needed context to understand why he forgot so much of his past. He never wanted to relive that shit after spending his entire life running from it. The titles, the clothes, and the dominance to overcome his personal history. Admittedly to compensate for—

His fist went through the nearest corrugated panel. It narrowly missed a suspicious control box. The wires no doubt alive and happy to electrocute him.

"You tire yourself out, yet? Eternity knows you've worn me down keeping up with you." Remorse called from around the corner.

As the Icarean General fought with the panel to relinquish his hand, he considered his blockmate. The man always slept when Korac wandered the halls. This was his first opportunity to glimpse his appearance. What race he hailed from.

Fucking circuit box.

Korac kicked a foot on the wall to pull with everything in him. "While I correct this minor concern, tell me about the big cell again." What the hell was this panel made from?

Remorse chuckled as if he caught the show from way over there. "I'll be happy to divulge the rest of my knowledge in exchange for a picture of our girl."

With a groan of mason and a shriek of metal, Korac peeled the circuit box, panel, and electrical channel from the wall. He rushed on black wings to the blockmate's cell. Someone called for an execution on Infernus block, and the Icarean General would gladly deliver it—

Stopped. Halted. The shock froze the blood in his veins. In a voice of three pitches, Korac remarked, "Remorse is an unusual name for a Tritan."

His blockmate spread his arms wide as if caught and unashamed of his crime. Mostly, he stared amused at the Icarus as he examined his wings.

Korac pressed, "I thought they kept your kind on Enki. Rather dangerous to leave one of you here." Deadly. It made him a target for more than one reason.

The Tritan referring to himself as Remorse approached the nacre-resistant barrier with his hands clasped behind his back. "Hence, Infernus block. I was originally in the big cell. But they migrated me up here a few months ago. After...say, how old are you, son?"

Korac retracted his wings and let his eyes return to normal. In his usual tenor, he answered, "Three million. Give or take."

"That sounds about right. Yes. You and the Executive Warden are investigating Inanis? You won't find anything. You certainly won't find those children."

In the light, the war criminal memorized the other man's features. As distinctive as features came on a Tritan. Seven-feet tall. Special jumpsuit. No way to see a compression orb, but all the Primaries were presumably accounted for in Enki. His skin a pale blue with darker navy scoring the striations of every sinewed muscle. He blinked dull black eyes, almost gray. Old. Older than Eminent Wiw, even.

The General wanted to know why the certainty—the absolute conviction—in those words. "What happened to the children that we won't ever find them?"

Remorse shrugged casually. "I don't know. You'll have to ask the last person to see them."

This was like pulling teeth. He disliked the gleam of anticipation in the Tritan's eyes as Korac asked, "And who would that be?"

"The Prince of Cinder."

Xelan.

EIGHT

THE PEACE IN ETERNITY

{???}

THE SAND CERTAINLY FELT BETTER THAN THE FLAMES. Without opening his eyes, Xelan took in his surroundings. The crash of waves. The scent brimming with salt and brine. The sea.

Gulls sung on their way by. Warmth unlike anything he experienced in his lifetime. He opened heavy lids to Earth's sun unshielded without a burn on his body. The horizon boasted the most beautiful blue sky with the occasional fluffy cloud. The ocean surged on the beach just outside arm's reach.

And he wasn't alone. The tinkling giggles of children, and the heavy laughter of men carried to him from the boardwalk down the way. Some wandered onto the beach to play in the sand. Others bought ice cream or won prizes to surrender them immediately to their small charges. All little girls. Fathers and their—

"Superman!"

Xelan's heart wrenched, and he forgot the strange rope in his hand. After living for three million years, he thought heaven or Eternity was a myth served as comfort for beings with shorter lifespans. Now, he wanted to believe. Standing to greet her, he smiled as she looped a chubby arm around his leg and spun. From between his boots, she gave him a grin sans a front tooth.

"Rayne, did you lose another one?"

"Hee." The grin broadened, letting him have a better look.

He made an exaggerated show of it.

"Two days ago. I didn't cry or nothing." Her dark hair in braids, four-year-old Rayne wore a purple swimsuit with a faux shark fin strapped to her back.

"You're a very brave girl, but it's okay to cry, Rayne." Whether this was heaven or an illusion, he refused to waste any of this precious time. "Do you have a bucket and a shovel?"

With a big, goofy nod, she darted off across the sand. Her tiny bare feet left adorable impressions for him to follow. Wearing black cargo pants and a white t-shirt, he plopped into the sand beside her. The supplies seemed plentiful for a single girl, but this wasn't reality. Young Rayne instructed him on how to collect the wet sand, shape and mold it, and use it to form walls and towers. Her voice so sweet it choked him.

Don't think. Just stay with her.

"And—and then we'll take the shovels…and we'll build the moat." Rayne pointed with an emphatic gesture at the churning sea. "The water comes in from over there."

A storm formed on the ocean's horizon in the direction she pointed.

After swallowing hard, Xelan offered, "You're pretty good at this." She hopped on her feet with the fluidity of a child that adult humans lose later in life and hobbled across to him. With some effort, she reached up on her small tiptoes and planted a kiss on his cheek.

She deserved a better smile from him. The pain lancing through his heart wilted the brilliance of it. So instead, he turned her around, plopped her back down in front of the castle, and kissed the top of her head.

"Is there room for one more?" The sarcastic tone of a third voice implied she already doubted it. It wasn't her fault. Twelve years old was a hard age for a young woman.

Xelan turned to face Rayne's second apparition. The reckless troublemaker who already sought her place in the world. She wore a black halter-kini with short-shorts, flip-flops, and pronounced white sunglasses. Her long hair dripped down her back with streaks of blue. Ahh... he almost forgot the fake tattoo phase. #Rebellion.

"You're always welcome to join us, Rayne. Do you think you could build the moat?"

Rolling her eyes, she groaned, "Yes. I know how to build a moat." She sank in the sand and started in with the shovel.

As he added some detail to the battlements, Xelan pretended not to examine her. An idea struck him. "One day you'll have a real tattoo."

She paused and peered up at him. "Really?!" A grin blossomed on her face.

He nodded and returned her grin. "I give it to you."

"Oh, my god! That's so cool. You're the best. What is it? Tell. Me. Everything!"

Some time past and Xelan regaled the girls with stories of his adventures with their older self. An interesting exercise in psychology, but a comfort to him nonetheless. Even as he lost himself in their precious company, he still feared the inevitable return to darkness. He peered out across the beach to the lowering sun.

Would all this vanish when night came? What about the storm? Was this really Eternity?

With a tug on the rope, something moved between him and the sun, cutting a silhouette. It started toward them. Using his hand for shade, he watched the shape take the form of a young woman walking across the beach. She wore a strappy blue sundress the color of her eyes. The only time he recalled her wearing color. It flowed to her bare feet. Carrying her shoes in her able left hand and the rope in the right, she took graceful steps across the wet sand as her long black hair blew in the salty breeze.

The girls stood with Xelan. They ran to her while he froze to the spot. He tried to place her age when a horrible thought struck him. If this was Eternity, why was she here? Rayne greeted her selves—also an interesting study in psychology. They danced around her until she stopped within arm's reach. Her peaceful smile gutted him as his mind reeled with the possible deaths that led her here.

"Superman."

The sound of Rayne's voice broke Xelan down. He swept her into his arms and held on tight. Distantly, he heard himself say, "I'm sorry I wasn't there to protect you. I'm so sorry."

She clasped her arms around his back and held on so tight he gasped. "Shh... sh... I had to learn to take care of myself. I have so much to tell you."

Xelan's heart jumped in his throat. He pulled away in a panic. "Tameka? Is Tameka alive?"

She beamed and nodded. Relief washed over him and sent him crashing into the sand. She knelt beside him. "And the rest are also fine."

"What happened? Why are you in Eternity?"

While the adults talked, the other two Raynes returned to constructing their sandcastle.

"This place?" Older Rayne glanced around at the beach and the boardwalk. Casual and unassuming, she answered, "I made it." She faced the sea then and pulled her knees to her chest.

Xelan mirrored her pose. "Where are we, Rayne?"

"I meant to do this on Father's Day, you know? But I couldn't find you then. You... You've been gone two years, today. I constructed this in my sleep. We're outside the Seam in a little pocket of reality." Idly, she twisted the rope in her hand.

A father and his daughter rushed onto the sand near their troupe. She gave him a high five as he fished a frisbee from the ocean.

"I made this place for daughters who lost their fathers."

Xelan whirled back to her. Every line of her face filled with sadness. He asked, "What about—"

Rayne's lips pulled into a tight smile, but she kept her focus on the ocean. "I've already seen Ray. He's doing fine. Passes along his thanks for keeping me alive all these years." She nodded over her shoulder to the younger apparitions. "I sent these two to keep you company while you waited." After a long pause, she gave him the full impact of her broken heart in her gaze. Tears brimmed her eyes. "You made a terrific dad."

As they both fell into a shuddering, tearful fit, Xelan pulled her to him and kissed her forehead. He whispered against her hair, "I'm sorry I never told you about the lineage." He leaned away to level his eyes with hers. "Come on now. Let's not cry. Do we have until sundown?" He peered over at the sun already setting and tried to ignore the pang in his chest.

"Yes. Then I won't be able to sustain it anymore without risking destabilization."

"That was a lot of words I won't pay too close attention to." She grinned at his insistence on positivity. He loved winning that smile from her.

Rayne spied something beyond him, her face contorting in confusion and a hint of fear. She jumped to her feet. Xelan whirled around, ready to take on the cosmos to defend this moment. When he spotted what caused that reaction, his own heart sank.

Nox stood on the boardwalk. The source of Rayne's fear. Made sense. But the confusion rested with what lay in his arms. The giant of an Icarus cradled a tiny bundle. His expression filled with peace. He refused to acknowledge anything else existed in the surrounding space. Only him and the baby in his arms.

"Xelan?" Rayne whispered.

Xelan stood and faced her. An unhappy memory, he swallowed twice through the thick emotions choking his tongue. "He and Celindria . . . uhm . . . " A sad story with an unhappy ending. Keep to the facts. "She became pregnant.

Nox wanted them to be a family. Celindria decided against it. She told him after the fact."

Rayne frowned, then peered back over his shoulder. "I knew that, but I never intended to bring him here."

It was Xelan's turn to frown, both at her lack of surprise and her choice of words. "How *is* he here?"

Staring back out at the storm over the ocean, she announced, "We don't have much time." She sounded tired.

The sky dimmed around them. The lights went out on the boardwalk. The darkness beckoned. Well, fine. But before that happened, he needed to know, "Rayne, are you all right?"

Radiant and beautiful in this illusionary place, Rayne probably thought she'd fooled him. Never. Sadness cast a shadow over every feature Xelan memorized of her face. A vast loneliness constellated in her eyes, and he never wanted to save her more. She clenched and unclenched her jaw and fists, trying to regain some composure. Even so, when she looked at him, tears glittered her cheeks around a fake smile.

"I won. I saved everyone. I'm fine."

Tiny Rayne clutched his pant leg and beamed that missing tooth at him. Preteen Rayne stepped up to his other side and took his free hand while staring into the darkening sea. Adult Rayne trembled from her tears standing before him. After thousands of years of Xelan living in lonely bitterness, this young Progeny woman banished all of it away with a single smile. And now—

He brushed a strand of her hair behind her ear. "You're a very brave girl, but it's okay to cry, Rayne. I miss you, too."

"This was a bad idea. I'm losing you all over again."

Xelan clutched her to him then and held on tight. "No. Never say that. I'll cherish this moment. Seeing you alive... hearing the others are fine. Don't you dare take that from me."

Rayne broke into a great sob pressed against his chest. She clung to him, but much weaker than before. As night encroached on the beach and father-daughter pairs faded, Xelan knew the tremor racking her body was as much from the strain to keep him here as it was from her tears.

Terrified of the dark but more terrified of whatever happened to her when she "destabilized," he spoke against the top of her head, "Rayne, it's time to let me lay down my sword."

"No!" she cried. She stared up at him, her face red with tears, and her eyes tight with strain. The ocean shimmered and winked until it disappeared.

The only thing left in her world was them. In a tiny voice that might as well have come from her four-year-old self, she begged, "Stay. Please."

Xelan pulled back enough to take her face in his hands. "I don't know what's happening in the worlds right now, but I promise you, you'll be all right."

She made to shake her head, but he insisted, "I've seen it, Rayne. You'll be all right." He glanced down when her younger selves went to her side. As her eyes shifted in form, he knew their time was up. "Tell Tameka I love her. Please. Give my love to the others. Punch Kyle in the face again for me. And Rayne?"

On a shaky breath, she answered, "Yes?" She tried to straighten herself for him, and he admired her courage.

Make this count. In his last moments in what passed for a pretty decent stand-in for Eternity, he shone her a brilliant signature grin. Then he told her what he wanted to tell her since the first time Xelan saved her life.

"Thank you."

Because Rayne, in turn, saved his.

NINE

THE KNIFE AT YOUR BACK REQUIRES NO CONSENT

{EARTH}

HEADS.

"Are you done yet?" Andrew groaned for the third time. He waited, sprawled across an armchair, and mulled over their mission for the millionth iteration. Every scenario he played against the Probabilities. Brief hints on which threads led to which outcomes. He strove to navigate them. To understand the paths and ultimately pave the safest road for their strategy to follow.

The nose bleeds sucked.

"She's almost ready, just one more spray. There." Of course Lucas helped her. That "dress" was made with more straps than bondage gear and covered even less.

Sagan laughed nervously from the bathroom. "I'm glad Tameka did my makeup and hair before I left her place or I would've hogged your bathroom for two more hours. I'm ready. What do you think?"

"Thank fuck," Andrew sighed and looked away from the infinity he imagined on the ceiling. To... Wow. "I think I'm mad you look so beautiful. Rayne did the same damned thing. What is with you two dressing up for the monsters?"

The Seamswalker glided in on actual glass slippers made in Pil. Little silver, glittery straps wrapped around her dainty ankles. Lucas sprayed silver glitter along her bare legs, hardened with toned muscle. Glitter on her arms and exposed chest. The dress belonged on a figure skater. Diamond studded straps laced across her neck, shoulders, and—ahem. The silver silk clung to her figure like a lover, deepening into a violet micro skirt that matched her eyes. Elegant. Ethereal. He approved. He disapproved of her jewelry. A cluster of diamonds spelled out GENERAL across her throat. Announcing her title and his. Loud. Assertive. Claimed.

Lucas followed her out with an expression of pride mixed with nausea. He even winced as he took in the entire ensemble. "He has a point. I wish you'd let me conceal or bedazzle that thing." With an elegant gesture, he indicated the nacre port cover over her sternum.

The beam she gave them matched the wattage of the necklace. "I'll take both your reactions as a compliment." She even fluffed her hair, adorned by the same diamonds Korac wore on Volcano Day.

"What will *he* think about it? You dancing with Razor in that?" Andrew despised the idea of a fight, but someone needed to play older brother here. He stood and took her hands in his. The silver nail polish even matched her Icarean lover's eyes. "Hell, what will Razor think? The moment he sees you, he'll know the statement you're making here."

Again with the sassy smile. "Let me worry about that."

"At least borrow one of my coats." Lucas headed for the closet, but Sagan touched his arm.

Tails. Throwback time.

Out of the bag she toted around for bigger things, she retrieved a black leather duster. Far too big for her. At least it wouldn't drag the floor with her on those four-inch stilettos. The scent of frost and spruce filled the air. "I've got it covered. Thanks."

Andrew blew out the air in his cheeks on a whistle. "Be safe."

After the star of the show doled out hugs and kisses, she left without her axes for a mission more dangerous than she realized.

In her absence, Andrew frowned. He turned to Lucas and asked, "How did you find an exact match of Korac's coat from Invasion Day?"

"It's a gift," the golden-eyed Icarus said with a graceful, dismissive wave. Within a second, his eyes hardened and shone with intensity. "Are we prepared to do this?"

"It's time we responded. Kyle identified the locations. We scouted them out. We act tonight."

Lucas walked out of the zeppelin first, dressed in another Armani suit. Andrew wore Iona security gear. All black. Shocker.

T.A.O. and Kyle waited for them at the burning fields. Andrew spared a thought for Silence. He wished she could join them, but the virus testing was more important. Pablo hoped to create a vaccine, more of a firewall, to block the nacre disabler. Let them keep at their work.

A war waited on the horizon of those black flames. The Shadow needed every weapon imaginable in their arsenal. Unlike the last war, they weren't Xelan's kids doing the best with what they had anymore. The Two Worlds depended on them. Hell, maybe all twelve considering the enormity of the threat they faced.

He clutched his chain. How would Rayne—

"Hey, man. You good?" Kyle fell back on his green crutch.

The smell of it antagonized Andrew's nerves rather than settled them. "Yea. How are you, T.A.O.? Are you ready for this?" The little woman would perform most of the work.

Known for her madness, the First Wave Progeny's single curt nod worried Andrew. But it would satisfy for now.

Lucas pressed a hand to Andrew's back. Comforting. Reassuring.

Yeah.

Only able to trust himself, Andrew flipped the coin again.
Heads. Exactly what he wanted to see.
"We start with Lukemore."

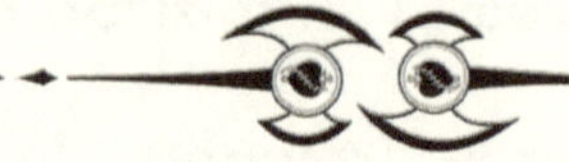

{Gait}

It took Sagan an hour to build up the nerve to Seamswalk to Lucas' zeppelin. Once mustered, she took one tiny step in and one quick step right out. Same for when she moved to Gait. No activity to report, but she refused to give the voices much opportunity. Not with her nerves somersaulting over tonight's impending insanity.

The Emporium looked lonely, with no one lining the streets for entry. Closed for the night. The owner waited for Sagan inside. He asked her to meet him early. Pulling the hood closed around her neck, she drew a deep breath of Korac's scent and crossed the street.

Only weeks ago, she made the same trek into Razor's den. And like then, he watched her approach from his favorite perch on the mezzanine's banister. Now, his eyes shone less with predatism and more with ownership. Proud of his progress on the Seamswalker, who arrives on time at his invitation. Who only eats in his establishment. Who speaks his name in her sleep.

Razor still underestimated Sagan. Good. Her eventual withdraw would surprise him all the more. As soon as she convinced herself of when that time would come. Anytime. She could stop anytime.

She walked onto the mezzanine. He already turned to greet her. A nice black coat that shimmered from his shoulders to the soles of his boots concealed his ensemble. Aside from the shiny top hat, of course. But no cane. Withholding her disappointment, she met his strange orange and green eyes. He lined them with kohl. Against his tan skin and the shocking red eyelashes, it worked for him.

"We think alike." Razor nodded to her coat. "Of course, mine actually fits."

Sagan smiled. Might as well enjoy the evening.

He cocked his head to the side and admitted, "I am curious to see what you found worth concealing."

"I look forward to the reveal." If only she could record his reaction.

Razor held out one hand wrapped in black silk up to his fingers. For the first time, she took it and allowed him to escort her down the spiral stairs. She imagined a satisfied smirk on his face as they went, but never glimpsed one.

"Matt?" Razor called across the floor as he led Sagan to the addition. His shoes tapped in a way that made her suspect he wore heels.

"Yea, boss?" The auburn-haired young man stepped out of the line of booths he maintained. He took one look at Sagan in Korac's coat and broke into a genuinely warm smile. "I don't think that matches the formal dress code."

She took in the carbon fiber jumpsuit and extra-gelled hair. He'd gone native. "I don't think that matches either. You're not joining us?"

Razor answered for him, "He's in charge of watching the Emporium while I'm gone. There's no place safer than the gala." He released his hold on her and took a step toward Matt. "If you don't mind, I'm running through the checklist one last time before we leave. We can finish while you eat." He gestured to a tray of nibbles on the kitchen counter behind them.

Her stomach growled ferociously.

Both men looked at her, equally amused.

"Yea. Let me eat while you do that."

"Hey," Matt called to her before she turned away. "You keep forgetting your chain."

Right. The port replaced the presence of the chain. Sagan stopped him from removing it. "Do you mind holding onto it for another night? It doesn't really go with my outfit."

"Yea. I got it."

The two of them left to discuss inventory or something while she stuffed her face without smudging her lipgloss. Matt planned to meet her secretly in four days to trade intel. Her skin crawled, imagining all the weird shit he'd seen in this place. But with that in mind, Razor treated her with respect. It was his own distinct brand of respect, but all the same—

"Do you require more?" The man on her mind returned and pointed to the already empty tray.

Sagan's stomach felt mildly relieved of its hunger. Enough to get her through the night. "I'm good. Thank you. It was delicious." Honestly, euphoria came to mind.

"I always appreciate your appetite." Now he smirked.

Under her lover's hood, Sagan's face burned. But since he brought up the subject, she asked, "When—"

"Three days. I'll even close the Emporium for your privacy. I think you might want the immersive booths for what will be the final curated experience." Razor gestured at the two special Divine Booths in the addition. Massive, they sat on a custom reinforced stage to hold their weight. Their white enamel casings shown with a pearlescent sheen. They looked like mausoleums.

And yes. Sagan caught herself glancing over at them many times. Fully. Immersive. What must that entail? And did he just say, "Final?" She asked it aloud.

The Pain Curator offered the Seamswalker his arm. The sadness of his smile shocked her. "I can't keep spoiling you like this. I enjoy your company, but exploring your pain consumes me. It's become an addiction of its own. I grant us tonight and three nights from now. And then I let you go. My clients need me. You don't."

Sagan closed her gaping mouth and glided to Razor. She took his arm, searching his eyes. Sad. He wanted her to know this saddened him. What was this? Was he developing feelings for her? Or trying not to? The intensity in his words, in his gaze, kept her from offering friendship. No. A man like him wouldn't settle for less than what he wanted.

But what did he want from her—

"The car's here." Matt's voice across the Emporium broke the spell.

An hour later, the anti-gravity limousine drove them through the conduit to Reipon. They sat across from one another in the spacious backseat, discussing the business prospects of a pain market on Earth. Thirty minutes into the conversation Sagan blurted, "Fuck this!" And threw the hood back, careful to conceal the choker with the jacket's lapels.

The divider between the driver and the backseat returned her reflection. The diamonds in her hair sparkled like the ones at the inner corners of her lined eyes. The white and gray eyeshadow—the entire outfit—was the shade of Korac's eyes. He'd love it. She planned to show him once the event ended.

"Breathtaking. I'm very intrigued as to the rest. Although, I hope you planned for a grander reveal at the gala."

Razor's teasing revived her congenial mood, and she laughed. "I'll be the most fun date that doesn't put out you'll ever have. Swear on it." She even crossed the jacket over her heart.

He laughed, friendly and rich. His downright professional treatment of her left a gaping hole of curiosity.

She pressed onward, "By your reputation I thought you'd get more familiar with me by now."

"What purpose would that serve? You're utterly taken and the last thing I need is an angry Seamswalker tormenting my business at any opportunity she'd like."

Sagan smiled—no—beamed at his perceptiveness and the honest compliment within.

Razor stared at her in such a way that he took in her eyes, nose, cheeks, and lips. Like he committed the expression to memory. "But that smile would almost make it worth it."

Her face fell.

"What bothers you more, Seamswalker? That I've not expressed any interest in sleeping with you? Or that it's left you disappointed?"

She looked out the window. The sprawling space-scrapers and white stone palaces interested her little.

Out of her peripheral vision, she watched Razor lean forward and ask, "Why do you think that is?"

"What?" She kept her gaze on the scenery.

"Your disappointment. Do you need to be wanted? Will that ease your troubles?"

Sagan softened and confessed while looking out the window, "Men in a position of power desire control through sex. It's a neat and easy diagnosis. Simple." Facing him, violet eyes met green and orange ones. "So if that's not your predation, then you want me uneasy for a more nefarious reason. You want me vulnerable." She leaned forward to meet him halfway across the car, searching his eyes. "Why do you want me, Razor?"

The longer they stared in silence, the more arrhythmic her heart beat. A flutter with a skip. On the fourth skip, he startled her by falling gracefully back in his seat with a forlorn sigh.

"It saddens me you weigh your brilliance down with such negative thoughts. We're business partners. Let's keep our arrangement professional. I'm merely looking forward to our evening together. Music. Dancing. Watching you enjoy the food. You're safe with me."

But not *from* him. It bothered Sagan that he refused to answer her question directly.

They arrived after a long time in silence. Razor left the car first and held out his hand. Sagan took the alien's hand and stepped foot onto a red carpet from a space limo and—

Wow... Her life was weird.

People from all over the Vast Collective worked and attended the gala with no limitation on species or origin. Two humans held the doors for them. One Mon3 drone offered to take her coat. A dwarf in a mechanized suit took Razor's. Simultaneously, the ushers revealed their clothes.

No. No, no, no...

In a bizarre twist of fate, they matched. Razor dressed as a ringmaster in all black. The hat stayed as the coat stripped away. A silk jacket fastened at his ribs by silver chains with long tails in the back. Leather pants fed into freshly shined knee-high boots. Silver chains adorned the pockets. A coiled whip hung from his hip.

Sagan dressed like his lead acrobat. Well, aside from all the obvious badges she wore in Korac's honor. And the port.

Razor's mercurial expression set her on edge. As he appraised her, hunger burned in his eyes. But when they focused on her collar, something else burned there. Not anger. Ambition. It bothered her more than his reprisal. Behind those peculiar eyes, he calculated the means to replace General with Razor.

Worse than any of it, he showed no trace of surprise at this disturbing coincidence. He sounded satisfied. "And here I expected to see the signature axes. But they were an understatement compared to this gorgeous ensemble. Did you tattoo his name somewhere on you in gold?" Once more, he offered his arm.

Sagan imagined all the places on her body where Korac would delight in branding his name as she took what Razor offered. "What an idea." She grinned playfully up at him as he led them down a spectacular black hall.

The colors in his eyes spun when he stared down at her.

Around them, the polished surfaces—similar to Earth's granite—shone like dark mirrors. More couples and trios followed behind them into the prismatic space. Sagan sparkled in the reflections as she caught glimpses of herself. And Razor.

The Pain Curator watched her intently. Leaning down, he muttered against her hair, "You stand out." He caught her eyes meeting his in the nearest reflective surface. Their proximity, their clothes—it painted an intimate portrait of them. Quietly, he elaborated, "Your eyes. Your race. And you're the only one not in black. I neglected to mention it with the invitation. Remember what I said about Seamswalking. No one will touch you with me, but if you explore too much on your own, I can't protect you."

She turned to meet his eyes. So close she could barely focus. "From what?"

"From Imminent. Welcome to our inner sanctum. Well, one of them, anyway." Razor faced forward and swept an arm out for her to see.

Rock. The entire building was carved into a cavern, polished and furnished. Everywhere she looked, Sagan's reflection stared back. A star in an inky dark sky. Bright and alive among black tuxedos and elegant gowns. Stand out? More like a diamond in a field of obsidian.

And most of them alien. On any other night, it wouldn't bother her. But after the Pain Curator's little proclamation, she wished she'd dressed more discretely. Maybe dyed her hair and worn contacts. At least then she might blend in with the other humans and Icari.

Stupid collar.

"Safe with me, remember?" Razor whispered once more at her side.

Sagan nearly glowered at him. What kind of trophy did she make on his arm? The Seamswalker at the ball with the Pain Curator. But how could she get angry? He said he brought her for this exact reason when he first proposed this idea. "I wish I'd known about the dress code."

Carefully, he swept the bangs from her eyes. "Your face is more known in the galaxy than the former King of Cinder. The only person more recognizable than you is the current one." He paused, looking thoughtful. "Actually, I think you and the Sovereign Ambassador are equal."

Her head spun, and her stomach turned. But don't cradle a hand to it. Don't let them see any weakness.

"The food is this way." Every touch, every word, and every look, Razor disguised as a caress from a lover. That's why the proximity and public affection. His eyes sparked with covert knowing.

Play along, they said.

Sagan kept her stride while leaning into him. She curved her arm around his back and allowed him to drape an arm around her shoulders. People stared at them and whispered. Ignoring it, Sagan gawked at the expansive buffet piled high with exotic eats. Heaven existed outside

Korac's arms. Minding her manners, she took lady-like nibbles off the first fourteen trays and beamed. Finally, food outside the Emporium that satiated her. She started to suspect Razor prepared magically addicting food, but this stuff tasted as amazing if not better.

"You're practically purring."

The Seamswalker met the Pain Curator's gaze to find amusement shining in his eyes. Beyond him, she glimpsed a black Lamia in human morph and a female Icarus with short hair. She reminded Sagan of Tempest, one of The Brethren who advocated for the Shadow on Earth's governing affairs. It wasn't her, for sure. But...

"They're related." Razor leaned down once more to speak in her ear. "Betton is Tempest's third sister's niece. She joined us about six hundred years ago."

Sagan tilted her neck, exposing more to him while reaching for his ear. Her lips brushed his skin as she whispered, "Tell. Me. Everything." Leaning back to meet his eyes, she intentionally let her lashes flutter slowly and parted her lips as if intoxicated with him.

"You're more convincing than I expected." Razor smirked with respect in his gaze. "Come on. After the one dance you promised me, I'll whisper your worst nightmares to you."

On the dance floor, Sagan expected weird alien customs, but their movements resembled human waltzing. Each race contributed their own spin to it, creating a dizzying, multicultural mix. Razor brought Sagan close to him, put her hand on his chest, and stretched the other out in a mix of modern slow and ballroom dancing. He clasped her hand on his chest with a conspiratorial wink and twirled them around the floor. Her tiny skirt and the longer tails of his jacket flared with the motion.

Playing the game, Sagan laid her head against his chest and let him take her around the room. One round, two... until their tandem movement seemed natural. The music played on foreign instruments in a four-beat composition that felt airy and ethereal. Perfect for the surroundings.

With the black rock and diamond chandeliers, they danced on the cosmos.

Razor whispered against her hair, "I studied human dancing when I learned you were looking for me. Should the occasion arrive..."

Of course he did. Quick study, too. "It paid off. But now you keep your end of this bargain."

He chuckled, and the sound rumbled against her cheek. It caused a pang in her chest. Sagan wished she was dressed up and dancing with Korac in a creepy black cave surrounded by sharks with her violet eyes like blood in the water.

The wrong smooth voice spoke against her hair. "The gala is a preamble of an annual fundraiser. It accumulates credits for the major 'charities' across the galaxy. I host the auction at the Emporium. But it's a front to appease the Vast Collective's leadership. They don't know this location is one of many hearts that beat for our cause."

Sagan set herself far enough apart to gaze up at him as they glided across the floor. Pragmatism poured from him and confounded her. Composing a mask of pure adoration, she asked, "Does Imminent funnel the credits into resources? What about the charities? And what exactly is your cause?"

Razor's eyes darkened. He gathered their outstretched hands and twisted them into a lock at the small of her back, nearly restraining her. Where his hand swallowed her smaller one at his chest, he shifted it to cup his face. He smoldered at her with desire, making for a truly convincing mask that set her pulse hammering. They spun all the while.

"Chaos." The octave dropped in the bass of Razor's voice, and it startled her. Closer, almost kissing now, he explained, "We require chaos to exist. So we push pieces of focus along the board to establish more lines. More Probabilities. Rayne is King. You and the Progeny are knights and bishops. Your people are rooks. The humans are pawns—The metaphor is working for you. I can see the connections in your eyes."

She swallowed twice before saying, "And the credits? What do you fund?"

"Everything. We are everywhere. We are Imminent."

Icy terror flooded her veins. The certainty in his eyes, the faith in his words—It froze her in his arms. And then they stopped. The dancers and attendees faced the entryway. A breath from Razor's kiss, Sagan inched her gaze away to the door. Eminents Wiw, Lance, Abresson, and Celindria entered the fray.

Gently, the Pain Curator brought her back to him with a single finger under her chin. His eyes asked something of her. "Remember. You're safe with me."

The dancing resumed with Sagan much less comfortable than before. Celindria, dressed in a black gown with revealing slits in strategic places, fixated on the younger Progeny immediately. Those bright blue eyes practically bore a hole in the Seamswalker's back. Razor drew her close and whispered in her ear, "Before she walked in the room, I was the second most powerful being in it."

She leaned back to catch his meaning. Her. The Pain Curator considered the Seamswalker more powerful than himself. Moving close again, she reached up to whisper against his neck, "Keep going."

"As the galaxy's primary pain merchant, I provide many outlets for business and operations. Sponsors and recruitment. Valuable services. Highly valued." The tone of his voice hardened as he explained the rest, "Until she seceded the previously most powerful Tritan coordinator. Celindria undermines my authority and demeans my contributions as limited, petty trade. She interferes with my empire, and I've worked far too hard for far too long to grant her that. For the last two thousands years, I've arranged the pieces in my favor. And only recently she discovered the intentional slights, the botched engagements, and the counter-espionage. She knows I've fixed the game to benefit the current generation of Progeny. And right now, at this very moment, you're aiding me in that game to bring her down."

Breathless and dizzy, Sagan closed her eyes. Overwhelmed but terribly curious, she asked, "How?"

"With this dance. In one of many bases of her operations. She's furious with me. But I'm afraid you won't be permitted to remember its location."

Razor brought their dance to a stop beside a Reipon Lamia. An attendant. He held out a device. "Madam, please unfasten your port for the siphon."

Bothered, Sagan peered at her dance partner, and he explained, "It's required of all non-member guests. We take the location from your memory bank. That's all. I promise."

No. She definitely wanted to keep this memory. Seamswalk. Ghost them—

A loud blast racked the cavern. Violent convulsions jolted and toppled them. A wall of fire and rock rode into the ballroom. Razor lunged for her and knocked them both down. Before they hit the polished floor, Sagan followed her initial instinct and fell into the Seam.

{REIPON}

Ross gripped her chain as Sagan and her mysterious dance partner completed another revolution around the ballroom. Beautiful and elegant, they made quite the match. Which surprised the younger Progeny as she recalled the Seamswalker describing her boyfriend very differently. For starters, this guy's hair was black, and Korac's hair was white. And the war criminal was a smidgen taller than the ringmaster. Never mind that.

She planned to wave this time around and get the more experienced girl's attention. This bizarre game of intrigue and life-threatening politics unnerved her. Ross required guidance before disaster struck—

Rumbling. Fire. Rocks.

An explosion knocked Ross into Iuo, who grabbed her and threw them both to the side. A pillar of shiny black rock fell and busted where they once stood. Morphed in his humanoid form, the Lamia raised off of her in a plank. With black and blue reptilian eyes, he scanned her for injuries.

"Are you all right?" When not shouting in concern, his voice sounded pleasant. "Ross?" Yes, his voice hissed her name in a serpentine lisp. All "S" sounds brought it out.

A tear in her silk pants split the material down one leg, displaying a few scrapes. But that was it, and they were already healing. "I think I'm fine. Thank you for saving me." Her voice shook, and her hands trembled as she tried to sit up.

"Wait a moment. Wait until the leads stand up and account for one another to avoid drawing attention to yourself." Smart man. He peered down at her shaking hands with a crinkle in what passed as his brows. "Are you in shock?" Without waiting for her to answer, he sat up and removed his jacket. The gentleman even draped it over her shoulders.

"Iuo. Thank you. But I don't think Tumu will kill you for something so far outside your control."

Oh, shit. He recoiled as if she slapped him.

"I'm sorry! I didn't mean to offend you. I'm only surprised you care so much for a girl you met a few days ago without...you know? Incentive."

Rigid and formal, he corrected her assumptions. "That's precisely what offends me. We may all be snakes on Reipon, but we're not all vipers." After another moment, he softened and helped her stand. "But you're young and raised on an isolated planet. So, I'll forgive you this once. I care about you and the other Progeny, Ross."

The silence after the explosion distracted her from the Lamia's kindness. No one screamed. What kind of people attended this party that no one seemed shocked at all?

"Eminent Wiw is dead," an unfamiliar voice echoed off the walls.

Ross' breath hitched. No. The wizened Tritan was so nice to her in Enki. She clutched her chain. If she'd used it, would he be alive now?

The woman who announced his passing took to the center of the room. Beautiful black skin. Long hair of varying styles and textures—braids, twists, dreadlocks—all black and woven with white ribbon. Shocking blue eyes struck Ross' recollection, but she was sure she never met someone who vibrated with such energy. Alive. Like electricity. A presence roiled beneath the surface. Something older.

Again, the unknown female called out to the crowd, "This is a charity gala to celebrate the upcoming auction. Who would attack such a haven of generosity and action? To kill an Eminent—A Tritan! Those responsible will know retribution and pain."

A second Tritan, a shorter one Ross recognized from Enki, went to her side and reasoned with her, "Eminent Celindria—" Oh, shit. So this was *her*. "We'll find the organization responsible and seek justice for Wiw. But first, let's take him to Enki. Let's take our brother home and say goodbye."

"Of course, Eminent Lance. Eminent Abresson, how is the state of security to evacuate…" They continued the conversation off to the side.

"Iuo, I liked Eminent Wiw." Ross needed to share that with someone.

The Lamia squeezed her shoulder. "We all did. We'll miss him very much. Especially now that Eminent Celindria is on the tribunal—"

"Did you say another Progeny was here? Other than the Seamswalker?" Celindria's voice rose in volume as that sentence went on.

And Ross' blood ran cold.

Iuo whispered to her, "Don't move. It'll only exacerbate matters. You're my guest."

But why was Tumu's Lamia contact here? Did he possess enough wealth to attend charity balls and auctions? What sort of connections brought him here?

"Ross, I intended what happens next. Please keep your faith in me a little while longer while you face your next set of trials." He pulled back and entreated her with those blue and black eyes.

She knew genuine terror.

He called out, "Eminent Celindria, this young woman is—"

"Ross Roberts," the ethereal woman finished for him.

Eminent Lance looked away from Abresson to gape at the young Progeny woman. "What in Enki's name are you doing here, child?"

Ross winced at the parental tone in his rebuke. She always hated getting in trouble. "Seeing the galaxy?" Her voice sound tiny and insignificant compared to the other woman's regal speech.

Iuo announced, "I found her meddling around Reipon and took it upon myself to investigate. I don't believe she's responsible for this act, but I suspect her involvement in its fostering terrorist cell."

Gaping at him, Ross scoffed, "You can't be serious. Iuo! How could you—"

"Take her into custody. We'll let Eminent Celindria interrogate her." Eminent Abresson dismissed her incarceration with a wave.

Ross dug in for one last glower at someone she considered a friend before letting the Mon3 drones pull her away. On the way through the cleared entrance, she overheard Celindria mutter orders to one of her guards, "I can't waste time with her. Assign her to Razor's custody until I'm available for more menial tasks."

Ross contained her anger. She learned through arguments with her brother that blowing up solved nothing. Bide her time. Wait until the perfect opportunity presented itself and take it. As she passed Celindria on the way to their super swanky space motorcade, the confident woman all but jeered at Ross. But the young woman gave her nothing in return. And, as they shoved Kyle's sister into the car, the Eminent looked bothered.

Good. They'll soon find out what Ross was made of.

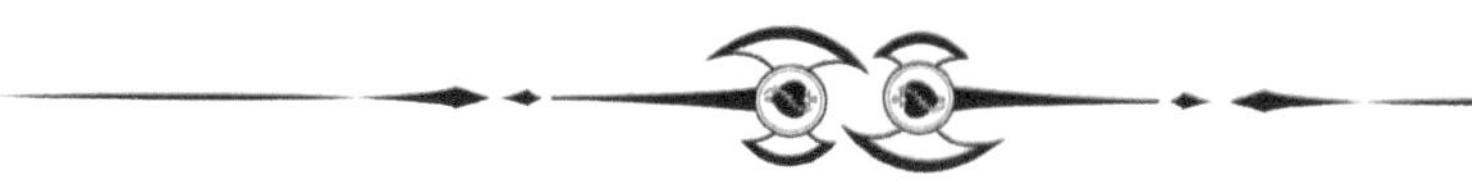

{EARTH}

The console projected the strategy screen between Pablo and Silence like a game of battleship. Both of them communicated with different squadrons of the Shadow's strikeforce. Their conversations overlapped as they maneuvered the pieces on the board with each update.

Pablo nearly fainted with relief as Lynn safely reported, "Lukemore complete. The charges on the eighteenth floor detonated as intended, and the silo collapsed cleanly. Over."

The recon footage of Abresson with Imminent soldiers below all those exhausted people sickened the doctor. "Understood. Meet you at the base. Over and Out." To Silence across from him, he asked, "Pil, confirmed?"

The Icarean warrior staved him with a finger as she listened intently to Smith on her device. "Go ahead."

Imminent housed one of its headquarters on Pil in the same plaza as the quantum engineers who temporarily resided on Earth for the global communicator. Bastards.

"Copy that. Over and Out." Silence gave Pablo the most awkward sideways thumbs-up with the most confidence he'd ever seen. "Leveled."

Pablo laughed, nervously. Exhaustedly.

Silence and Twenty-One made for good company through the tests. But she interested him in regards to the studies of their species. Quick. So very smart. At times, Pablo wondered if Silence showed signs of telepathy. But suspected both Icari belonged with the Shadow. The ancient soldiers lived by a code of just determination he only saw in members of their family. He opened his mouth to say so, "Silence—"

"Doc, come in. It's Fury. Over."

"Go ahead, Fury."

"That operation the Shadow is running tonight, I thought you canceled Reipon for lack of sufficient evidence?" The concern that wavered her voice chilled him to the marrow.

"You understood correctly."

"Someone bombed a gala that the Eminents were attending. Doc, the blast killed Eminent Wiw."

As the doctor's eyes no doubt bugged out of their sockets, Silence cocked her head curiously to the side across the console. He swallowed hard before confessing through a tight voice, "I don't understand. How could anyone know to coordinate with our strikes? We didn't do it, Fury. I swear."

A dead Tritan. A dead important Tritan Pablo met on one occasion and liked instantly. It hurt to know the wizened alien—who lived beyond Pablo's understanding of a lifespan—was the first casualty of this war.

"I believe you. But I'm worried about the ramifications. I'll report to you any news I hear. Please let the others know for me. And doc, let them know we honor that man. He did nothing to us."

That we know of hung in the air.

"Copy, Fury. Over and Out."

Silence's voice reached him through the gloom, almost innocent in her lack of awareness. "He was a good man?"

Pablo hung his head and muttered, "I think so."

"They often die first."

Xelan. Pehton expressed exactly the same sentiment about Wingmaster after his passing. The older warriors would know. Which brought up an interesting question. "How old do you think you are? How old do you feel?"

Dressed in a bikini and a labcoat, she pulled her knees to her chest and looked thoughtful. "Without memories, it's hard to say. But...in my sleep, I sensed the state of things. The shift of Icarean life. I knew of Umbra. Sometimes I think I remember seeing his face in person. I understand that was very long ago. Yet, I think I'm much older than even that."

Most of the Shadow, including Pablo, read Nox's Verse. Nox being the son of Umbra, the first King of Cinder. At least six million years old. Any older and Silence might know Elden. Pablo shook his head, unable to fathom it. "Come on. Let's tell the teams about Reipon. I can't believe—I guess there's nothing to do about it now."

Kyle's voice broke onto Silence's comm. "Reipon complete. Over and Out."

The female's stony gray eyes crept over to meet Pablo's. Her chest heaved as if her heart pounded. "Holy. Shit."

Yea, the doctor couldn't put it any better. He took the comm from her and called into the mic, "Story Taker, we canceled Reipon. Under your orders. Why target it? Over."

T.A.O. came on then. It struck Pablo as odd that she hardly left Kyle's side since joining the mission. "We suspected a spy and wanted to redirect attention away from the intended target. Do not take it personally. The mission was successful. That is all that matters. Radio silence. Over and Out."

The doctor almost threw the comms device. Out of frustration. Out of rage. Out of the futility of their current shit storm. He gripped the curls of his black hair and pulled. Ready to scream—

Across from him, an unexpected sight interrupted his tantrum. A tear rolled down the Icarean warrior's cheek. And another fell from her lashes. All the while, she stared up at the projection as if unaware of her expressiveness.

Silence met his eyes and repeated, softly, so very softly, "Yes. The good ones go first."

"I'm getting the impression you're no longer referring to Eminent Wiw. Silence, what do you think is wrong with Kyle?" Pablo stared intently until the hair rose on his arms and something tingled on the back of his neck.

Not three pitches. Silence's voice split into six as she recited, *"No man may own another nor impress his dominion over them. For only in forfeit of volition, can one assume control over the other."*

Holy. Shit.

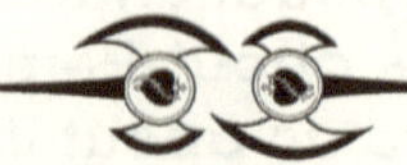

{GAIT}

Pehton knew of the only back door into the Emporium. Near the kitchens and close to the basement entrance. The Pain Curator sealed it with adhesive made from nacre fibers. And the Executive Warden of Gait knew the exact trick for it.

Even in the dead of night, the light pollution illuminated Gait's purple skies. The trash receptacles hovered overhead, clunky and smelly. Various manner of refuse painted the back alley in viscous blue and green fluids. Her carbon fiber boots splashed in it. Black silk wraps hid her orange feathers and arm gliders. She retracted her Lyriki armor. The bright blue was too arresting against the shadows she aimed to tread. Instead, she concealed her pitch-black muscle and curves beneath a mesh bodysuit. When she dressed, a thought occurred to her which made the petite female cringe.

Razor would approve.

Shaking off the shudder, Pehton approached the door and softly sang against it. The resonance told her to tweak the pitch until—Bingo. The nacre glass shattered, and the adhesive flaked away. She slipped inside with a good sweep to the left and right. Nothing. Entering the basement, the darkness swallowed her current choice of gear.

Not a stitch of color anywhere. Black walls, floors, ceiling ducts, metal pillars, and beams. Catwalks of black metal led forward and a mesh stair led to Hell's lower circles. Affording only that brief glimpse, she kept onward with this floor and doubled back to the Emporium proper. The frosted glass ceiling, disguised as parquet flooring, provided the only light in this abyss. But it also oriented her to the desired destination. Below the mezzanine, now, she recalled Razor leading her from a stair in his vault to the bedroom suite.

As Pehton slinked below the building currently closed for the owner's night off, she silently repeated her objectives. Maintain perspective. *What counts.*

One, raid his desk, libraries, archives—whatever to learn his plans for the Seamswalker. And anything else about the mysterious "others." Two, anything at all hinting at Inanis and this Atheneum mystery. How did these things involve the taken children? Three, investigate suspicious accounts of slave intake linked to the Emporium.

The Executive Warden was aware of the unfortunate people who signed over their lives to the Pain Curator in exchange for credits at the end of their service. Unfortunately, that was perfectly legal. But the slave work? Him and her went a few rounds about that in the past. When she was first promoted to Executive.

Was she ready to go toe-to-toe with him again? About enslaved workers? Damn fucking straight. Pehton would happily unleash the Chorus for that offense. Of course, resorting to that weapon would kill the slaves along with everyone else on the planet, but she'd make her point—

Fuck!

Pehton ran into a blacked-out obstruction and almost knocked herself unconscious. It hurt her head so badly that even with a nacre she took a step back and cradled it while fighting not to swear aloud. It was a wall. With one hand stretched out, she followed along until it came to a corner. Turned and continued to follow. This was it. Razor's bedroom.

Did she miscalculate? Was the only way in through those stairs in his second-floor vault? When inside, Pehton swore she noticed another door—

There. Her hand brushed the seams of the entryway until she found exactly what she wanted. Sealed. With nacre filaments.

One soft song later, the Executive Warden entered a space that should never see an ultraviolet lamp. Upon her entry, perimeter lights illuminated along the walls. All black like the rest of the basement. Except the bed. Pehton frowned. The sheets were white. He changed them. Oh, and where were the—

Sixteen women, all pitch-black with varying height, descended on the Executive Warden. Their pretty faces hissing as they opened their mouths to sing.

Pehton ordered, "Stop. Return to your stations and await your owner."

Without hesitation, the women with orange, yellow, and red feathers for hair dispersed deeper in the room until they melted into the darkness. Only one remained, but she wasn't hissing.

Triss, lovely with the brightest red feathers, glided toward Pehton completely naked. Confident and alluring, she smiled seductively. "Hello, replacement. Did you come all this way because you missed me? Because you're tired and want to step down and restore the title you stole from me?"

The current Executive Warden wanted to swallow hard against her apprehension, but stopped herself. "What happened to your volition? How did you break the bonds?"

"Oh, Pehton. You should know better. The Executive Warden never signs over her volition. Not even to the prison. Obviously, you didn't." Triss threw the first punch.

The orange-feathered Lyrik blocked with her gliders and ducked with a leg sweep. "What about Razor? How is he controlling you then—"

"He doesn't. I love him." Triss avoided the sweep with a backflip.

Pehton couldn't hide the recoil or keep her lips from curling in disgust.

The more the Executive Warden reacted, the more fevered Triss became until she traced hands over herself like a lover and bit her full lips. "I worship the ground that man walks on and whatever he wants, I do it. He never has to ask. You gave me a gift. I can help him ignite the world around us and watch it burn safely from his lap." Incoming side kick.

It caught Pehton square in the chest and sent her to the floor. Unnerved more than injured, she tried for logic, "You must know he doesn't love you. Men like Razor can't feel that way."

Hands on hips, Triss shrugged. "He favors me. That's all that matters. I'm the only Lyrik he fucks. He won't even fuck that little Seamswalker he brought down here the other night. Because he wants me only." She glided over to the door that Pehton entered. Her voice hardened into icy condescension. "Keep the promotion, Pehton. Leave the Lyriks here with us until you need them to flaunt the prison's security like last time. Never return here. Consider me letting you live as my payment for the favor you've done me. I no longer serve the Tritans as their guard dog. As you do. I serve a real god."

Pehton stared, aghast. This couldn't be it. "Triss, my children—"

"Are dead." No pity. No compassion. "Forget them and hold onto your life a while longer. You don't want to experience Razor's wrath. And it's like I told your ex that came around here recently, nothing will turn me from him." The impatient Lyrik folded her arms and leaned back against the wall, waiting.

Ex? No. "Celindria?" Why the hell would the First Progeny try to recruit from within the house of pain?

"Yea, that's the one. Have a nice life, Pehton. While he lets you have it."

And that's how the Executive Warden found herself shuffling back through the basement with her tail feathers between her legs. Her only opportunity thwarted by the surprise of Triss' compliance. How could Pehton get so many things wrong? How far did Razor's claws dig into Gait? And why didn't she simply kill Triss? The woman deserved it long ago.

No. The Executive Warden was completely blindsided. Shocked. She never imagined such a circumstance would overcome the prior Lyriki leader. What was this feeling? Guilt? Complicity? Triss was in this position—this madness—because of Pehton. Now Pehton's mission took on one more objective. Putting that bitch out of her misery.

She imagined all the delightful scenarios as she exited the basement. Beheading. Fire. No, fire wouldn't work—

Shit. She wasn't alone.

"I was hoping to find you here." The auburn-haired human leaned against a wall, eating a strange yellow fruit from Earth. He peeled the outer layer down and took a bite.

Caught. Again. Elden, this was demeaning. "Yea?"

"Why were you in Razor's suite? And what did you and Triss talk about?"

An opening presented itself. And Pehton would certainly take it.

TEN

WITHOUT A WILL, IS THERE A WAY?

{???}

HEADACHE. Dizzy. Sagan groaned, unwilling to open her eyes. Something heavy landed on her. Landed? Why landed?

The explosion. The last thing she remembered was the wall of fire, Razor threw them out of the way, and...the Seam. The firm stone beneath acknowledged it. Sagan opened her eyes and...cried out.

The Seam. The stone everywhere she looked was purple. Like her eyes. Startled, she tried to sit up and finally examined the heavy weight anchoring her down.

Razor groaned at her jerky movements where he'd fallen on top of her.

In the Seam.

Razor was in the Seam with her.

Sagan didn't cry out.

She screamed.

Her voice echoed through the cathedral and startled him awake. He gazed around, unawares and possibly concussed given their circumstances. The moment he looked down and saw himself laying on her, he quickly moved off and onto his back with another groan and a wince.

"If I apologize, will you promise not to scream again? No one will hear you, anyway." He sighed and covered his eyes with one hand. "Are you all right, Seamswalker?"

"That depends on your definition of all right. How. The hell. Are you here, Razor?"

He frown-squinted at her, perplexed. That's when she noticed the hand at his face. The nails beds were bleeding. Yellow.

Rudely, she pointed at him and accused, "You're a Thailean Mystic." She held up his hand as evidence known to her from Nox's Verse. "I thought you were all short."

Razor chuckled. Inappropriate given their circumstances. "I assure you, I'm no priest." Stiffly and with many grunts, he rolled over and pushed himself onto his feet. He took in their surroundings. "Monarch Hall. It's been a while." Gazing down at Sagan, he sighed. "How could I ever forget that shade of purple? I need only look in your eyes to see it." He offered a silk-wrapped tan hand.

Between them, his whip lay on the floor. Two-pronged. In Nox's Verse, the King of Cinder, Nox, gifted his General a two-pronged whip. Korac later used it to punish Celindria. It couldn't be...

In the middle of a personal crisis, Sagan reached for her chain. All she found was the cover on her nacre port. She closed her eyes in defeat when she found it missing and remembered Matt kept it for her. No axes either. How could she be so naïve?

"No harm will befall you. I swear. And not only because I need your help to leave this place."

The Seamswalker opened her eyes to find the Pain Curator smirking down at her, hand outstretched like a lifeline. She could walk out of here and leave him to die.

As if he read the thought behind her eyes, he knelt to level his gaze with hers. "Ask yourself what's changed since you trusted me at the gala. I've done nothing to you.

I won't. Now you know I'm different from others you've met before, but you already suspected that."

"I want answers. Honest answers, Razor."

He gave her a genuine smile at that. "I owe you that much."

Sagan searched the cathedral beyond him and reached out her hand. "But not here."

He clasped it, and they stood together. Peering about, the tightness in his shoulders implied the Seam made him as uneasy as her. "My suite in the Emporium. It's the only place I know without Imminent surveillance. And here..."

She shook her head and fought a shiver, unwilling to stay. "We're making a stop first." Sagan walked them out of the Seam and into the coat check at the gala.

They stood close to prevent unwanted attention. He smiled at her once more. "Of course, you'd return for it. He is a very lucky Icarus."

"I love him, Razor. I'm like this with the people I care about. Do you understand what it is to love someone? To be foolish and risk yourself for a jacket because it belongs to them. Because it holds meaning between us?"

"Your innocence is enthralling." He searched her eyes with utter emptiness in his own.

Sagan's heart broke with Razor's words.

Irredeemable.

A small fraction of her held out hope she could sway him to the Shadow's side. To work for good. In that moment, her disappointment decided for her. She'd never save him, and it was never up to her, anyway. He was no friend of hers.

With that knot in her gut, the Seamswalker snooped around the closets until she found Korac's coat. She spared a few risky seconds to breathe deep of his scent and reveled in it. A man worth fighting beside.

She found Razor across the way retrieving his coat, and that's when they heard a sound neither of them appreciated. Celindria's voice cut through the halls. "Eminent Wiw is dead."

They froze and stared at one another with wide eyes. Before they overheard more, several Mon3 drones dispersed and swept the area. Without another moment's hesitation, Sagan took Razor's hand and led them to the mezzanine at the Emporium. He took her into a vault big enough to stand inside. There, he sank into a blacked-out staircase in the floor. She followed, confident in her ability to Seamswalk if shit went sideways.

The "suite" spanned the entire bottom floor of the main Emporium. Steps led down to an Olympic-sized bed with shiny white sheets. She tried not to notice they were the same sheets she bought for Korac's bed. Her cheeks burned.

Razor led her to an equally impressive desk that might double as a boardroom table. All the while, he stripped out of his jacket, unfastened and rolled up his sleeves, and ran a hand through his bright red hair. Mussed. When he started unbuttoning his collar, she worried he meant to strip entirely.

He caught the look on her face and smirked. "So skittish. I think I'll call you Pain Kitten."

If Korac suggested the name, Sagan might like it. But given the supplier, she only shook her head. "You wish."

With a chuckle, he threw himself in his enormous chair and leaned back with his boots on the desk. Arms folded, he put it to her, "What would you like to cover first?"

"How can you be in the Seam?" This mattered to Sagan. Until recently with the voices, the place was so lonesome and empty to her. None of her friends could join her there.

He took his boots off the desk and leaned across it, meeting her eyes. "I was born there. Impossibly long ago. I won't bore you with the entire story. The people I hail from originated in the Seam and eventually migrated to Thailea. The people known as Aegis."

Sagan never heard of such a race. "How many of you are there? Where are the rest?"

"I am the last."

She recoiled despite herself and spiraled on the proper way to respond. Eventually, she offered, "My condolences. May I ask how it happened?"

"You may ask me whatever you wish to know. We were hunted and exterminated like vermin. Which is why I'm not forthcoming with the information. And also why my rank in Imminent is so significant. Very little prevents Celindria from reducing my contributions to nothing and painting me as unnecessary to the cause. As expendable."

"About Imminent... Razor, I need you."

At her words, he closed his eyes and inhaled deeply. When he opened them again, the irises twirled. "Whatever you want, I'll grant you. I only ask for your discretion in return."

Lean into it. "I want full dossiers on every known agent of Imminent."

He stood up so abruptly it startled her. He shook his head to disguise the delight at her "skittishness" but not very well. A second vault stood sentinel along the wall beyond his desk. Opening it with a retinal scan, he stepped inside for only a moment before returning with a drive of some sort.

"Any Enki tech console can read this. The password is Aegis Atheneum. It contains what you seek."

That word. From the Seam. It all pieced together with Razor at the center of the puzzle.

He handed it to her. But when she took it, he held onto his end. They gazed at one another over the precious device.

"I wrote it when I first heard you came looking for me two years ago. You were everything I'd hoped you would be and for that I'm grateful to you, Seamswalker."

Staring into his eyes left her dizzy. Or maybe the shock of surviving an explosion. Or maybe the discovery of an entirely unknown race with ties to the Seam.

System overload.

Razor touched her elbow to steady her and offered, "You can stay here tonight. I'll sleep upstairs. Matt will guard you."

Exhausted, Sagan looked at the bed. So close. No doubt comfortable. But then she remembered whose bed it was and the leather bundle she held in her arms. "I appreciate the offer, but I need to report to my family and return this to Korac."

"Come here anytime you need shelter. My life is in your hands now, Seamswalker. There are few games left to play between us."

Sagan shook her head, disheartened. Genuinely, she asked, "Why couldn't you be a good guy, Razor? Why did you have to be a villain?"

For the first time, Razor smiled in a way she would actually describe as sexy in its devilish charm. "Because villainy produces far greater thrills and even richer rewards." Then he gently took Sagan's hand and pressed the back of it to his lips.

Rolling her eyes, she withdrew her hand and stepped into the Seam. "Good night, Razor."

Bone and shadow once more, she gazed at the empty world. Aegis. She thought of a hundred more questions to ask him, but not tonight. The drive mattered more.

As if he sensed her thoughts, Razor's voice resonated from the ceiling. "Good night, my Pain Kitten."

Why did part of Sagan take comfort in it?

{ENKI}

Physically, Tameka felt amazing.

Sip.

Even better now. Mentally, her mind knotted up into an enormous ball of churning anxiety. The Shadow killed an Eminent. Kyle acted on his own again. And here she was sneaking around Enki trying to work on a map to their most sacred grounds.

"Steady." Caedes' gruff, yet reassuring, voice in her earpiece eased her some.

Talk. Take her mind off the mess. "Jack is so busy here. John has his hands full watching over him. But I think he enjoys feeling useful."

Caedes responded with a taciturn, "Humph."

So much for diverting conversation.

"Take this conduit and head right. Expect some traffic in that area. Watch your back."

"Got it. Thanks." Tameka followed his instructions and kept an eye out for passing Tritans. All the surfaces around Enki were white stone and glass. Sometimes the walls were glass and the floor was stone. It reminded her of the Seam. Several conduits led to stone platforms on the ocean. They labeled these as landings. Caedes' calculations estimated over seventeen million of them in this labyrinth. Designed to confuse and exhaust their enemies. It certainly discouraged her.

"Keep going, Tameka. You're making excellent progress."

Right. Exactly what she needed to hear. Close to something Xelan would say, but with less cheese. She missed the cheese. That grin when he took pride in the cheese...

Intently, Caedes explained, "From here, we have nothing. Tell me which conduit you choose. The device will map your location for us."

Fury idly twisted her chain and considered which of the thirteen conduits to choose. Far left.

Sip.

"It's a shrine." Tameka took a step onto an almost invisible barrier between her and the empty at the Dyson's Sphere center. "I assume you want me to poke my head through and see where it leads?"

Again, Caedes encouraged her, "Only if you feel comfortable—Hey, we weren't expecting you. Again."

Sagan's muffled voice came over his mic. "I need to talk to you and—where's Tameka?"

There was some quiet and movement on the comm device before Sagan came loud and clear. "I have a lead on Imminent, but we can't completely trust it. I'm handing off a drive from my source to Caedes. Open it with caution. Off system."

"Sagan, something awful happened tonight. Eminent Wiw died in a bombing."

"I know. I was at the gala the terrorist group hit."

Caedes informed her, "It was Kyle and T.A.O."

"No fucking way? They almost killed me."

Tameka bit her lip. Killed an Eminent. Almost killed Sagan. Confirmation. They needed confirmation. "Sagan, this is important, was it an Imminent location after all? If you were there..."

"Yea. It was. Razor took me to the party for undercover work. Let's hope the drive pays off. I'm sorry about Wiw, Tameka. I know you were fond of him."

"I think his loss was likely a genuine tragedy." Some part of Tameka wanted to turn Kyle over to Enki. Or kill him. But... "I wish we could ask Rayne—"

"—What to do next? We know how she'd handle this, and it's part of the reason she's in the Complex. Her way is definite and permanent. We need flexibility here to unite the Vast Collective against Imminent."

Tameka nodded at the truth in Sagan's words before remembering the blond couldn't see her. "She's not the way for that. We'll meet soon to decide how to handle Kyle's punishment. And I think he deserves one."

"I agree. I'll be there. Just tell me when and please let it be after tomorrow. I need to sleep. Oh, and sorry for not knocking the other night, Caedes. I'll uhm... practice more discretion." She snickered like the carefree girl they missed, and then silence blanketed the mic.

The bald Icarus tried his best for a clinical feeding experience. The purring was an autonomic response from the intoxicating affects of Tameka's blood. He slept it off in her bed. The surprise on his face the next morning when he realized—he looked venerated.

Sip.

"Uncle Caeda!" The most precious change of subject ever. And Caedes always let him in. "Hee. Mommy?"

After a shuffle of the mic, her baby's voice came through her ear. "Mommy."

"I'm here, sweetie. Do you need me?" Tameka scanned her surroundings, feeling ridiculous standing in a shrine outside of Elden knew where. And taking a mommy call. Working mom hustle.

"Lines. Same."

A little distant, Caedes explained while he maneuvered the obviously wriggling toddler, "He's pointing to the model. At the conduits. No, Pax. Please don't touch that." Even his stern "Uncle voice" was less gruff than his casual talk among the Shadow.

Warmed through, Tameka gave in. "I'm heading home. Maybe I'll take him out for the next one. He wants to feel a part of this, and his..." She closed her eyes tight and took a deep breath through the impending attack. Eventually, tightly, she finished, "His father wouldn't want me to hide reality from Pax." Or at least she thought so.

"The lines, mommy!"

Caedes pressed softly, "Before you return, do you feel up to checking where the shrine leads?"

"Not a problem." Tameka, Fury, Sovereign Ambassador of the Two Worlds walked right out of Enki and into a weird room. Empty. Black metal floors, walls, and ceiling. Corrugated and industrial. The space reminded her of the resident bunks in the Ecology. The far side shimmered with energy. A nacre-resistant barrier. Where the hell was she?

Stepping back into Enki, she reported the details back to Caedes. All the while, her hackles raised and that anxiety knot twisted. Listening to her instincts, she booked it back the way she came. "Something feels wrong about this."

"I agree. Keep steady."

Sip.

"Sovereign Ambassador."

Shit. Tameka stopped and turned around. "Eminent Lance, I'm so glad you've returned unharmed."

"It's fortunate I found you about." The Tritan caught up with her and touched her elbow gently. "The remaining

Eminents are grieving. And I'm afraid that's left them quite dangerous. Avoid confrontation with anyone unless I'm present. How is Pax? And Caedes? Is he recovered?"

Caedes stayed quiet all the while, but his breathing changed at the mention of his name.

"We're all fine. Thank you for your concern and your advice, Eminent." Lance was the next most tolerable member of the Tribunal. Gently, Tameka offered, "I'm sorry for your loss."

"The Vast Collective's loss. Wiw balanced justice and peace within the Tribunal. Without him and with the other two promoted, I'm afraid my voice counts for nothing." The Tritan kept fidgeting with his sleeves as if uncomfortable speaking with her.

Ice filled Tameka's veins. Coincidences and schemes stacked on one another. And they all threatened to topple and bury the Shadow.

"Be safe, Sovereign Ambassador. And never find yourself alone with them." With that grave warning, he swept away in his robes and disappeared through a nearby conduit.

"You get all that?"

"You know it. I'll stay on the line until you get back."

Tameka rushed home through the conduits, clutching her chain. In her bones, she felt it. She knew. "Soon."

Sip.

{Cinder}

Bones spent the better part of the day in a crawler several miles below the Earth's surface. He and Colton took turns unearthing the stronghold's entrance while Cypher and Lamassau guarded the King. The excavators damn near threw a party when they dug up the last rock. Relief and celebration. Until they reached the living area.

Finesse. That's what they needed.

Now, he rested in the pit on King duty. The light rains outside suggested Rayne's disposition calmed down compared to earlier in the week. But her majesty still suffered a melancholy of sorts—

"Yo, it's your turn." Lam gently nudged him with a boot under the table.

Bones put a stern finger in his opponent's face. "Don't try that footsie shit again. I like Tumu. And I don't appreciate being used like a piece of meat between two tigers."

"Beefcake . . ." Lamassau batted those membranes on those eyelash-less voids in what passed for Tritan flirtatious allure. "You know I'd never treat you that way. You're special. Raise or call?"

"I bet you say that to all the muscle." Beefcake. Please. Bones was—at the very least—a rare slice of chateaubriand. He slapped down two cards and drew two more. Hmm. "I'll raise you."

"I like to hear that. How many this time?"

"Two bags of Cheetos and a pickle."

The Chef whistled, impressed. "I don't know. That might be too rich for my blood."

"You learned how to play this game twenty minutes ago. I was there. I was the one that taught you. Now, call or fold." Please don't raise.

"Well, you may have only taught me a few minutes ago, but I've won the last three hands."

Stupid expression-lite Tritans. Lam's fucking poker face was killing Bones' snack trove. Frito Lay died during the initial Icarean Invasion. Only a precious few expired bags of Cheetos remained.

"Lamassau. Come in." Tumu's voice emitted from the Chef's palm device.

He grinned and answered, "Tumi, I've only barely kept the Icarus off me. But I did so in honor of you. Expect reparations."

Bones rolled his eyes at Lam's exaggerated wink.

"Eminent Wiw is dead."

The green Tritan sobered to downright professional as if someone flipped a switch. "Cause?"

"Crushed in an explosion at the Reipon gala." Was that a waver in the Officer of the Third's voice?

"Do we suspect Imminent?"

Bones nodded solemnly. The enemy. It fit their modus operandi to strike at Enki while the Shadow conducted their own counter-attacks.

Tumu confirmed, "We suspect both Imminent *and* the Progeny. Representatives from the latter will come before the Tribunal within the next few days."

No. Oh, no. This was a brilliant maneuver. Frame the Progeny for Eminent Wiw's death. Divide and conquer.

Lam closed his eyes tight like he was praying. "Is this worst-case scenario, Officer?"

"The very worst. Don't let them near the King of Earth and Cinder. Protect her with your life. Radio silence beyond this point."

"Tumu, wait!" The Chef turned away and muttered in the guise of privacy, "Be careful."

"You, too."

Of course, Bones worried about the Shadow tonight. Their retaliation missions aimed at the hearts of Imminent. But now they found themselves in even hotter water. Boiling hot.

"You know if your people killed my friend, there will be a reckoning, right?" Said the green Tritan that apparently breathes fire.

"No one with a brain for warfare wants a dead Tritan. Especially not one with a history of siding with the Progeny." Pragmatic assurance? No. "That's the truth. It makes no sense for the Shadow to make an enemy out of their most powerful ally." Not that it mattered anymore, but Bones threw down his hand. Two pair. Sixes and eights.

"Practical warrior you are." Lam laid down his cards. Full house. Aces and queens. Shit.

"Bones, this is Cypher. Over."

After the milestone in the excavation project, Cypher and Colton took over guarding the Icarean migration at the conduit. Almost to the point of pouting while the Tritan scooped away his snacks, Bones grumbled, "Cypher. Go ahead. Over."

The pretty decent human with a crush on King Rayne sounded exasperated, "You won't believe the garbage we just took out."

The Chef cocked a non-eyebrow and leaned forward to listen.

"What's that?"

"Some group called Natural Humans vs Nacre Humans marched a parade across the fucking desert to protest Icarean entry at the conduit."

Incredulous, Bones met Lam's black voids, who shook his head at the stupidity of some people. Gruffly, the Icarus responded, "Please tell me you broke their asses on the way out?"

The Tritan chuckled and opened a bag of Cheetos. A soft cry eeked out of the Icarean warrior in protest.

"They vowed to return every day until they die on this hill. And they will die. They're not bringing provisions. These people aim to martyr themselves for this cause. To prove they can survive fine enough without Enki technology. It put us in the uncomfortable position of providing for them to prevent the bad publicity. We need King Jack. Or King Rayne. Or Tumu. Anybody."

"Man, Cypher. They're beyond busy right now." Bones rubbed the stress out of the back of his neck as he considered the pile-up of bad news.

"I hear ya. Just thought I'd warn you of what we have to look forward to in the coming weeks."

"Thanks, man. Watch your back out there. Over and Out."

Bones almost asked for a Cheeto when he looked over and saw Lam staring at the Martyr Complex. His rich green complexion paled to pastel. The Icarus tried to speak softly to avoid startling the Tritan, but failed. "It's like she's a ghost. Easy to forget she's there until she makes herself known."

"I thought I heard..." He shook himself and returned to eating the Icarean guard's beloved snacks.

"King Rayne talks to us in her way." Bones shuffled the cards, ready to win back his trove.

After some wordless crunching, the Chef finally asked as if his curiosity got the better of him, "What does she say?"

"Soon."

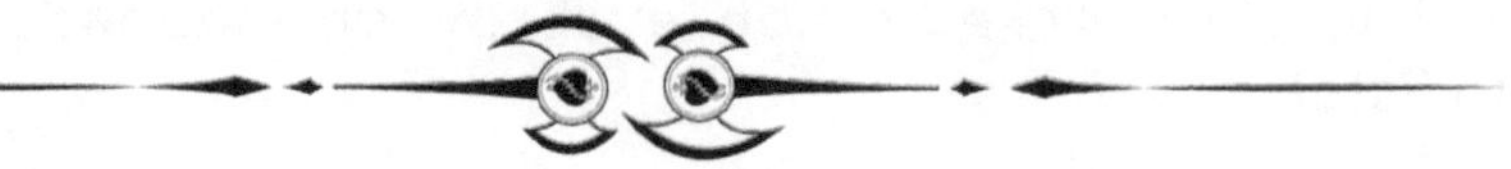

{ENKI}

"But…And I'm sorry to ask this way, but what does that mean, Tumu?" John asked after shaking off the shock.

The entire hospital room went speechless at the news of Eminent Wiw's passing. The Officer of the Third arrived seconds ago to inform them. John liked the old Tritan. He treated everyone with respect and fondness. Para and Karter exchanged knowing looks. Chris and Jack ducked their eyes as if shocked beyond bewilderment. This was awful.

"He was so nice…" The King Regent of Earth faced Tumu with genuine grief in his hazel eyes.

The Tritan softly agreed, "He was. And John, it's left quite a dangerous imbalance within the Tribunal. A power vacuum until they find his replacement."

"You could do that." Chris gestured at the Tritan. "You have our vote."

The ancient alien—former Primary—shook his head. "I don't qualify. Remember, they're like saints to your people. They accomplish so many good deeds—miracles if you must—before they're elected."

"You helped us organize a resistance against Nox's forces." Karter jumped on the bandwagon.

Para followed soon after, "You restored Earth with the Progeny and helped establish the migration efforts. You're overseeing Rayne's sentence…"

Before John opened his mouth to add more, Tumu held up a hand to stop them. "Once demoted from Eminent, it's nearly impossible to regain that status. And I'm fine with that. But I actually came here for you, Karter."

The black and green of the woman's eyes widened. "Me?"

"The Icari could use representation, and I can't think of anyone more qualified than you. You've survived the main eras of this race. You saw the expansion of Li. And all the while you fought for the betterment of your people." Tumu made an excellent case.

The Osage human in the room considered the history of Cinder. Of all the men and women mentioned throughout, Karter's name recurs with mostly positive mentions. The only exception was the Tritan-backed coup. But no one should know about it since Nox's Verse was illegal.

Chris took Karter's hand. "I support whatever you want to do."

Para took the other one. "We'll get a place in Enki. All of us as a family."

Mostly distracted by the warm spectacle happening right in front of him, John barely noticed the shift in Tumu's countenance. But he caught it. The Tritan looked desperate. The Educator asked, "What's this really about—"

"It should be my sister."

They all turned and stared at Jack. Chris sighed. Karter, Para, and Tumu looked more sympathetic. John's eyebrows tried to reach his hairline.

But the King Regent set his jaw in determination. There was fire in his eyes when he faced Tumu. "It should be Rayne. She's given everything for the people of both worlds. She *is* a miracle. What's it take to exonerate her? Tell me, Tumu. What miracles did Wiw or Lance accomplish to gain that status? I don't care to hear about Abresson or Celindria. We know how they rigged their elections."

"Be. Quiet."

John's eyes widened so much that tears fell from them. Terrified, his heart raced. The Officer of Third's voice came from inside his own head. The Tritan never moved his mouth. Could they read minds? Or only communicate with telepathy? Was it only Tumu? Cause Abresson would have said something by now if he could hear what they really thought of him. Could he hear John's thoughts right now?

Chris and Para hopped out of their seats and assumed a fighter's stance. Karter unsheathed a concealed knife from who the fuck knew where within the resurrection casket.

But Jack was a Callahan through and through. He faced Tumu, unafraid. Notably, with his mouth shut.

Again came that eerie disembodied bass in their heads. *"Be careful what you say. Enki has eyes and ears as well as an unfair sense of judgment. No Tritan will understand your ire in the face of their loss."* And in a shock so vacuous it made their ears pop, Tumu spoke aloud, "Wiw was a good friend and a great man. He made discoveries that prolonged the life of our species to continue our research. But he also established the true integration of the test planets into a Collective of people. Initially, the humanoid, intelligent populace of the planets we seeded were only considered experiments. Clinically and inhumanely treated. Wiw is the reason any of you have rights. That you exist as free peoples. Mourn his loss, for that's truly what it is. Our loss."

John searched the faces around the room to gauge their level of impress. Each of them looked properly affected.

The Tritan rotated his neck as if working out the tension in his shoulders. "That said, under normal circumstances, your sister qualifies as a spectacular candidate. But she is not a person from whom one seeks council. She is the person for whom one seeks execution."

Jack conceded with a duck of his head.

Tumu squeezed his shoulder with genuine warmth and consolation. "This brings me to my next concern. The remaining Eminents will bring the Progeny before the Tribunal. There is evidence as to their complicity in the matter. Obviously, not King Rayne. All of you must lie low until after this formality is observed."

John brought Jack back out of the way with him and patted the younger Callahan on the back. Why couldn't their lives be simple?

The Officer stepped around the group and held out his hand to Karter. Softly, the Tritan smiled with a lipless mouth, and helped the Valkyrie out of the casket. "Please consider my offer. It's much to consider, but I mean it genuinely. You make an excellent candidate."

Chris and Para both stood at the taller Icarean female's side. She gazed at Tumu as if measuring his sincerity. Strong and sure, Karter acknowledged, "You came to this decision based on what I told you about my child. You're arranging us into a stratagem." She held up a hand to stop the incoming protest. He nodded for her to continue. "I accept your proposal for candidacy as the first Icarean Eminent and the first Icarus of the Tribunal."

Tumu closed his eyes and sagged with relief. John swore he deflated and blew out a black cloud of stress.

Chris' chest puffed out as he beamed at her. Para looked less happy and more resolute, as if she knew better what lay ahead for them.

"I have conditions before I combat the current Tribunal for this honor. You said you knew what happened to my baby. Before I take this position, you'll tell me. I don't care what fate they met. I want to know." The powerful woman never wavered.

Jack walked over and whispered in her ear. John overheard Ross' name.

"We also want Ross returned. Safely—"

Tumu interrupted her to explain, "I just heard word. Iuo set Ross another step closer to finding her sister. From here, it gets a little dark. But I'm positive that she'll find Bethany."

"Without harm?" John needed to clarify that.

The Tritan hesitated and chose his next words carefully. "It's a dangerous mission. She agreed to face potential risks. I can't promise unharmed. But I can promise alive." He stopped and turned toward the door. Placing a finger to his lips, he asked them for quiet.

The room held a collective breath.

After a few seconds passed in silence, Tumu looked back to Karter. "You're free to return to Tameka's apartment. It's getting crowded in there. I'll arrange another—"

"We want the entire wing," the taller Valkyrie demanded. Chris barely concealed a proud chuckle. Para beamed.

"Yes. Of course. I'll head that way when I finish my rounds. Thank you, Karter." The Tritan left a little lighter in his step than when he arrived.

They all turned and looked at John, who shuffled on his prosthetic and brushed his ear. "Did you get all that, Caedes?"

"Yea. We did. Fury wants everyone back. Now. She has a plan."

{GAIT}

Wearing Korac's leather duster, Sagan stepped into the Seam and sagged to her knees with a thud. Her muscles felt too heavy and sore for her bones to hold them up any longer. She sank forward and rested her head on the stone. So hungry. So tired. Close her eyes and take a brief rest—

"Beautiful."

"Razor?!" She startled awake, lying on her side in the Seam. The voices. Were they back? How long had she slept in this monochromatic wasteland? Elden, she felt like shit. With a grunt and a groan, she rolled onto her stomach and forced herself to stand.

Dizzy. Back on her knees, she vomited. When the waste dried to ash and dissolved into the stone, she skid back with a cry of alarm, "What the fuck?!" Open a conduit. Leave. Now.

Nothing happened.

Terrified, Sagan clawed at the stone until she stood and tried again. "What..." She couldn't Seamswalk. Was it her current state of weakness? Or was the Seam refusing to let her leave? Either way, Sagan couldn't get out.

And she screamed. Trapped. Unable to leave. A place of ash and bone. No escape. Her worst nightmare. Sagan screamed. Until she fell. Until her throat burned. Until her exhausted mind gave up and choked on the futility.

"Sagan."

Not the voice she feared. The voice she wanted to hear. "Korac!" On an instinct that fired her blood, Sagan ran through the hall and into Korac's arms. She knew from the scent of snowfall in the dead of night. Tears poured from her eyes. Sobbing hard against him, she held on as if sure he almost lost her.

"I heard you clear through the ether. You were screaming. What happened?" The Icarean General. The war criminal. The man famous across the Vast Collective for his cool facade. For his elegant cadence in that smooth tenor. Trembled with fear. His entire body shook with it.

Sagan told him everything. Every moment of the night. Except one detail. She kept Razor's secret. With Remorse and whoever else listening, it seemed wrong to out the man as the last of his kind. A hunted kind at that. No, she'd keep her promise.

At first mention of the Pain Curator in her recount of the events, Korac stood Sagan up with him as support. He stripped the leather duster from her shoulders and let it pool on the floor. While she told her story, he stepped back and appraised the dress with admiring appreciation. When he got to the collar, his eyes flicked up to hers. The smoldering smirk was pure commendation. Pride, even.

Sagan flushed as his reward.

Korac knelt and took her leg so he could remove one glass slipper. Then the other. Every touch further sensitized her skin and shot through her. The stimulation made it difficult to concentrate on her storytelling. And he enjoyed that. With every word stumbled, he smiled in wonder at her responsiveness.

She loved him for it. For their way of being together. "All night I wished I was dancing with you." Okay, blurting that out wasn't smooth, but she needed to say it.

Standing, Korac kissed Sagan's nose and took her by the hand. Near the shower, he slipped the first set of straps from her back. Then her shoulders and biceps. Every strap. Until only a whisper held the dress on her. Korac bent to kiss her nacre port, and the dress fell. "The collar stays. And I expect to see it with my axes next time."

Sagan finally smiled for him. "Yes, Master."

The war criminal stopped smirking. He stared hard at her until her skin burned under the intensity. The blood rushing all over reminded her of the dizziness. He caught her gently as she faltered. Despite her weakness, Sagan took notice of his bare stomach and the light-weight sweats hanging off his hips. Celebrating her escape from the Seam, she kissed his ribs. When he shivered, she licked. Her hands wandered—

"Not yet. Let's get you showered and fed first. We need to anchor you." Korac peeled her off of him and gazed into her pouting face. He put a stern finger between her eyes. "After that, I'll give you a night you'll never forget, General."

Sagan skipped to the tile under the shower. Neither one of them said it, but she smelled like a mixture of Korac and Razor. The dancing left vanilla and darker things on her. With the perfect restraint of a gentleman, he washed her sore muscles without a single unprofessional touch. Unfortunately. Afterward, he handed her a wrapped sustenance bar.

When she raised a questioning brow at him, he shrugged. "I'm not touching you until you eat that entire thing." At her pout, he chuckled. "I have some Vittle supplement to spare, if you really want to experience torment."

Unwrapped and in her mouth before he forced her to endure that frozen spinach crap.

"That's what I thought." Korac smirked and prepped the bed.

All the while, he never dressed and walked around as tantalizing incentive for her to choke down the tasteless brown brick. Well, two could play at that game.

Sagan sat on the floor with an oversized towel draped over her. She let it slip and expose her shoulders.

He noticed. She caught the slight falter in his fluff of that pillow.

The Progeny General also didn't miss the sway to his bare ass when he folded the sheets back.

Okay. Hard ball. The Seamswalker leaned back, supported by both hands flat on the floor. Knees up and legs closed, the towel fell off, leaving her naked to the air still humid from their shower.

Korac glanced behind him and did a double-take. He stood straight and narrowed his eyes at her. "Woman, you finish your food yet?"

Sagan bit her lip and opened knees. Closed. Opened. Closed. "Half of it. Is that enough, Master?" And it was a rough half. All nutrition and no flavor.

His physical response complimented her efforts. A raised flag of surrender. She won. Korac opened his arms to her, and Sagan jumped up into them. He set her down on the bed. She didn't expect any play tonight. Her man was in caretaker mode, and Sagan loved him for it.

As if he read her thoughts, he knelt between her knees. "You need anchoring and feeding. I can't let the Seam take you, now can I?"

No interruptions this time. Even if Pehton brought the entire warden squad, Sagan was drinking from Korac. She brushed her fingers into his silver hair, so happy it was growing out. Gazing into his eyes, they looked colorless. But really they were white with dark gray flecks. And for her, they were always open to his soul.

"I love you." Again, as if he read her mind.

Sagan choked and fought back tears. "Do you think Pehton will officiate a union for us?"

Korac pressed a finger to her lips with a mischievous gleam in his eyes. "Shh. I've imagined our union many times for us. I have plans. And we will *not* spoil my plans on this cell."

She giggled for him, and he thumbed away her tears. After which, he cupped her nape and brought her to his carotid. Atramentous. Without a reflection, Sagan knew her violet iris swallowed her eyes. Her fangs extended, and she teased out breaking his skin. Suddenly, he jerked her off the bed and onto his kneeling lap. At the sweet taste of his blue blood, the Seamswalker moaned into the war criminal's neck. Great draws of the stuff. He groaned through his teeth and repositioned her until she straddled him on the brink.

Against her ear, he growled, "Your permission. Do you give it?"

Sagan stopped drinking only long enough to say, "Always to you, Korac."

Slow. He lowered her slowly onto him. Drawing it out like she drew on his life. She couldn't fight throwing her head back. With his voice rough, Korac confessed, "I look forward to the day I drink from you like this." He settled for kissing her throat in its ecstatic arch while moving for her.

Softly, she cried, "Please."

"You're weak. You need—"

"Please, Master. Take me."

Korac latched onto her shoulder and sunk his teeth in. Sagan cried out his name. He drew on her in time with his thrusts until he gripped the bed behind her and used it for leverage. The bunk's frame pounded against her back until it bruised. And she asked for more.

Unaware of how much time passed, eventually Korac finished with her name on a growl. They finally made it to the bed with him intoxicated.

Obsessed with her skin, he brushed, kissed, and sucked on her shoulders, arms, and neck. She giggled and tried to peel him off. But not really. "Are you sure you'll be okay?"

"I should sleep the effects off by morning—You have a freckle here, too. Let me get that for you." He kissed it among others to the sounds of her girlish laughter.

Spooned against him, she put up no resistance. This made her happy. This was her haven. Not the planet with skies as purple as her eyes. Not the Emporium with its exotic experiences. Not the prison with its cells full of war criminals. Her haven was right here. In Korac's arms.

And no one could take Sagan away from him.

ELEVEN

DUSK WAITS BEHIND THE FIRE

{Gait}

Another Rayne promotion played on the projected screens. Matt touched the chains hidden under his shirt—his and Sagan's. The packed Martyr Complex Bar & Lounge displayed an ad every hour. He kept his watch by it, as he shadowed Razor across the dance floor.

The Pain Curator greeted the regulars of the more casual establishment. No tuxedos or cufflinks here. Carbon fiber pants and black tees for the employees. Black slacks and an open button-down for the boss. The bright orange of it contrasted starkly against his navy skin and paler hair.

No nacre port. And no... navel. Not something Matt thought he'd notice, but there it wasn't.

Men and women alike from all over the Vast Collective tried to explore the oddity for themselves. They reached for him. Matt snatched many hands away and left them with a menacing glare. They always cowed.

After the most recent attempt, Razor chuckled and threw back his green drink. "I'm delighted you take your role so seriously, Matt."

"That's right, boss."

With another chuckle, Razor led them to the bar and chatted with the bartender about inventory and trending drinks. "And how is the Seamswalker doing?"

Matt made to answer what little he knew of her when the other employee cut in with, "Sold out. Not enough purple Vittle punch."

"But you saved enough for me." Razor wasn't asking a question. He was stating a fact. And the sudden darkening in his eyes suggested only one answer would suffice.

With a curt nod, the mixologist set to making one for the boss.

To Matt, Razor elaborated, "I invented the drink after that dramatic display with the Icarus and Peh Peh. The clients asked for Seamswalker-themed goods. I asked her permission first, of course."

"Of course." Yea, right. It's not that Matt thought Sagan would care, it's that Razor wouldn't want her sharing in the profits. When they rendezvoused in two days, Matt definitely planned to mention the Pain Curator's obsession with her eyes.

The alien held the colorful drink to the pendant lights. It shone like stained glass, twinkling in that trademark shade of mauve. Enraptured, Razor announced, "Two days."

The redhead hid his surprise as he wondered not for the first time if telepathy was in the mix with his boss. "Sir?"

He gave Matt the full weight of his gaze. Gray as steel, but less tempered. "You're working a special, annual auction in two days. A demonstration of fortitude for those who survived the terrorist attack."

Rich reprobates flaunting their excellent death-evasion skills. They would brag about how close they came to the blast when they hadn't even arrived yet. Matt nodded once. "Sure, boss. Likely one of them will make an attempt on your life and keep me from getting bored."

"That's the spirit."

They both shared that odd smile between them. Respect. Acknowledgment of similar humors. But also the hint of a threat. Like Razor waited for Matt to try it. Not only because he'd enjoy putting the younger man down, but because he'd finally see how Matt would go about it. After Matt's talk with the Executive Warden, the play was in motion. Hopefully, it took the Pain Curator by surprise. If not, both he and the Lyrik would see the inside of a cell in the basement. And that's if they were lucky.

Matt's shift with 324 started soon. That person wasn't Lucy. But he believed they were someone she'd want him to keep watch over. The way they begged contrasted too sharply against the other Numbered. Pitiful. They didn't belong there. And Razor's intentional method of abuse coincided with an ongoing theory.

Allies. The key to each of Lucy's insurrections was her ability to create an army within the Cult's own following. Maybe Matt should befriend Puk—

All the projections glitched at once—flickered—and settled on a white screen.

Razor stood and took a few steps toward the nearest one until he stood under it. He gazed up expectantly with his eyes narrowed in suspicion. The crowd watched him, not the screens. The room held a collective breath.

A black shapeless shadow consumed the screen. An effect distorted the voice into a demonic depth. "Night Rayne dies in two weeks."

The Pain Curator disturbed Matt with a grin. Mania flickered in his eyes.

Concert footage of impressive pyrotechnics and a stage soaked in blood played across the screen. "We invite you to kill us during the premiere of our newest—and final—song. You know you're on the guest list. One song. One battle. No encores. See you in two weeks."

The Rayne promos returned to the screen. But it focused on a specific moment when she ripped someone apart at IONA-29 and smiled for the camera. With no one at the DJ booth, Night Rayne played over the club's speakers. Matt damned near jumped when Razor gave a slow clap of his hands. Everything about his demeanor denoted respect and a sense of impress.

His voice went to that eternal depth, vibrating in the bodyguard's chest as he called into the crowd, "I'll be there."

The club cheered and returned to dancing. It surprised Matt that the boss left the music playing. Charged. That's the word. Razor looked electrified like someone called "clear" and hit him with the paddles.

"We'll go to that show. It's been so long since I've killed someone myself. I can't wait to wring that impostor's neck."

They headed out into the street as Matt followed him.

Conversationally, he looked at the redhead as he vented, "Fourteen. That's how many of my prime clients Night Rayne have killed. But now I feel like you. A killer in his prime. All I can think about is technique. What's the best method? What would give me the most satisfaction? Any suggestions?"

"Is this a bad time to warn you it's probably some kind of setup, and, as your bodyguard, I strongly discourage you from attending?"

Razor stopped in the middle of the street and faced Matt. "Not at all. Never apologize for doing your job." He patted the younger man proudly on the shoulder. "Consider the concert a proper challenge to your abilities."

The boss took off again with a spring in his step. The bodyguard answered his question, frozen to the pavement, "I like crushing skulls with my bare hands."

The older man stopped.

Matt elaborated without waiting for him to turn around. "I like that the nacre strength lets me face them while I steal their life away one thrilling crack at a time. The blood from their eyes. The futile twitching... This gives me the most satisfaction."

The Pain Curator kept his back to him. "No wonder the basement can't touch your appetite. Nothing on this plane will ease your troubles. And one day, you'll revisit the eyes of those whose lives you stole, and you'll know Eternity."

"I suppose you look forward to that day for yourself."

Not his usual chuckle. After a forlorn "heh," Razor assured, "Eternity won't have the likes of me." He brought his hand up, fingers curled, and stared at the missing nails. "Skull crushing suits me just fine. If you don't mind me stealing your signature?" Turning, he faced Matt with infinity swirling in his gaze.

The redhead grinned congenially and joined him the few steps closer to the Emporium. "Pay me five hundred extra credits next week, and we'll call it even."

"Deal. Now head downstairs early. I want you to spend extra time with 324, tonight."

"You got it, boss."

{GAIT}

The Nice Man gave 324 hope. They knew it was a man by the blows. Women stung. Men bruised. Women lost their temper. Men got off. Both broke things. But not the Nice Man.

He led them upstairs into a zone. Another empty black space with the quantum resonance of agony and loss. 324 went without tears, without sagging and dragging. He would hurt 324 like all the others. But unlike those abusers, he would first lean into them and whisper...

"Another will help."

Always a message. This one stirred more than hope. 324 clenched their fists and grit their teeth. Not to fortify against the pain. But to fan the flames of determination. The fight slowly restored to them.

Soon.

Survive the next six hours. And the next six after that. Eat. Sleep. Prepare. They'd reunite with their family. Soon.

Thanks to the Nice Man.

{GAIT}

Sagan's time with Korac revived her some. But that nutritional brick left her starving for food with actual flavor. Why not pop into the Emporium for a quickie—Not that kind of quickie. Food. She wanted a full stomach for the Tribunal on Enki. If everything went sideways, the other Progeny relied on her to help them escape. Although, she heavily considered leaving Kyle.

She frowned. Messy. Complicated. Everything got so mixed up so quickly. Remorse was a Tritan imprisoned in Gait. And squatted on a heap of intel regarding Inanis, the prison, and even Xelan like a dragon hoarding treasure. Korac asked her not to confront him. But once she knew, Sagan couldn't just sit there saying nothing. Restless, agitated, she needed to prepare for the next morning's events but also let off some steam. Hence the Emporium.

But which entrance to take? She considered the front door, but nah. Better to keep things fresh. Not the mezzanine. The kitchens were too obvious. Bedroom?

The Seamswalker never wanted to return there. Even the big sweater Korac loaned her couldn't fight off that chill. The shiver left goosebumps all over her. Her exposed legs were proof. The glass slippers reminded her to keep a second pair of shoes and clothes in the cell.

One other place came to mind. More or less harmless. Sagan walked into the shop with all the nacre glass curios. After midnight, she expected customers to wander their way through the wares. But the store with its boutique glass shelves and jewelry lighting sat empty. What a shame. Left all on her own to snoop. The first night she came here, the prices interested her.

Why were nacre glass plates and vases so expensive? Was it because the ore came from Thailea? Unbreakable also upped the price, surely. But—

"Hmm..." Sagan crossed the white tile space to a set of plates. A small name card denoted YU in fancy script. Was there an odd number of them? Seemed strange for a dinner set. One. Two. Three. Four. Five. Six. Seven. Eight. Nine—

"Seamswalker."

"Yip!"

Razor startled Sagan so bad she knocked over the plates like dominoes. Caught snooping amid his wares, she whirled with a burning face.

Leaning in the door frame, he looked utterly bewildered until he burst into laughter. Holding his sides, genuine and loud—way too loud—

"Razor, are you drunk?"

He held up a fancy diamond-crusted bottle. "Guilty." He stumbled over to her, almost pinning her to the shelf. "And you're skittish as ever, my Pain Kitten." The two-toned effect of his eyes twirled so fast they almost flashed white.

While Sagan normally tried her best to ignore any attraction to him, the mussed fiery red hair and open shirt—a bright orange that complimented his tanned skin—really worked with the evil business owner vibe. His breath did not.

With a scrunch of her nose, she pushed him off. "Whoa. Ease off." Her *and* the booze.

The Pain Curator gave no resistance, almost as if their proximity were simply an accident of his intoxication. "I sensed you in the Seam from the first moment you went into it. So lonely, this place." He tapped the center of his exposed chest.

"Your heart?"

"My bones. I can feel you in my bones." Unexpectedly, Razor snickered and pointed. "Your nose does this cute scrunchy thing when you hard think. But I worry anything I compliment you on that you'll stop doing it around me. Please don't. I'm not so bad once you—"

He laughed into his bottle and took another drink. When finished, he continued the thought, "So big a lie I couldn't say it with a straight face. I'm a bad man. You should stay far, far away from me, Kitten."

Sagan reached for him, ready to tuck his arm behind her neck and shoulder him. "Here, maybe we should get you to bed—"

With no effort, the Pain Curator grasped the Seamswalker's arm, twisted it around, and twirled until he held her close to him. One hand against his chest beneath his shirt. The other stretched out. With a wink, he led them in a dance out of the shop and into the addition.

She glanced around nervously, aware of the amount of people in the space. Not afraid. Just cautious.

"You're safe with me," Razor reminded Sagan.

The young woman relaxed into the dance by inches. Into the main Emporium, they went among a throng of aliens. The people watched, enraptured. Some of them gazed with almost carnivorous expressions. Hungry. Ready to feed.

On her.

Safe with him. Not from him. "Why the drinking and dancing?"

He smiled, delighted and warm. "I'm celebrating. A competitor chose to step down from the business."

She shared in the smile as if happy for him. "I'm sure it's a hard market to dominate."

Razor smirked at Sagan the way Korac did when she selected her words without thinking. Dizzy. Everything made her dizzy. She stopped and rested her head against him. This time she almost let her knees fall out from under her. Heavy.

"Shh." The Pain Curator scooped the Seamswalker into his arms and carried her to the kitchens.

Sagan resented it. She could lift entire cars over her head and open conduits to Hell. But here she was, in the arms of her frenemy, being tended like a child. A damsel in distress, even.

Trays of hor d'oeuvres covered the counters. At the smell of roasted meats and toasted cheese, her stomach growled so hard it concaved into knots. Razor sat Sagan down on a bar stool and gathered a small plate of food.

Before she took a bite, she stared into his strange gaze. Always perplexed by the man's odd nature. Still, manners mattered, "Thank you, Razor."

"I'm always happy to ease your troubles, Seamswalker." Back to the original nickname. Was Kitten something he only wanted to keep for them in private? Somehow that felt more intimate—

"You're frowning again. Eat, now. Overthink, later." Again, that knowing smirk.

How well did he think he knew her? How well did he actually know her? Was Sagan so transparent? And how bad a thing was that—

A cracker with some smoked salmon and cream cheese waved under her nose. Oh, this was embarrassing.

"Even if I have to feed you myself, you'll leave my establishment satisfied."

Sagan peered up at Razor, and—yup, his phrasing was intentional. What a smart ass grin—

Crunch. "Mmm..." She moaned and took another bite from her own hand.

He sat down beside her and watched with his side leaned across the counter, head in his hand. Fascinated.

So drunk and attentive. Question time. Quietly and between bites, she whispered, "Can you enter the Seam at will?"

"Nope."

Well. Was there more to this? "Why not? If you were born there?"

"Long story."

Two more toast points bit the dust. "Before I brought you there yesterday, how long had it been for you?"

"Very."

Damn. His mysterious mode never shut off. Sagan thought of the voices. "Is there anyone else there?"

"In a manner of speaking."

Her frown deepened until she caught him smiling at her nose. And he was right. She wanted to stop doing it now that she knew.

Before long, she ate the entire plate and two more worth. Finally full, she made to leave when the bright white booths caught her eye.

"Two days," Razor reminded Sagan. The special finale. He stood and stepped around until he was behind her. In her ear, he whispered, "Would you like an appetizer?"

Hilarious cause she ate all those hor d'oeuvres. "Ha ha." She punctuated it with a roll of her eyes. And a prayer that he couldn't sense the quickening of her pulse and the shallowing of her breath.

Against all her hopes, he chuckled and walked ahead. "Two short ones. I come along for the ride. You're far too skittish. The Tribunal will eat you alive. This should help you relax."

Did she mention the Tribunal to him? Must have. And it's not like word doesn't travel fast. The entire Progeny not currently serving a sentence investigated for terrorist acts and the death of an Eminent. A liked one, at that. Yea. Razor would know about the Tribunal.

He held out his hand to her. In a softened voice, he offered, "Don't worry. Consider yourselves an endanger species. Protected. They won't lock all of you up."

Sagan took his hand and accepted his gracious behavior as genuine. "I suppose it's normal to be nervous."

Razor led her to the booths featuring port access. Supposedly, it enhanced the experience and eliminated the fog that lingered afterward. Guess it's time to see if it's worth the upgrade.

He expertly diverted the subject. "How is the King of Earth and Cinder, by the way?" Once inside, he placed her under the bars and handed her the goggles.

While she messed with them, Sagan thought on his question. "She sleeps. Honestly? Rayne has no patience for games. I think if she were on Enki with Tameka or here with me, there'd either be two fewer planets in the skies or two more in her kingdom. I suppose that's one reason she went to sleep."

"For some, diplomacy is slow and intentionally complicated. I happen to enjoy the chase." He smiled at her while Sagan considered exactly how badly Rayne would've killed him by now.

He connected a cable or hose of some sort made from nacre glass filaments to the booth's output. The other end, he brought to her. Razor suggested harmlessly, "Might as well try it before we take it away."

When he brought it to her chest, she frowned.

"What is it?"

"My necklace. Matt still has it."

"He's busy downstairs. Next time, I'll make sure you take it." The smile he gave her was warm and genuine. Friendly.

"I want to like you," she blurted.

The smile saddened a touch as he connected the cable to her chest. "It's so unfortunate that fate would make us enemies."

She touched his arm then. "Razor, have you ever seriously considered leaving Imminent? Saving others and redeeming yourself in the process? You could have a home with the Shadow."

The Pain Curator took the Seamswalker's hand from his arm and kissed her knuckles. Softly, sadly, he confessed, "Another lifetime, maybe. But this is how it must be. And it's not safe for you to like me. We're not friends, my Pain Kitten. We're business partners. And our contract ends soon. Until then, enjoy yourself."

Why did that hurt so much? Because she failed to make a friend of an enemy? Or maybe because she'll have to locate a non-Imminent food source?

Sagan sighed, and it was big. He sat down in the chair that popped out of the floor and looked to her for the signal. At her nod, Razor sent her into the experience...

...And into Hell.

The liquid poured on Sagan's body, scorched until it blistered and bubbled. The port allowed her to smell the cooked meat under the burning sweetness. Caramel. Sugar.

She shrieked and grabbed onto the bars. The hood over her head suffocated her. It prevented the long inhales she needed to draw enough breath for another scream.

As the sugar cooled, a breeze fanned her skin. The nacre healed it. The scalding lessened into a sear. The relief, the serotonin that pumped straight into her port, rewarded her for surviving the pain.

Live through the misery and experience elation unimaginable outside this given situation.

The hot sugar came again. She screamed in agony. The relief always followed. And she soaked in the clarity.

Sagan got high. Higher than ever. The artificial stimulation overrode her tolerance. Until the dark space spun, and a crowd formed in the night surrounding her. They watched from below. An execution? Or a public—

The whip cracked and split the skin to her bone. She never screamed louder. Again. And it wasn't healing. The sensation only hurt with no relief. The blood cooled as it spilled down her sides. A male voice—one she never expected to hear again—cried out, "Why?"

And then the evil bitch's voice entreated, "I am like you. I am not like your Icarean masters—"

No. This was Nox punishing Celindria for her betrayal. Sagan read about it in his Verse. Korac delivered the punishment, eagerly.

Sagan fell to her knees, but Razor caught her. She ripped the goggles off and found him holding her like one of the earlier experiences. He let her go without being asked.

Before it slipped away, she questioned him, "Why did Celindria come here, and what did she trade her pain for?" Definitely less foggy with a port.

He took a deep draw on the bedazzled bottle. After a messy swipe over his mouth, he returned the favor. "What do you know about her relationship with Pehton?"

Well, the galaxy was small after all.

{ENKI}

Tails.

Right on time, Sagan knocked on the zeppelin. "I got it," Lucas announced as he answered.

Andrew listened to the muffled voices as he finished dressing in the bedroom. Warm chatter and a request for her axes and coat. When she appeared in the doorway wearing a man's sweater and the same man's axes on her hips, Conscience shook his head. "Which one of them ripped off the collar—never mind. I don't want to know the answer."

She blushed, and now he knew. But quickly she changed the subject. "Do you think they'll punish us?"

"If Kyle admits to his responsibility in the matter, the Tribunal will likely only punish him," Lucas explained.

Nah. "No way. If they decide there's fault on our end—of any kind—they'll use it to take us all down." Andrew did not like this. Kyle jeopardized not only the mission, but their lives.

Sagan took his hand and smiled sadly at him. "Are you ready?"

Her pupils looked blown. Her chain was missing. And when Andrew gently tested her intentions, he came back with a mixture of exhaustion and self-loathing. Like after instant-regret sex. He pulled her in for a hug. Hiding the wince at the slightness of her usually muscular frame proved difficult. Against her hair, he whispered, "I'm always here for you."

Leaning away with a smile, she assured, "I'm the one that does the saving, remember?" She turned to Lucas. "How are The Brethren in their recovery?"

"The chateau is lost, I'm afraid. We salvaged what we could from the libraries and such. Fortunately, the quantum facility is retrievable with an impressive amount of excavators and two crawlers. Imminent sank it without damaging it. But it'll take some time." The Icarus smiled genuinely for her.

The hope that sparkled in her eyes warmed Andrew through. Sagan pulled both of them into a hug. "We can do this."

With the power of thirty excavators, yes, they could do this.

Heads. Doable.

"Ready?"

They nodded, and she took them through the Seam.

Tameka waited, leaned against a glass wall with her arms folded. She looked pissed.

Across from her, Kyle and T.A.O. looked unaffected.

"What is T.A.O. doing here?" Sagan gasped.

"Yup. Yup. Already did this," Tameka grumbled with a "hey" to Lucas.

The joint in Kyle's hand only slightly excused his serene demeanor. Even stoned, he usually rose to the bait. Instead, he cooly explained, "T.A.O. is here to appeal to the Tribunal for her freedom. Isn't that what we wanted for the First Wave Progeny?"

The ancient Seamswalker remained silent, evidently fine with Kyle speaking for her.

Andrew shared an incredulous look with Lucas who offered, "I await you with Caedes."

"Hug Pax for me." They went in for a quick squeeze.

"You *will* hug him, yourself," Tameka ordered.

Andrew chuckled at her bossiness. "Well, this way he gets two from me."

Heads. Shit.

"It's time," Tumu cut into the mostly warm conversation.

Sagan headed through the glass corridor first. The rest followed, with T.A.O. bringing up the rear. Andrew kept between their girls and Kyle. He wanted to form a barrier in the tunnel. Beneath their feet, a forest of cranberry-colored trees stretched forever in a sea of red leaves and black branches.

Tameka and Sagan whispered to one another. Andrew caught words like "Cinder" and "Li." He'd ask later.

The corridor opened into a stadium with glass rows. The three surviving members of the Tribunal stood at glass podiums. They didn't waste time.

"Progeny, we consider today your complicity in an upheaval that disrupted the fabric of Tritan society and resulted in the demise of a beloved member of our Tribunal." Eminent Abresson, the darkest and shortest of the three, glared down at them.

Andrew stood straight and kept his chin high. This wasn't the Probability he hoped for, but dammit, he'd face it with his family head on. Although Kyle he might consider leaving. The bastard stood beside him, as smug as Celindria. Whom he refused to acknowledge as Eminent.

"After which, we'll consider Tumu's matter," Eminent Lance added. The others turned on the kind Tritan with narrowed gazes. So much suspicion among equals.

A warmth brushed Andrew's hand, and he open it to grip Sagan's. The Seamswalker also took Tameka's. And in a show of solidarity, Andrew took Kyle's. He was their responsibility.

Celindria's cadence always came on high like some celestial being. She dressed almost exclusively in white in an attempt at an angelic aesthetic. Or something older than angels. She graced them with her voice and its slightly murderous tone, "We know everything. Our investigation was thorough. You retaliated against Imminent and struck several of their bases. Impressive. But, unfortunately, the Eminents were inspecting a known location for their operation. You interfered, and it cost Eminent Wiw his life."

Eminent Lance shifted uncomfortably. Eminent Abresson nodded dubiously.

Andrew made to defend them, but Kyle spoke up, "I acted alone, and I alone hold responsibility. Eminent Wiw was a good man, and I deeply regret my part in his death."

Tameka's eyes widened as she and Sagan gaped at him.

T.A.O. kept her solid eyes front.

Lance nodded along solemnly, and when Kyle finished, he offered, "We understand completely. Earth's defenses are desperately in need of our help. Which is precisely why we've agreed to officially grant Earth entry into the Vast Collective and all the technology that entails."

Sagan punched the air with an emphatic, "Yes!"

Tameka kept her eyes narrowed. Both she and Andrew waited for the other shoe to drop. They gripped their chains. Except Sagan. And Kyle, who also lost his somehow.

Eminent Abresson mastered smug face. "But in penalty for the loss of our dear Eminent Wiw, we fine each of you with one year service under Eminent Celindria starting once your affairs are in order. A few weeks should suffice."

Tumu scoffed, "You can't be serious?!"

Even the mostly serene Kyle took up an argument, "What about T.A.O.? We—"

She touched his arm and shook her head. "I accept the penalty."

"Well, I don't. What about my son?" Tameka failed to veil the murder in her eyes as she glared at the First Progeny.

Sagan squeezed their hands, waiting for the signal. With two squeezes from either Andrew or Tameka, she'd get them all out. And then they'd live as fugitives.

Andrew shook his head at her and let go of her hand. They couldn't do this. If they left, it likely nullified the acceptance of Earth into the Vast Collective. They needed that.

"The son will join the mother in my lab," Celindria stated formally. Cold and clinical.

Sensing the shift of power in the room, Andrew went around Sagan to take Tameka by the shoulders. "Don't. Not yet. Think about Earth."

The redheaded Progeny opened her eyes and revealed that green Atramentous. Shit.

"Fury, listen. This won't be the end. It gets better. Hang in there." Andrew knew. He knew for certain. It *would* get better.

"What about Rayne? We're her guards." Sagan reminded them.

Automatic, as if on reflex, Celindria and Abresson simultaneously declared, "Rayne is safe."

What the fuck did that mean?

"Quiet," Eminent Lance called for order. "Our friend was several cosmic years old. And you snuffed out that life. It doesn't matter your intentions, there must be a punishment." He held up his hand to stop their protest. "We will reconvene with the Primaries to discuss alternatives for your service to us. I, for one, agree a lab is no place for a child." Shooting an uncomfortable look at Celindria, he continued, "After we decide a proper atonement, we'll grant you two weeks to prepare."

Was this really fair? He made an excellent point about Eminent Wiw's life and death, but dammit. They didn't do it. Kyle did. And they weren't through with their retaliation against Imminent, yet. One more job. Shit, Andrew planned to kick Kyle's ass as soon as they got back to Earth—

"As to your petition, Officer of the Third," Eminent Abresson sneered. "We reviewed the case, and we unanimously grant it. In three days, we'll formally induct the Icarean warrior, Karter, into the Tribunal."

Okay. Everyone without "Eminent" in their title turned and gawked at Tumu.

He paid them no mind. "Thank you, Eminents. I look forward to passing on the news."

Well, Andrew didn't see that coming.

Tails. Not again.

{GAIT}

A commotion stirred from the lobby where everyone waited upstairs for the Progeny to return from the Tribunal in Enki. Everyone but Silence. Watching something parade around in Kyle's bones sent her eavesdropping from the floor below. The sight and sound of the charade hurt her teeth and twitched her eyes. Either few others noticed, or they were much more capable of hiding it.

Still, she kept the chain *It* gave her. All the Shadow carried them. The significance of it wasn't lost on her. She only wished it'd reverse whatever happened to him—

"You cost us worse than our lives, Kyle!" Conscience.

The unmistakable thud of a fist to a face resounded after.

"If Celindria gets her hands on my son, I'll kill them and all of us. Do you understand me?" Tameka sounded beyond infuriated. Almost scared, even.

Sagan interrupted, closer to the stairs. "It won't come to that. I'll get us out."

Again, Andrew growled in that cold calm of his, "We can't. We risk them rescinding entry of Earth from the Vast Collective. And possibly Karter off the Tribunal."

Such interesting revelations.

"Earth? They accepted?" Lynn's excitement infected Silence.

And apparently Pablo, too. "Well, at least some good came out of it—"

The Tritan, Tumu, cut through the celebratory din, "We can't let them have you. You'll need to create a suitable enough punishment. Like King Rayne and the Martyr Complex. But something that also leaves you free."

"I'll volunteer myself to Celindria's lab," Kyle's controller announced grimly.

Tameka, the first of many footsteps on the stairs, huffed at him. "Yours is definitely an ability we don't want her to have."

"There is no other way." The tiny Seamswalker. She appeared beside Silence with a strange expression. Familiar and conspiratorial.

What the fuck?

The others made their way down while continuing their argument. Some celebrated the entry into the Vast Collective. But Silence only clamped her jaw and focused at the wall straight ahead.

Don't. Look.

Hide. That was better. She bolted from her seat and stiffly made her way to the labs. Dr. Suarez was kind enough to grant her entry into the main area so she could examine the machines as they calculated the results. Entering Med Lab 2, she reached the detainee pods.

Twenty-One looked up from his bunk. In good humor, he asked, "What the hell is your name?"

Softly, she answered, "Silence."

"No smile today?"

She shook her head.

He sat down on the floor with only the glass between them. "You haven't smiled in a few days. What's wrong?"

How to phrase this? "I see a change in someone I care about that no one else notices."

"I've noticed. What little I've seen. It makes my skin crawl." He popped his neck. Left, then right.

So it was obvious. Silence chafed her arms and bit her lip as she considered the best course of action.

Twenty-One frowned while he scrutinized her more closely. "You look familiar."

She laughed. "Well, I thought I was more memorable than that—"

"Unforgettable." He gave her one hell of a grin. "But that's not what I mean. I think I met someone who looked similar to you on Cinder. A very long time ago." Indicating her expression, he elaborated, "A similar sadness."

"How unfortunate for us." Silence looked away.

"Ask me."

That brought her back around.

"You came here to ask for my help. Ask me." Twenty-One stretched his legs like tree trunks in front of him and tapped the soles of his boots together. Patient. Anticipatory.

Was she apprehensive? No. Until she witnessed something piloting around her only friend, Silence didn't understand fear. This hesitation made her recall the conversation with Andrew. What would he want her to do? She asked, "When it's time, will you help us?"

"Anything for the Shadow. Iona is the best thing that ever happened to me. I haven't been this sure of my next meal or slept with both eyes closed since before Umbra ruled Cinder."

An azure pulse traveled under her skin. A vague inkling nudged her. Itched and scratched for recollection. Why was Umbra always the trigger for these "almost" moments?

"We can't keep you two apart." Kyle's voice sounded wrong, flat. Too high and off key.

And Silence's skin shriveled off her bones. Even Twenty-One gazed up at him blankly from the floor. Why was it easier for others to hide their revulsion?

"Silence." Please let the monster never say her name again. "Can you come with me? I want to break the news to you, myself."

The news she already guessed from a mouth she couldn't bear to see move. "Of course."

With a wave to Twenty-One, she let the impostor lead her into an empty lab. But before she gave *It* a chance to speak, she said, "I know you're offering yourself to Celindria's employ for punishment. I want to know why you bombed Reipon—why you lied to us—in the first place."

The puppet raked a hand through Kyle's curly brown hair. Gruffly, *It* explained, "I can't tell you, yet. But I promise. Everything will make sense soon."

"Fine. May I go now? Dr. Suarez needs to see me as well." Silence made for the door, but a heavy hand slammed against the wall and stopped her. She turned back to him with an eyebrow raised all the way up.

"Spend the night with me."

Bet they heard that slap all the way upstairs in the patient rooms. Kyle's head nearly turned completely around. When the thing turned back to face her, *It* was slow with little creaks and crackles. Blood dripped from his nose. But . . . the eyes. The green glass sparked and fizzed out. Lit and extinguished. His entire body trembled.

Teeth clenched, muscles contracted, *It* spit out the word, "Sorry." And left as if fleeing the room.

What the hell was that all about?

TWELVE

SUN SETS AND THE FUN BEGINS

{ENKI}

"**YOU LOOK AMAZING, FURY.** That's all we're saying. The glow to your skin. The shine in your hair. Although, I take some credit for that amazing haircut."

Sagan affectionately mused her way down the vacant colony's corridor while she and Caedes tag-teamed Tameka in a compliment sandwich.

The softening of the gravel in his voice belied his crush. "She's right. And—ahem—as much as we appreciate the work you put into yourself, maybe cut back a bit to avoid detection."

"I can't help that I look good." No shame in the redhead. "But for the mission's sake, I'll reduce my consumption. A little."

After a night's rest in the bungalow, Sagan traded Korac's sweater for her Lyriki coat and trademark boots. When she awoke tired and craving more appetites than she could juggle, she resigned herself to visiting Doc Pablo. But first, she and Tameka traversed different routes to map while Caedes and John recorded them from "the room." Jack, Karter, Chris, and Para worked out their living situation and future steps with Tumu. Meanwhile, they awaited word from Ross. It was a crazy day in Enki.

"Third conduit on the left, Seamswalker. Fury, you're approaching unchartered waters. Tell me which conduits you choose and where they lead," Caedes instructed. He healed up nicely after feeding from Tameka. No obvious bruising or soreness. Sagan thought he even shaved and shined his head recently.

Through the Icarus' mic, they overheard John groan, "How long will this take?"

"Until we find it. I took the second conduit on the right, Caedes. It leads to another landing. Once again, no discerning features." The powerhouse Progeny sounded discouraged.

So Sagan changed topics. "How do we feel about Pehton and Celindria?" The most recent conduit took her to another corridor with each door lining the hall locked behind nacre-resistant shields.

Tameka clicked her tongue and weighed in, "I want to say that's their business. But..."

But they couldn't afford any conflicts of interests with their allies. That being said, "The First Progeny sure burned her fair share of powerful allies."

Caedes gave an approving, "humph," before changing the subject. "I'm working on beefing up security within the system before I test the drive you gave us."

The approving note from Tameka reassured Sagan. "Can't be too careful."

So much happened in the last few days. Touching her axes for comfort, Sagan reflected on the conversation with Razor earlier. About the experience she remembered. She knew so few things about Korac. And everything was always too hectic for her to stop and get to know him.

"Still no Tritans?" John asked over Caedes' mic again.

Sagan frowned as she observed, "Notta. Feels weird slinking around their sphere without bumping into anybody."

"Almost like there aren't enough of them to bump into," Tameka said what everyone was thinking, as usual.

This time, John sounded more excitable. "Seamswalker, how old is Razor?"

"No idea. He won't tell me."

"I'm sorry if this is intrusive, but could you ask if he knows about the number of Tritans?" Was John onto something?

Not that it mattered. Sagan almost admitted to losing the upper-hand in the arrangement when an idea struck her. "Sure. I thought of just the thing to make him tell me."

A strained silence stretched between them. Eventually, Tameka broke it with, "Seamswalker, don't you think—"

"Uncle Caeda! Play?"

Auntie Seamswalker grinned. Pax had that affect.

"Come on in, Pax, we—Hey. Don't touch that kiddo. Wait—" Sounds came over the mic of a struggle with a tiny person no one wanted injured.

"What's wrong?" Tameka sounded both concerned and beguiled.

Caedes grunted while wrestling his charge before explaining, "It's the map again—"

"The lines, mommy. On the paper."

Sagan stopped square in the middle of the most recent landing. "Wait. Caedes, ask if he means his dad's paper?"

He relayed the message, and the wriggled struggling intensified.

"Mommy. Daddy's house."

The Seamswalker knew instantly what he meant. "Fury."

"I heard."

Sagan let the excitement into her voice. "Would it align with Caedes' mapping system, do you think?"

Tameka's voice denoted a grin. "Only one way to find out."

"How is that?" Caedes asked as Sagan Seamswalked into the stronghold.

When no one came over the earpiece, she tested, "Anybody hear me?"

Nothing.

Sagan entered through her bedroom on the stronghold's third floor. And immediately jumped back with a "Yip." Someone was in her bed.

"T.A.O.?"

The dark woman lay there with her eyes in permanent Atramentous open to the ceiling. Her breathing came heavy and even as if in deep sleep. Sagan walked over and gently, cautiously, touched her arm. She gave no response and continued to hibernate. A chill traveled down the younger woman's spine. This was not natural.

As if locked in a room with a cadaver, Sagan quickly exited via Seamswalk to Xelan's museum. Climbing the glass stairs which appeared underfoot became easier overtime as the Progeny acclimated to the novelty of it. At the top, pressed between two pieces of glass, was a sheet of paper with lines on it. The first time Tameka brought Pax here, before the explosions, he tried to show it to them. They paid it no mind, but...

The lines. They looked exactly like the conduit plans Caedes drew on his model of the Dyson's Sphere. Sagan pressed the release and retrieved the sheet with a delicate touch. She turned to Seamswalk and almost kissed a nightmare.

T.A.O. stood behind her, staring as if she traded Sagan for the bedroom ceiling.

"What're you—"

The woman clasped a hand over Sagan's mouth. "The Seam calls for you. It asks for the archive. She desires it. Do not let her have it." Blood dripped from her nose, slow and viscous, like molasses. Those solid purple eyes glanced down to the blond woman's nacre or the port at its place. "I will watch over you. Do not let her have you. Or it. Him." In the same instant she removed her hand, she disappeared.

The younger Seamswalker's heart pounded in the abandoned stronghold. She was almost too scared to travel through the Seam. With a deep breath and a whole lot of faith, she took one quick step in and one quick step out.

Enki. In Tameka's bungalow. Outside "the room." With shaking hands, she knocked on the door. Not that Caedes and John got up to anything incriminating, but she needed to practice her manners.

"Come in," the gruff Icarus called.

Upon entry, Pax flushed all the way to his freckles, hopped out of Caedes' lap, and hid under the desk. Both the human and the Icarus shook their heads with gentle smiles at the cuteness.

"I got it." Sagan handed the sheet carefully over and watched with bated breath as Caedes held it up to their current map system.

"Holy shit," John gasped.

Tameka came over the earpiece once more, "What? Is it a match?"

In a voice mixed with pride and wonder, the Icarus announced, "Pax found it. He found the Pantheon."

{GAIT}

Two and half million years ago, Junior Warden Pehton hated her job. Every day, the other Wardens sanctioned atrocities committed by the prisoners. It repulsed her. Especially the ones they afflicted on the Prisonborne children. Their screams...They never stopped.

Shrill. Helpless. Hopeless.

Not one more day. She refused to standby and do nothing for one more day. No. Someone finally armed Pehton with the leverage to cut-off the source. But she'd show enough respect for the Executive Warden to offer one last chance.

"Triss." No knock on her private house at the highest peak in Gait. No formal title. "Have you discussed freeing the children with the Pain Curator?"

The red-feathered woman sitting behind the desk stared upside Pehton's head like she grew a second one. But after another moment, the ire melted into...what was that? Desire? "I drove a hard bargain, but Razor's negotiation skills proved...most impressive. We maintain the status quo."

The Junior Warden grew more agitated. "I implore you to reconsider—"

"Do you understand the unrest this prison will face if you take away their toys?" Triss stood and stepped around the desk to face Pehton. "They'll force us to incinerate possibly twenty-eight percent of them before the others learn from that example. Enki will punish us for killing their precious specimens."

The older Lyrik placed a finger on the younger one's lips before she could argue further. "You are young. Barely two million. Trust me, the screams will bother you less in another million years. Unless, you find yourself concerned for the children of Gait for another reason." She glanced down at Pehton's swelling stomach and when her yellow gaze returned, it was full of a knowledge she shouldn't possess.

That was it. That was the last flame that needed igniting. "Goodbye, Triss."

Pehton turned on her heel and left. She marched straight to the warehouse currently under renovation on Mercy Row. The new Overseers clunked overhead with their shiny exteriors. Against the purple sky, they looked hopeful, not oppressive. The sign of Gait's future in prison control and Prisonborne cataloging. Separating the inmates from the citizens.

Like her.

The promises of her new ally emboldened the Junior Warden to seek the most notorious villain on Gait. For them. She touched her growing belly. Before entering, Pehton fashioned her armor to best disguise her condition. No need to let him know. Pushing aside a flap of plastic, she entered the dim space. The clack of her boots resonated off the beautiful wood floors.

"Not that I need to extend manners to a trespasser, but how can I help you?" A man stood on the mezzanine with brown hair and brown skin. He looked handsome in a slimy way. Polished on the surface, all blemished underneath. As she expected the Pain Curator to look.

"I am Junior Warden Pehton. I want to negotiate removing the child labor force from Gait."

He headed down the wrought-iron spiral staircase without looking up from the forms in his hand. Unconcerned, he dismissed her. "The Executive Warden and I have an arrangement. As your employer, she holds you to it."

"Not Executive for much longer."

Piqued, Razor finally looked up with a raised brow. "Is that so?"

She straightened her shoulders and stood taller. "It is. And you will remove the children."

"You ask a lot with nothing to offer, Peh Peh. Do you mind if I call you that?" He came closer, and her skin wanted to escape.

One baby kicked as if reminding Pehton why she played this game. "I know it would never matter to you if I mind or not. What do you want that I could offer you?"

What made the grin so terrifying was the menace beneath the allure. "As Executive Warden, the Chorus is yours—"

She shook her head, and the gliders flared on her arms.

Massive Tritan satellites circled Gait. They controlled the constructs within, including the cells of the prison, the Overseers, and the Lyriks. With the Chorus activated, the Lyriks' resonance weapons would amplify until their voices shattered every nacre on the planet.

"I will not give you that—"

He held up a hand to placate her, while the hard ambition in his eyes softened to understanding. "No, of course not. I have no interest in its primary function. But the secondary."

"...You—You want the Wardens?"

Brown fire burned in Razor's gaze as he turned on the convincing charm. "Give the idea time. You can free the children and get your promotion—"

"You can have them."

The man genuinely startled. His eyes widened, and it took him time to recover his congenial smile. "I thought you might appreciate more time to consider it. The decision is planet-altering, after all. No need to be rash."

"I want those children out of my prison now. After the last one leaves, I deliver the Wardens to you." Those bitches let monstrous men and women torture those children. One day—her children. No. Let Razor have them.

"I like you, Executive Warden Pehton."

"And that's it. Once the twins came, the Primaries elected me Executive Warden. They outlawed slave labor and underage sex-work across the Vast Collective. The day of the changeover ceremony, Razor came to free the children and collect the Wardens. I accepted my promotion, walked down the steps, and crossed the street. I held my babies' hands so tight…And then they were gone."

Korac didn't offer a warm hand or a kind word. Only a companionable silence.

"I wish I'd known that, as Executive Warden at the time, Triss wouldn't be under the influence of the Chorus. I never imagined a scenario where she'd go to him willingly." Pehton ran both hands over her feathers, seeking any comfort. "I can't tell who's the worse villain here. Her or me?"

"Razor." Korac's gaze froze into a sheet of white ice. He looked into the distance beyond Pehton, not seeing Infernus hall but something else.

"You were labor here." She knew that, but… Oh, she never gave thought to which kind of labor. "Korac…" How does one ask what haunts a warrior of this magnitude? One bearing a reputation of such regal standing and ruthless strategy? What would make eyes freeze over that once saw billions fall to his army?

"You're not telling all of your story." He accused her of exactly what she was silently accusing him.

Chilled, Pehton shook her head. "I can't tell you that. Please don't ask—"

"How were the children connected to your promotion, Executive Warden?"

{GAIT}

Korac sat on the trunk across from Pehton. Her pitch complexion melted into his black sheets where she sat on the edge of his bed surrounded by the black metal walls, floor, and ceiling. The abyss couldn't compare to the cloud of darkness that followed her. The downpour weighed heavily on their mission.

The electrified question sparked the air the longer it lingered between them.

The panic in her voice set the storm free. "I can't tell you that. This prison can hear. I'll lose my title."

Pehton left her race's volition to the likes of the Pain Curator. Korac's honesty shouldn't phase her. "You lost control of this planet the moment you handed over your people's will. And any inkling of control you've had since was a delusion. A delusion afforded to you by Razor."

Pehton sharply met his gaze, and those red eyes of hers hardened into rubies.

With reason and understanding, Korac pressed, "I respect your reasons. But we can't solve Inanis while you withhold how your children and the promotion were related."

The determination faded. How long did she keep this secret? How lonely was it to mourn offspring that barely existed relative to a lifespan like theirs? The Executive Warden leaned forward and pressed her lips close enough to almost touch his ear. She whispered, "A Primary approached me with the offer of promotion if I gave him children."

"Which one?"

"Rem." When she leaned back, she looked anywhere but straight at him.

Which suited Korac fine since he slammed his eyes shut to absorb this catastrophe. Pieces fell into place and made for an ugly picture. He expected Remorse to interject half-insights any minute now—

Remorse.

The Icarus left the Lyrik in his cell. She cried out in alarm as he stepped right through the nacre-resistant barrier. No time to spare for that talk. He stormed his way over to his blockmate's cell. Ready to wring the bastard's neck—

Empty.

Korac half-expected as much. He hung his head and laughed bitterly at their misfortune. *"This prison can hear,"* she'd said. No, but Tritans could.

Pehton called to him from down the hall, "It's you. I heard about you." There was sadness in her words. He hated hearing it.

He ignored her and stepped into the cell. Standard. Absolutely no sign of residence. But the back wall looked wrong. Light and energy fizzled and crackled. When he shoved one hand through the disguised conduit, Pehton gasped from behind him. Korac walked through it and into an unguarded shrine in Enki.

He needed to warn Sagan.

Korac returned to find the tiny woman orange-feathered woman he left behind fuming at him. With her hands on her hips and one boot tapping, she looked utterly adorable. The hard edge to her voice was not. "You've withheld vital information from me, as well." It softened to a whisper as she got closer with one finger in his face. "Like you don't have a nacre. And you neglected to mention a partner inside—"

"Executive Warden, stop. I told you from the beginning I'm here on my honor. Remorse wasn't my ally. I thought he was another prisoner. He was a Tritan and—"

She groaned. "No." The horror of it widened her eyes.

"—Exactly. I've good reason to believe he's the same man who opened the conduit to Earth from Cinder. Who worked with Celindria to manipulate Nox. Why was he here?"

Pehton quit listening. She marched through the conduit. Korac rushed to follow. He called after her before she left the shrine, "Where are you going?"

"To kill him." Her words rang across the stone slab surrounded by the ocean.

He grabbed her arm. "Stop. He's a Primary and—"

Korac's hand burned where it gripped her elbow. Smoke rolled off the Lyrik. Her orange feathers swayed in the kerosene-smelling fumes. Flames flickered in her eyes. He wasn't aware of an Atramentous for her kind, but Pehton certainly activated her dark mode.

"Executive Warden, this is no time for a suicide mission. Now, as much as I'd like to see this bastard burn for his crimes, it won't happen on Enki. He's far too powerful here. And if you pursue him, they'll kill you. Then you'll never know what happened to your children." Despite the searing pain, he refused to let go. With a gentle squeeze, he tried one more avenue to reach her. "They survived Inanis. Remorse—Primary Rem told me, himself. Xelan was the last person to see them when he ransacked the Pantheon. That was only two thousand years ago. Sagan and I will work with you."

The tiny woman finally looked up at him and met his gaze. Damn, Lyriks were scary.

Respectfully, Korac released her and took a step away. "The decision is yours. But I want you to know I don't want to watch you die. Or myself. Because if you go, I'll go in after you. We'd both leave Sagan alone never to know what happened to us—"

"Why? Why would you go in with me?" Pehton gazed at him, earnestly searching his eyes for the truth.

The war criminal shrugged casually with a smirk for his warden. "I won't let that hedonist die without getting at least one good swing in."

A pitiful laugh burst from her. The Executive Warden choked on it until she shook with sobs. The smoke and fumes dissipated and left a broken woman in its wake.

Korac startled her with a groan. "Ugh. No. I've been around the Shadow far too much. I almost offered to hug you." As she sniffed and wiped her eyes, he carried on, "Can you imagine? The awkwardness of it." He shook his head incredulously and waved the image away.

Pehton giggled, and her shoulders eased.

"Come on. Let's get back to the prison before we're overtaken by the only two Tritans that patrol Enki."

As they made their way back through the conduits and to the shrine, Pehton confessed, "Since you were so forthcoming with me, I want to return the favor. And you won't like what I have to tell you."

"You don't have to say it. I already know you're in love with me. Sagan thinks it's cute, too." As they crossed back into the Primary's cell, Pehton stopped walking in step with him. He turned and found her looking at him rather seriously. "Tell me."

The Executive Warden chafed her black arms and chewed on her lip. Eventually, she spilled the bad news. "I've been avoiding telling you this but...Razor has sheets he dyed the same color as Sagan's eyes. And I think he let me see them, so I would tell you. I think he wants you to know." After dropping that bomb, she paced into a logic frenzy. "Okay. But he had to have them dyed a while ago. Like before she started coming around the Emporium. And that's not all. Her Lyriki coat? Triss and Oleen made it like over the last two years, right? He owns them."

"Fuck," Korac spat and clenched his jaw as he fumed. He hated the way the Pain Curator looked at his woman. Like he wanted to give the Icarean General a run for her. But that's not their relationship at all. No one owned anyone. They were equals.

Pehton punched one tiny fist into her other tiny palm. "I'll warn her when I see her next, but she gets around so fast. And I can't hang out at the Emporium waiting for her. Triss will tell Razor I was there. But I have a plan." She crossed the distance between them and brought him down to her height. In his ear, she whispered, "A source on the inside—Sagan's human friend—discovered evidence which makes me believe Razor broke the slave labor laws. Matt asked for my help. I'm asking for yours. Would you like to help me bring down the Emporium?"

Korac looked into her eyes from only centimeters away. Grinning, he assured, "With pleasure." He held up a finger and leaned forward to whisper, "Quid pro quo. I help with the Emporium. You get me in the big cell."

"Deal."

King Rayne might soon inherit another planet.

{EARTH}

At the double sinks of Pablo's apartment bathroom, the happy couple brushed their teeth. The two made eyes at each other as they washed the taste of the other one out of their mouths. It seemed the polite thing to do before facing the high-strung crowd of soldiers, strategists, and barely twenty-year-olds running the Two Worlds.

Lynn asked as she finished dressing, "Are you ready for this?"

Pablo spit in the sink and answered honestly, "Never. I'll worry about you constantly."

"Don't." She kissed his shoulder. "We're getting it right this time. Conscience said so."

"Has the arsenal responded yet?"

She emerged from the walk-in closet in an all-black carbon fiber jumpsuit. Catsuit was more like it. Partially unzipped, the woven material gripped to her curves like his hands wanted to right now. "Not yet. But they will. And they'll say 'yes.'" She even fired a finger gun at him with a wink. After bundling her locs into a tucked bun, she blew him a kiss. "See you at the meeting, my sexy fantasy doctor." All that beautiful cleavage left with her.

Damn, Pablo loved her. And that outfit distracted him from the worry so badly, he forgot to say goodbye. What was maturity?

No time to chase her. His super secret patient probably arrived downstairs already, waiting on him. He grabbed one of many lab coats to cover his gray scrubs and headed for the sublevels of Med Lab 1. He locked all the doors behind him with a blood seal to protect the patient's privacy. As he walked to the exam room, he tried to keep the excitement out of his step. It wasn't everyday he got to run a pregnancy test.

Sagan already sat on the exam table when he opened the door. She set the trademark axes aside. "Thanks for meeting me, Doc."

"Anytime—"

"I'm just so nervous, you know?" Her voice grew more shrill the longer she talked. Hand gestures more frantic. "Everything's going down and there I am passing out like my blood sugar is low. Hearing voices in the Seam. I've been having so much unprotected sex with Korac. And we tried this one position that I'm pretty sure did the job—"

Pablo pressed a hand firmly over her mouth. "Please stop." He removed his hand at her nod. "Deep breath."

She did.

"It's very unlikely you're pregnant." He wheeled over on the stool and took her temperature. "Nacres function differently for women. They constantly monitor your hormones in a way that replaces your menstrual cycle. When your mental state and your hormones align, the nanocomputer allows fertility. Basically, you have to consciously and subconsciously invite it."

Sagan's nose crunched when she frowned as she processed it. "Tameka wanted—I mean, I love Pax, but—"

"Fury kindly shared her experience with me for medical knowledge. She conceived pre-nacre. Apparently during that eighteen hours on the train. She also over-shares." Pablo gave Sagan a smile. "After the nacre, she chose to keep him." He wheeled away and returned with the blood sample gun. "Just a pinch, and I can run some tests."

Sagan held out her arm and looked anywhere but at the gun. Tightly, she considered aloud, "Of course, she did. She loved Xelan—loves, I mean. Besides, getting an abortion amid Volcano Day…Impossible."

"No, that's not what I mean." He rolled over and placed the sample in vials containing test liquids. "Women can choose to terminate the pregnancy. Like Celindria did in Nox's Verse."

"How?"

"Opposite of the circumstances of conception and incubation. Consciously and subconsciously end it. Hormones out of balance, malnourishment, and...almost *willing* it to stop existing. The computer recognizes the signs and recycles the energy."

While silence stretched between them, the tests ran in the centrifuge with a gentle hum.

Out of nowhere, Sagan confessed, "I'm thinking of getting a tattoo like yours. For me and Korac."

Pablo laughed. "Copycat." He glanced down at her chest. "Where's your chain?"

"Oh, Matt's holding onto it for me. I keep forgetting it. Probably the light-headedness." She played with her overgrown bangs while they waited. Her violet eyes crossed cutely as she focused on them.

Still, her carelessness concerned Pablo. "Rayne wouldn't like that."

After an emphatic chuff, Sagan agreed, "No, she certainly wouldn't. I promise I'll get it back. I haven't visited her in a few days. How is she?"

"We're testing her blood samples against the virus and the disabler. Our hope is that the latter can stop the Weapon. Or—at the very least—lessen the side effects."

That got Sagan grinning. "Fingers crossed."

Pablo returned the smile and explained, "The vaccine is another matter. We're almost there. Silence and Twenty-One are invaluable." He chuckled as he reflected, "Lynn thinks we're adopting them—Oh, we're finished. Hmm..." He frowned as he scrutinized the results. "You're severely malnourished. Are you skipping meals or forgetting to hydrate?"

"Doc."

He turned around and faced her. "Sorry, what?"

"Am I pregnant?" Sagan looked beyond exasperated.

Shaking his head, Pablo answered, "No. I'm not sure if you'll find that good news or bad."

With a relieved sigh, she nodded. "Neutral, I promise. This isn't the best time for it when I'm ferrying people around." The neglectful Seamswalker hopped off the table and clapped once. "Well, I appreciate your help—"

"Sagan. You're starving. You're not leaving here without a banana bag. Maybe three." Pablo suspected as much and brought some of the vitamin-packed bags for that exact reason. He nodded to the plate on her chest. "And I'm testing that thing. I need to know if it's draining you. Plus, you never know. That kind of technology might prove medically useful."

"Okay. No arguments from me. Set me up." The Progeny woman hopped back onto the table and held out her arm, looking away. To distract herself, she asked, "What about Sol's radiation? Did we ever solve that?"

Pablo concentrated on the line insertion without further agitating her obvious phobia. He found it endearing that Sagan feared needles, given who she was dating. "We're making improvements, and so far the planet isn't in major decline. Between Xelan's journals and my work with Andrew, we're figuring out how to convert light from Li through Elden's Sphere to imitate ideal growth conditions on Cinder. But don't tell anyone. That's a long-shot, and I don't want to get anyone's hopes up."

She beamed again. "Wow. Imagine that? I've always admired the way Elden and Xelan described Cinder. Or I guess Xelan's mom. Savis passed it down to him. And then he passed it down to us. Do you think this is what he wanted? Us to save it?"

With the first bag hanging for the IV drip, Pablo set to cleaning the room. "I want to believe we're on the right track. I think…" He cleared the emotion choking his voice. "I think Rayne is where we failed the most."

Sagan snapped to him. Her eyes glistened already. "What do you mean?"

The words he left unspoken for years rushed out of him all at once. "I don't think he'd want her in that box. Alone. In pain every hour. I haven't gone to see her in two years."

"Oh, Pablo..."

Once the train got rolling, Pablo couldn't make it stop. "I can't look at her like that. She went through so much for us. From the very start, she led us through this bullshit—Sorry. I don't talk much about it. We have so much else to keep us busy."

The Seamswalker took the doctor's hand and squeezed it. Now her voice was thick with emotion. "She chose that for us. Believe me. She wouldn't want us wasting a second grieving her decision. Not when that energy could be spent solving problems, right?"

"Right."

She gave his hand an encouraging shake. "So, we press on. One day, she'll get out. And because of your research, you could make it happen. Don't let it discourage you. Let it do the opposite. We fight for her. And we fight for Xelan."

"And we'll never stop—No. Sit your ass back down. I'm loading another bag." He hopped and started the next one.

"Yes, Doctor Spazoid."

"I love you, too, Seamswalker."

{Enki}

Sip.

At midnight, Tameka fluffed her jaw-length curls that foamed out from her face in a thick mass. "Space hair," Pax called it. With a sigh, she applied eyeliner and mascara. Thanks to her nacre, her skin never required foundation. She could think of a few years in a highschool when she needed that. Despite her excitement of finally solving the Enki labyrinth—with Xelan's help, no less—the mirror reflected sadness. This time of year hurt the most, and the misery weighed heavily on her—

"Mommy?"

For one moment, Tameka closed her eyes and soaked in all the love from that tiny voice at the door. He repaired her. That and—

Sip.

The lights dimmed. Oh, shit. Too much this time?

Caedes' voice called through the door next, "Everything okay in there?"

She rushed to answer and as Pax latched onto her leg, she let all the terror show on her face. "Caedes, will they know?"

"It's a good time to find out. Better now than while we're running a secret mission. From hereon, try to dial it down. How's it treating Pax?"

"Hee."

Tameka beamed down at her precious son. His skin glowed, and his eyes sparkled. Like his mother. "Baby, how are you feeling?"

"I can fly. Watch!" He spread his arms out wide and zoomed around the room, making whooshing sounds.

She melted. As did Caedes beside her. Softly, she said, "I think it's working."

"Great. And no Tritan patrols at the door, yet, so maybe we're all clear."

"Hello! I'm in the living room." Sagan's voice rang through the open bungalow. "Totally nowhere I shouldn't be without knocking."

Caedes chuckled while Tameka rolled her eyes. "We're up here."

Pax darted into her closet so fast he almost left a waft of cartoon smoke.

The Seamswalker entered the hallway looking healthier than the last two visits. "Hey, where's Jack and John?"

"They moved next door with Karter, Chris, and Para," Tameka explained. "It's temporary. Eventually, we hope to open the entire wing."

"Cool." To Caedes, Sagan asked, "How's the drive coming along?"

The Icarus gestured for them to follow him to "the room." "I'm trying it out tomorrow. Let's hope it doesn't melt the colony."

With a deep breath, the Seamswalker looked over at Tameka. "Are you ready to do this?"

In light of her son's cuteness, Tameka beamed. "Absolutely."

Sip.

Caedes went over the plans for the Dyson's Sphere's map in "the room." "And when I apply...uhm..."

"You can say it." Still, Tameka braced herself. Sagan spared her a pitying look.

"Wingmaster's schematics, we get this." The lines that were on the paper layered over the conduits currently marked on the three-dimensional model. Perfectly. Until only a few undiscovered conduits remained between them and the Pantheon.

Sagan frowned and pointed at the display in the center of the desk. The girl's axes shrank the tiny closet space. "Where do all these go?"

"Shrines, it seems," Caedes offered. "Of course, we'll review everything, but I think you should try to locate the Pantheon tonight. For confirmation, only."

"Let's do this." Tameka was ready. Finally, they'll discover whatever secret the Tritans hid there, so important they made Xelan a fugitive for it. Some part of Tameka wondered if she should tell Tumu. But given his history of ambiguous help, it seemed better to move forward without him. Besides, this was recon only for tonight.

"All right. Which landing is that?" Sagan asked about the nearest explored point to the Tritan temple.

Caedes blew out the air in his cheeks. "If you find the right one, I'll be impressed. Your ability is based on visuals, correct? Those landings are intentionally identical. That makes it different to pinpoint the exact location. Try... here instead. Have you ever been to John's lecture hall?"

She nodded.

"Okay. Gear up and try for that. I'll guide you from there."

"Thanks," Tameka offered him an appreciative smile.

He looked away with a curt nod.

Sip.

They Seamswalked into the amphitheater John used to educate the Tritans on human existence. Tameka asked, "Are we in the right one?"

Caedes assured, "Congrats, you made it. Luckily, there are fewer of them to pick from. Okay, take the second conduit on the right of the hall's entrance."

Tameka and Sagan went hand-in-hand. Even with the map, they explored for what felt like hours. Glass corridors. Ocean landings. Colonies of stone and glass. And ceilings too low for their supposed makers. The repetitive similarities of every space spiraled the labyrinth into dizzying madness. They distracted themselves with conversation.

"So there's nothing wrong with the port, and if he can imitate the technology, it actually might improve memory bank exploration and upgrades?" Tameka tried to ignore the other part of this discussion where Sagan mentioned the pregnancy test. The thought of the Seamswalker bearing Korac's children terrified Fury.

"Isn't that wonderful news? Something good came out of this it." The blond poked it.

And the redhead refused to shudder. But one thing struck her. "Where's your chain?"

Sagan rolled her eyes. "I am aware that I left it with Matt. I plan to retrieve it tomorrow. I know I'm irresponsible and an asshole. Okay? I'm sorry."

Tameka held up her hands to ward her off. "Whoa, sorry. I'm not trying to harp on you. I guess Pablo already gave you the talk."

"And three banana bags."

What the fuck were banana bags? Never mind. Not important. "Oh! Speaking of forgetting. I remembered. On my last solo walk, I found a weird room on the other side of a shrine. Black metal floors, walls, and ceiling. A bunk like the detainment pods in the Ionas. And a nacre resistant shield made up the opposite wall. Ring any bells?"

Tameka heard Sagan swallow from two feet away. When she answered, her voice wavered, "The room you described. It sounds like a cell on Gait."

The redhead recoiled. "Fuck. Really?"

The blond girl frowned as she considered the implications. "Wow. I... I have to tell Korac or Pehton. Maybe Razor knows something—"

"Okay. Stop." Tameka dropped her sister's hand and faced her.

Sagan shrank back. "What?"

"Stop with the Razor 'enemy of my enemy is my friend' crap. He's completely untrustworthy. And no offense, but the more you trust him, the more I'm convinced you shouldn't."

"Hey!" The Seamswalker folded her arms and went into defensive mode.

Fury tried to diffuse the bomb. "I trust your judgment, I do. But you and Rayne have this thing in common with bad boys and redemption arcs. Not everyone is worth saving—"

"Progeny."

The girls straightened to attention before they remembered Caedes couldn't see them. "Yes?"

Gently, he pressed, "You're two conduits away."

Upon his instruction, they stepped into the next conduit and entered a surprisingly familiar space. Of course, they instantly tried to retreat, but the conduit sealed behind them.

Sagan mouthed, "Shit."

Yea, that about covered it.

The last time they came here was two years ago. Xelan wasn't allowed to join them. He stayed back while the Progeny learned the history of Enki's manipulation of Cinder and the Icari. Primary Rem's sanctuary and its impressive waterfall of Cascading Light. All white stone composed the entire colonnade surrounded by the ocean at Enki's northern-most point.

Looking up from here dizzied her, so Tameka kept eyes front. But Sagan's eyes danced with it. The entire Dyson's Sphere, upside-down. A beautiful wonder and one hell of a headache. It distracted them from the important question.

Tameka mouthed, "Where's Rem?"

They cautiously stepped closer. It wasn't likely they could miss a sixty-five foot blue alien in the center of the Greek-style columns. Boldly, they walked up the steps to the center. Absent.

Sip.

Caedes whispered over their earpieces, "Contact."

Tameka and Sagan shared a look before Fury quietly answered, "Right, Caedes, we found Primary Rem's sanctum."

He sounded terrified. Quietly. "Well, Elden, get the hell out of there—"

Sagan shook her head and stood at the glass lift that raised for the Primary's audience. "He's not here. Although, it's no surprise he's the final boss before the Pantheon. It leaves me wondering how Xelan ever got by him. Naked..."

Tameka lamented, "We'll never know."

"Bet I can Seamswalk here now. That makes it easier to do multiple trips—"

Knocking sounded from Caedes' end. The gruff Icarus made plenty of noise as he exited "the room" and headed for the front door to the bungalow. "Yes?" How did he increase the gravel in his voice for an extra grumpy effect?

"We discovered the source of a power delay."

Oh, shit. Tameka recognized that voice as one of the so-called "maintenance" Tritans.

The inconveniently timed interruption continued speaking, "It came from this apartment. We need to diagnose the problem."

Both Sagan and Tameka glanced at one another in perfect agreement. Within the same second, Fury was back in the master suite of her home. Softly, she warned, "We're back, Caedes," before he made excuses for her absence.

Sagan locked herself in "the room." To which the door camouflaged into the wall. It was okay for Tumu to know she Seamswalked around Enki as she pleased, but not randoms.

As the snoops tore all over the apartment searching for the cause of the power surge, Caedes and Tameka discretely went into the kitchen with Pax. Quietly, she griped, "We were close."

"Should we try again?" Sagan squeezed out.

Caedes pretended to rummage through the cabinets and used the sound to disguise, "When?"

The Seamswalker answered after a pensive pause, "Tomorrow night. I have a quick thing at the Emporium. Then I can join you, say nine-ish?"

Fury almost rolled her eyes. She loved her sister, but Elden dammit, she wanted to choke some sense into her. "Be careful. I'll see you then."

"Always."

After Sagan left, Tameka grumbled, "Rayne wouldn't let her get by with this shit."

THIRTEEN

THE ANGER IN ME

{???}

RAYNE LEFT NOX IN THE DARK TO PROTECT HER SANITY. Living through Xelan's death in both their heads—their hearts—almost killed her. How could someone feel so much grief and remorse for a murder he committed while feeling so much exhilaration and righteousness during it? And in her grand plans for justice against the Tritans, how long before she put herself in the same position?

It was too much. She needed to see Xelan. To hear his encouragement and feel his kindness. Until she lost him again.

That, also, almost killed her.

Now, Rayne wanted to return to Nox. To complete the sharing of lived experiences. To witness the last scene contributing to their unspoken conflict. Everything else she understood. But…

Damn, she wanted to beat the hell out of him. Came close to doing it, too. As she stared down at him in tears on his knees, Rayne wanted to kill Nox all over again. But then she thought of how his entire life people stronger than him took out their rage and frustration on him. When he was weak. When he was strong. Did it amount to anything?

Rayne already killed him for his crimes. What good would beating him serve?

His tears told her that their shared emotions were enough. He suffered for his sins in his afterlife. What further amends could she ask for?

They could progress to the next level of consciousness. No interactions; only share in his knowledge. But . . . when the dust settled, the sun set, and the night filled the sky—Rayne didn't want to be alone. And in his wholehearted attempt at rehabilitation, Nox made for decent company.

She wasn't prepared to touch on his presence in the father/daughter afterlife bubble. The sight of him cradling the swaddled infant probably swayed Rayne's decision to return. For the last testimony.

The lights switched on in her conscience. Rayne entered through the center of the room. Not for the first time, seeing him stole her breath away. Only this time, it was because he hadn't moved. Nox knelt where she left him near the screen with that horrible image on replay. He stared down at his hands in his lap like something covered them. When the younger version of him lit the Icarean firestick, the man before her turned away.

"Forgive. Me."

So quiet, Rayne almost missed it. So quiet, it wasn't meant for her. She interrupted a private conversation between Nox and his brother.

Closing her eyes, she prayed to Elden for the strength to get through this. Nox wanted to face the wrong in himself to evaluate the worth of his life. To measure his deeds, the good and the evil. In his six million years, the former King of Cinder committed plenty of both. The current King of Earth and Cinder acted as his moral guide. Not his savior. But joining him on this journey meant confronting the worst of it together.

Rayne was ready. She folded to her knees across from him and offered, "I don't have to imagine the hell you're inflicting on yourself. I can feel it." Self-loathing, pain, and grief. "Before we find your place here, there's one more trial for us."

Her fallen enemy finally met her gaze. Even here, in this sacred space of her mind, blue blood stained his eyes. The black of them flickered like night in a mirror. She sensed his apprehension, but also his resolve.

Nox was ready. On his assenting nod, the scene on the screen changed. Li still burned in the sky, but from a different vantage. An observation platform in a blocky castle of black stone. Millions of Icari gathered. For the spectacle. For the conduit.

The Kings of Cinder in her mindscape refused to look. They locked eyes as the event played in their periphery. The first of her recalled negative emotions—anxiety—made Nox frown. The next one…they both broke down simultaneously as his younger self swallowed Xelan's nacre. Unable to contain it, this version of him howled with her pain.

Rayne closed her eyes and let the tears roll down her cheeks. For one second. One moment to prepare herself for the rest. A moment she never allowed herself to process, to accept. Resolute, she opened her eyes and refused to close them again. Nox never gave in. Never looked away.

Her emotions from the time of the non-consensual act slammed into her in a specific order. Sorrow. Anxiety. Fear. Disgust. Resolve. Rage. Confusion. Desire. Self-loathing. Rage. Loss. Hurt. His emotions shocked her. Pride. Desire. Love. Confusion. Regret. Anxiety. Hope. Pride. His felt subdued compared to hers.

The two Kings were overwhelmed by the torrent in her. Until the wave of his shame overtook them both. Drowned them in his current remorse. In his love for her. In his understanding of his unworthiness. They never looked away. They both cried, rocked with the violence of their emotions.

Until they reached Rayne's desire. Nox frowned at first, confused. Her horror and shame for enjoying even a fraction of it—for still wanting a man she once loved—broke him apart. "No. No. Don't you dare blame yourself for this. It's biology. Friction. Rayne, I went out of my way—"

"Oh, believe me, I figured out pretty quickly how thoroughly you studied my notebooks. You made sure I'd compare everyone that came after to you. Knowing they'd fall short. And now I get to ask you, how could you do that to me? You made me love you and then you made me want more of *that* from you." Rayne spat out the words and pointed at the screen. To the exact moment she would never come back from. To her climax that he took so much pride in.

Nox finally faced the image before looking back at her. Astonished, he cried, "Is that why the Rites? You considered yourself a traitor?"

At last, Rayne looked away.

When he fell silent, she sought his conscience. And found a whirlwind of hatred, disgust, and regret. All of it aimed at himself like the blast after a bomb. Shrapnel and glass. Inside his head, Nox tried to phrase the solution without implying obligation or malice. His usual go-to whenever he wanted to apologize, which she noticed was fairly often.

Eventually, he reasoned, "Let me go. Whatever benefits you gain from my being here cannot possibly outweigh the harm. I don't deserve to be here. I'm no different—"

"You are not your father." A different man entirely, but what of the monster in him? Selfishly, Rayne admitted, "And if I let you go, I'll be alone. Would you ask that of me? Ask me to release you to erase your discomfort and leave me to face everything on my own?"

Nox winced. She knew it went deeper for him. He hated that he hurt her. But, in life, he never cut her any breaks. She gave him plenty until he reduced her to killing him. He owed her this.

Even kneeling, he towered over her. Searching those remorseful eyes, Rayne demanded answers, "You promised to take me when you invaded, Nox. Not take me apart and give the pieces away."

With shame on his face, he still never looked away. In that deep baritone of his, Nox genuinely submitted, "If you need to kill me again, do it. I'd give my life to take your pain away. I deserve worse for causing it."

Fresh tears scalded Rayne's face. His became a mirror of hers. With pain and confusion strangling her, she squeezed out, "I want to know why."

Nox's succinct answer came in a rush as if he considered this many times, "I couldn't separate you from Celindria. From all the terrible things that happened to me because of her. From all the things that she did to me. I saw all of that when I looked at you. Eight thousand years is a long time to plan your vengeance, Rayne. A long time to harbor a hatred that would never die. And there you were. A being of light. You were happy with your friends and your family. I couldn't let that happen. Do you understand? Couldn't tolerate that she would be happy while I still suffered, miserable and alone."

The truth. Every word. Even his recollections of the moments flashed on the screen. The next scene was of him locking her in the Martyr Complex. The first time her eyes shone with Li—a broken, lonely star.

He looked upward and closed his eyes, as if warding off the memory. "I keep reliving the momentI knew you weren't her. I tried to strip the disguiseand expose the monster beneath. The look in your eyes when I tried to take your goodness away...Pure resolve. You would never relinquish your light to me. I could hurt you physically, but you'd die before you'd let me ruin your kindness."

Rayne swallowed hard against his regret in her heart.

Nox turned his gaze back to her with his eyes like mirrors. Atramentous. His grief reflected in her. "That's when I knew you weren't her. And that you would stop at nothing to kill me. Not for revenge. No. You are above that kind of pettiness. You'd kill me to stop me from hurting someone else the way I hurt you."

The former King of Cinder stood and held out his hand. The current King stood gracefully without taking it. The sad smile he gave her coupled with his genuine emotions squeezed their hearts.

"Six million years I've lived, and if there's one thing I'll do for the rest of my existence, it's to never stop regretting what I did to you. And you share in my mind. You can feel my soul. You know that I'm telling the truth. I regret looking into your kindness and seeing only hatred until I had to make you like me. I'll regret it until I'm gone, until I'm dust, and long after."

Rayne found it difficult to look at him with that much of his crushed heart open to her. She glanced down and hid her hope by pushing her hair behind her ears. After considering their situation, she wanted one thing clear. "Your regret does not obligate my forgiveness."

"Absolutely not."

At this, she wanted eye contact to get her point across. "And while I agree Celindria is a bitch, I wouldn't wish what you did to me on anyone. Killing her is enough. It's what her actions deserve. What you did was small and petty. The actions of a monster, not a man. She made you into her. I will not let you do the same to me." That flame ignited once more, and she pounded a fist to her nacre.

Nox winced but took the truth she offered. "There's no way to make it right. I know. But what can I do then? Why am I here?"

"You think this is Hell?"

On more than one occasion, Rayne sensed Nox's confusion over this arrangement. The limbo frightened him. In his honesty, he confessed, "Eternity was too good for me. Here I relive my worst moments with your careful gaze always assessing me. To what end?"

With all the complicated matters between them more or less resolved, their current circumstance proved easier to explain. "You make a powerful ally, Nox, but you need to appreciate the shift in the balance between us. To say I saw something in you worth saving is inaccurate. But I did see a man who wanted to try. And... That counts for something."

Hope glinted in those obsidian pools. In his thoughts, she detected a sense of pride and renewal. But he'd earn that redemption. She wouldn't grant it to him so easily. Hell, she wouldn't grant it at all. A second chance was between Nox and himself. But she held out hope.

"I told you before that I'd die before I'd forgive you. And even though I see—and I want you to know that I do see—a change in you, I won't be your redeemer. If that's the path you want to take, you're on your own. I'll give you the arena for it. Here. In my mind. But I won't give you my hand. That said, this—" She waved a finger between them. "—Settles the business between us. Although I have every right, I'll never throw your misdeeds in your face. My righteousness knows some boundaries, and it wants me to let you earn this. You can't do that if I'm constantly reminding you of your sins. Can you do this? Can you stand with me knowing that you love someone who can't forgive you?"

Nox, the former King of Cinder, went to one knee and placed his fist over his nacre. The vow required no words. And she felt his sincerity in his marrow.

Rayne beamed at him and watched that gallant exterior shift. Her expressions moved him too much. She couldn't help but sense it. But with every effort he put forth not to show it, she couldn't hold it against him.

With the last vestiges of their conflict settled, it was time to get to work. The storm was coming.

"On your feet, soldier."

FOURTEEN

PLAY A GAME WITH ME

{EARTH}

LYNN EVICTED HERSELF FROM THE TENSION UPSTAIRS. Originally, she sought Pablo in his apartment, but he left for work already. Too bad. She liked the way he drooled at her in this suit. Instead, she headed down to Med Lab 2. Her mind formulated a plan, and it involved further research before she pitched it to the others.

The detainee pods glowed from their perimeter lighting as Lynn wandered the corridors. Icarean warriors who volunteered for this fate to avoid Gait. Here they served medicine. At the Arsenal, she and the scientists tested biological and chemical weapons on them. Only on volunteers. Facing a new war, she wondered if there was some way—

"Chief Lynn," Twenty-One called from the first pod in the hall.

He saved her life only last week. It took nothing for her to spare him a few minutes of conversation. "Yes?"

"I wouldn't do what you're thinking."

Lynn rushed to his cell and stared up at the massive Icarus. Almost as tall as Nox and similarly built. "Why's that?"

Twenty-One smiled kindly down at her. His disposition radiated respect and appreciation. "You've fed and sheltered us. That engenders some gratitude. It certainly does from me. But we're old, Chief. Some require more time than others. And most aren't ready, yet. Give it... another hundred or so years?"

She closed her eyes and processed his logic. They couldn't afford to wait that long. The Ionas needed a militia to defend it. And she came down here to consider them as volunteers for it. But Twenty-One made sense. Was it too soon to expect former enemies to side with them? Against a threat capable of freeing them from the Shadow? But was it fair to ask all those free Icari and humans of Earth to face war once again after only recently settling into reconstruction?

The human woman sat cross-legged on the floor and speared fingers in her hair, frustrated. Across from her, with glass between them, Twenty-One mirrored her. Only he looked serene. The quiet stretched between them. Not awkward or stressful. More like companionable.

When the massive Icarus broke it, she snapped to him. "After testing the disabler on me, what was your next step in the experiment?"

"What do you mean?" It's true, they wanted to test the integrity of the perfect defense virus against the nacre disabler's design on him. But that was it.

Twenty-One ran a hand over his black buzzed cut hair and fidgeted with his nails nervously. "Well, let's say you test it on me, and the virus proved resistant to your new toy. What happened to me next? Or let me put it another way. What would the enemy do next in your place?"

Lynn hugged one knee to her chest as she considered. "The ecology planned further testing for the virus if it proved resistant. Would it allow upgrades? If not, they'd consider the nacre cold and outside manipulation. Not necessarily a good thing. Pablo—Dr. Suarez—would start over at square one to create a less resilient virus."

That was the surface. But as she thought deeper and let Twenty-One's words sink in, more ideas became clear. Not all of them good. "Likewise, the Arsenal—I—would have to design a more effective disabler." She crawled closer to him and frowned. "You'd become the sole test subject, and your nacre…If it fails the disabler, then we've inadvertently frozen you out of the upgrade cycles. Twenty-One, you'll never progress from this point if we can't find a way to hack your operating system." This bothered Lynn.

"I'm aware."

The door to the detainee hall opened, and Pablo stepped through. He looked slightly ashamed of himself. "Sorry. I couldn't help but overhear the last part. We told him of the side effects at the start."

"But…" It bothered her. She gazed back into the cell of this pleasant Icarus and considered the rest of his existence. No upgrades. Logic, healing, fighting—Frozen forever. "No. We have to do something. And we have to stop advancing the disabler. It's already powerful enough. Make the virus strong enough to resist hacking, but not so strong that it shields against intended advancement."

"Hey." Pablo sat down and took her hand. "That's exactly what we're trying to do. But Twenty-One, I think you're holding back on us. Tell me what else is on your mind." Together, they both gazed at the Icarus for answers.

The giant leaned forward and spoke quietly until they barely heard him. "What would it take to recreate the Weapon?" Proper noun.

Rayne.

Lynn recoiled, stunned. No. No one wanted that. Except… Her husband kept his gaze down without facing either her or Twenty-One. "Pablo?"

He swallowed hard and licked his lips before answering, "Pax's blood opened up some possibilities."

"Twenty-One, can you please excuse us?" She forced her husband to his feet and dragged him to an empty lab. "Okay. I want you to tell me everything. Right now."

He held up his hands in defeat. "I planned to tell Tameka before I even considered telling Tumu, but Pax has Tritan genes in his DNA. It's faint, but—"

No.

"It opens up possibilities for upgrade research. Including what makes Rayne the way she is—"

"Stop."

Pablo did. His warm brown eyes darted around the room, avoiding hers.

Lynn crossed the room and took his face in her hands. He finally met her eyes. Firmly, she said, "We tell Tameka. The very next chance we get. Put aside any thoughts of testing on him for now. Let her decide that. And forget the Weapon, do you hear me?" She kissed this brilliant man before reiterating, "Forget it. 'Can' and 'should' are not the same. This is our line. No one should live with a planet-destroying bomb in their chest."

He pulled her to him and held on so tight. "You're right. You're so damned right. I'm sorry."

A few heartbeats passed as they calmed down. Eventually, she asked with her voice muffled against his chest, "This may sound silly, but should we apologize to Twenty-One?"

Her husband's rich laughter soothed any residual anxiety as they stepped back into the main lab.

And froze.

Kyle stood in front of Twenty-One's detainment pod. The Icarus stood at attention like the proper soldier he was. Meanwhile, Story Taker, in all his recent weirdness, grew more agitated with the conversation. To the point of slamming his fist on the glass.

They both rushed into the hall. When Kyle faced them, Lynn recoiled. Atramentous. A rich green with a brown pupil. But why such strong emotions?

"Is this about Silence?" Pablo asked, looking between the two.

Huh? Oh. Was Story Taker into her? Twenty-One looked more bothered than if this were a conversation about a woman. In fact, his eyes kept darting to Lynn's. Like he was trying to tell her something. What the fuck was going on?

"Yea. A little healthy competition never hurt anyone, right, T.O.?" Kyle stepped away from the glass and headed for the exit. "Are you two ready for tonight? The last hit. After this, we can let Enki take over with Imminent."

Lynn didn't like this. She opened her mouth to say so when Andrew and Smith came down the stairs. "Hey, I've been looking all over for you. Lynn, we'd like to upgrade the rifles with the disablers. Can we do that? And Pablo, Silence is waiting for you in the exam room off Med Lab 1. She's running a fever."

"I'll check out the weapons." Duty calls. Lynn countered, "What about Lucas? Any word?"

Smith smiled at her with all that heavy eyeliner accenting the good-natured sparkle in his brown eyes. "The Brethren will give their address at the agreed upon time. Now, come on. Let's go beef up some guns."

Amid their family, Lynn kissed Pablo goodbye as they went about their separate duties. This last job didn't worry her. They all knew their parts. No. What bothered her was what happens after. Could they face their greatest trial, yet? Risk everything?

Well, in a few hours, they'd find out. Lynn just hoped she heard from the Arsenal by then.

{ENKI}

"Karter, the Tribunal asked you here to consider your candidacy for Eminent."

Sure, Lance seemed like a genuinely decent Tritan, but god damn Chris was a nervous wreck. Jack wasn't. The kid stood beside him, in their little cheerleading section, beaming for the Icarean warrior standing all by herself before the most powerful council of the Vast Collective.

Well, not really by herself. Para stood on the other side of Chris, grinning like a woman who faced many armies and won. Tameka, Sagan, and John made up the row behind them. Each of them oozing with excitement.

Yup. Chris was the only one dancing with anxiety.

Eminent Celindria was a beautiful specimen of African heritage. But he wasn't fooled. Her blue eyes, so similar to Rayne's, sparked with malice. In a regal voice, she listed Karter's qualifying miracles. "Establishment of the Valkyrie. Raising the Icarean princes. Siding with Enki during Umbra's revolts. Volunteering for stasis to prevent reducing food supplies for your species during famine. Joining the fight against Nox immediately upon waking. Aiding in the reconstruction of Earth. Protecting the King Regent, including risking your life during a cave-in. Karter, you are an impressive example of compassion and strength."

Eminent Lance eagerly nodded his agreement as he looked approvingly at Tumu, who stood beside the Tribunal. "Indeed."

Eminent Abresson looked less convinced. "What can you offer the Vast Collective?"

Chris grinned when his girl didn't hesitate. "Enki and therefore the Vast Collective declared war on Imminent. The organization targeted the Progeny. Those people who dedicate their lives to uniting Two Worlds torn asunder by war. And they're not alone. That force has terrorized the Collective for a million years at least. Bombings, corruption, manipulation—It has to stop. As someone who's fought several wars, I can contribute my strategic expertise to uniting the Twelve Worlds against a common enemy. We will defeat them. All of you are officers, but none of you are warriors. Let me aid in this."

The dark blue Tritan with his white scars frowned at her, as if he wasn't sure she meant that as an insult or not. Lance beamed with optimism and pride. Celindria turned into a statue. Could she blink?

Para's warm hand brushed his, and Chris took it. He turned and looked at Jack, who shared the same expression as Lance. They believed in her. But despite that, Tumu's fixation on Celindria unnerved him. Like he held his breath and waited for her decision.

Shit, this really was fifty/fifty. Fingers crossed. Chain gripped. Please.

Abresson smugly offered from behind his glass podium, "Perhaps, we should recess and discuss this again among ourselves—"

"I require no additional deliberation. What of you, Eminent Lance?" Celindria stared at Karter. Something like three minutes now without blinking.

Lance winced at his name from her mouth, but nodded all the same. "Yes. I'm ready."

"Agreed." Abresson was less than convincing.

"Karter, Valkyrie of Cinder, we grant you status of Eminent and invite you to sit on the Tribunal."

The Tritan Eminents both gaped at her. Lance recovered quickly with a fantastic grin. Abresson visibly paled the longer he went without breathing.

Chris broke all protocol and ran to Karter. She jumped in his arms, and he spun her while sharing in her delighted smile. He dropped her so the shortest Valkyrie could join in their hug.

Jack hooted and hollered. Very unKingly conduct. Sagan, Tameka, and John high-fived with their own shouts of joy.

Then Chris glimpsed Tumu. He wasn't celebrating. That careful black stare considered the First Progeny. While Chris could guess at why, he chose to remain positive. They'd worry about Celindria's ulterior motive later. Right now, he wanted to celebrate with the women in his arms. They would definitely relocate Jack and John to another apartment for tonight. Loud and messy. Yea. That sounded good.

"Rest up and celebrate, Eminent Karter. Tomorrow you begin a more arduous journey than you imagined." Was Celindria threatening her?

Karter didn't seem to give a shit. She cried out to the entire Tribunal, "Thank you! I look forward to it!"

Lance chuckled and went aside with Tumu. The two whispered among themselves while Celindria and Abresson melted villainously into the shadows. Figuratively speaking.

Back at the colony wing, they gathered in Tameka's place for lunch. Honestly, Karter couldn't get enough of Pax.

"Auntie Kar, fly me again!"

Tameka clicked her tongue and pointed a stern finger at her son. "What do you say, Pax?"

The intimidation was almost unnecessary with him as he added, "Peas," as if he innocently forgot to say it the first time.

Karter looked over at Tameka. "Can I?"

"Always." The redhead beamed at her and went back to the kitchen with Jack. "Any word on Ross..."

Their conversation faded in the background as Chris went out on the terrace with Karter and Pax. The toddler held out his arms and hopped. The powerful Valkyrie picked him up and held him securely in her dark gray arms.

"Ready?"

"Wee! Les go!"

Her beautiful black wings opened and carried the future of the Progeny race into the sky. As she flew the giggling child around, Chris thought of Karter's story. That Aegis couldn't choose a better woman to mother his child. And Chris wished she'd had the chance. Once things settled down and Rayne reclaimed her crown, that'd make the perfect time for them to build their own family. Until then, they awaited word from Tumu on how that situation played out.

"I promise, Tameka. I'll be back on time. Let me congratulate Karter and then I'll visit Rayne." Sagan stood halfway out of the kitchen and onto the terrace saying her goodbyes. "Yea, of course I'll pass on your love." She turned to Chris and walked over to him with her arms open.

His pre-apocalyptic family wasn't small, but he never received this many hugs. Each of them warm and full of sincerity. The Shadow loved each other—

Another set of arms circled them, and a brunette head rested on Sagan's shoulder. She giggled. "We love you, too, John."

"I just wanted in on the moment. And dinner's ready." He patted them both and headed for the kitchen.

Karter alighted with the tiny Progeny full of giggles and delighted cries. "Again!"

"Your momma said dinner's ready, sweetie."

The moment Sagan called to him, the boy's freckles blushed. He got so quiet.

Too precious. Chris chuckled and picked Pax up to sit around his neck. "I got you, sport. Let's go eat." He winked at Sagan on the way inside, who waved goodbye. He went faster, and the toddler gave a high pitch squeal of laughter. The weight of the boy made him feel taller and stronger. Like he could take on the world defending this kiddo.

Yea, Chris could do this with their own. Soon.

{GAIT}

Matt descended into his least favorite place in the Emporium. His boss's suite below the vault. It wasn't the blacked-out everything. Not the harem of Lyriks that saw to Razor's every whim. No. It was the scant lack of furniture. Bed, desk, and two chairs. That's it. The alien never slept or watched TV. All business. That level of focus was dangerous.

"No, Triss. She'll share our bed until she conceives, and then it's just you and me again. I'll never have her without you present."

Oh, and Matt always seemed to interrupt something down here despite the summons. Razor pressed Triss against one of the metal pillars. At the human's throat-clearing, the boss held up one finger.

The red-feathered Lyrik never acknowledged the interruption. Her gaze never left Razor's. "Do you know how long we have together before...?" She looked down at her abdomen with tears in her eyes.

This was the most affection—genuine affection—Matt ever witnessed from Razor. He pressed his forehead to hers with his eyes closed. His voice even croaked as he said, "I wish you'd reconsider. I'll miss you terribly."

"Well, maybe you should take your time with her then." Triss glared at him as she spat the words like an accusation and moved to get away from him. "Keep her around for after I'm gone since you seem keen to replace me—"

The boss gripped the side of her face and slammed her back against the column. He swallowed her gratified sounds with a kiss. The two smacked so long Matt headed back upstairs.

"It's fine, Matt. We're done." The boss turned back to Triss and promised, "I'll see you soon."

What the fuck was this soap opera? The old alien shocked the younger man with the genuine emotion warming his gray eyes. Interesting.

Triss slunk into the shadows, and Razor waved Matt down the remaining stairs. "We have some business, today, that will guarantee to test your loyalties. If any of the engagements disturb or anger you, let me know, and I'll accept your resignation in exchange for a memory debriefing. Are we clear?"

"As long as I don't have to watch you make out with anyone else, I should be fine."

The two men shared their odd smile of sociopathic familiarity until Puk came down the stairs with a surprise. The oldest of Kyle's sisters stepped onto the board, another piece for Matt to ponder Razor's intended use in the game.

The black formal suit looked cute on her and terribly out of place in Hell. All that wavy brown hair draped passed her shoulders. No sign of tears from those hazel eyes. Only weariness weighed her down, as if she came a long way without any sleep. Still, he gave her credit for those straight shoulders and that lifted chin.

When Ross faced Razor, recognition flickered, but when she laid eyes on Matt, it flared. Shit. He hoped to keep their connection a secret for an advantage.

"Oh, I'm not surprised you two know each other," the Pain Curator offered in a congenial tone. "It's perfectly reasonable. Hello, Ms. Roberts. It's a pleasure to make your acquaintance. Do you know who I am?"

Ross looked between the men across the desk from her. Uncomfortably, she guessed, "I think so. Is your name

Razor? I saw you dancing with Sagan at the Reipon gala." That frown made sense. Why would a member of the Shadow dance with a man of such a notorious reputation?

"Ah, yes. The Seamswalker and I are business partners. Please." He gestured for her to take the seat across from them as Razor claimed his own. At Matt's reassuring nod, she sat while the boss continued, "It must surprise you with everything you've no doubt heard about me that Sagan would entertain my presence. And you *were* warned about me, weren't you?"

She nodded, sitting straight in the chair but looking less and less certain the longer she sat in the blacked-out pit.

"And you didn't listen, did you?"

Ross sighed as if she found this bothersome. Making herself more comfortable, she stripped out of the jacket. Matt worried her tan skin exposed by the black silk camisole might prove more enticing than she intended. Irritated, she explained, "The Eminents arrested me. I wasn't looking for you. They said you have the honor of interrogating me."

How could Matt miss Razor's assessment of the barely legal girl across from him? With those gray eyes filled with purpose, the boss assured, "We know who assassinated Eminent Wiw. Your brother and the rest of the Progeny already met with the Tribunal. Quite messy business. But that's not why you were there."

Once again, Ross glanced at Matt, the familiar face in the room, for guidance. But the energy vibrating off his boss left him nervous as to the direction of this conversation. Matt nodded to reassure her.

She leaned forward with her hands clasped on the desktop. "I'm looking for my sister. She was taken from Earth during the Icarean Invasion. I've since learned she was brought to Reipon as a slave and sold to the textile mills on Lukemore. But she's no longer there. She hasn't been for almost two years."

Razor let her tell the story with encouraging nods for her to continue. When she finished, he sat forward excitedly.

"Was she working in the cotton dyes? Like for sheets and shirts?"

With hazel eyes sparkling, Ross stood and cried, "Yes!"

Matt witnessed a transformation taking place in his boss that unnerved him. An electricity hummed from Razor, winding up the voltage with every question he asked. "Young thing? Brown hair like yours, but straighter? And honey brown eyes?"

She stopped breathing. Within a heartbeat, she rushed around one end of the desk and fell to her knees at the Pain Curator's feet. Taking his hands, Ross lost all her composure. "Please. Please. Mr. Razor, sir. Do you have my sister? Please, let me see her. I need to hold her. I—" The young woman's voice shattered as sobs wracked her body, so fragile and small next to the alien.

Razor took one hand and placed two fingers on that wrist. With that out of the way, he pushed Ross' tousled hair from her face. So pretty and innocent, like many girls Matt forcibly recruited to the Cult of Night. With her here, he could count another soldier in his army to bring down the Emporium—

"Matt, please bring me 324."

No.

Small and slight of frame.

Oh god, no.

At the young man's hesitation, Razor pushed. "Come now, Matt. Don't let this beautiful young woman wait to reunite with her sister any longer."

The blood in Matt's veins went icy, and he considered decapitating his employer for the first time. Stiffly, he went upstairs and through the Emporium to the basement. He ignored the hood and suit. It no longer mattered. This was always Razor's intention. This climax. Matt's body never felt so repulsed by its own actions as it did in this moment. When he opened 324's cell, the person reduced to little more than a tortured animal beneath the hood flinched.

Next to her ear, he whispered, "We're going for a walk."

She relaxed at the sound of his voice.

God damn him.

Matt gripped the Numbered—no, not the Numbered—the fifteen-year-old girl by the arm. He considered taking the hood off now, but it was dark down here and bright in the Emporium. Better to walk her all the way to the vault. There he led what he really hoped wasn't Kyle's youngest sister into the suite.

Both Razor and Ross stood from the desk. But the hopeful smile on the older sister's face faded as Matt presented the hooded person, shrunken and sulking. Ross looked back at the Pain Curator, who nodded for her to proceed. The boss watched on so fascinated that some of his mania leaked onto the outside. He looked hungry, like when he asked Matt to kill that assassin a week ago.

Ross reached for the hood, and the wild animal inside flinched from her touch. A broken sob fell out of the older sister before she choked out, "Bethany?"

The shrunken human howled. So much worse than the whips and scalding water. This was the siren of a tornado of emotions clashing at once. Matt glared at Razor across the room as Ross removed the hood and fell to her knees. "No."

Bad bleach job.

All this time, the young girl begging for Razor to "make it stop." The suicidal Three Two Four. All along it was Bethany. Two years of daily torture. Left on the brink of insanity.

Ross didn't know that. And she wasn't on her knees crying at her sister's feet over the bad bleach job, either. No, the look in Bethany's eyes... Those beautiful honey brown eyes...

She was long gone. Feral. Unreachable. Every touch made her screech like an animal. Shrink and hide. Even the pitiful light in the suite made her squint and blink excessively.

Razor broke her.

"Matt. Puk. Lock them in separate bunks on separate floors. Assign Ross a number and start her on daily rotation tomorrow. She's eighteen, so don't exempt her from the sexual experiences—"

Unbidden, Matt remembered being born. The face of the doctor as he cut the umbilical cord. His mother's ecstatic smile as she held him for the first time. His dad's scowl. A few birthdays. The first frog he mushed and opened to see inside. Snakes. Rabbits. The first girl he kissed. When he hit his first home run in little league. His mother's funeral. It rained, and all the flowers were white. Meeting Lucy in the middle school library. Cutting open that Icarus at Fair.

His consciousness slammed back into his body hard enough to leave him—everyone—on the floor. Fuck, that hurt. He couldn't even move. Breathe. Focus on breathing. His lungs throbbed with each painful gulp of air.

Imbued with her brother's ability, Ross shrieked, "Bethany, come on. Let's get out of here!"

The younger girl howled.

Ross screamed, and Matt shifted in agony on the floor to see. Razor twisted her arm behind her back and pulled her against him. He muttered something in her ear. Something awful, if her increasingly frightened eyes were any sign. Tears poured, and she closed them as if to ward him out. But the devil made himself damned clear because she cried out, "Stop! I'll do whatever you want. Please, just leave my sister alone."

"No one will touch her as long as you hold up your end of our bargain. Do not fight my people. Your nacre will heal you. And when I call on you, you behave. If not…" He whispered the rest, and Ross sagged hopelessly in his grip.

As if desperate to make him stop, she breathlessly agreed, "I understand."

Matt finally rolled onto his hands and knees. He glared at his boss as the new orders came in.

"Remove 324—"

"Bethany," Matt corrected.

After a considering pause, Razor grinned. "Bethany from rotation. I'll leave designing our new asset's daily routine to you. You can call her whatever you want."

Ross cried pitifully in his arms and gazed at Matt beseechingly.

God damn it.

"Yes, boss."

The hope drained out of her and left her too heavy to carry herself. Puk took Bethany, who never once reacted to her sister's face. Matt carried an unconscious Ross up the stairs.

Razor called out as they ascended to the vault, "You did excellent, Matt. I can't wait for tonight."

How could tonight possibly show up this catastrophe? Matt found himself reluctant to find out. Good news: Ross could aid him from the inside. Bad news: the damage to her sister—damage he helped cause—was irreparable. At the first opportunity, he'd inform Sagan and Pehton.

Tonight.

{CINDER}

Bones missed King duty with Para. At least he was having fun when naked with her. Lamassau sat across the table from him, fully clothed and collecting the Icarus' entire snack hoard. Meanwhile...boxers and socks. That was it.

"I secretly hope Tumi visits with you like this. Quite the scandal." The Tritan's non-eyebrows bounced with mischief.

Refusing to give up, Bones tossed in his socks. "Call."

"I don't need those, honestly. But I'll take them." Lam threw down his hand. "Three of a kind. Two's."

This was it. His moment. The Icarus proudly showed the winning hand. "Flush in spades. Pay up, cheater."

The green Tritan touched a hand to his chest dramatically and scoffed, "I never cheat!" An ace—actually, completely, really—fell from the sleeve of his robe.

Bones quirked a brow before gesturing for the other man to fork over the pool. Which he did while grumbling about wanting to see boxers come off.

And that's when Sagan walked into the pit. "Hey gents, I—Oh. Dammit." Hands on hips, and the nose scrunched with the frown. "I have to knock now before entering here, too?!"

Well, not since he and Para realized Rayne could hear them getting it on. He and Lam exchanged a look before both bursting out in side-splitting laughter. Until the cheating bastard made a move for the pickle. Bones slapped his hand with a stern, "Hey!"

The axes made a trademark clinking as Sagan approached. He never realized until now how comforting he found the sound. Like things were all right in the world with that noise nearby. She looked a little thin and somewhat tired. But that's war. Stress and no time for rest. The silver disc on her chest appeared fairly recently. Ugly thing.

Sagan caught him looking, and her face fell.

Bones started, "No, I was just wondering about your necklace—"

"Look!" Lamassau cried out and rudely pointed at the Martyr Complex.

It glowed with a warm light.

"She knows you're here." Bones smiled for her, and it brightened when the Seamswalker returned one of her own.

The smell of sand, ocean, and cotton candy chased away the ash. Warmth filled the room like Earth sunlight in summer. Not that Bones ever experienced the full brunt of it. Not that he could without combusting.

Sagan waved to them before Seamswalking to the island. From then on, he and the Tritan tried to ignore the private conversation within hearing range.

"They made Karter an Eminent. Can you believe it, Rayne?"

Hell, Bones couldn't. He wanted to punch the air and cheer for his race and for Para, but that'd giveaway his accidental eavesdropping. The Tritan didn't bother covering his shock. It bothered the Icarus. The other man looked horrified rather than excited.

Ask later.

"Jack is doing great. You'd be so proud. And Tameka is doing lovely. I'm so glad she finally told you about Pax. He's so smart, Rayne. He's just like his dad."

Ouch. Bones came in after Xelan passed, but every Icarus knew of the Prince's great deeds. Only they were considered sins for most of Bones' life.

"Andrew is much better. Kyle helped orientate him to this reality. Only... well, now Kyle is acting weird. We're checking on it soon. And do you remember Pehton? She kind of arrested you? But she's super cool. I promise. Anyway, we're helping her look for these children that all disappeared off Gait at once. Korac was the only one who wasn't taken when he was little. It's all tied together somehow. I was working with Razor to solve it, but..."

A heavy sigh sounded from the island. What sort of weight did the Seamswalker carry on her shoulders? Only two of her kind existed, and one of them exhibited shifty allegiances.

"My last pain experience is tonight, and I think after this I won't be around him so much. That's good. I know it's good. I need to kick this habit and get rid of this port. But I don't know. There's something there. Rayne, I wish I could ask you. Was this how you felt about Nox? That maybe deep down there was something worth helping? And then he crossed a line and disappointed you too badly to come back, right? I'm afraid of what the line is for me, and how long before Razor crosses it."

Lamassau and Bones both avoided looking at each other with matching faces that said, "Not my business."

"So, I'm cutting myself off tonight before it's too late. Then I'm meeting Tameka, and I think I'll come right after to see you again. I miss you—" A sniffle, and the scent of salt carried over to them. "I love you. I can't wait for you to get out of this coffin. I know you think the world is too delicate for you to touch it without breaking everything, but I know that's not true. I trust you. I love you, and I trust you. Tomorrow. I'll come by tomorrow."

Both men tried to straighten themselves as if they overheard nothing. So by the time Sagan Seamswalked beside them, Bones was dressed and Lamassau was asking how to play Twister. Yea, right. Like the Icarus wanted Tumu to catch them playing that.

"Thanks for everything you're doing, Bones. Chef." Sagan hugged them both to Lam's obvious astonishment.

The green Tritan flushed black as his blood.

It made her giggle, and Bones laugh into his bag of Cheetos.

"Ahem. Thank you, Progeny."

Sagan shoved her hands in the pockets of her Lyriki coat and twirled like an anxious kid. "Well, I guess I'm off—"

"Won't you stay for something to eat? We haven't talked in a while." Bones tempted her with a precious extinct Cheeto. She was worth sharing with.

As if sensing its significance, Sagan giggled and kissed his cheek. "Thank you. But I gotta head to Gait and then to Enki. Big night. I'll be back tomorrow to see Rayne, and we can catch up, then?"

Lamassau took the Cheeto and grinned. "It's a date." Crunch.

Bastard.

"Tomorrow."

And then perhaps the most innocent of the Progeny disappeared.

{EARTH}

The signal.

Lynn gave Andrew a thumbs up. He turned to the group. "All right. Saddle up, everybody, let's go!"

Everyone assembled to load up at the Arsenal before heading to Reipon for the main event. The Chief Weapons Engineer and Smith toted ahead. Andrew walked alongside Kyle to the conduit. The Doc brought Silence along for some testing that Lynn originally wanted to run on Twenty-One with the Perfect Defense virus. Lucas saw them off with a promise to hold down the fort until they returned with news of the Imminent raid.

The conduit opened into the sky, miles above the ocean.

Andrew whistled. "This alone would deter me from fucking with this place."

Kyle shrugged and offered, "I guess some people are more determined than others."

Lynn communicated to some kind of camera in sign language. Smith relayed his own code. Silence watched with rapt attention. Pablo leaned into her and explained, "They're using their hands to form words. It's how we communicate with hearing-impaired individuals. Of course, that may not be as common once Enki disseminates nacres to humans."

The Icarean female borrowed a pair of his scrubs. The bottoms stopped at her knees. At least the top looked cropped on purpose. One day, they'd find time to get clothes that fit her. Especially with her growing into the Shadow like one of many adopted strays. She tied her black hair into a high ponytail, but left the blue streak in her face. Hopefully, they'd open her memory soon and discover her lineage. No doubt an interesting one, given her unusual features.

Silence caught Andrew looking as the lift took them down the glass cylinder below the ocean. She nodded once to him. A confirmation of sorts.

Good. He needed it. Everyone had to play their parts.

Lynn led them through the guard posts and down a high-security hallway. "And this takes us to the disabler research labs where we can upgrade the guns. Come on."

They followed. Once inside, she and Smith upgraded six of the Imminent rifles and passed them around. "Everybody got one? Great. So now—"

T.A.O. appeared. Not in the plans. Kyle shot Andrew, simultaneously disabling his nacre and knocking him on his ass. More weapons discharged.

Silence screamed, "Pablo!" A thud followed.

As Andrew faded in and out of consciousness, Lynn fell beside him. Knife in the chest. Brown eyes, unseeing.

No.

Pablo fell next. Skull bashed in.

Barely enough strength to roll over, Andrew found Kyle standing over him with Silence in his arms. At the counter beyond, Smith upgraded more weapons at the point of T.A.O.'s gun.

Betraying them again. Lying about the bombing. Setting them up with the Tribunal. Andrew asked the obvious question, "Why?"

Kyle's voice came in three pitches, "Chaos."

That's what happened if Andrew flipped tails. The coin went up and up. Inevitably, it pitched down. All the while the metal sang to him. A promise that this time, things would go right.

Heads.

FIFTEEN

WILL YOU OR WON'T YOU?

{EARTH}

KYLE RAILED WHEN CELINDRIA PUSHED SILENCE AWAY. But volition bonds crippled him. He screamed and strained against the mental shackles.

Andrew! Silence! She plans to kill you all!

But the words never left his actual mouth. No matter how hard he cried. He made no further breakthroughs. Celindria used his lungs to smoke enough pot to subdue him. Nothing affected her, unfortunately. His physical metabolism, his hindrance. Her body occupied space elsewhere, uninhibited.

He hoped she left it on some tracks somewhere, and that a train would take her out soon.

The Shadow entered the cylindrical lift to the Arsenal's entrance. Andrew whistled and muttered beside him, "This alone would deter me from fucking with this place."

Celindria shrugged his shoulders and offered, "I guess some people are more determined than others." She shot a sinister smirk over her shoulder at the host from which she infested.

He rolled his eyes and forced gagging sounds.

The crazy bitch threw her head back and cackled. Fuck, he hoped someone rescued him soon. She mused, "You're so similar to Devis. Strange how certain personality traits pass through ancestral lines."

"Rayne is nothing like you."

She kept her eyes on the visual, never missing the details. In an icy tone, she offered, "I don't know. She and I both enjoyed sex with Nox."

The gagging sounds were no longer fake. Until the day Kyle died, he'd relive watching Nox's conquest when Rayne's eyes shifted from fear to ... to ... Elden, he wished he could vomit. Brain bleach, please.

The lift slowed. Lynn and Smith went ahead to the guard post. Next they headed down a corridor lit from beneath the mesh walkway.

"Not long now," Celindria muttered with anticipation.

Kyle groaned into the floor until his voice went into a hoarse scream of powerlessness.

"Quiet. You'll miss the game."

The group entered a hexagonal room glowing in red light. It reminded Kyle of the backup lights at J.A. Fair—

An invasion. A force. A will not Kyle's own asked him to stay.

Celindria froze into an ethereal statue. The body, in fact, stayed in place as the group exited through the next set of doors. He looked closer at the walls through the visual. The ceiling. The floor ... Holy shit.

"Nacre glass," she hissed.

Kyle chuckled once. Twice. Gradually, it stretched into quiet laughter and then maniacal delirium. Relief unlike anything he felt before washed over him.

They figured it out.

Lynn's voice came over the speakers. "This is a Faraday cage. When we built the Arsenal, Sagan tested it for us. No Seamswalking allowed."

The manifestation of Celindria's nacre-hacking invasion clenched her fists.

"We know that's not Kyle." Andrew's proclamation injected Kyle with hopeful adrenaline. "Is he dead?"

Somewhat.

"No. He's in here with me." Celindria looked back at him with an evil gleam in her blue eyes. She forced his body to press his arm against the wall and used the other one to punch it. Bone cracked.

Kyle screamed. The only one of the two of them connected to the nervous system, he cried out, "Stop!"

"And I can do whatever I want with him unless you let me out."

The door opened, and Silence stepped inside. She looked beautiful in those ridiculous scrubs. Her gray eyes held so much confidence and fearlessness.

Celindria bowed Kyle's head in greeting. "I'm so honored to properly meet you. It's not everyday one faces a legend."

The powerful Icarus demanded, "Stop hurting him and answer their questions. If not, I'll disable his nacre and send you back to where you come from."

"You think that will work?" The First Progeny looked so smug.

"We shall find out. And if it doesn't evict you, I will render him useless to you when I put him in a coma."

Damn. That...was hot.

"He likes you, you know?" Celindria's voice dripped with venom. "He noticed immediately how the cold of the room affected your breasts. The poor boy almost cried when they caught you fucking that prisoner. But then you don't know how often women he loves have fucked other men over him."

Silence surprised them both with that movie star smile. "Then please assure him for me he'll get his chance to impress me once I beat you senseless."

Kyle hoped he beamed as much on the outside as he was on the inside.

Tense quiet stretched on another moment. Two. And then Celindria went to Kyle's knees and held out both hands, squeezed at the wrists. Hesitantly, Silence approached while retrieving nacre cuffs from Elden knew where. Applying them, she searched his eyes as if looking for signs of him in there.

He loved her then.

Celindria looked from him to her and shook her head, almost sadly. To Silence, she said, "How could I fight you, Mother of my people?"

What...

Silence's eyes. A beautiful blue swallowed them, the pupils went thin and gray. Her Atramentous. Her skin pulsed the same cobalt before fading to gray.

And then she fainted, leaving Kyle on his knees in chains.

{GAIT}

"Sold to Prince Iuo, expert on all Yun artifacts, for seven hundred thousand credits."

The Reipon Lamia looked pleased with his new plate set. Matt couldn't fathom it. He watched from behind the curtain where the curios were staged for bidding as ten elegantly dressed and masked clients flexed their wallets. All of them, high rollers in the Vast Collective. Dressed as a ringmaster in white, Razor personally oversaw the annual auction for that exclusive Pain Curator touch. He spared Matt the occasional glance, as if assessing how well the younger man processed this afternoon's drama.

Razor glimpsed his bodyguard taking in the spectacle and smiled with the affection of an instructor to a pupil. After waving on a nacre glass fountain as next in line, he asked Matt, "What troubles you, tonight?"

The freckled human spared his boss their secret smile for reassurance. "Nothing. I'm learning the system. Everything makes sense to me but the actual merchandise. Why are plates so fucking expensive?"

Puk chuckled knowingly, as he toted the fountain by them and onto the stage.

Matt raised a brow at the humor.

"I explained this to the Seamswalker earlier. How familiar are you with the Brothers of Yu?"

Right. Nox's Verse wasn't legal, so best keep that a secret. Instead, Matt offered, "Legend has it they were slain by Nox. Legir's sons, right?"

Razor gestured at the plates as more Mon3 drones returned with them backstage for packaging. "I searched the Vast Collective all over for their nacres. An unlikely circumstance led me to them. They're illegal to possess or sell. To get around that, we collectors fashion them into everyday items. Iuo is an old business associate of mine. I practically made them for him."

Some dots connected, and Matt didn't necessarily like the pattern they made. "Celebrity takes on a different meaning in the Vast Collective from Earth."

But the alien looked off elsewhere, as if listening to something the younger man couldn't hear. His voice went super deep again. "Matt, grab Puk. Change into the gear from the basement. Wait five minutes and meet me in the first of the immersive Divine Booths. Go, now."

"Sure, boss."

The shift was intense. Matt kept his eye on Razor all night after the alien promised more trauma for the evening. Was it time, then? Matt clutched both chains around his neck and reminded himself to return one to Sagan the next time he saw her. He waved for Puk, and they headed to the basement.

Fuck this place.

They both changed into black carbon fiber gear and a hood. He opened the door back into the kitchen, finding an unexpected sight. The Seamswalker was sprawled on top of the Pain Curator. Both crashed to the floor. She looked terrified.

Matt almost intervened, but Razor glanced his direction and waved him back. He stayed hidden and eavesdropped.

"Sorry. I—Just now. I couldn't leave the Seam. I was so scared." Her voice wavered and everything.

The redheaded human watched the masterful sociopath gently sit her up straight, pull her in for an innocent side hug, and chafe her arm. Careful around the twin axes.

With much concern, he asked, "Has anything like this happened before?"

Damn. The most innocent Progeny looked up at him with those violet eyes big and fearful, appreciating his comfort. She shivered in her Lyriki coat. In his arms. "Yes. Recently."

Razor helped Sagan stand. "Well, you need to eat. Keep your strength up. I have an auction going right now, but I can set up a spread for you once you finish the last experience." He kissed both her hands before releasing them.

The girl blushed and followed the man to the booth. Matt shook his head. This was a mess.

As they entered, she mused, "How many colors does that outfit come in?"

He laughed charmingly and bowed for her with the top-hat off and everything. "You liked it at the gala. I wore it especially for you. I want our last experience to be special."

"Oh, it's always special with you, Razor." The Seamswalker implied one thing, but the Pain Curator's wink implied another.

Five minutes.

Matt waved for Puk to follow him, and they crossed the kitchens into the addition. Outside the booth, he heard Sagan ask, "So, I know you've been around a while."

"Hah!"

She giggled at his burst of laughter. "Do you know much about the Tritans? Like how many there are?"

"Less than you think. But I believe they keep that number to themselves for an important reason. Here. The goggles. And I'll connect your port."

Puk cracked the door. Sagan set the axe holster aside and slipped the goggles over her head. Once on, Razor waved them inside. At his signal, they went in. Matt frowned at the polypropylene rope the boss produced from a hidden compartment in the floor. He tossed a bundle to both men and waved for them to start.

Start what?

Sagan froze as Puk drew closer. "Is there someone else in here with us?"

"Yes, Pain Kitten. But they're here to help make the experience special."

What...

Despite the warmth of how Razor said the unusual nickname, Sagan stiffened. "I didn't think you'd call me that around anyone else. What's going on?"

He whispered one word next to her ear.

She fell to her knees. Not screaming, but she shook her head as if disoriented.

"Now," Razor ordered.

Puk took her arms and tied the rope around her wrists.

"No. No, don't do this, Razor! What—why?! Stop touching me!" Despite her protests, Sagan put up no resistance, as if her body refused to respond to her.

Matt grit his teeth and tied her ankles around her boots. Without a struggle from her, they easily stretched the rope to the far sides of the booth and fastened it to the walls.

All the while, the most powerful being in the room kept still, as if rendered powerless. "Razor, you just crossed the line."

"Much to my regret, but it is necessary."

That's when Matt noticed the feed projecting her captivity in the booth to the auction hall. Ten individuals watched enraptured as the events inside unfolded.

Sagan's last experience was the finale of tonight's circus.

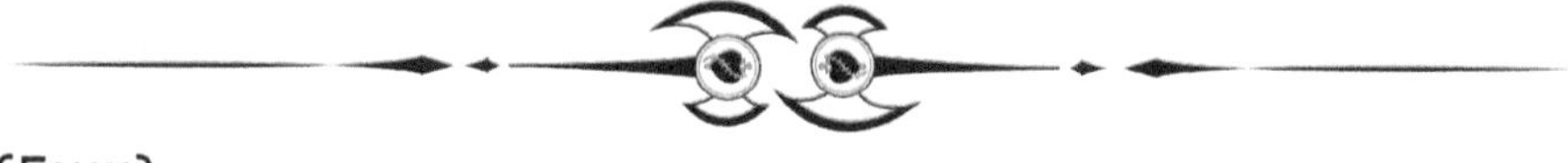

{ENKI}

Tameka took another drink from her new favorite source. Power surge be damned. She already waited around the apartment an hour before insisting on taking the long way to Primary Rem's sanctum.

Where the hell was Sagan? The Seamswalker visited pain experiences the way an addict bumped coke. It made the redheaded Progeny uncomfortable enough that she planned an intervention for tomorrow.

"She'll be fine," Caedes insisted over the earpiece. "There's nothing that warrior can't escape from."

He was right. And it calmed Tameka a little as she approached the final conduit. "Okay. Going in alone behind enemy lines. Wish me luck."

"Be careful, Fury."

Tameka grinned. "They should be careful of me. I got this." Once again into the breach. The beautiful colonnade surrounding that waterfall of Cascading Light. Empty. Still, she whispered, "Where is Rem?"

"Taking a vacation from Primary duties." His grin broke into his voice, warmer than gravel on a hot summer's day.

She soaked it in for one second. But that wasn't her right. His wasn't the grin she wanted. "Moving forward."

The conduit to the Pantheon looked no different from any other. Broad and sparking with energy. Through the blurry barrier, another colonnade waited.

Deep breath.

"Hey, the drive finished loading—"

Sip.

The Pantheon—columns, daises, squares, shelves and shelves of paper records—spanned as far as Tameka could see. A continent's worth of archived texts and tomes. Billions of lives stored and collected. Their experiences laid bare on the page.

"Caedes, you won't believe this—Caedes, are you there? Did I lose you?" Tameka pressed her earpiece and waited. When only silence returned, she made to leave. It wasn't safe to proceed without backup.

A light flashed, and she fell back on her ass, startled. Thinking quickly, she scuttled behind a wall.

"Progeny designation Fury. Messaging sequence activated. Standby. Sovereign Ambassador."

That was Eminent's Wiw's voice. With her heart in her throat, Tameka slowly turned and looked around the wall. A screen projected an life-size image of the Eminent standing with his hands clasped behind his back, as always. Or was always? Forever now.

His warm voice pressed on, "I imagined you'd find your way here one day. You're a bright girl with brilliant companions. I enjoy every one of our talks."

Grief tugged at her heart. She'd enjoyed them as well.

"Times will get dangerous ahead. I don't expect to survive. Should you see this message, follow this map to the location I've marked. There I hope you'll find answers you and the Seamswalker seek. Beware of the Overseers. They fly above the stacks and monitor the facility."

Yes, sir. The screen flickered off, and Tameka headed down the correct aisle. The screen switched back on, and for the love of Elden, she controlled her startled squeal.

"Tameka, protect Pax. He's more special than you know. Goodbye, you brave young woman. I was honored to know you." The projector powered down and disappeared.

Okay, there was definitely a tear now. The good die first.

An hour passed of following his directions and hiding in holes from the Overseers—large clunky machines in the sky. This was nothing like the more public-facing archives. Every book in this place was white and massive. Two feet tall, and three feet wide, with spines deeper than a D-ring binder. The bland tomes blended into the white shelving, white floors—everything pale and as much a labyrinth as Enki itself.

Tameka found the location on a humongous stack designated Wiw. His Verse, so to speak. Pretty long. Another hour later, she scoured roughly the area he designated in the map she memorized with no luck.

"Damn it." Let them catch her. At this point, she was lost in this mammoth library with no idea what to look for—

A flash of red caught Tameka's eyes. She whirled. A set of books, tucked behind another bunch, sported red ribbons between the pages like bookmarks. A curl blew into her face on the breeze that smelled of dust and the lost. The same color red.

Fury slid to it and hid inside the shelf, forming a little nook. The hefty text laid flat, and she opened it to the first marked page.

2.6778.9890 | K

We celebrate today our first venture into life cultivation and the progression of reinstating our species. My heart is heavy at our victory. The cost was high. I and the other Eminents pray for peace with what remains of our enemy, the proud people who saved us at significant cost to themselves. The Aegis. A bright white light intervened like a miracle, granting us the advantage of seizing six continents and four oceans. Little by little, we gain more of Enki. They grow more desperate with each loss. I blame them not. Peace, please.

2.6779.6253 | L

The Exalted met with Primary Tumu today. The greatest leaders from both our sides. I hope for peace. They threaten our people with the Chorus. But they aren't prepared to self-decimate. We hold the advantage with over half of Enki in our control. There is nowhere left for them to run, but we still have so much to learn from them. We should broker peace. Primary Rem is unsure.

2.6779.6255 | L

The Exalted's three hundred and twenty-fourth son approached me with prospects of an accord. Shunned for the ability to control an undesirable phenomenon, this young man presented with great potential for the makings of the first ally to bridge our peoples since the beginning of the conflict. The boy harnessed the ability on his own, practicing in secret for fear of his father's wrath. But without proper guidance, it grew outside of his control. After an accidental unleashing of the phenomenon—the white light—they punished him by removing his fingernails.

Ghastly. With much pity in my heart, I revered his story and passed it along to the Primaries. They see an advantage to his abilities and will communicate further on the matter.

2.6779.6278 | M

Three Two Four (324 hereon) parlayed with me again. For the transgression of meeting with me without the Exalted's permission, the Aegis threatened to exile him from the void between Probabilities that they considered their home. Primary Remorse took pity on him and offered him asylum among our people. But Primary Tumu suspected him of a double-cross and consulted as much to me. It is an uncomfortable situation for me as an Eminent between two Primaries. So we petitioned to the oldest Primary for council.

He asked for time to think on the matter and will reconvene when he returns from the First. He cannot be swayed from it.

2.6779.6279 | M

Tumu is now the oldest Primary. Quet died on the First. A terrible death. I shudder to imagine it. The Primaries democratically settled the matter of an alliance with 324. All but Tumu voted in favor of it. At the next talk with the Exalted and his council, 324 will harness the phenomenon and test its usefulness. I pray Primary Tumu reaches peace before Primary Rem signals the young man.

2.6779.6281 | M

May the cosmos forgive us for reducing such a beautiful people to the same fate we suffer. Only sons. No daughters.

We must learn what unmade us. Perhaps we will find a way to save both our races.

The account stopped in this volume. While scanning her surroundings, Tameka retrieved the next one and opened to the bookmark.

2.6780.1355 | N

We search daily for the library of bones. With all but a few Aegis in hiding, we cannot operate most of the facilities on Enki to full capacity. Or correctly. Their archives spoke of a library—the Atheneum. It housed a DNA repository to reestablish the recycled lives of lost Aegis. Possibly, including the females removed at the hands of 324.

Once we captured the Exalted and the elders, we locked them in a prison of our making. And made 324 the Fifth's first citizen for overstepping his place and condemning both our species to the same Hell—

Tameka cried out as someone touched her arm. Dropping the books, she made to crawl out of the shelf. The Tritan proved stronger. He hauled her up by the waist and ignored her powerful kicks and blows. With a deep breath, she calmed and opened the well inside her. Half-full from her regular sipping. Her body went stiff as she prepared to drain this motherfucker—

"Stop."

"Tumu?" Tameka stopped struggling and faced him.

"At least you're not naked." He grinned.

She smiled.

The Tritan's kind expression vanished. "Keep your faith in me a little while longer."

"What—"

The world went black, and all the while Tameka wished Sagan kept her promises.

{Gait}

"My friends are expecting me. Tonight. Tomorrow. They know where I am. You can't keep me here."

Sagan's heart slammed into her chest. The goggles left her blind. In the dark. Her pulse ran faster with each attempt to break the rope. She could lift entire cars filled with people and supplies. But this rope only tore into her skin. It wasn't enjoyable.

Seamswalk away. Get. Out. Escape, dammit!

Nothing.

"What have you done to me? Razor? Fucking answer me!" She hated the terror in her voice.

When the Pain Curator spoke, his voice came from right beside her. "I reduced your nacre's effectiveness by fifty percent. Your friends did an outstanding job with this technology. I assume with help from Xelan's own research, of course. Brilliance breeds excellence."

No. Sagan wet her drying lips and asked the hard question in a small voice, "Why can't I Seamswalk?"

"A fail safe I installed with your port. Fear not. It's not permanent." His leather pants creaked this close as he knelt low to elaborate in her ear, "Wouldn't want to damage my investment."

The Seamswalker turned her face away. How could she get out of this? Pehton? No. She's probably tucked into bed in the prison. An idea came to mind. "Matt! Matt, help me!"

"Shh. What do you think I plan to do to you, Pain Kitten?"

She spat, "Don't call me that! And if you know what's good for you, you'll let me go." Pulling on the ropes only shivved more of the splinters into her wrists.

"Imminent has use of you. *I* have use of you." He practically purred it against her ear.

"You'll use me to hurt Rayne." Because why else would they want Sagan?

Automatically, Razor recited, "Rayne is safe." That's exactly what Celindria said at the Tribunal. Like they knew it for certain.

At this point, Sagan's head spun. She felt dizzy, suspended in the room with goggles covering her eyes. Trying to remain calm, she focused on her breathing.

"Feeling woozy, kitten?"

Hot tears poured unbidden down the sides of her face. What had Sagan allowed him to do to her? "The food? Was it poisoned?"

"No." Flat. Honest.

So much relief at that.

To her horror, the Pain Curator tested one of the buckles fastening her coat. Idly, he explained, "The food is low calorie and produces extra endorphins for an addicting experience with no weight-gain side effects. But it's not sustainable. Perfect for parties. I've seen no one take to it quite the way you did. Except T.A.O. She also loves it." He quickly released a clasp at her breasts.

Sagan swallowed before asking, "Razor?"

He stopped. "What?"

The harmlessness almost made her scoff with incredulity. "Stop. Please. My coat . . . I'm—"

"Trust me, I've noticed. Everything you wear. The dress at the gala. That collar. You've kept me on edge. A being as old as myself appreciates the exhilaration. Such an innocent thing with the cutest kinks. Oh, that night that you nursed my concussion. I think I decided I liked you then. Or was it the first time I saw you eat? It makes all this other business quite unfortunate." By the time he finished, he reached the final buckle all the way down at her hips.

Keep him talking. "What about your people and the Seam? The drive?"

Razor planted his chin on her shoulder and changed the subject. "You asked me once about my predation. Why do I want you? I knew the answer then. Would you like to hear it now?"

Oh, Elden. Sagan wasn't sure she liked the change in direction of this shit. She tugged on the rope again.

"I'll take that as a 'yes.'"

The coat opened almost entirely. The cool air touched her bare skin and teased her bellybutton. Razor's nail-less fingers grazed her collarbone. The nacre port. When he trailed them between her breasts, her breath hitched in fear. In response to her skittishness, he assured, "I want nothing as mundane as sex from you." Over her abs. Circled her bellybutton. If he went any lower . . .

He flatted his hand over her stomach, which twitched at his touch with her relieved gasps. Relieved that he went no further. With his presence leaning over her, the Pain Curator announced, "I want your soul. Assign me your volition, Sagan. And the others can have nothing from you. You'll be mine. Safe with me."

A long time ago, when she first started dating an Icarus with a preference for control and pain, Sagan researched Elden's Tenement's of Volition. She meant it as a present for Korac. To show him the depth of her love for him. One forfeits control of the user interface within the nacre to a new controller. Her idea was that they shared in sex through her body along with her lover's full control over her.

Legends and rumors suggested the control lacked authentication from the user. That another component was missing to immerse the full experience. Maybe Imminent discovered that component.

The Shadow without a Seamswalker. Not exactly neutered, but close to it. Not to mention Imminent would gain one. Or another Seamswalker, if the Shadow's theories about T.A.O. were correct. Either way, this hurt her family. And Sagan was made of stronger stuff than that. She wanted more information first.

"Why, Razor? Why you, specifically? Why not another member of Imminent?"

The sweet scent of vanilla filled her senses the closer he drew. Razor whispered, "It's been so long since I could go home. You can take me there. Give me a child that can go there." Knuckles brushed her face, and she fought the urge to jerk away despite the horror of his proposal. "Unfortunately, you likely wouldn't survive the first pregnancy to bear another. Regretful, truly."

Sagan hated how rushed and shrill she sounded. "I thought you said no sex."

Razor moved back and laughed softly. "Reproduction without sex is much less fun. I prefer the more direct means to this end. Enough postponement. Pain Kitten, what say you?"

"Fuck you."

The Seamswalker heard the smile in the Pain Curator's voice, "I expected nothing less." He ripped the coat open and fully exposed her. She sensed those green and orange eyes rove over her naked skin. His voice seethed with anger and bitter disappointment. "If I can't have you, I'll settle for ruining you. Commence program."

This experience started on a scream. A howl of pain and agony unlike anything Sagan ever felt. Fear, terror, and disappointment.

The heavy metal of the riot gate crashed into her left arm. A sickening, guttural pop erupted from the smashed appendage. Her entire body spasmed in pain.

The Seamswalker bit her lip and tasted blood through her teeth. Fully. Immersive. She lived this experience.

"Powerless." That was Nox.

Sagan was Rayne. Invasion Day.

"No!" She swallowed three heaving breaths, pinned to the spot, and he slammed it down again. Her body jumped and writhed.

"Hopeless." Solemnly, he raised the gate again.

No, no, no, no...

"Accepting." Gazing into her eyes, he rolled the gate down one more time.

Sagan felt Rayne's hatred of the tears. Hated the way her limbs flailed outside her control. But most of all, she hated that the pain dissipated in its entirety. Numb was bad. Her arm stopped responding. Her mind begged her not to look.

That was it. Rayne believed her arm would never work again. And still, she burned with the desire to fight. It fueled Sagan's resolve and filled her with pride. The Shadow could do anything.

The scene of the school burning around them faded and transitioned into a structure of black rock. It was hard and porous, cutting into her back. The visual changed, and the person she existed through looked out.

To a sea of Icarean faces. Millions of them watched.

A man's weight settled on her.

No.

No.

Sagan did *not* want to live through this.

Resolve like a fire burned in her. The woman lying on this throne—helpless—plotted her retribution. It tasted sweet.

Rayne.

Boundless courage and strength. Even now, as Nox took her clothes from her, she never doubted her revenge. It gave Sagan hope of surviving the ordeal with her.

People paid money for this shit?

Something...unexpected filtered through.

Desire.

Rayne... Oh, Elden. No wonder she hid it from her best friends. This was how the rumor of their love story perpetuated.

Push the memory aside. Don't experience it.

The scene refused to relent and played on. Sagan wept and fought. And lost.

Eventually, a beautiful mountain spring with stout evergreens and clear water surrounded her. She lay on a rock shelf in the spring after Korac carried Sagan there. The scent of pine and frost comforted her. This was an enjoyable experience to relive. Their first time together outside of her dreams.

The axe. The fire. Her perfect trust in him. His love for her.

Sagan wasn't ready, however, given what Razor was subjecting her to. Yet, the experience continued without her consent. Contaminating her relationships with the two people closest to her.

Monster.

"But keep your eyes on me."

"Yes, master."

Korac and Sagan kissed, and she held on for what came next.

The Seamswalker never screamed so much in her life. Never felt a pain so searing. It wasn't the trusting play from her memory. But the fires of Hell blistering and splitting her skin with Korac smiling over her—

Razor ripped the goggles off. And she wanted to vomit. The rancid smell of cooked flesh warned her not to look.

Please don't look.

Gulping and sobbing, Sagan looked.

Two men in black jumpsuits and hoods pressed the scorched blades of her axes into her stomach and thigh. With her nacre only at fifty percent. The soft tissue repair system wasn't keeping up, and they weren't pulling away to give it time to cool.

Blood spilled from the charred wounds and dripped off her exposed skin.

Pain for pain's sake was not her thing. There was no trust in this. Only burns and a smell she'd never forget. Her wrists looked like meat after tearing into that rope. The Seamswalker sagged sickly in her bonds.

"Matt," she called weakly. "Help. Matt!" The words barely left her lips.

Razor pressed his ear close to her mouth to hear her and when he looked at her, he smiled. Rushing across the booth, The Pain Curator unmasked one of the men. Auburn hair. Freckles. Near black eyes—

"No . . ." Sagan groaned.

How could Matt not help her? How could he do this to her?

Expressionless, he peeled the blade from her.

The bastard responsible for this situation gazed down at her with eyes that shifted and flashed. "Will you reconsider, Seamswalker? I'd hate to make this a nightly occurrence." He indicated the projection feed.

A masked audience of Imminent assholes watched eagerly from the auction hall. Each inched to the edge of their seats, practically salivating over her pain.

Sagan sounded tired and weak to her own ears. "Razor, never let me go. Because once you do, I'll rip your world apart." Shrieking as Puk ripped off the other axe hurt her intended effect.

"We'll continue tomorrow then." Razor gestured for Matt and Puk to cut the ropes.

She fell to the floor and hissed from the searing discomfort. As the Seamswalker rolled onto her knees and elbows, she tried to let the coat fall closed and protect her modesty.

The Pain Curator went to his knees beside her and untied her wrists gingerly. Over his insanely contradictory behavior, he ordered, "Lock her in the basement. We'll pick back up—"

Sagan cried out as her shins disappeared into the floor. With bleeding hands, she clutched desperately to Razor, terrified of the Seam taking her away.

He held onto her and calmly explained, "The Seam wants you. I can feel it. And you're so weak. Too weak to leave it when it claims you. Say it, Sagan. Say it, and I'll save you."

With her body half sunk into a conduit in the floor, the Seamswalker stared into the Pain Curator's eyes. Frightened, bleeding, and alone, she ground out, "I only belong to him."

White. His eyes went solid white with two crescent pupils in each eye. Then Razor dropped her as if it burned him to touch her. He called Matt over who knelt beside his boss. They discussed matters as if she wasn't sinking into oblivion, and she refused to be wrong about two people this night.

With everything left in Sagan, she reached up and clutched the younger man's hand. For one kind moment, he squeezed back. And she knew. Not alone, after all.

And then Matt pushed her into the Seam.

"Rayne!

"Korac!"

Forever, she fell into nothing.

Razor's voice echoed, "Now, you've gone where he can never find you."

{GAIT}

Two and half million years ago.

"The nacre-less boy. I want that one. Beautiful, isn't he? Yes, that's my request for Razor this month."

Triss, the red-feathered Lyrik, chuffed. "You wish. You can't afford him. And there's nothing you can offer that's worth Razor's time."

Korac silently thanked whatever divine entity fucked him over this badly, because at least he wasn't forced to entertain that sweaty slob. And they always sweat on him. The swine.

Footsteps sounded down the metal hall. He recognized them. Good shoes were hard to come by, and he wanted a pair so badly. Shiny, the way the man in nice pants polished them. The footfalls rounded the corner. White pants this time. Yes, one day, he'd wear white pants like those with shiny black shoes.

The man pressed the Lyrik against the wall, and Korac shrank into his rags. He hoped to disappear. Poof. Gone.

Muttered exchanges. Not all of it about sex. As they finished, the man said, "I'm taking him outside, and then things will be different."

"I'm ready." She sounded quite ready and smelled like it, too. Roses filled the air.

Their lips smacking ensued once more, and Korac knew to keep his eyes low. Never look anyone in the eyes. Never see faces made to haunt his dreams into Eternity. Never let them have his gaze.

"*Contaminant*, come with me."

With the voice more clear, Korac nearly recognized it. A smooth tenor that might produce rich laughter. So close to naming him—

The white light in the prison yard.

The four other children disappeared.

Korac lay on the ground, staring into the purple sky. A frightening pale blue face stood over him. The fucking Primary. Remorse. He called to the man in white pants, "We relocate the Atheneum once I receive confirmation of the payload." The snow crunched as he walked away.

Korac still couldn't move. The man in white pants knelt at his side with the sun spearing the boy's gaze. In a deeper voice, he proclaimed, "Now, they will never find you."

"Korac!"

"Sagan?!"

Korac woke to Sagan's screams.

He expected her to Seamswalk into his cell. But she never came. Only her crying and begging for him. Was she trapped?

Not bothering to throw on a shirt or shoes, Korac stormed out of his cell in sweats. He charged through the nacre-resistant barrier on his cursed blockmate's false prison. All the way through the conduit.

Primary Rem waited in the shrine on the other side. Thirteen feet tall with black robes and a compression orb. The man aimed some kind of gun at the Icarus' chest.

"Remorse. Where is she?" Although his voice came out icy, Korac's body trembled with a rage hot enough to scald.

The ancient Tritan frowned in an attempt at genuine sadness. He lowered the gun with a sigh. Even his voice filled with it. "Now, you'll never find her, son. Razor ate that heart of hers. And I am in no position to get it back."

Korac's eyes flicked to the weapon. He looked back up at Remorse's voids. "That won't hurt me."

The Tritan raised it once more. "It wasn't designed for a nacre-bearing Icarus. It's much older. And it'll work just fine. Go back inside for your own good. Don't make me shoot you, son."

Korac took a step toward the Tritan, testing him.

"This gun will turn you inside out."

Korac clenched his fists and jaw. He could still hear her screaming. "I have to save her."

"Consider yourself lucky to have known her. And let her go. Convince Pehton to stop aiming for Razor's empire. Both of you relax and play nice like the pawns you are. Leave the fighting to the knights and the bishops."

He scanned the Tritan's body language for sincerity. Finger on the triggering mechanism. Aim perfectly square at the Icarus' brain. Breathing steady. With all that in mind, Korac smirked. "That's not really my style." He lunged.

The gun went off.

EPILOGUE

{GAIT}

WHITE. Green and orange. Gray. Red. Brown.

Pale. Tan. Blue. Pale. Brown. Pink.

The Aegis known as Razor saw the last of his Imminent guests out of the Emporium and locked its revolving door. A metaphor for the sinners of this galaxy. They just kept coming back for more.

Next, up the wrought-iron spiral stairs and into the vault. The sunken stairs carried him into the dark. A persistent buzzing greeted him and elicited a satisfied smile.

At last.

Oleen appeared and removed his white jacket. Miy took his gloves. All the Lyriks removed his clothes. All of them lovely.

Their souls tasted sour on his palette.

No, the Aegis known as Razor preferred sweeter fare.

Triss sat on her knees in the center of the bed, tattoo gun in hand. A sort of welcome for his newest prize. The Lyriks took their time with his new acquisition, breaking her in. Naked, mussed, lipstick smudged.

Sagan stared into nowhere. Red tears streaked her cheeks. A sign of the struggle to fight his volition. Brilliant girl, but she needed to keep still for the branding.

Triss swiped away the last of the blood and ink and turned to him with a wicked grin.

RAZOR across Sagan's throat. A more permanent collar.

The Pain Curator climbed into the center of the bed. A fine tremor plagued the Seamswalker. The closer he drew to her, the more her naked body trembled. Fresh blood spilled from her eyes.

Always a fighter.

He liked her.

Brushing back her growing bangs from those violet eyes, he sighed. He wished he didn't like her.

"She's very pretty," Triss proclaimed with no trace of jealousy or malice. More like an echo of the regret he already felt.

He raked his fingers through those bright red feathers. "It's terribly tragic the women rarely survive the labor."

"What about that Icarean woman?"

That's right. One of few and unfortunately, he'd rather she perished. "Father chose well. Not that my brother benefited from it." He gazed into Triss' yellow eyes before capturing her lips with his. The bed shook from their third's growing anxiety.

He broke away and glanced at Sagan. Softly, he confessed, "I wished you'd reconsider. Then we could keep her as a pet."

Triss placed a hand on her black stomach. "You deserve a child, and you won't let me keep this one. We don't know if I'd die—"

Another kiss to stop that line of thinking. No fatalism allowed.

Up for air, they both looked at Sagan. The only viable option remaining. A child produced with her meant a greater chance of the offspring traveling into the Seam. His home.

"I'm very sorry about this, Pain Kitten, but I promise to make it enjoyable for the three of us. And look!" The Pain Curator pointed at the various cameras in the space. "I'll send the feed to your lover so he knows you're safe and having a good time experiencing what remains of your young life."

More shaking and fresh blood. Triss took Sagan's face in her hands and kissed her. He allowed the blond woman's autonomic functions of the lowest level to operate at their own will, and the Seamswalker kissed back. Blood smeared on their face from her tears, and the Lyrik purred into it. He kissed the Seamswalker's shoulder up to her neck and pulled her into a kiss with him. She rose on her knees to meet him with a matched intensity.

Leave his taste on her.

Leave his mark on her.

Send Sagan back to her lover with the footage and compel her to end the relationship with the *Contaminant*. She won't be needing him anymore. She'd have everything she wanted here. Pulling her hair, he separated them by inches.

"I'll take from you what I like. You'll give to me anything that which I ask. Until Eternity takes you, you're mine."

"Yes, Master."

He jerked her roughly to him, her back to his front on their knees. He turned her head to look forward, facing the nearest camera. Against her ear, he commanded, "Say it again."

Sagan locked her gaze with their audience. Blood spilled from her eyes until she lost the battle of wills and repeated, "Yes, Master."

The Aegis known as Razor claimed her where Korac hadn't. All the while, she cried out the Pain Curator's name and begged for more—

Triss swallowed down with a delighted moan. Her throat convulsed around him most pleasantly. The Aegis known as Razor pet her red feathers approvingly. "Thank you, gorgeous. Tonight was stressful, and this was exactly what I needed."

She set back on her heels under his desk and corrected on a purr, "It's exactly what you deserve."

Thinking of Sagan's short blond hair, he brushed aside the Lyrik's feathers. "Yes." He smirked for her. "That's precisely why you're my favorite."

"Razor, I know you're disappointed the Seamswalker escaped—"

"Escaped? She fell into the Seam while weakened with a reduced nacre. Our last chance at a child—my last chance to see my home—dies in a few short days from dehydration and starvation in an empty world." He shook his head with what little sorrow he could muster. "She deserved better."

"A warrior's death?" The Lyrik offered as she hopped back on the desktop.

He granted her a solemn smile and stood between her parted thighs. "Yes. A fighter to the very end." Cupping Triss' face, he kissed her softly. The device in his palm vibrated, and he broke the kiss with a snarl. "I have to report."

Without him asking, she kissed his cheek and disappeared into the dark.

Perfection.

Engaging the screen built into his desk, the Pain Curator met with the Tritan. "You lost the asset," the Primary accused.

"Nice to see you, too, Remorse. What of the Atheneum?"

"It suffers."

The Aegis known as Razor shrugged and offered, "I've weakened the Progeny. The library pays for it. That was our agreement. There is nothing left between us."

The Tritan slammed his fist on a column in his sanctum, shattering it. "We needed a Seamswalker. Now, Celindria owns the only one remaining. You know that puts us at a disadvantage."

"Celindria was always your undertaking, old friend. We'll see how well she performed in her attempt to acquire Conscience and the Mother, tomorrow. If that will be all? I was in the middle of celebrating my triumph."

"...Does the girl suffer?" Soft, quiet, sad.

Yes. Sagan's kindness infected them all on this mission. He wished they lived in any other Probability. The Matrix underestimated her attachment to the *Contaminant* in this one. "No," Razor lied. "She fought like a warrior to the very end."

"There's fire in these girls. Excellent stock."

"There's danger in considering them as anything else. We'll keep our distance from the next one. Minimal contact with her to prevent contamination of our motivations."

"Agreed. Congratulations, 324."

"Good night, Remorse."

With the Atheneum returned to his ward, he could ensure its suffering. But as Sagan screamed and wept in the Seam, the Aegis known as Razor lamented the lost potential of the forgone Probabilities.

How long will it take her to die? How long must he sense her suffering? All the while knowing what the Pain Curator lost in his Seamswalker.

Better that than knowing Sagan's wrath.

AUTHOR'S NOTE

I promised shrapnel and tears, and I delivered. But don't lose hope. The Shadow always rallies in the darkest hour.

Continue reading for a sneak peek at Restraining Silver.

RESTRAINING SILVER

{GAIT}

"THIS MISCALCULATION CONTINUES TO COST ME."

Korac—badass, convicted war criminal, and former General of the Icarean Army of the planet Cinder—lay beside the resurrection casket on the icy floor of the big cell. Pitch darkness shrouded the prison's basement on Gait, the planet he regrettably called home. The nacre glass—unbreakable bonds—shackled his naked ass to said cold tiles, leaving him with no means of escape. The eerie field of nacre-deterring energy that blanketed the floor harmlessly skittered across his skin, hungry.

For a week, Korac railed and fought until his wrists and ankles bled. Until his hulking efforts broke his back and paralyzed him.

To save her.

Sagan's screams died in the Seam—the world between conduits—two days ago, taking Korac's sanity with her. Only she could enter there. It's why they called her the Seamswalker. In recent visits, his reason for any hope in this world confessed the monochromatic space tried to claim her. It whispered to her. Called for her to find the Atheneum—the lost library of the Ancients.

So, Korac helped Sagan anchor to this reality. Food, touch, sex, blood—all of this kept her with him. When suddenly, she stopped eating. Her duties to her people, the Shadow Progeny, kept her busy and exhausted. Each attack from their enemy, a terrorist group known as Imminent, meant ferrying her friends across the Vast Collective to their next missions. She rarely slept. He imagined she never tried outside of his arms, when he managed to keep her still. The innocent seductress knew how to distract him from his more tender duties to her person.

And somehow, all these current disruptions tied back to Razor, the Pain Curator of Gait.

Korac's blond-haired, violet-eyed lover recently pursued the monster for intel on Imminent, the Tritans, and the entire Vast Collective.

Razor's existence went back longer than the Icarean General's memory. He got his claws into Sagan. Into her responsiveness to pain and control. With trust, her desire for it made for a perfect marriage of bliss and ecstasy. But the Pain Curator knew nothing of cultivating trust. Only of breaking it.

Now, he'd broken Sagan. And Korac couldn't reach the door, let alone the Seam to save her.

Remorse.

That fucking Primary Tritan. After the Icarean General lost the confrontation with the Gargantuan god, Korac found himself here. That bastard. Haunting and stalking them since the former King of Cinder, Nox, was a child. Six million years at least, manipulating this operation for what he desired. Which was what? The pieces of this multi-sided puzzle interconnected somehow, centered on their lives in ways Korac could only speculate.

From his minute perspective.

On this cold fucking floor.

"You must know something. Why else would they lock me in here with you?"

The resurrection casket, his only cellmate, remained silent.

In the long hours of losing his mind, Korac took to speaking to the Tritan artifact. The machine reduced an entity to its nanite-controlling computer in its chest—its nacre. And likewise, when reversed, it reconstructed a person from their nacre. Made of an amber glass, this tiny pearl maintained the complex functions of most living beings in the Vast Collective.

Korac was the only known exception. He never needed a nacre. His body processed upgrades, transferred through exchanges of blood, without the need for one. Upgrades allowed compatible nanites to increase speed, agility, strength, soft and hard tissue repair, and, for the Icari and Progeny, granted them retractable wings.

This war criminal was a paragon of a specimen unlike any other entity in the Twelve worlds. Not only was Korac nacre-less, no one else looked like him. White hair and nearly white eyes marked him as exotic—A trophy to obtain. And yea, sure. He played it up. Dressed for any occasion in high-class fashion or warrior gear tailored to emphasize the predatory beauty. To entice. To lure.

But it wasn't like that with Sagan. The Seamswalker had a way of looking at the Icarean General that stripped away his careful pretense. Because, for her, it wasn't about the clothes. It wasn't the arrangement of his hair or the stances he posed. The beautiful young woman—the successor General of his armies—melted at his smile. There weren't words to describe the genuine virtue in her sweetness. In her love.

Korac strained against the set of chains on his left side, turning, pulling as far to the right as possible.

"Fucking unbreakable glass. Pehton! Pehton, where are you?!"

No sign of the tiny Lyriki warrior. Although she was the Executive Warden of Gait, the war criminal currently serving time in her prison recently spent much of his sentence with her. Together they aimed to solve several of the planet's mysteries. Mysteries that once again revolved around Razor.

Where was Pehton? Surely, she'd think to check for him all over the prison. No. Korac suspected that somehow Remorse was responsible for her absence. As much as he was responsible for putting the Icarean General here.

Elden, please, let the dying of Sagan's screams mean she settled into distraction. That she's solving her own mysteries. Please don't... It couldn't mean...

No. Never her.

Korac howled into the four walls of the dark cell. It carried and resounded back to him. He sounded desperate. And heartbroken—

The lift whirred.

For seven days, he waited to hear the air brakes on the only way in and out of this place.

Finally.

It was too dark to make out the figure paused on the machine. He sniffed, taking in their scent. Recognizing the faint sexual neglect, Korac called out, "Executive Warden."

No lights to see, but he remembered her pitch-black skin and fiery orange feathers. So short, she barely reached his elbow. Those carbuncle red eyes of hers took in everything. Even in the dark.

Pehton's breath hitched, and salt filled the air. Tears. Whispering between sniffles, she confessed, "I'm not supposed to be here."

Korac closed his eyes and let the relief wash over him. She wasn't yet his enemy. Cutting to the chase, he started, "Pehton. Sagan…she needs our help—"

"I can't. I'm sorry. I can't." Pehton shuffled and activated the lift.

"No! Come back!"

"I'm so sorry, Korac."

"Elden, damn it! She might die without us! Pehton! Pehton!" But his words fell on no one's ears. She'd already gone.

Oh, not for the first time salt burned a trail from the corner of Korac's eyes to his hair. Very little made him cry. The thought of the woman he loved dying alone and afraid left him lost. That Razor and Imminent gained from her death burned his heart.

Did the white hats defeat Nox and Korac on Volcano day for this? To waste Korac betraying his King and his nobler efforts for the side of good by losing to Razor and Imminent?

Korac pulled, tore, and bent in his restraints. Nothing deterred his attempts. Not the gashes exposing the veins in his wrists. Not the snap of bones in his extremities. Nor the popping of his ligaments. In his madness, he considered chewing off a hand. But even nacres didn't regenerate amputated limbs.

Far away, a tiny voice whimpered, "Korac."

Sagan.

Alive.

Korac felt it in his bones.

"Whatever it takes... whatever I have to do. Amos, I promise with everything in me, I *will* find you."

www.ingramcontent.com/pod-product-compliance
Lightning Source LLC
Chambersburg PA
CBHW020459310726
48979CB00016B/2721/J

* 9 7 8 1 7 3 5 6 7 1 3 6 9 *